SEEK

CATWALK SERIES - BOOK FOUR

S.Q. ORPIN

Published by Wild Hibiscus Press

PO Box 1761 Lafayette CA 94549

Cover created by Fresh Design

*To my 'family' at Berkeley Adult School
who constantly supports me and cheers me on.*

Thanks for believing in me.

CATWALK SERIES

The Catwalk series was inspired by the exciting but perilous world of modeling in Los Angeles. Dream was motivated by an accident that redefined the life of the author's model-niece, Sterling. Wanting to give a voice to additional characters and in response to a 'What next?' storyline, Catwalk expanded to a five-part series. The stories encompass a deep examination of characters struggling to find meaning in life and love.

The books are written from multiple viewpoints allowing the reader to explore the diverse characters, while delving into the deep, and sometimes dark, human existence and tumultuous relationships. The series contains adult situations and language, including sex, trauma, and violence.

DREAM introduces the cast of characters and the relationship developing between Casi and Kyle. It layers the superficial world of modeling with the lifestyle of a small-town man, creating challenges and pitfalls. **HOPE** continues as reality and conflict consume the couple and supporting character storylines develop. **TRUST** explores the emotional rollercoaster of love, career, loss, and coming to terms with the past. **SEEK** reveals secrets and backstory, helping the characters move forward as emotional scars are healed. **LOVE** is the final book in the series which spans five years, achieving triumph and finding meaning in life and love. The series primarily focuses on the main characters of Casi and Kyle, but supporting characters are intricately woven throughout the five books.

CAST OF CHARACTERS

Casi (Roberts): A former swimsuit model in LA. Born in Burnaby, Canada, and now living in Blackberry Falls, WA, with her husband, Kyle.

Kyle Jensen: A master woodworker with his own business in Washington State. Married to Casi.

Jake: Kyle's older brother and business partner.

Gail: Jake's ex-wife and mother of his two children.

Olivia: Jake's daughter.

Reid: Jake's son.

Austin: Jake's son with Lia

Tommy: Jake's youngest son with Lia

Mary Ann: Gail's best friend. Briefly dated Kyle.

Lia: Lauren's older sister. Divorced from Jake.

Lauren: Lia's sister. Dated Kyle for three years. A chef in Seattle.

Fran: The mother of Lia and Lauren.

Anna: A lumber rep in Seattle. Briefly dated Kyle. In a relationship with Jake and they have a daughter, Charlotte.

Georgia Jensen: Kyle's and Jake's adoptive mother.

Peter Jensen: Married to Georgia, and the adoptive father of Kyle and Jake.

Tara: Biological mother of Kyle and Jake. After their musician father, Tommy, died, she turned to drugs and lives on the streets. The brothers were put in foster care when they were one and four years old.

Jack Roberts: Casi's father. He owns a restaurant and brewery in Bellingham, WA. Divorced from Casi's mother, Sonya. Married to Ava.

Ava: Jack's wife and Casi's stepmother.

Sonya: Casi's troubled mother who died of a drug overdose.

Mary: Casi's mentor and Ava's close friend. Owner of McCrae Skincare.

Alix: Casi's ex-boyfriend. Celebrity, graphic artist.

Dylan: Casi's best friend from LA. Also, her hairdresser. In a relationship with Brian.

Earl: Peter's best friend and former partner in a plumbing business. Married to Libby.

Libby: Peter's sister. She is a writer and came back to Elmvale to take care of Earl.

Grady: Kyle's best friend from high school who was killed in a boating accident.

Brian: The Jensen brother's accountant. In a relationship with Dylan.

Amber: Kyle's high school girlfriend.

Nicole: Kyle's high school girlfriend, after Amber.

Amy: The receptionist at the wood shop. Dating Riley.

Riley: The apprentice at the wood shop.

Ray Dawson: Casi's former doorman in LA. He's an avid cook.

Dawn: Casi's best friend from high school. Married to Joey.

Joey: Casi's high school boyfriend.

Katie: Casi's friend from high school.

Dingo: Kyle's German short-haired dog.

Jezebel: Casi's calico cat.

Dare to Dream, Hope, Trust, Seek, and most of all, Love.

PROLOGUE - DREAM

Cassidy Roberts had stars in her eyes when she was scouted for modeling at seventeen, on the beach in Burnaby, Canada. She moved to Los Angeles with her mother, Sonya, and changed her name to Casi. She distanced herself from her father, Jack, and stepmother, Ava, determined to reinvent her image and leave her old life behind. Sonya micromanaged Casi's career and immersed herself in the chaos of Hollywood life until Mary stepped in as Casi's mentor and redirected her to a better path. Her career blossomed in the world of lingerie and swimsuit modeling, accenting her curvaceous figure.

A dozen years later, as an experienced and in-demand model, Casi lived with her celebrity artist boyfriend of four years, Alix Grey. She created a life of excess, parties, and glamour, but was unfulfilled and petrified about turning thirty. When she met Kyle Jensen, a craftsman from Blackberry Falls, WA, she became instantly smitten. After she broke her pelvis in a car accident, her career was jeopardized and Casi spiraled down, becoming lost and confused about which direction to take. She bought a loft in Hollywood, and focused on her career, capitalizing on her success, while also finishing her business degree. She followed her heart and pursued a relationship with Kyle, ignoring the issues involved with moving to a small town, and dealing with Kyle's untrusting brother, Jake.

An opportunity to be part owner in a surfing line, Sand and Surf, with ex-boyfriend Alix, promised to be lucrative and provide extra income. Casi naively accepted the deal, assuming everything would fall in place. Passionately in love, Kyle and Casi married in Hawaii, determined to prove everyone wrong and live a happy life, with their cat Jezebel and dog Dingo, in their house on the lake in Blackberry Falls.

PROLOGUE - HOPE

Casi discovered marriage was more challenging than she anticipated. Kyle became frustrated with her living in LA while he remained in Washington. When Casi came home for Christmas she tried to tell him about the failure of her business venture with Alix, but she was rushed in for emergency surgery for a ruptured ovarian cyst. Reacting on advice from the doctor, Kyle signed for a tubal ligation, believing it was in her best interest. Feeling disconnected and angry with him, Casi fled back to LA.

Jake had a fling with Sonya on the beach in Hawaii, acting out when he felt Lia was being clingy. Lia informed Jake she was pregnant and was surprised by his reaction. When he failed to commit to her, she questioned whether she should keep the baby.

Sonya convinced Casi to do a racy editorial, not telling her about what else she planned. When Alix realized the trouble Casi was in, he called Kyle to come to LA. Jake and Kyle discovered her unconscious with signs of an assault, and Kyle orchestrated her leaving LA. After a scuffle getting the pictures from the editorial, Kyle was shot and ended up in the hospital. Once returning to Washington, Kyle took charge, overwhelming Casi with his controlling behavior. She grew closer to Jake as he comforted her and confided some of his secrets and anxieties. Mary stepped in and offered Casi a position in her skincare line, wanting her to be an independent woman. Her new profession suited her, and she soon blossomed into a successful businesswoman. She became close friends with Anna, the woman Jake had fallen in love with. Anna helped Casi create a professional appearance and shared her trade experience.

Casi met Kyle's ex-girlfriend, Lauren, at Lia's baby shower and was mortified to learn he kept secrets from her, while over-sharing with Lauren. After Lia gave birth to Austin, Casi convinced them not to give him up for adoption. She took care of the infant while Lia wrestled with postpartum depression. Jake stepped up and became an involved father, turning to ex-wife, Gail, for advice.

Casi's father, Jack, and stepmother, Ava, faced new problems as Sonya intervened in their close relationship, creating a wedge between them as she ignited past sorrows. Kyle took a stand against Sonya's meddling, settling her in the loft in LA, and away from Casi.

While Jake's love for Anna grew, he discovered Lia was pregnant, again. Anna revealed she was marrying a wealthy business tycoon, which devastated Jake. Lia wanted to terminate the accidental pregnancy, but Jake insisted they should become a family and raise the two children together. They married in Vegas, realizing that the union was most likely doomed.

PROLOGUE - TRUST

Casi continued to thrive in her career, traveling more and focusing on professional opportunities. Her mother, Sonya, claimed to be abandoned in LA once everyone dismissed her drama.

Casi bought a cottage in Blackberry Falls in hopes of relocating her mother and providing a stable and safer environment. After a painful night in LA rescuing her from a nightclub, Casi realized there was little she could do to change Sonya's behavior. She called Kyle for help when she realized Sonya would not come willingly. He rushed to her aid with Jake in tow to assist, but instead discovered Sonya overdosed. Alix stood by Casi while she struggled with the reality of her mother's death. Casi insisted on walking the runway at a lingerie show to prove she left LA on her own terms. The video went viral when she dominated the catwalk.

Kyle planned a cruise for the families to spend time together and included Anna with Charlotte, on Lia's insistence. Lies and confessions unexpectedly unravelled on the trip after Casi tried to figure out what was causing her night terrors. Kyle confessed he had been falsely accused of rape in college by a disgruntled classmate who later tried to make amends. He also revealed his party lifestyle, including using and selling cocaine until he collapsed and began using Adderall instead to handle his intense class schedule. Jake was angered by the information and betrayed by his brother's secret drug use.

Jack revealed the truth about his brother, Jamie, who was married to Ava. He was killed in a car accident and Ava lost her unborn child. Ava also confided how her relationship with Jack began and the deep love she had for Casi since she was born. The truth brought the families closer and new bonds were formed.

1
———

DOCKED

The river churned faster, stained ruby red as it infused with blood, and Kyle tumbled through the rapids, helpless to the tug of the undertow. He slammed against a jagged rock, tearing his flesh and snapping the bone below. Gasping for air he reached frantically for Grady attempting to halt their passage to the spinning vortex waiting to swallow them. His hands clawed the water, unable to grasp his friend while his lungs ached for oxygen. Like a steel blade, the granite sliced through his rib cage to expose his youthful organs. The sinewy roots clutched him at the cusp of the whirlpool, taunting him before the sacrificial release to his death.

Kyle gasped and sucked in air, waking from the terror. The night sky glowed silver from the full moon studded with brilliant stars, and he eventually succumbed to the rocking of the ship, easing into a peaceful slumber. Casi breathed softly against his neck, snuggling deeper to his chest. He kissed the top of her head, reveling in their connection and releasing the pain and uncertainty of the prior weeks which disrupted their perfect marriage. He longed to keep her locked safely in his arms, protecting her from past demons. As he embraced her tighter a shiver trembled through his core threatening a premonition of impending doom and unrest in the year ahead.

I

"Excuse me, Sir," a soft lilting voice repeated.

Kyle rubbed his eyes, trying to comprehend his surroundings and why a uniformed man stood beside him, concealing a smile. He breathed in the crisp sea air, confirming he was still aboard the cruise ship. "Good morning. May I have a vanilla latte, please?"

"Shall I bring three?" The server glanced at the dozing pair snuggled against him.

"Um, sure." Kyle cringed at the arrangement. "My wife and brother fell asleep while we were stargazing last night," he said, quickly relaying the relationship status.

"It happens. We are docked now. Perhaps you should take the drinks to your cabin to prepare for disembarkation?"

Kyle tenderly stroked Casi's face to wake her and smiled as she burrowed deeper, wrapping her long limbs around him. "Sweetheart, we need to return to our cabin." He shoved his brother. "Wake up!"

"How come you're sweet with her and I get hit?" Jake yawned, not in a hurry to disengage from the warmth of his sister-in-law.

"Do you realize how this comes across?" Kyle yanked the blankets off. "We're in Long Beach. We need to finish packing."

Casi stretched and located the source of the heat pressing against her back. "We can't ever cruise with this line again. They will suspect we are deviants. First a racy sex tape and now a threesome, tsk, tsk." She mocked Kyle's pained expression. "Coffee!" She bolted upright to receive the steaming cup.

"Damn, I was completely out. I can see why you enjoy sleeping with this girl, she's a lot softer than she looks. Like a warm, cozy pillow. I might have to move in the bedroom when we get home. The couch seems lonely in comparison." Jake chuckled.

Kyle eyed the camera on the overhang. So obvious now. "I'm sure our activities on the upper deck the other evening will get a lot more views than the recording of us sleeping last night."

"Perhaps more happened." Jake shrugged. "Sometimes my hands wander in my sleep. You can't hold me accountable if I'm unconscious."

"I'll render you unconscious if your hand moves any farther." Kyle pinched him as he stroked Casi's bare, tanned stomach. "You have a girlfriend to fondle in your cabin. And a wife at home."

"Can we keep sailing? I'm not ready to face the reality of my life on shore."

"I want to stay here and drink lattes and eat pastries," Casi chimed in. "Although, I do miss my job and Austin." She giggled when Jake raised an eyebrow. "And Tommy. I always forget the new addition to our clan."

"I'm ready to get home to my dog." Kyle grinned. "Oh, and your cat, who rarely acknowledges me."

"Jezebel is quite particular," Casi agreed. "Alright, let's go home and check if Lia burned down the house while we were gone." She smiled back at Kyle, hearing him gulp. "I'm kidding, I'm sure it's fine."

Jake embraced Charlotte, breathing in the sweet scent of the baby before handing her to Anna at the SeaTac airport parking lot. "Do you think she'll forget me?"

Anna smiled, hiding her devastation from saying goodbye and mourning the loss of the close-knit group and their daily interaction. "You'll see her all the time. She knows you're her father." She hesitated, "I'm unsure what happens next. Obviously, I want you in Charlotte's life, but I'm not ready to fall back in a relationship. The cruise was amazing, but my life is in Seattle and you belong in Blackberry Falls... with all your other children and wife."

Jake sucked in his breath, not liking the reality of the situation. "Lia and I are proceeding with the divorce. We don't have to be together constantly, but I love you, Anna. This doesn't end here."

She stepped forward and kissed him. "No, it doesn't. We're both Charlotte's parents. I love you, too. We'll figure out how to make this work in our own twisted way."

"I'm starving!" Casi whined as they took the off-ramp for Blackberry Falls. "I miss the endless supply of food."

"I'll miss the buffets," Jake agreed.

"You were certainly in your element." Kyle chuckled as his brother flipped him off. "It was wonderful having choices every night. Now, it's back to our cooking schedule. What's that smell?" He stepped back when they entered the house, surveying the laundry strewn about the living area, dishes in the sink, and overflowing garbage.

Jake shook his head and gathered the trash, tying it closed and replacing the liner. "Where's Lia?" He turned toward the sound of Tommy wailing.

Casi strolled to the bedroom and immediately retreated. "She's in bed... but not alone!"

The cries escalated, and Jake stormed in and extracted his infant son from the portable crib. He glared at the sleeping couple, oblivious to the commotion. "Austin, come here," he whispered, scooping the toddler from the makeshift bed beside the crib.

Kyle read the anger on his brother's face when he emerged and intervened. "I'll take Austin while you change Tommy."

"CeCe!" Austin launched himself into Casi's arms.

"I want a new bed." Casi shuddered. She softened her scowl in response to the defeat present on Kyle's face. "I'll begin the laundry if you want to clean the kitchen?"

Kyle nodded and started a pot of coffee with a sigh. He opened the fridge and paled. "Ugh, even this is a disaster." He sniffed the spoiled cream before pouring it down the drain.

"Take the boys with you to the store and stock up on groceries while Casi and I whip this place into shape," Jake said.

"Excellent strategy." Kyle hurried to the door with the children. "I'll pick up donuts as a reward."

Casi grinned when he exited. "He hates when his house is violated." Jake nodded, busying himself with loading the dishwasher. "What's wrong?" She rubbed his back. "Are you bothered Lia has a boyfriend?"

He shrugged. "I don't care who she's with in bed, but I'm pissed my sons were there. She didn't wake to Tommy crying or notice we took them. What if one of them ended up in the lake?" He gripped the edge of the counter and attempted to regulate his breathing. "I don't claim to be a terrific parent, but the safety of my kids is at the top of my list."

Casi shook her head noticing the sliders to the deck were partially open. "We'll talk with her. Let's not dwell on what could happen and be thankful they're both fine."

He leaned against her. "Were you afraid when your mom left you alone?"

"Not when she left me in public places. My dad always showed up, and I entertained myself by watching people and the surrounding commotion. The scary times were when she slipped into depression and became a zombie. The house was messy like this, and I was afraid to set her off. She smoked back then and would pass out and burn holes in things. I stayed in my room and played, which is probably why I possess an active imagination." A deep sadness penetrated her smile.

"I don't want Austin to experience the fear I had when we lived with Tara. It took me years after we were adopted to trust adults wouldn't hurt my brother." He grabbed a stack of dishes and shoved them in the dishwasher. "Kyle claims he built this house to take advantage of the gorgeous view, but deep inside he was affected by the chaos we came from and it created a desire to control his environment. This isn't just a mess, it's an attack on his well-being."

Casi's eyes widened. "Kyle is our rock and we can't allow him to be overwhelmed."

Kyle returned to the hum of the washing machine and the house in proper order. "Thank you. I appreciate you guys tackling the disaster. I wasn't sure where to begin."

"No problem. I wanted to ensure my area was tranquil." Jake arranged pillows on the sofa while Casi finished polishing the coffee table.

Kyle began unloading groceries, chuckling when Austin pushed in front to help. "That's so cute," Casi giggled, taking pictures of the toddler haphazardly stacking ingredients in the fridge with his uncle's assistance.

Jake sat on the edge of the bed, rousing Lia. "You're home," she yawned. "I thought you came back tomorrow."

"I'm sure you did." He eyed the man beside her.

She blushed deeply. "Where are the boys?"

"Eating breakfast, although it's after lunchtime." Jake harnessed his annoyance. "Wake your friend and inform him it's time to leave."

They emerged within minutes and Lia avoided Kyle's glare as she poured a cup of coffee, glancing briefly at the fresh quart of cream. "Was the cruise a blast?"

"It was fantastic!" Casi turned and exclaimed when she recalled the man from the fungus lecture. "Mushroom man! Or do you prefer Fun-guy?"

Lia giggled, "Yes, this is Trent."

"Radical house." Trent grabbed a donut.

"It was," Kyle mumbled, moving the plate away to avoid the crumbs filtering through Trent's beard making contact.

Jake picked up an army jacket and guitar and handed them to Trent. "Why don't you take your breakfast to go? I'm sure you must have a job or other obligations." Lia expedited Trent's departure, shuddering when he asked to borrow money for a train ticket. Before she could reach for her purse, Jake handed him a twenty-dollar bill. "Lose this address."

"Jake, I..." Lia attempted after Trent left with the flash of a peace sign.

"No." Jake indicated a chair at the table. "You don't need to explain your lover. We've agreed to go forward as friends, and you don't criticize my relationship with Anna."

"I like Anna," Lia said meekly.

"That makes things easier. We share a daughter, and therefore she's in our lives one way or another. We should discuss this in private except Kyle and Casi are involved in decisions we make for the children. Is Trent someone you want around our sons?"

"I don't care much for him." She winced.

"Blech, good!" Casi expressed.

"Lauren introduced us. She said it would be wise for me to meet an intelligent man and assumed we would hit it off."

"I don't believe your sister had your best interest in mind," Jake scoffed. "Do you have anything in common with him?"

Lia shrugged. "He was interesting when we chatted online, but then he asked me to pick him up at the train station. It was lame."

"He doesn't own a car?" Kyle interjected.

"He has a work truck, but he's not allowed to use it for personal errands."

"Hooking up with you was an errand?" Kyle fumed. "What made you consider it a smart idea to bring someone like that to my home?"

Jake narrowed his eyes at his brother. "Yes, your house is much more valuable than my children."

"To me," Kyle said under his breath.

Casi elbowed him. "He's a loser, I doubt he'll come back and rob us."

"It would be difficult to take much when you have to hitchhike." Kyle grinned.

Casi stifled a laugh. "Lia, we're your friends, can you share what's going on with your moods lately? You're not committed to the bungalow if you've changed your mind."

"Or the divorce. Do we need to revisit what will be the best decision?" Jake rubbed his temple.

Lia wiped tears sliding down her cheeks. "It was difficult to be alone while you were all together. The trailer leaks and smells of mold. I loved being in the bungalow, and it's heartbreaking to not live there right now. I find it hard to manage the boys on my own, and my mother reminds me constantly of the poor choices I've made. Work used to be my escape because it was social, and I kept busy, but our new manager criticizes the way I do everything. I'm a complete failure." She covered her face with her hands and broke down in sobs.

"You're not." Casi rushed to hug her. "We'll help you figure out what the best plan is and support you."

"You can make a mandala with her," Kyle poked Casi in the ribs.

"The process did help me put a few things in perspective. What are the primary areas overwhelming you, Lia?" Casi urged.

Lia shrugged. "Can we hold off on the divorce? I want to be settled in the cottage before I can imagine starting over. Does that impact your relationship with Anna?"

"Anna's focusing on her life and career in Seattle. I'm not sure where I stand with her, but Charlotte is a priority for both of us."

"The bungalow will be move-in ready by the end of the month," Kyle confirmed. "Jake, you're welcome to stay here until your house is finished, which should be by the end of summer."

Jake nodded. "Sure, that's fine."

"I'm happy to have you spend some nights with me. It'll be beneficial for the boys to transition slowly," Lia beamed.

"Thank you, I appreciate that." Jake smiled.

"Can we burn the trailer down?" Lia grinned at Kyle.

Kyle scowled. "That's our hunting trailer! It'll be moved back to our property once the foundation work begins."

Jake stood behind Lia, caressing her shoulders. "I'll patch the roof today. Kyle and I will expedite the bungalow to make it livable."

"Can you find another job?" Casi asked.

"I've put in a couple of applications, but there aren't a lot of positions available for my limited schedule and skill set."

"You could take online business classes," Casi suggested. "You said you would like your own coffee place one day."

Lia blushed. "That's not realistic. I'm not smart enough."

"Sure, you are," Jake praised. "Casi can help you figure out what classes would work for you. You have enough experience; you only lack confidence."

Lia eyed Kyle, expecting him to nix the idea. He smiled. "Since Coffee Junction was bought last year, it hasn't been the same. I would be happy to take my business elsewhere and support you in your endeavor."

"You make everything seem possible."

"Hey, we're headed to Canada to bury my mom. You can come with us and it'll be really fun!" Casi exclaimed.

Kyle wiped tears of laughter from his eyes. "Yes, disposing of your mom will be a blast. Let's ensure she stays put."

Casi giggled. "That came out wrong."

"Your dad said it was fairly far north. We can make a long weekend trip and stop to visit your friends," Kyle suggested.

"That would be ideal!" Casi said.

"We agree you'll lose Trent's phone number and ditch the online romance?" Jake patted Lia's shoulder.

"He doesn't believe in cell phones. He professes they cause brain cancer." Lia smiled. "I only talk to him online."

"He doesn't think computers are dangerous?" Kyle raised an eyebrow.

"He inputs his orders for work, but he goes to the library because he's convinced the government is spying on us and collecting data." She shook her head. "He seemed cooler online."

"Was he at least decent in bed?" Casi shivered.

"Don't answer!" Jake shoved Casi.

"No! He wasn't worth the effort." Lia rolled her eyes. "Maybe I can meet someone in Canada?"

"Most of my friends are married, but you never know what will happen along the way. The planets were in alignment when I met Kyle in LA. I mean, how random was that?" Casi threw her hands in the air.

Jake pretended to gag while Kyle grinned and took her hand. "It was definitely written in the stars."

2

SACRIFICE

"Casi, we're only going for three days." Kyle frowned at the giant suitcase she heaved toward the car.

"I'm unsure what to wear." Casi dissolved into tears.

"She was your mother, dress how you want." He carried the bag back to the house. He undid the zipper and spoke calmly. "It's a nine-hour drive to Prince George and we'll meet our folks. Your dad booked a motel because apparently your mom's town is so small, they don't have lodging. Tomorrow we'll do the service thing and depending on when we get done, we'll consider spending the night near Vancouver and you can visit with your friends. Did you call Dawn?"

"Yes, and I told her I would give details on time once we figured out what we were doing. Basically, I need a dress and something to wear to Swiss Chalet."

"Plus, dinner tonight." He lowered his voice. "Jake wants to create a small get-away trip for Lia. Will that be awkward for you?"

"No, I prefer if we can make this easy-going. Lia is sliding into a depression again and if the untimely demise of my wretched mother can lighten the mood, why not?"

"That's a joke, right?" Kyle said cautiously.

Casi giggled. "I've been a psycho about her death. I want it done and over with. Is it weird I'm excited about seeing Dawn and oblivious to the magnitude of burying my mom?"

"I believe you have accepted she is gone, and this is the final step in saying goodbye."

"Do you think the people will have a ceremony after the service?" She gathered items and put them neatly in a small overnight bag.

"The people?" he chuckled. "They're your family."

"I'm not sensing I'm welcome in their town. Ava's controlling information regarding them and holding back details."

"She's protective of you, and even your mother. She didn't seem to appreciate their tone about our arrival. She urged me to let her send the ashes, but I reiterated the importance for you to deliver them yourself." Kyle put his hand on her shoulder. "Let's consider this is not easy for Ava either. A lot of turmoil and tragedy unfolded in her past, and I'm sure she would prefer for this to happen swiftly."

"What do we do with Crazy Pants?" Jake shook the small wooden box as he unloaded the bags at the hotel.

"Leave her in the car." Kyle cringed when tears came to Jack's eyes and he turned away. He shoved his brother. "Stop screwing around with the ashes. You're being insensitive."

Ava gave them a sympathetic smile. "It's difficult to see the remains. The finality is heartbreaking."

"Sorry, we stashed the box at the wood shop. She's become a fixture on the shelf, and we forget how it affects others." Jake cringed.

"I'm used to her living in LA and I'm still in shock. How are you, Sweetie?" Jack put an arm around Casi's shoulders as she stumbled out of the car.

"I'm unclear if I'm nauseous from the long car trip or the thought of giving my mother to strangers," she breathed.

"Her family requested them, and since she didn't express anything different, it's the right thing to do." Jack kissed her cheek.

"Where are the boys?" Georgia asked as she greeted everyone.

Jake grinned. "Our sons are with my first ex-wife, who adores them. We felt the trip might be too long and questioned the nature of the welcome they might receive at the funny farm for the funeral."

Peter shook his head. "You have a complicated life, Son, but you run it as a well-oiled machine."

"It's not easy juggling three women and five kids but I've got a system in place." Jake's grin faded when Casi staggered forward. "Kyle, your woman is about to chuck."

Kyle quickly directed her to the bushes and rubbed her back as she vomited. "Jake, give me water."

"Please." He chuckled and patted Casi on the backside as he handed Kyle the bottle. He shook his head and turned to Jack. "That tweaker damaged her and still has a hold on her from the afterlife."

Jack nodded. "I'm hoping once we put the ashes in the ground, the tie will be broken. That's why I asked your parents to come. I want her to have as much support as possible."

Casi sipped the water and shivered. "I'm fine. I ate a donut for breakfast, and I guess it didn't sit right with the long trip."

"I told you to sit in front," Jake challenged.

"I suggested oatmeal, but you were hellbent on donuts and have refused to eat anything else." Kyle wiped her face.

"It all comes up the same," Jake snickered.

"I'll be better when this is over, I'm having a difficult time eating regular food. Is it too early for a cocktail?" She giggled.

Peter winked at her. "Canada is a different time zone, so I'm sure it's appropriate."

"You're lying to make me feel better." Casi smiled.

Georgia nodded. "You need a proper meal. Let's get settled in our rooms and find a place for dinner."

"I made reservations," Ava asserted. "You'll enjoy it. They have a decent happy hour we can go to beforehand."

"Have you been here before?" Casi grasped her hand.

A shadow passed over Ava's face, masking the smile plastered in place. "Briefly, a long time ago. I came with your mother for the weekend to visit her sister."

"You've met her family?"

"Only her sister, Simone. This is not a regular town we're going to." Ava hesitated. "You might consider it more of a compound."

Casi smoothed her floral cotton dress as they stood beside the car. "Where's the town?"

Ava cringed and pointed toward a tall stucco wall obscured by trees. "As I mentioned, it's more of a community. Simone will meet us at the gate."

"Can you call and tell her we're here?" Casi asked.

"They don't use phones. My communication has always been by mail."

Jack grasped Ava by the elbow. "Sonya claimed her family disapproved of her marrying outside her faith, which is why they wanted nothing to do with us. What's the real reason?"

Ava flushed and bit her cheek, and she considered the answer. "She was married when she left here. They don't accept you or Casi as members of their family."

"Our marriage wasn't legal?" Jack's eyes widened.

"But I'm her real daughter. Why doesn't that count?" Casi's eyes welled.

Ava led them along a well-worn dirt path through a dense stand of trees. "This ends here. Your mother had no other ties outside of this compound." She approached a wooden door and grasped an immense iron ring, sending a thunderous vibration through the silence of the forest. The click of numerous bolts and clasps being unlocked indicated a party on the other side. A frail woman similar in stance and coloring to Sonya appeared through the crack of the gate, hesitating to open it and reveal the background behind her. "Hello Simone," Ava greeted.

The woman's eyes darted to the group, and she became agitated. "I asked you to come alone."

"Sonya had friends who wanted to say a final goodbye." Ava plucked the box from Casi's grasp and shoved it through the gate.

Casi burst into tears. "My mother…"

"Is gone." Ava spun to face her and put a finger to her lips to use caution. "Thank you, Simone. Please take care of your sister from here."

"Wait, what about a ceremony?" Jack blanched. "We came all this way to leave Sonya with a family who never cared for her?" Simone glared at him and slammed the gate, re-locking the bolts before they could challenge her.

"This is bullshit! Why did you give her the ashes? What kind of place is this?" Casi stomped her foot with disgust.

"Honey, I…" Ava started.

"I thought we were here for a funeral. We may not rate in their world but Casi is Sonya's only child, and she has a right to dictate how her mother is put to rest," Jack fumed.

Ava narrowed her eyes. "Keep your voice down! I explained last night this is different from what we're used to. They do things in their own way and don't want people from the outside intruding."

"Casi, no!" Kyle rushed toward the wall. He reached it too late to prevent her from scaling the thick cement border and landing with a thud on the other side. He observed the group with confusion, analyzing how he should respond. Sheer terror tore across Ava's face, convincing him his wife was in grave danger. "Damn it, Jake, give me a hand." He eyed the slick boundary with confusion of her easy hurdle.

"Kyle," Ava called before he plunged to the other side. "Don't let her talk to anyone and please stop her from mentioning she's Sonya's daughter. There could be severe consequences." She turned to Jack and shook her head. "This is not a religion you want to challenge. They possess strict beliefs and there's a valid reason Sonya severed her ties with them."

"Why did we come? We should bury her at home!" Jack paced the length of the wall.

"It was the protocol, not a request to bring the remains. If we put them in a cemetery, they would exhume them. All children in this religion are born here and are buried here regardless if they separated from the community in their lifetime." Ava wrung her hands. "I should have done it on my own. I wanted Casi to have closure."

"It could have saved us a lot of hassle if they picked them up from you. Why did we come here?" Jake shook his head.

"I promised I would deliver them. I don't want anyone around our home. Or near Casi." Ava surveyed the trees around the compound. "Simone promised to take care of Sonya's ashes with respect if I brought them."

"Why is Simone the spokeswoman for the group?" Jake asked.

Ava took a deep breath. "She's the only one Sonya kept in contact with. She has put herself at risk to keep secrets."

"Like Casi being her daughter?" Jake concluded.

Jack's eyes went wide as Ava tensed. "Yes."

"Wait," Kyle called in a hoarse whisper.

"Don't stop me," Casi sobbed, frantically searching through the maze of stark white buildings.

"I'll help you accomplish whatever task is necessary, but you aren't staying here alone. What is our mission?" he joked.

She gave him a pained smile. "I can't leave her here. She had nightmares about a place like this. I believed I was bringing her home, but I sentenced her to hell. Although she was a terrible mother, I can't live with myself if I allow this to be the end."

"Can you let me take the lead? No offense, but with your sense of direction we may never leave this place," he insisted.

She grasped his hand and submitted to his request as they pressed themselves against the cold cement and navigated alleyways built in a circular pattern around what appeared to be an altar. They locked eyes at the sea of worshipers swarming, adorned in long white tunics and bare feet. "Hare Krishna?" Casi guessed.

"I've never witnessed anything like this," he admitted in awe of the buzz of activity around the central sphere.

"What is that?" she whispered.

"An obelisk, but I'm unclear on the meaning," he said, extracting his phone to take a covert picture. "Odd, no cell service, and my phone is blocked."

"This is a cult," Casi concluded.

"Definitely. There's Simone," Kyle whispered. "I'll get her attention when she walks by. Stay hidden and be prepared to run if she alerts the others. There are hundreds of people here, and I gather we're not welcome. Perhaps they practice human sacrifice."

"Gross," she scoffed.

Kyle gathered pebbles from the ground and carefully tossed them at the hem of Simone's tunic as she moved in the crowd. Her eyes widened when she spotted them, and she shook her head indicating they should stay hidden. With a glance over her shoulder, she casually strayed from the group while keeping her chin up and hesitating nearby without turning toward them. "How did you get in?" she hissed.

"Over the wall," Kyle said. "We need Sonya's ashes. We were misled about what this community was."

Simone's dark eyes welled with tears and she exhaled. "Our worlds are different. You don't belong here."

"As nutty as Sonya was, she doesn't belong here," Kyle stated, regarding the sorrow etched on Casi's face. "We must give her a proper burial."

Simone glanced at Casi briefly, then turned back to the crowd as she spoke. "I know who you are. Ava has protected you all these years. Stay hidden," she said before she rushed toward the throng of people.

"Why would I be in danger?" Casi questioned.

"Let's heed her warning. They're not the back woods country folk we assumed we were coming to meet." He crouched lower in the alleyway and pulled Casi against him while they waited. The crowd moved in unison in the courtyard, as if choreographed. The spark of a flame was ignited and chanting ensued, rhythmic and intense. Kyle rocked back on his heels, startled by the sudden appearance of Simone at his side. "What's going on?" he asked, gesturing to the scene.

"It's the ceremony to release Sonya's soul to our ancestors."

"Where do they think she's been all this time?" Casi asked.

Simone's shoulders slumped, and Casi had a fleeting moment of kinship with the woman she realized was her aunt. "Women are permitted to go to town for supplies only. Sonya slipped away on one of the shopping days, and I didn't report it until it was too late to find her. Commending my sister's spirit to the gods will repair the damage she did when she left."

"Gods?" Casi whispered. "What is this religion?"

Simone shook her head. "I've shared too much. You're an outsider and it's prohibited." She suddenly appeared alarmed. "Did your mother mention a journal?"

"No, I don't think she was one for writing things down," Casi pondered. "Would Ava know about it?"

"Forget what you witnessed here. Don't ask questions and never come back," Simone instructed as she attempted to open the lid. "You may have the contents only."

Kyle produced his pocketknife and pried it open, scowling at the interior. "Um, what do we put her in? I figured she would be in a bag." He assessed Casi's distraught face and realized she might pass out. He pulled off his shirt and poured the contents in the center, quickly wrapping it into a carrier. "This should hold her." He gathered pebbles and dirt to rebalance the weight before securing the lid of the box.

Simone clasped it to her chest, visibly shaken. She reached out and stroked Casi's cheek. "You were lucky you never made it here. Enjoy your freedom," she said, whisked away to the flurry of activity.

They watched her straighten her back and rejoin the group. "We should leave while they are preoccupied," Kyle warned.

"One minute," Casi said entranced by the commotion as the group parted and Simone strolled to the altar and knelt before a man, holding the box up to him. "I wonder if he's her husband?"

"Or her father?" Kyle whispered, curious at the demographics of women of all ages but only young boys and older men. Kyle held Casi closer to his bare chest and slid a hand over her mouth to muffle her sobs when the man set the box on the altar and it was engulfed in flames. As the chanting intensified, Kyle backed down the alleyway, forcing her to come with him as she clutched his twisted shirt. When they reached the wall, he hoisted her to the ledge, hoping someone was on the other side to aid her dismount while he scrambled next to her.

"Damn it, I was ready to come after you," Jake chastised when he grabbed Casi from the ledge and eyed his brother. "What happened to your shirt? Were you assaulted?"

"They made me their love puppet," Kyle joked, grasping his brother's hand to steady himself. "By the way, we still have our nemesis. Casi couldn't let her go."

Jake scowled at the bundle. "And she's escaped her constraints, we better put her in the trunk."

"One of my favorite shirts is ruined," Kyle lamented.

"I can clean it for you, Honey," Georgia urged.

"We'll dump it with the remains." Kyle surveyed Casi's broken demeanor and embraced her. "I'm taking a stand since no one wants to be the bad guy."

"We can make a group decision," Jack offered.

"We are past that point," Kyle challenged. "Ava is bent on hiding the truth, which I'm sure is in Casi's best interest..."

"I was obligated to bring the ashes here. I tried to do it on my own," Ava panicked.

"I understand, and aside from the hassle of driving here and our Olympic feat of scaling the wall, we accomplished the mission. They're doing their little fire and brimstone ceremony inside and commending her spirit to the gods, so we're in the clear with them."

"You're being dramatic," Jack said.

"No, it's a hardcore religious nut-fest in there," Kyle confirmed. He shook his head and eased the ashes from Casi's grasp and shoved it toward Jake. "Two hours back to the motel to pack up our things and then another eight to the crossing. You have ten hours to decide what to do or I'm chucking her on the side of the road. This ends today. I won't have her undermining our lives in Blackberry Falls. She stays on this side of the border one way or another."

3

SWEET RELEASE

Kyle surveyed Casi in the backseat with her knees to her chest. He winced when he noted the sign for the border crossing, adamant about not backing down. "Casi, we…"

"Take this exit," she blurted, bolting upright in her seat. Kyle complied, waiting for further instruction. "Pull in the lot beside the beach." Before he could put the car in park she leapt out and raced toward the railing. "This is the place."

"It's dark. Should we get a hotel and finish this in the morning?" Jake yawned. "I'm starving. You said we would stop for dinner two hours ago."

"It must be done now. She'll change her mind again if we wait." Kyle moved out of the way as Jack parked beside them.

"Good call, Honey. You kids always wanted to go to Kitsilano, but she would wander off here and sit for hours on that point." Jack motioned to a rocky ledge jutting out over the water.

Ava shivered. "This is perfect."

Casi strolled back to them and gave a sad smile. "I'm ready to let her go. This feels right. I would prefer to do it on my own. Can you guys go to dinner and come back to get me?"

"No problem," Jake said.

"Why don't we all go eat together," Jack suggested.

"I'll stay with her and you can bring something back for us." Kyle shook his head when Casi protested. "This is not up for discussion. I won't leave you alone by the ocean."

Jack nodded. "I saw a steakhouse a few exits back. Shall we try it?"

"Sounds ideal," Jake agreed.

Casi clutched the shirt with the ashes to her chest and whispered, "Don't worry, Mom, I sensed this is where you wanted to be. You may have been a horrible disaster in life, but I'll set you free."

❧

"Ava, what has captured your attention?" Jack nudged her.

"Huh? Oh, sorry." She squinted at a figure across the room. "Is that Roxy?"

"From the old restaurant in Burnaby?" He peered through the crowd.

"I haven't seen her in years." Ava jumped up and wound through patrons toward a server putting drinks on a tray. "Roxy?"

"Just a sec, Hun," the woman said, almost dropping the tray as she turned. "Ava! Where the hell have you been?"

"I moved to Bellingham." She smiled. "And I married Jack."

"You took the scoundrel back?" Roxy narrowed her eyes. "Has he been good to you? That son-of-a-bitch had a lot of making up to do. He was practically run out of town after he fell apart when you left."

Ava laughed. "I guess he couldn't live without me. We have a restaurant and brewery. You should come visit."

"Did Cassidy ever get in touch with you? She came by the restaurant to find your contact info. I told her you abandoned me." Roxy frowned.

"I'm sorry." Ava leaned in and hugged her. "I wasn't thinking rationally. I needed to get out of town and start over."

Roxy put a hand on her hip. "Yet Jack found you and convinced you to marry him. That two-timing louse!"

Ava laughed. "Casi tracked me down."

"Casi? La-di-da." She rolled her eyes.

"She changed her name for modeling. It really suits her."

"That beautiful little brat. I heard she was super successful in LA. I guess she finally grew into those boobs and long legs." She rolled her eyes. "She was too damn pretty for her own good."

"She did well with modeling. She's married and has moved to Washington. She's in marketing and promotions for a skincare line and is very happy."

"Any kids?"

"No." Ava glanced away.

"I meant Cassidy." She smoothed a hand over Ava's arm.

Ava smiled. "She doesn't have children either."

"Good, then her marriage stands a chance." Roxy threw her head back and laughed. "How's her crackpot mother?"

"Sadly, we're here because Sonya passed away and we're finalizing things."

"Drugs? Or did someone kill her for screwing their husband?"

"The former," Ava whispered. "Come say hi to Jack."

"Look what the cat dragged in." Roxy shoved him roughly when she approached the table. "What's up, Jack-off?"

"I haven't missed that nickname. I thought you'd still be talking smack at the old place. Did someone finally sue you for misconduct?" Jack stood and gave her a hug.

Roxy swung an arm around Ava's waist. "I needed my partner in crime. Things went south when she left. You're not the only one who missed her." She surveyed Jake and grinned. "Who's this handsome devil? Back in the day, I would offer you a wild ride."

"I'm flattered and I'm sure you could deliver on that offer." Jake perused her curvy figure barely secured in tight clothing.

"His brother is married to Casi and they are at the beach." Ava introduced the rest of the table.

She cocked her head and eyed Jake. "Is your brother as gorgeous as you?"

"Much better looking." Jake grinned.

"Are you working or socializing?" a man yelled from the side.

"Go suck a dick, ass-wipe," Roxy shot back. She ran her fingers through Jack's hair. "I'm surprised you still have your golden locks. I figured you'd be fat and bald like the rest of my men."

"I was never one of your men," Jack insisted, smoothing his hair back in place. "Not that you didn't try."

"Sure, but you only had eyes for this goddess." She winked at Ava before flipping off her manager. "Hey, are you hiring? I'm not a stellar waitress, but I can work a bar like no one else. Pair me with Ava and we'll run those tabs up. You owe me for all the times I covered for you while you two were playing hide the sausage."

"We're fully staffed." Jack shuddered.

Ava handed her a business card. "I would love to catch up."

Roxy wrapped them in a hug before stomping back to the bar. Jack elbowed Ava. "Why did you give her our number? We should let that cluster-fuck live out her days on this side of the border."

Ava smiled. "Perhaps it's time to shake things up."

❧

"A ton of people come here at night." Jake scanned the full parking lot.

Ava nodded. "It's a pretty remote beach for this kind of turn out."

They followed the sound of laughter and glow of a fire at the edge of the shore. Jack stopped in his tracks when he recognized a few of the party goers. "Joey? Did Casi tell you she was here?"

"Hey, Mr. Roberts. Yup, she sent Dawn a text about spreading her mum's ashes. We wanted to be here for her when she gets back."

"Back? Where did she go?" Jack's eyes darted over the beach.

Joey pointed toward the inky sea. "I'm guessing out that way. We found clothing on the shore."

"She went swimming?" Jack gasped.

"Damn it!" Jake rushed to the water's edge. "Where did they swim to?"

Ava came to his side and slid an arm around his waist. "She most likely swam out to the buoy." She indicated a faint orange outline in the distance.

"Most likely? I can't just stand here and hope they make it back!" Jake began to hyperventilate.

"There they are!" Ava rubbed his back and brought his attention to dark figures bobbing in the waves.

Dawn squealed and rushed to the shore with a bundle of towels. "Our girl is a loon!"

Joey grinned. "We built the fire to guide them in case they got turned around out there."

"Good idea." Jack exhaled as the couple waded to shore.

"Why did you go out so far?" Jake demanded.

Kyle shivered. "She wanted to spread the ashes from the point to the buoy. I tried to explain the tide would take them there, but she insisted she had to be the one to deliver them." He secured a towel around his hips and draped another over his shoulders with Dawn's undivided attention.

Joey cradled Casi in his arms, while another friend blotted her hair with a towel. "Come sit by the fire, Angel."

"We have a surprise." Dawn stepped aside.

Casi's face lit up, and she burst into tears at the sight of her old friend. "Katie! Where have you been all these years?"

"Busy with life and stuff." Katie hugged her as the tears flowed freely. "I've missed you. I heard about your mum through Facebook and I finally broke down and messaged Dawn to find out what was going on. She texted me you were coming this weekend, and I hoped to put the past behind us."

"I'm sorry for everything!" Casi sobbed.

"I was in a bad place back then and I blamed you for the crap in my life." Katie hugged her tightly.

Casi wiped her nose with the back of her hand and giggled when both Joey and Kyle pushed toward her with a tissue. "This is my husband, Kyle."

"Uh, of course, super-hot," Katie sighed.

"Are you married?" Casi asked.

Katie shrugged and glanced over her shoulder. "Sort of."

"What does that mean?"

"I have three little girls," Katie beamed. "They're the best part of my life and help me stay on track..." She shifted her weight in the sand. "Did your mum tell you I got fat?"

"Who cares? Obviously, you did something about it." Casi noted her slender figure.

Katie shrugged. "Partially because of her."

"How did she inspire you?"

"More like tormented me. She saw pictures of me on Facebook with the kids and commented on my weight."

"She was never kind." Casi winced. "I hope you unfriended her."

"She trolled me!" Katie exhaled. "Casi, I married Shane."

"Shane?" Casi blurted, then covered her mouth. "In a drunken haze?"

"I hit rock bottom and ended up getting pregnant. The baby changed the direction of my life."

"And you're still with him?"

"Kind of." Katie exhaled.

Jack raised an eyebrow at the burly man beside him. "Your reputation continues. How's business?"

The man narrowed his eyes at the pair of women reuniting. "I work for Boeing in Seattle. I'm an electrical engineer. My poor choices are behind me." He eyed Jake and Lia, keenly listening to the conversation, and extended his hand. "Hi, I'm Shane, the most embarrassing man you could marry."

Casi turned to the sound of his voice and giggled. "Shane! I never pictured you as a dad. I figured you would be in jail."

"I served my time." He rubbed his belly. "I'm well fed, a father, and a hard-working man. The husband part is questionable."

Jake nudged Lia as he observed her scanning Shane with interest. "I guess you will meet a man in Canada."

Lia blushed. "He's married."

"It doesn't sound permanent." He gave her a wink.

Jack embraced Casi. "Is everything done the way you hoped for?

I'll leave you to reminisce with your friends and the four of us will head home."

"Thank you for understanding what I had to do." Casi hugged him tightly.

Jake set clothes on a log by the fire. "Probably a good time to get dressed before you freeze to death."

Kyle stood and dropped his towel, unabashedly getting changed as Casi followed suit. Dawn giggled, "Cassidy, you're still as carefree as you were in high school."

"She's still my same beautiful angel," Joey admired. "Although the tattoos are new and very sexy!"

"I love them!" Dawn agreed, turning her eyes to peruse Kyle.

Katie frowned at the perfect figure dressing before her. "Obviously, you don't have children."

Dawn patted Casi on the backside. "She's blessed with a gorgeous body. She also has a hot husband and a stellar career."

"What are you trying to say, Dawn?" Shane teased as he shook his hips and rubbed his belly.

The women giggled as they watched his performance by the fire. "You're still a goofball," Dawn confirmed.

Shane chuckled and regarded Jake and Kyle. "Brothers?"

"Yes, I'm Jake." He extended his hand and grinned. "This is Lia, my soon to be ex-wife."

"Wow, Dude, you're mega-handsome but I don't roll that way." Jake's face contorted and Shane smacked him on the back. "Just joshing with you, bro. Nice to meet you, Lia." He grasped her hand and smiled as she blushed deeply.

Kyle noted the chemistry between them. "What were you in jail for?"

"You cut to the chase." Shane grinned. "Are you concerned about the epic relationship stirring between your brother and me?"

Kyle chuckled. "My brother can take care of himself."

Shane noted his glance toward Lia and nodded. "Dealing and driving around with underage girls. Nineteen, and the girls were fifteen." He pointed across the fire. "Cassidy, Dawn, and Katie. High as kites, and I supplied it. I did five years."

"Did Casi rat you out?" Jake asked.

"Nope, and her dad refused to press charges. He advised me to get my shit together and stay away from his daughter and his wife, although she was an ex by then."

"You slept with Sonya?" Jake snickered.

Shane shrugged. "Who didn't? Honestly, that's why I came tonight. I wanted to pay my final respects." He poked at a burning log and frowned. "We kept in touch on Facebook, and I loved seeing how Cassidy excelled at modeling. I remember her in second grade, sassy attitude and long legs."

Casi smiled when she heard her name. "Why didn't you contact me?"

Shane shrugged. "I was forbidden. Katie didn't realize I was friends with your mum until a few years ago."

Katie rolled her eyes. "Yes, when she commented on my family photos calling me a porker. Oh, and then she sent nudes of herself to Shane."

Casi's mouth dropped and Jake roared with laughter. "Trust Sonya to stir things up."

"Jesus Christ, that woman had no boundaries." Kyle shuddered.

Shane chuckled. "She's jealous because your mum was way hotter in her fifties than Katie at thirty."

"Whatever," Katie snapped. "Cassidy, tell me everything about your life."

Casi glanced at Dawn, who gave her a knowing smile, understanding the happiness and complexity resulting from reuniting with their old friend. "LA was fine for a while. I did ok with modeling." She smiled at Kyle. "I live in Washington now," she continued, the joy coming through in her voice as she talked about their home and her career. "I'm close with Jake's and Lia's boys."

"She helps raise them. They love her," Jake interjected, and Lia nodded. He cocked his head. "Casi, why did you address your mother as mom if you're Canadian?"

She sighed. "I only called her mother when I lived here. She hated 'mum' and certainly was never a mummy. She thought it was stupid, like we were trying to pretend we were British. I tried not to slip and call her that by mistake." Her eyes welled.

"I suspect she reinforced her opinion?" Kyle clenched his jaw.

"When we moved to LA, she decided 'mom' was appropriate. It was weird at first, but she felt it made her sound younger and more hip."

Jake rubbed her back. "I'm sorry I asked."

"It's fine." She cast a glance to the sea. "She's gone now."

"Let's go for a walk on the beach." Katie grabbed Casi's hand.

Casi hesitated and reached for Dawn. "Come with us."

"Your wife is a piece of work," Jake said when they walked away.

"She's a bitch." Shane shivered. "She and Cassidy used to be best friends with Dawn in high school. They had a falling out after Cassidy moved to LA and Katie flew off the rails. I ran into her at a bar and we hooked up. That sums up our life since then. I was the pity fuck who got her pregnant, and when life didn't offer her much more, we stayed together. Things were better when she was chunky. We actually had some fun times," he sighed. "Then she went on this mission to lose weight, and although she's been successful, it's made our home life miserable. I'm in Seattle weeknights but I come home on weekends to be with the girls."

"Sounds brutal," Jake said.

"Our kids are great. That part is worth it." He continued talking about his life as he poked at a log in the fire.

Kyle nudged Jake. "Let's go check out the pier."

"Are you trying to get romantic with me?" Jake grinned. Kyle cocked his head toward Lia and Shane, lost in conversation. "Sure, that would be cool." As they walked away, he glanced back at the couple. "Are you advocating for this to turn into a relationship? He seems like he has a screwed-up life."

"You do too," Kyle said. "Lia appears interested. It would be good for her to date someone other than the leftovers in town."

"Remember I have children with her," Jake cautioned.

"Would you prefer Trent?"

"Perhaps you're sympathetic toward your fellow drug dealer?" Jake followed his brother's gaze to where Katie, Dawn, and Casi strolled hand in hand down the beach, kicking at the waves. "Wait, a second! You're using Lia as bait because you don't trust that woman with your precious wife."

Kyle grinned. "I think she's trouble and Casi has remorse about their lost friendship. I'm concerned we just got rid of one leech and may be gaining another."

"You're throwing my naïve wife to the wolves to spy on them?"

"Shane's cool. He can teach your kids how to play hockey," Kyle chuckled. "Lia likes her men husky, and he seems genuinely interested in her. I fear Katie might embed herself in our lives, but if Lia and Shane get together, there will be a filter."

"Plus, Shane will innocently tell you all the dirt on Katie, so you can protect Casi," Jake concluded.

"I just got her put back together. She can't come unglued again."

When a blanket of fog enveloped the beach, the party moved to Dawn's and Joey's basement. Beer and tequila shots made the rounds, and Casi discovered a karaoke machine. Dawn raced to join her on the makeshift stage while Katie reluctantly completed the trio with less enthusiasm. Kyle performed a sexy rendition of a Pit bull song, making the women swoon until Shane's impression of a backup dancer had everyone rolling with laughter.

"You were always hilarious," Casi giggled.

"Still am, but now I'm better looking," Shane replied, gyrating and posing.

"Can you believe how fat he got?" Katie scoffed.

"I have to admit the extra weight suits you." Casi scanned his physique. "You were pretty scrawny before. You are more like a man now."

Shane bellowed with laughter, catching Lia's admiring eye. "Some women prefer a burly fellow."

The evening wore on and Casi announced a pajama party, rekindling the memories of youth, as they recollected the fun times spent in basements in a nest of blankets and pillows. Kyle smiled at Dawn's attempt to extract herself from Casi's clutches as she draped across her lap. "She has no problem falling asleep on people." He swept her hair from her cheek as he gazed at her with love.

"She never did." Dawn sighed and squeezed Casi's hand. "I'm working the night shift otherwise I would leave her on me. I miss her so much."

"You have to go to the restaurant?" Casi yawned.

"Cassidy, I haven't worked at Swiss Chalet in years!" Dawn giggled. "I'm an emergency room nurse and I have night shifts this week. My parents are watching the kids because Joey's on swing shift at the factory."

Kyle swung Casi in his arms and carried her to the bed he created on the floor and settled her between blankets, frowning when Katie scooted beside her claiming his spot. He stepped over her to wedge himself between the wall and Casi.

"You don't care for the floor either?" Shane cocked his head as Jake paced the perimeter of the room. "My back is messed up from hockey, so this does a number on it." He flopped beside Katie on the edge of the blanket.

"Football." Jake nodded, hiding the real reason for his anxiety.

"Move, Shane! You snore." Katie elbowed him away.

"Where would you like me to go?" He jumped up and grabbed a blanket from the sofa, relocating to a chair.

"Jake, why don't you and Lia take the pullout?" Joey offered. "I'm heading upstairs to grab a few solid hours before work."

"Shane, would you prefer the bed?" Jake asked.

"You keep trying to hit on me. Perhaps you'll wear me down in time with your electric blue eyes and promise of sexy tattoos over rippling muscles, but for now you should sleep with your wife." Shane bit his bottom lip and groaned deeply.

Jake grinned, amused by the good-natured ribbing. He surveyed the distance from the door to Kyle several times before reclining beside Lia. She smoothed her hand over his back and whispered, "Are you ok? You're shivering."

"It's cold down here," he lied. "Are you warm enough?"

She cuddled against him as a long, muffled growl vibrated throughout the room. "Wow, he snores like a bear!" She laughed into Jake's chest.

Giggles and chatter continued for several hours, punctuated by Shane's snorts, releasing another round of laughter until exhaustion overcame them. Casi woke with a start, confused by her location, feeling Kyle's warm breath on her neck in contrast to Katie's chilled cheek on her shoulder. Anxiety gripped her, and she feared being trapped, pinned against the musty damp floor. She crawled out and crept to the stairs, gasping for air. "Are you alright," Jake slid beside her as she crouched in the dark.

"I couldn't breathe," she choked. "Sorry if I woke you."

"I never fell asleep."

"Is Shane's snoring too loud?"

"I'm used to it from hunting camps."

She assessed his discomfort. "How do you deal with your anxiety when you're camping?"

Jake smiled at her perception. "I only require two things; I must face the entrance and those I care about are behind me."

"Is that a foster kid thing?"

He rolled his eyes. "You throw that term around like it's normal." His lips curled into a smile. "Juvenile hall did a number on me. The older kids were always sneaking up and covering your face with a pillow or messing with you. I'm perfectly fine at home and I'm not afraid to sleep alone, but I'm uneasy when I'm in an unfamiliar environment and I must protect people."

"Like Kyle." Casi glanced at him asleep against the wall and realized his neck would have a severe cramp when he awoke.

"And you, or my kids." Jake smiled.

Casi hugged him. "Thanks for looking out for us. Do you want to get donuts?"

"It's five in the morning!"

"Tim Horton's drive-thru is twenty-four hours."

The headlights illuminated Kyle's distraught face as they pulled in the driveway. He rushed to the door and yanked it open. "Where were you? I woke up next to Katie drooling on my pillow and I couldn't find you anywhere. I figured you were together when I noticed the car was gone."

"Coffee and donuts." Jake held up a bag.

"I'm sorry I abandoned you." Casi handed him a tray of coffee as Joey appeared with a yawn. "Where are you going?"

"Early shift at the factory. Dawn will be back in a bit. She'll pick up the kids on her way home." He eyed the donuts and wiped a crumb from Casi's cheek. "How are you not fat?"

She threw her head back and laughed. "My husband monitors my nutrition normally. I had an early morning sugar craving and my brother-in-law complied with my request."

"I am concerned for her health. It's not about her weight." Kyle blanched.

"Chunky monkey." Jake poked her in the ribs.

Joey grinned. "I loved the girl, but you claimed the woman. You're the ideal man to take care of my sweet angel."

4

SONGS OF THE HEART

"What did you think of Katie?" Casi asked mindlessly, rolling a staggered line of periwinkle blue paint.

Kyle redirected her stroke, trying to keep her focused on the task. "She seemed alright. It's terrific, you're friends again. Why don't you and Dawn catch up with her at the house?"

Casi giggled. "You sound like my dad. He says Katie's trouble and Dawn is the sweet normal one keeping everything in balance."

"Your dad and I have a lot in common," he agreed. "Like loving you so much we don't want to see you get hurt."

She nodded, swiping hair from her cheek with the back of her hand. "Katie isn't perfect, and it's been years since we've been friends..."

Kyle grabbed a cloth and gently wiped the paint smeared on her cheek. "You're on an amazing path and I don't want you to get talked into harebrained ideas."

"You've been speaking to Shane."

"A little. I'm vetting him for Lia."

"Liar!"

"Honestly? I leave for the island in two weeks to start that job I told you about. I'll be back and forth but spending most of my time there until the work is finished, which might be six weeks. I'm concerned you might take my absence as a reason to renew your friendship with someone who is not the best influence."

Casi smiled. "Are you appointing Jake as my babysitter?"

"To a degree," he teased. "It's not that I don't trust you, I'm worried about stuff you may not consider a problem until it's too late."

"Like checking my tire pressure and gas?"

"Plus eating a proper breakfast. And feeding our animals."

"I made a list of all the things you do for me and I'll make sure it's handled. It was surprisingly long with subcategories."

"That kind of talk turns me on." He pulled her toward his chest. "I also require you to keep an eye on Jake. He's focused on helping Lia move forward to the life she desires, but he hasn't grasped he'll be alone. This is bad timing with me leaving town."

"Do you anticipate a panic attack?"

"Quite possibly. We're moving the trailer this weekend, which means he'll be basically homeless."

She raised an eyebrow. "What if we put a futon in your secret room nook? We will camouflage it with fun pillows to hide the fact he sleeps there, but his bedding will provide a defined space."

"Excellent idea! We'll tell him we bought it on sale and suggest it would be practical to move to his house for one of the old kids."

"Perfect, but let's call them by name to make it less tawdry."

Lia arrived with curtains. "Casi, won't these be darling in the front windows?"

"Kyle, tell Lia the paint should dry before she installs curtains." Jake frowned at Casi's haphazard application.

Kyle took the roller from Casi's hand. "Why don't you and Lia make lunch and we'll finish painting. You might be better at the detail work." He eyed the patchy paint job. "Check out that sale you mentioned. We could store a few things at our place if you decide there are significant savings."

"I assumed painting would be more exciting. It might not be my forte." Casi grinned. "But shopping is totally my thing."

Kyle stood at the edge of the property, clipboard in hand. Jake strolled over and surveyed the empty lot, glancing at the paperwork his brother held. "Do you want to go over the plans one more time?" Kyle asked.

"I don't care, I want it done." Jake rubbed his arm.

Kyle grasped Jake's wrist to halt the compulsive action. "We designed this as a two-bedroom, one bath. We should consider long-term and the amount of kids you sired. Let's add a bedroom and a second bathroom."

"Whatever," Jake mumbled.

"Have you spoken to Anna?"

"She's staying in her condo for now. She wants to be close to work and Charlotte's daycare is nearby."

"Ok, but she'll visit, right? Charlotte needs a place and the boys will live here half the time, at least."

"I want to live at your house." Jake grinned.

"Consider this an addition with a road between."

Casi surveyed the organized stacks of paperwork set out on the dining room table. "Can we move these to eat dinner?"

"I will after everything is in order." Kyle moved papers from one pile to another. "I went to Costco and got the basics, so you guys should be able to manage for a while."

"We can feed ourselves even when our fearless leader is out of town."

Kyle smiled. "I didn't mean it like that. Your work is busy, and Jake has a lot more pressure with the wood shop. We've put Riley on for full-time, but the frames must be built for the custom work, in addition to the regular orders on the dockets."

"Who will take care of my sexual needs," she purred.

"You have two hands. And a shower head."

"I like your hands on me."

"Let me finish my paperwork and I'll put my hands all over you for the rest of the night," he promised.

"I moved the last of Lia's things to the bungalow. The boys are taken care of, so I can settle into my homelessness." Jake helped himself to a beer..

"Cool, now we can plan all kinds of fun things to entertain ourselves." Casi gave Kyle a wink. "Let's bring the boys over this weekend for a sleepover. I'll rent animated movies and make popcorn."

Jake nodded. "Get the one about the fish. They would like that."

"Sure, and when we want them to fall asleep, we'll put on Kyle's documentaries." Casi laughed as Kyle smacked her behind. She turned and waved to the space beside the computer. "Lia and I were shopping, and I found this futon. Kyle picked it up and we will store it here until your house is finished. It was too good of a deal to pass up. Plus, it will be nice for extra space for our sleepover parties while Kyle is out of town."

Jake sighed and smoothed his hand over the perfectly coordinated sheets, pillows, and comforter. "It's a similar pattern to my room at the farmhouse, interesting how it was all on sale." He turned and smiled at them. "Thank you. I appreciate the warm welcome."

Kyle covered the microphone on his phone and sighed, pausing mid-step as he left the parking garage. "No, it's fine," he lied. "That's awesome Katie found a last-minute sitter for the kids and can meet you after all."

"You sound disappointed," Casi said. "Is dinner made?"

"I'll grab something on my way home."

"We can do happy hour another time," she insisted.

"Go and enjoy. I realize it's difficult for Katie to get away and your schedule is ramping up as well."

"I won't be too late. Maybe Jake wants to hang out?"

"I'll call him." He hung up, not bothering to call his brother, already aware he was with Anna.

An upbeat rendition of a Stevie Nicks song caught Kyle's attention as he strolled a side street and he jogged down the steps to the underground club to check it out. He found a table at the corner of the stage while his eyes adjusted to the dim lighting. His jaw dropped when the sultry woman belted out the tune, and he stammered his order to the waiter. "Um, a martini," he finally whispered. "Hey, does she sing here every night?"

"Her band plays here the first Thursday of the month. She's awesome, isn't she? They don't make them like her anymore," the waiter stated.

"She's amazing." Kyle reclined in his chair to enjoy the show. Several songs and two drinks later, he brought out his phone and recorded the performance to send to Jake. "Look who has a nightclub act."

"Holy shit!" Jake replied. "How did you find out?"

"I came in for a drink and discovered her on stage."

A round of applause erupted, and Kyle slipped his phone back in his pocket. The lights dimmed on stage while the bar was illuminated. He watched her intently, wondering if she would notice him and considering if he should leave to allow her the privacy of her performance. "Kyle?" She cocked her head and moved toward him.

"Hi, Ava." He stood to greet her. "I came for a drink and was pleasantly surprised. I had no idea you were in a band."

"No one does, not even Jack." Ava gave him a wink. "He thinks I have a book club meeting every month."

Kyle grimaced. "I shared a video with Jake. I didn't realize it was a secret. He said you were incredible by the way."

Ava smiled. "Thank you. Is Casi here?"

"She's at happy hour with Katie. I was already in Seattle, so I figured I would check out a club."

Ava smiled. "Because you didn't want to disappoint her by admitting you drove here to meet her."

"Something like that." Kyle grinned.

"Katie, huh?" Ava sighed.

"Bad news?"

Ava signaled the waiter and ordered a whiskey sour. "You don't mind if I join you? We're taking a thirty-minute break." She smiled. "They have good food here if you would like dinner."

"That would be great."

The food and drinks arrived, and Kyle grinned. "Do we start with why you're sneaking around on your husband or why I'm afraid to confront my wife about her troubled friend?"

Ava laughed and took a sip of her drink. "I've been in this band since I moved to Bellingham." She eyed the lead guitarist and shrugged. "When Jack came here, he was a wreck, and I ended a relationship to take him back." Her eyes faded to silver. "It was a hard year for me...the last of my miscarriages." Kyle slid his hand over hers and waited for her to continue. "Jack and I made each other, and the restaurant, our priority, but I desired something that was still just mine. These are my close friends and they have no connection with the rest of my life. There's no point to keeping it private other than it is something from my past I wanted to hold on to. I always figured Jack would find out at some point and part of me is disappointed he wasn't jealous enough to investigate my book club claim, especially when I come home smelling like tobacco and whiskey."

"I wonder if Casi feels like that. She breaks dates and makes her career a priority. Am I being challenged and I'm too dumb to see it?"

"Too polite," she agreed. "Casi loves her life with you but be aware of Katie. She's a master manipulator."

"I'm listening."

"Part of my issues with Casi as a teenager were because of Katie running her mouth. Casi is sweet and wants to please everyone. We would have a lovely weekend and hoped we moved past a rough spot and then bang; Katie filled her head with negative things about me or her dad. Dawn is a doll and I love Joey, but we struggled with the horrible backlash of Katie's desperate desire for attention."

"What about Shane?"

"He's harmless." Ava winked. "I used to buy pot from him!"

"Wow, scandalous!"

"He played hockey with Joey and was a party guy," she hesitated, examining the ice in her drink.

"He told us about going to jail."

"It wasn't fair. He took the blame for everyone, even though Joey was in the car too. Jack and Dawn's parents wouldn't press charges because they knew the girls were the instigators. They used Shane to buy alcohol and supply drugs, and he was a goofy guy who liked being part of the group. Katie lied and said she had been coerced."

"Isn't it surprising she ended up marrying him?"

"I'm sure no one else wanted her," she said bitterly, then smiled. "I realize that sounds catty. Katie put so much pressure on Casi to bring her to LA when that poor girl could barely take care of herself and Sonya. When things fell apart, instead of supporting her, Katie turned on Casi and tore her to shreds. Dawn and Joey stepped in and basically banned her from the group, which is how she ended up in Gas Town. I'm friends with her mother. She went through hell trying to help Katie straighten up and in return her selfish daughter lied about her home situation, pretending she was the victim. I'm unsure about the sequence of events leading her to get together with Shane, but I'm assuming he was the only one who would have anything to do with her because he was unaware of the drama."

"I hate her," Kyle seethed.

"She might have changed. Shane seems to have taken a positive path, and perhaps she matured. It's unfortunate she's in Seattle; it would be better with her on the other side of the border to create a buffer."

Kyle nodded. "There seem to be a lot of impromptu plans."

She glanced at her watch. "Are you staying for another set?"

"If that's ok, I enjoyed listening to you."

"I would love it. I'm getting together with Casi soon to show her scrapbooks. Maybe I'll take her to a Karaoke bar."

"She's not aware you sing?"

"I don't think she would remember." Ava smiled sadly. "We had moments of pure bliss when she was a teenager, but I fear the memories were overwritten by the negativity Sonya fed her."

"Casi has a remarkable memory. Perhaps those times are tucked away and can be regained in time. I'm leaving next week for that job on the island, but I would love to hear you sing together at some point."

"We'll make a date. I'll invite Jack."

Casi squinted as she turned the page. "I remember almost nothing from back then. Are you sure this was my life?"

"I assumed that would be the case," Ava sighed, moving the pile of scrapbooks. "I have videos but they're all VHS."

"Why don't you convert them?"

"How do you do that?" Ava cocked an eyebrow.

"I noticed a place in Seattle offering the service. I'll get more information." Casi took a sip of tea.

Ava reached over and smoothed her hand over Casi's arm. "Do you need to get home soon?"

"Nope, Kyle's on that island finalizing the deal. I'm not sure what time he'll be home." She ran a finger over the edge of her cup.

"Are you nervous about him being away?"

She shrugged. "I'm not looking forward to it and I'll be glad when it's done. He's been anxious lately, and I hope it's due to the job rather than something between us. What time does Dad get home?"

Ava rolled her eyes. "Who knows? He's training a new bartender, and she seems to be a slow learner."

"Why is he training her? The bar is your thing."

"Apparently, I lack patience with her." Ava stood. "Is it my fault she's as dumb as a doorknob?"

Casi laughed. "Let's hit the town and enjoy a girl's night out!"

"Ok, wait," Casi giggled, grasping her stomach. "Her name is Karma, and she's twenty-two? Is Dad having a breakdown, again?"

Ava wiped tears and erupted in another fit of laughter. "I'm labeling this one his midlife crisis. He actually tried to comb his hair over a thin spot, and I threatened to shave his head in his sleep!"

"Please tell me he's only flirting like an idiot and not sleeping with this woman." Casi's face contorted.

"I'm certainly not getting any." Ava covered her mouth. "I'm drunk and revealing things I shouldn't." She furrowed her brow. "I found a sample bottle of Viagra and flushed it down the toilet in a fit of anger. Two years ago, he performed just fine for your mother but now he requires medication. I'm assuming it was for me," she mumbled.

Casi took her hand. "He turned sixty and Mom's death made him understand he's mortal. The flirting and bedroom issues may be due to his inability to handle the natural aging process."

Ava nodded and ordered another round. "Did Kyle mention anything about last Thursday?"

"Oh God, is he cheating on me?" Casi clasped her chest.

"He was with me last week."

"I understand you need to get your kicks, but can you take Jake instead?"

"You're hysterical. Although if your father doesn't get his act together soon, I may take your brother-in-law up on his offer."

"I might vomit."

"Come with me." Ava pulled her over to the band.

"Ava, no, not when you're drunk!" Casi stopped in her tracks.

"Tell me if this prompts any memories." Ava smiled and took the microphone. Casi hesitantly stepped into the spotlight, squinting at the crowded room. Ava began Juice Newton's 'Morning Angel' softly as Casi's jaw dropped. After the third line, she sang the chorus accompanying her perfectly pitched stepmother. The crowd erupted with applause and cheered them to keep singing. Ava turned back to the band, and they nodded, continuing the impromptu concert.

"I forgot how we sang along with the radio in the car when I was a teenager," Casi recalled as they left the stage. "I have to pee."

Ava guided her to the restroom, chatting as they entered the stalls. "Do you remember any of the fun times we had?"

"I've been thinking back over things. Kyle suggested I focus on positive times in my past and release painful memories. You were a huge part of what was good." Casi stepped toward the sink and washed her hands.

"And perhaps a bit of what was bad, but please consider it from my perspective and understand how much I loved your dad, and you."

"Kyle has made me realize what it's like to be insanely in love with someone and I relate to the position you were in." Casi regarded her in the mirror. "Honestly, it hurts Dad was in love with you while he was married to Mom. It makes me worry about Lauren and if I should be concerned about her friendship with Kyle."

Ava nodded. "Every partnership is different. Your mom and dad had a physical relationship, but nothing else. You have a deep emotional connection with Kyle that began the moment you met him. It's not about sex, but knowing you're whole when you're with him." Ava tossed the paper towel in the trash and leaned against the sink. "I didn't try to steal your father. After the accident, our lives were completely shattered. It affected your mom too. When she lost her son, she couldn't find her way back to who she had been." She cast her eyes to the floor tiles. "That's when my relationship with her truly ended. She morphed into someone I had zero respect for." She squeezed her eyes shut and exhaled. "I should have been aware she was hurting you."

Casi slid beside her. "You couldn't have known." She smiled and took Ava's hand. "I do recall when you came back. It was like I could breathe again. I stopped being afraid because you made everything better. You moved me from that school I hated, and suddenly I had tons of friends. Dad was happy all the time and there was laughter in our world again."

Ava stroked her hair. "I love you so much, Casi. I hope you know that."

"I do." She leaned to hug her and tripped over her own foot. "We can't drive home. Should I call an Uber?"

Ava checked her watch. "Dad must be home by now, I'll call him."

"Is he home?" She surveyed the anger rising in Ava's flushed face.

"Jack, don't bother, we'll make our own way." She shoved the phone back in her purse. She took a deep breath and turned to Casi. "Karma was having car trouble, so he's giving her a ride."

"How convenient. Where does she live? Let's go over there and kick the shit out of her!" Casi sent a text. "Our ride will be here in thirty minutes, let's have another drink."

"Why not?" Ava nodded and led the way back to their table. She considered condensation on her glass and spoke carefully. "The reason I'm bothered by the Karma situation is not the flirting." She smiled. "You remember when I worked at the bar? I was young and vibrant and had my whole life ahead of me. I loved shit-talking with the customers, dressing sexy, and being bold. I've turned into a middle-aged woman who's in bed by ten and has more cross-stitched pillows than I know what to do with. I should start wearing quirky sweaters, get twelve cats, and call it a day."

"Are you jealous of Karma or missing your bad-ass self?"

"When we were in Canada, I ran into Roxy at the steakhouse. It brought back so many good times, but it left me a little depressed. Perhaps it was a wake-up call. Karma's not even pretty, and she's arrogant with the customers. She would rather be on her phone than serve drinks. She doesn't understand that no task is menial when you're creating an environment for people to escape to from their daily lives." Ava grinned. "Since I moved to Bellingham, on the first Thursday of the month I tell Dad I have a book club and I sing with my band. Kyle saw me last week, and it was terrifying yet exhilarating to get caught. For one night I'm still her and it's amazing."

Casi gave her hand a squeeze. "Don't give up on her, she deserves more than one night a month." She smiled. "Our ride is here."

Jake slid beside Ava and casually put an arm around her shoulders. "I hear there are damsels in distress?"

Ava blushed. "We've had a few drinks."

"Drunk women are my specialty." He stood and offered her a hand. "Monkey, you can ride in the bed of the truck; I want alone time with your hot step-mama. That video Kyle sent me was a total turn-on."

"Not a chance." Casi shoved him.

Jack rushed from the house when they parked. "Why didn't you answer your phone?"

"That's Karma for you." Casi snapped her fingers. "Remember to get medical help if you have an erection lasting more than four hours," she slurred as Ava giggled and tried to cover her mouth.

"What did you tell her?" Jack scoffed, attempting to untangle Ava from Jake. "Thanks for picking them up."

"No problem, we'll retrieve Casi's car tomorrow." Jake shoved her back in the truck before she could protest.

Ava winced as the sunlight probed her eyelids. She clasped a hand over her eyes and sensed the weight of someone sitting beside her. She peeked through her fingers and cringed. "I'm sorry about last night."

"Which part? Telling my daughter about my issues in the sack or the alleged affair with an employee? Do you want to go back farther and apologize for the lies throughout the years, including your fake book club?"

"You're aware?" Ava wedged herself up against the pillows to ease the pain in her head.

"I've known for years." Jack smoothed a hand over her tattoo and sighed. "I followed you one night because I was convinced you were having an affair. I realized who the guitar player is and assumed he had been the father of the child you lost."

"Jack, I..."

"Ava, I didn't tell you I knew because you deserved to have that piece of your life untouched. You sacrificed everything for Casi, me, and Sonya. When I saw you singing on stage, I was mesmerized by your beauty and confidence. It reminded me of how carefree you used to be, singing and playing your guitar. I had no right to ruin that with jealousy."

"I love our life. I'm not trying to escape."

"Jake sees it," he asserted.

"What?"

"Your wild spirit. It's still there. You've experienced a tremendous amount of pain, some of it because of me, but you're a fighter and that light inside you will never dim. I'm sorry if I don't always recognize it." He leaned forward to kiss her. "I'm not having an affair." He blushed. "The flirting made me feel young again. I guess I missed our youthful times."

"I want to work the bar a few nights. I'm tired of doing the breakfast crowd and taking care of paperwork in the office."

"I agree we should make changes. Breakfast is losing money and I think we could consider bringing Roxy on board. Your band would be a nice addition to liven the place up a few nights a month."

"That's a brilliant suggestion." Ava smiled and slid the blanket aside. "Kiss and makeup?"

"You read my mind." Jack grinned.

5

_____

KARMA

"Why are we going to Jack's place tonight?" Jake asked.

"Casi sent me a text and said they've made changes recently and she wants to check it out," Kyle answered.

"Wow, this place is hopping." Jake snaked through the crowd to the bar. "Holy shit!"

"What? Oh." Kyle grinned at Ava's edgy attire of a rocker t-shirt and tight jeans. "She was dressed like that at the club."

"Sexy." Jake pushed toward her.

"Hi boys, what will it be?" Ava expertly poured a string of drinks and slid them down the bar.

"Four more whiskey sours." Casi winked at the brothers.

"Are you working here now?" Kyle raised an eyebrow.

"Just for the night," Casi replied. "Ava's getting back in the saddle and I'm her sidekick."

"You're the hot ticket who lures men in and then the experienced women take over." Roxy smacked Casi's behind. "Go work it sassy Casi. Let me drool over your ruggedly handsome husband while you reel in customers."

"I don't care for my nickname," she giggled.

"Once I've named you, you're stuck with it." Roxy leaned forward to expose her generous cleavage. "A girl could get a lot of action around here."

"She seems like a perfect addition and rocker chick suits you," Jake praised, watching Ava bend down to get a rack of glasses.

Kyle elbowed his brother, then noted the row of onlookers waiting for her attention. "Is this one of the changes?"

"Jack and I wanted to shake things up. He's known about my escapades with the band for years. Instead of leading a secret life, we've decided to ditch things that weren't working and incorporate new ideas. We're no longer serving breakfast and I wanted to do more in the bar. We ran into our old friend Roxy in Canada and thought she could infuse positive energy." Ava nodded to an eager patron waving money to buy drinks.

"I'm not old, more like seasoned." Roxy shook her hips.

"Appears to be beneficial for business," Kyle agreed.

"Jack and I always loved the social part." Ava poured a round of drinks. "Over the years we tried to expand to capture the needs of the community, but a terrific small breakfast place opened up and rather than competing we gave them the time slot." She smiled and glanced at Jack across the room. "I proposed the idea, and he wasn't fully onboard until the morning after Casi's and my drunken night."

"You won him over with a wild time in the sack." Jake grinned. "I hope you didn't distract him by calling my name."

Ava laughed. "I passed out. If he had a wild time it was by himself. I normally run the breakfast shift and he handles the evening, but he let me sleep and when we arrived later, we found the crew standing around, talking on their phones, and socializing. Jack blew a gasket and threatened to fire everyone. I told them we were making changes and downsizing staff. That got their attention, and after a little housecleaning, we kept the dedicated workers and contacted Roxy."

"What about Karma?" Casi frowned.

"We'll see." Ava indicated a dark-haired woman approaching in a huff.

"Am I late?" the woman grunted, glaring at Casi.

"No more than usual," Ava mumbled. "You can take the dirty glasses back to the kitchen and refill the ice."

"I'm not the bar back. Why isn't she doing it?"

"This is Casi. She's Jack's daughter, who is helping out for the night." Ava turned to grab a bottle. "Roxy and I are the bartenders tonight and will be on many occasions." She checked her watch. "Reset the trays and prepare for a rush, it's been busy."

"I'm talking to Jack." Karma stormed toward the front.

"Be my guest," Ava sighed.

"I'm going to knock her out," Casi asserted.

"Do it," Jake encouraged.

"He'll do the right thing." Kyle shifted to watch the interaction.

Karma pointed to the bar expressing outrage, and Jack listened calmly and nodded. Ava inhaled sharply. "If he gives in to her, I'm walking out."

"Screw that, I'll help you bury his body," Roxy snapped.

Casi put a hand on her arm. "Let's do our thing first."

Ava nodded and motioned to a handsome waiter at the side of the bar. "Carlos, tend the bar with Roxy, please."

"Yes, Miss. Ava," he replied, efficiently taking over her position.

Ava and Casi joined the band as they finished setting up. Casi indicated which song they would lead with and Ava smiled, focusing on Jack as she sang the first verse of Selena Gomez's song, 'It Ain't Me'. He rolled his eyes when Casi belted out the chorus, holding up a middle finger to demonstrate the point.

"Ava oversees the bar and Roxy is a permanent hire with years of experience, if you don't like it, find another job." Jack shrugged.

Karma cocked her head. "You implied I was the lead bartender."

"When? I trained you and gave you a ride home when you had car trouble. If you are reading more into that, I apologize. Our relationship has always been and will remain as boss and employee."

Karma surveyed the sultry wife on stage and Roxy behind the bar. "I'm not the bar back. Make that old lady the step and fetch, if she can keep up."

Jack squared his shoulders. "Around here, everyone pitches in. I don't have use for a prima donna who expects to run a bar at twenty-five. Ava has much more experience and is the co-owner of this place. Roxy can run circles around you and haul tips better than someone half her age." He jutted his chin toward the bar. "Even on your best night you couldn't fill the room like they can."

"I quit," Karma challenged.

"I'll cut your final paycheck."

Ava observed them walk toward the back office and nudged Casi as they returned to the bar. "Your dad may require a place to stay."

"He can sleep on the sidewalk." Casi narrowed her eyes.

Karma bolted through the room as Jack strolled over to join them. "Carlos, can you pick up extra shifts?"

"You fired her?" Ava asked.

"She quit." Jack smiled. "I explained the rules, and she didn't like them. I also assured her my interest didn't go beyond the workplace."

"Good." Ava swiped a towel over damp glasses.

Jack slid behind and wrapped his arms around her as he whispered, "Why were you worried? You're my entire world."

"You snatched her back right when I was about to make my move," Jake teased.

"You never had a chance, buddy." Jack chuckled.

"I'm available," Roxy said with a wink.

Jack grasped Casi's elbow, directing her to the side and out of earshot. "Sweetheart, I realize I've let you down over the years, but I don't appreciate being flipped off and demeaned. Ava shared things that should be private between us, and although I'm thrilled you're getting along with her again, my role as your father has not changed."

Casi smiled and cocked her head. "Isn't it a little late to be the stern dad?" She noticed the lines around his eyes deepen with regret and kissed him on the cheek. "I love and respect you. I'm sorry I was rude. The other night I was drunk and tonight I'm only teasing."

"I understand drunk talk," Jack grinned. "You've cut me a lot of slack over the years and I appreciate the second chances." He tapped the end of her nose. "In return, I have never judged you either. Thank you for looking out for Ava, but don't shut me out."

꧂

Casi mindlessly applied her face cream, mulling over the tasks she planned for her meetings. Kyle came behind her, resting his chin on her shoulder. "Are you going to miss me?" he asked.

"I'm not sure if I'll notice you're gone."

He frowned. "Do you know what I'll miss the most about you?"

"I can guess," she commented as he moved his hand to her breast and nuzzled her neck. "My hot body."

"Yes, but I'll miss having you in my arms at night. I love how close we are when we're in bed, even when we're pissed off at each other."

"True. It's our safe place."

"Jake mentioned how he missed our treehouse at the river. It was where we went to escape from the world. We never fought and no one else was ever allowed to come there."

"Not even Grady?" She studied his reflection in the mirror.

"It was only for me and Jake."

"Will you take me there?"

"You wouldn't like it, there are spiders," he said.

"What if I said I didn't mind?"

"You'd be lying. And, I can't betray the oath."

"My feelings are hurt," she pouted. "I don't like being excluded."

"Vows are important to me." His eyes turned ice blue.

"Are you seriously worried I'll cheat while you're away?" She stormed to the bedroom.

"No, it's not that." He sat on the bed and grasped her hand. "I'm unclear how to explain it, but I'm out of sorts lately. There are so many important decisions to be made with the business and Jake's house. The more he retreats emotionally, the more pieces I must pick up. Olivia called me to ask for money for a program she's interested in but is still avoiding college. Gail is miserable at her job and wants advice on whether she can cash in some of her bonds. Anna is giving Jake the run around about when he can see Charlotte, and I'm leery about this new relationship Lia is pursuing with Shane. He's not divorced, and he has three kids. His wife is your friend, and I think she has a boatload of problems."

"Hmm, it sounds like you have too many women in your life."

"The only one I truly care about is right here. My biggest concern is she's getting shortchanged because I'm trying to solve everyone else's problems."

She stroked his cheek. "Take a breath and let's enjoy the time we have. This bed is our sanctuary where only you and I exist."

He brought his mouth to her breast as she moaned with pleasure and relaxed under his touch. The rhythm of the lovemaking began, and she arched her back, encouraging him to explore her. Kyle gazed in her eyes as he thrust assertively, conveying his desire. Minutes melted into hours as they brought each other to climax and tuned out the world. "I love you, Casi," he breathed, resting his weight on her in a blanket of adoration.

She put her hands to the sides of his face and locked eyes. "I love you. We can handle this separation. We will be fine."

He kissed the tip of her nose and smiled. "We are sensible adults who can handle problems as they arise."

"Damn, we're screwed," she giggled.

"Then let's make love all night so we'll have the memory to retreat to when the world closes in."

"Are you clear on the directions to your meeting?" Kyle asked, leaning against her car outside the ferry line.

"Yes, and I'll be early since I'm starting from Seattle," Casi replied. "Unless you want to have sex one more time?"

"Don't tempt me." He noted the line easing forward. "I must leave." He gazed at her with desire tempered with sadness before he turned and jogged to his truck.

Casi watched him board the ferry, feeling a tug at her heart as the whistle blew. She waited for him to come to the railing, realizing the difficulty for him to leave as well. A premonition swept over her that his promise to come home on weekends would be compromised by deadlines and unforeseen circumstances. She parked near the headquarters for the department store and checked the time, deciding a text to Katie would be quicker than a phone call. Although their relationship was on hiatus for over a dozen years, they quickly rekindled their friendship. Even with the significant changes in Katie's life, Casi suspected a lot of her old insecurities and negativity remained. The remorse over the loss of the friendship filtered the memories, masking the irritating anomalies of a woman with low self-esteem. In contrast, Dawn mastered adulthood with joy and maturity, resulting in a happy marriage and a fulfilling life. She had taken Casi aside at the bonfire and reminded her how cloying Katie's neediness had been.

"Are you in Seattle this week?" she texted, trying to recall the schedule she verbally relayed.

Katie replied immediately, "Yup, let's go to Happy Hour! Is your gatekeeper gone?"

Casi sighed, unsure how to respond to the jab. "Kyle left on the ferry. I'm available." As she hit send, her phone rang. She grabbed her laptop case and strolled toward the building as she answered, "Hey, Anna, what's up?"

"Are you abandoned?" Anna teased, punctuating it with her husky laugh.

"I'm trying not to be sad."

"Do you want to go out tonight and drown your sorrows? I can get a babysitter for Charlotte."

"Um, actually, I just made plans with an old friend I met up with when we went to Canada. She's part-time in Seattle until her citizenship paperwork comes through."

"Damn, your people are invading."

"Come join us, you might like her," Casi offered.

"Might?"

Casi giggled. "I haven't been around her in years, but she's a bit of a downer. Her marriage is messy, and oh, guess what? Her soon-to-be ex. Well, actually he's a guy from high school... so weird they got together! But, anyway, Lia likes him."

"Casi, you're talking in circles," Anna laughed. "I'll come and meet this woman who thinks she can replace me, so I can set her straight. I'm curious to hear about this ex and Lia."

"I'll explain it... No! Grant is at the damn meeting." Casi spotted him entering the building. He turned and smiled, holding the door as she struggled with her cell phone, laptop, and a box of samples. "Meet me tonight. I'll text you the address."

"It's been a while." Grant smoothed his hand across her back.

"Yes. I've been busy with marketing." Casi tried to sound pleasant rather than pissed off. She hoped he had taken her lack of communication as a sign she wasn't interested, but realized she would have to spell it out for him. She chastised herself for the hundredth time for kissing him, regretting hurting Kyle and allowing herself to act unprofessionally.

"We can catch up over drinks?" he suggested

She smiled. "Grant, I'm not interested in you outside of work. I'm sorry I sent you a mixed signal, but I'm married and completely in love with my husband."

"Sure, that's what you say now..."

"No. That's my forever answer. We have a new representative, Anna. Perhaps she should handle your stores from now on?" He nodded, displeased with her answer, and found a seat at the conference table, jutting his chin out as he texted, sullen and put out. Casi rolled her eyes, anxious to tell Anna about his reaction to her rejection.

Casi made the introductions, smiling inwardly as the two women sized each other up. Katie immediately fell into the drama with her marriage as Anna listened intently, kicking Casi under the table to acknowledge her disdain for the woman.

"I'm unclear what the hell Shane is doing. Lia is pretty, but he needs to get our shit sorted before he rides off into the sunset. I don't trust him to stay focused, so I'm spending half the week in Seattle now with the kids. He needs a reality check on how hard it is to be a parent." Katie regarded the chicken wings with a furrowed brow. "These are fried, huh?"

Casi shrugged and Anna answered, "Yes, that's what makes them delicious." Katie took a wing with resolve, ordering another round of drinks as she continued to rant about her life.

"You said you wanted a divorce. Why can't he date Lia if you're not interested in him? He seemed sad under his jolly exterior," Casi surmised.

"Who the hell cares? It's Shane!" She shivered.

Anna raised an eyebrow and Casi filled her in. "Shane was a few years ahead of us in school. He dealt pot and bought us booze." She smiled at the memory. "He was a long-haired goofy guy who hung out with us because he didn't fit in with kids his age."

"Why is Lia interested in a loser?" Anna asked.

"He's not a loser," Casi said. "Well, not anymore. Katie, you had a valid reason for marrying him."

"I got pregnant," she snapped.

"There's only one way that happens," Anna surmised.

Katie narrowed her eyes and assessed the lovely woman across the table. "My friends moved on and I was left with nothing. He was just a guy in the backseat of a car." Casi caught Anna's eye as she continued. "You don't understand what it's like to be a mother and worry about everything your children require. You have a hot husband and the luxury of a great career. It's different when you're a mom, life isn't about you anymore, there are more important things to focus on."

Anna grasped Casi's hand under the table. "We all deal with bullshit, Katie. You're clueless to what Casi has done for the people in her life, especially the children. Your world revolves around you and you should adjust your perception and notice the universe is full of people who lead complicated and diverse lives."

Katie shrugged. "Whatever. So, you're Lia's husband's lover?"

Anna smiled. "Jake and I are parents to a daughter. I live in Seattle and our relationship is complex. I respect Lia, and I'm in no hurry to push her toward a divorce."

"Jake is ultra-sexy. If we're sharing lovers, I should get in on the action," Katie challenged.

"Your prerogative," Anna said, not taking the bait.

"Let's change the subject," Casi said. "I'm still hungry and there's no one at home to cook for me. Let's order more appetizers."

"Where's Jake? I heard he was babysitting you while your husband is out of town," Anna teased.

"He's at his first ex-wife's house. Olivia is threatening to move out, and he's trying to convince her to go to college." She threw her head back and laughed. "Ok, seriously? Jake has the most convoluted life of anyone."

Anna brought her glass to Casi's. "Cheers to that. Our boy should be wrapped in caution tape." Katie excused herself to go to the bathroom, and Anna glanced at her watch. "That's the third time, exactly fifteen minutes after she eats. Is your friend bulimic?"

Casi furrowed her brow. "I'm beginning to wonder. I understand she's paranoid about gaining weight. She was up and down in her teens, but she struggled with it more after having kids."

"It does change your body," Anna agreed. "I don't care for her. You're too awesome and I'm not willing to share you."

"I'll always be your friend, Anna. And Lia's. It's weird because when I get together with other old friends, like Dawn, nothing has changed. I don't know Katie anymore, and that's tragic because I'm wondering if I've transformed that much. Did I evolve into someone drastically different from who I was as a teenager?"

"As we age our attributes are magnified, Katie appears to be consumed with negativity. Life throws curve balls, and some people can't figure out how to duck," Anna assured her.

6

DEPTHS OF DESPAIR

"When is he coming home?" Casi demanded, noting the shadow of sadness pass over Jake's face when he hung up the phone.

"Maybe this weekend," he sighed. "Do you want to go out for Mexican food tonight? We can order the giant margaritas, again."

"We've gone out four times this week. We've seen every new movie and I'm tired of the bar." She wrung her hands. "He's been gone a month! It's not even the sex I'm missing. I hate going to sleep and waking up by myself. I'm even sad about the stupid things like talking about our day over coffee or watching him work while I'm in my office. I'm lost without him."

"Those things aren't stupid. I miss him, too. I love spending time with you, but there is a definite hole in our threesome." Jake frowned.

"Why is this dumb job taking so long?"

"Permitting issues. He's working on staining and finishing details in the entry. But the dining hall ran into compliance problems. Until the paperwork is finalized, he won't require additional materials, which means it doesn't make sense to come back to the shop." Jake squeezed her hand.

"He doesn't want to see me?"

"Don't be a whiney baby. You know that's not true. It's killing him to be away from you, and especially me." He grinned. "He doesn't have the luxury of driving back and forth. Plus, I think it makes it harder for him to be with us and then have to leave." He raised an eyebrow. "Now you know how I felt when he spent all that time in LA on that endless job."

Casi's eyes watered. "Because he was with me! Do you think he's met someone?" Tears rolled down her cheeks. "Is Lauren there?"

"She's not. Only a team from the resort. They're preparing for a grand opening at the end of summer." Jake pulled her into a hug.

"Fine, Mexican food. I'm getting drunk."

"Even that has become routine," he chuckled.

Casi stretched out on the dock, letting the sun warm her chilled skin. Jake reclined beside her, dripping water from his hand in her belly button. "Stop!" She pushed him away.

"You looked hot."

"That's what Kyle always does and you're making me miss him more."

Jake glanced up the walkway and grinned. "Whatever, I'm going back in the lake. You can stay here and sulk."

"I said, stop!" She screamed when the warm calloused hand smoothed over her stomach.

"You didn't miss me?" Kyle breathed in her ear.

"Kyle!" She burst into tears as her eyes flew open. "You're home!"

"Briefly. I needed to see you."

"What's wrong?" She bolted upright.

"I'm finding it difficult to be away. We're working around the clock to get everything done, but then I stay awake at night thinking about you. I hate being away from the lake." He chuckled as Dingo mauled him and pawed at his arm for attention. "It's brutal to be separated from our family and the life we built."

Casi held out her hand. "Let's enjoy this gorgeous day. I won't waste a minute of your visit being sad."

"Why don't we barbecue later? From the photos you guys text me, and the stack of takeout containers in the trash, I'm figuring you don't cook much lately?"

"Casi would eat potato chips every night for dinner. I've done my best to at least make her have a meal," Jake challenged.

"We can't function without you," Casi giggled.

Kyle threw her over his shoulder and jumped in the lake while Dingo barked, attempting a rescue as she screamed and splashed. They swam for the rest of the afternoon, pausing to sun themselves and indulge in margaritas. Casi refilled the blender while Kyle floated in the inner tube across the rippling water, and it eased him into a gentle slumber. Casi returned to the dock and set the pitcher on a table before diving in the water. She haphazardly hoisted herself on the tube to join him, shocked when the rubber twisted and sent them plunging in the lake.

Lost in a deep sleep, Kyle gulped at the water, lashing out as he attempted to orient himself in the liquid world. Casi dove deeper in response to his struggle and was met with a heel to the face. Jake halted mid-pour on his drink when he heard the commotion, alerted by Dingo frantically barking. As the splashing intensified, he raced to the scene and pulled Casi away. "Go to the dock!" he ordered, realizing she was becoming a victim to the panic. He grasped his brother's arm to direct him to the surface and Kyle gasped for air, wild panic etched across his face. "You're ok, hang on." Jake felt the tremors racing through his brother's body as he assisted him to the inner tube. He rubbed Kyle's back, patiently waiting for him to cough up the water he ingested.

Kyle pressed his cheek against the warm rubber and exhaled. "I was confused which way was up. It seemed like a nightmare." He grabbed Jake's hand. "I was in the river, searching for Grady."

Jake smoothed his hand over his shoulder. "Panic attacks suck, huh? Can you swim to the dock?"

Kyle nodded, slipping back in the water and swimming gracefully. He sat beside Casi, giving her a sheepish smile. "Sorry."

"I didn't mean to freak you out." She hugged him. "It capsized when I got in. I've been eating out too much."

"The balance got thrown off, and I was asleep, so it overwhelmed me." He glanced at his shoulder and pulled back in alarm when he saw the blood. "Did I hurt you?"

Jake joined them, checking her nose for damage. "Not broken, but she might get a black eye," he assessed.

"It was my fault. I swam under your foot," she claimed.

Kyle frowned. "I'm so sorry."

Jake put his hand on Kyle's shoulder. "It was an accident. She's a tough little nugget. I'm going to the store to get steaks for dinner."

Casi laced her fingers through Kyle's. "Let's take a shower and relax on the deck while your brother cooks."

"One more thing I've missed." He wrapped her in his arms under the warm stream of water.

"Showers have been super lonely. What's your room like there? Do you have to bunk with other people?" She lathered soap over his body.

"Yes, I have twelve gorgeous women with me." He kissed her neck. "It's a generic hotel room with a decent bathroom and a pretty view. I spend minimal time there. I'm trying to get this job completed so I can come home."

"To me?" She slid her hand over his thigh.

"My one and only." He leaned her against the wall and grasped her hips.

They lost themselves in the union of their bodies, enjoying the orgasm radiating as the sensation of the shower made it more intense. He smoothed her hair back. "I can't believe I gave you a black eye."

"Kyle, if you had done it on purpose you'd never walk right again, and I would be filing for divorce. It was a stupid accident." She sighed when his eyes filled with sympathy. "You're curious why I never told anyone about my mom and why I didn't fight back?"

"You're so strong, and yet she had the ability to crush you instantly. Why did you let her get away with it?"

"When I was little, I couldn't protect myself. I tried to behave to minimize the abuse. She would fly into a rage, and I learned I was able to outrun her by the time I was six. In my teens, she lost interest in me until my dad left. I knew it was my fault, so I accepted my penance."

"That's horrible!"

"Once I started modeling, she limited it to mostly slapping me." She averted her eyes. "Kyle... I encouraged her to do drugs. It mellowed her out, and she stayed out of my life. It's my fault she died."

"No, she made her own choices. You're only responsible for yourself. Her overdose was a mistake because she lost control."

"What if it wasn't? What if she did it on purpose to punish me?"

"Don't let her. Her contribution to this world was bringing the most beautiful, kind, and incredible woman to this earth. After that, she only caused misery and pain." He ran a thumb over her bottom lip.

Jake smiled as they came out to the deck. "Hank hand-cut us beautiful thick steaks." He transferred them to a platter. "I made salad and potatoes. Casi, this might be a shock to your system to have real food again."

"I should be able to speak Spanish with all the Mexican food we eat."

Jake smiled and regarded his plate. "Years ago, I was unable to pay my bill at the grocery store. We were living in a crap apartment with one child and another on the way. I had a complete meltdown, and thankfully, Jeannie took care of paying when she witnessed me falling apart."

"Like she did for me? She's my favorite checker."

"Yes, she's awesome. I collapsed when I got home, and Gail called my parents in a panic. I was sprawled on the floor having a full-blown anxiety attack by the time they arrived, and my mom rocked me in her arms to calm me. Finally, I told them what happened and mentioned I hadn't realized I'd spent so much money on lunches during the week. My dad assessed me and guess what he said?"

"Here's some more money?" Casi shrugged.

"You should lay off that taco truck. I don't think it's helping with your situation." He shook his head.

Kyle grinned. "He didn't mean it to be derogatory. You gained a lot of weight and he suggested it contributed to your panic attack."

"Food was the only thing that made me happy back then," Jake sighed. "My ultimate joy in life came from a six-pack of beer after work and greasy Mexican food for lunch."

"That's so sad, Jake." Casi hugged him.

"Why is my kitchen full of junk food now?" Kyle cocked his head. "Are you lost without me? I'm sensing a correlation."

"Kind of!" Jake nudged Casi. "When Kyle was about twelve, all his pants fit as floods because he was so skinny."

"I didn't care. It worked great for skateboarding. When I got them long enough, Dad complained they hung low on my hips and he said I looked like a redneck," Kyle shared.

"Mom tried to sew extensions on his jeans." Jake chuckled. "Dad refused to let him wear them."

"He took me to a store in Seattle with a better range of sizes and told me to stop growing and to eat more." He smiled at his brother. "Life was simpler back then, huh? Now my pants fit fine, but I have a million more problems to worry about."

"I think your jeans fit better than fine." Casi gave him a wink. "You don't have problems, only trials yet to conquer and a few dragons to slay before you can return to your kingdom. I have confidence in your abilities."

Kyle gave her a kiss. "I'll be home soon. These steaks are awesome, thanks for making dinner." He refilled everyone's glass and made a toast. "To the two people I love most on the planet. Give me the strength to be away from them for a few more weeks and remember this will be worth it in the end." He frowned when Jake chuckled at a text on his phone. "Are we boring you?"

Jake's eyes crinkled. "Someone sent me something funny."

"Please tell me you're not involved with another woman. Casi, you're supposed to keep an eye on him." Kyle frowned.

"He's been getting a lot of texts." She grabbed his phone to check the contact. "Shane? Really?"

"What? He's a cool guy and we have common interests." Jake snatched his phone back before she could scroll through his messages.

"I see how easily I'm replaced," Kyle sulked.

"I'm sure he's using me to find out more about Lia."

"I'll bet he has a crush on you." Casi poked him in the ribs.

"You're twisted." Jake shoved her.

Kyle eyed his watch and sighed. "Thanks for making dinner, it's wonderful to have a home cooked meal."

"It's time?" Casi's eyes watered.

"Yup, I need to catch the last ferry." He stood and gathered plates.

"Leave the dishes. Go kiss your wife," Jake ordered.

They shared a lingering kiss at his truck, and he touched her face gently. "Please accept my apology. I'm glad you understand it was an accident, but it tortures me to have injured you, especially on your beautiful face."

"You're forgiven. You are a gentleman and would never intentionally maim me. I know how real abusers behave." They shared one more kiss, hesitant to break the physical bond as their lips finally parted. Casi smiled and waved goodbye, masking her heavy heart and devastation as she watched him drive away. She returned to the house and dabbed at her eyes with a paper towel.

Jake noted her flinching with pain and smoothed his hand over her back. "He feels like shit for doing that."

"I know." She shrugged. "It really isn't a big deal. I'm a master at camouflage, no one will know."

Jake exhaled and leaned against the counter. "When Gail was pregnant with Reid, after my major panic attack, my parents worried I had difficulties coping. They explained to her if I started to get anxious, just leave me alone. I became overwhelmed because Kyle hadn't come yet, and I questioned whether he still wanted the business with me. Gail was irate about me not helping enough at home and I tried to calm Olivia, who had croup. She kept badgering me and I tuned her out, which pissed her off. She slapped me across the face and went ballistic like a rabid animal. I meant to push her away but ended up backhanding her. I had Olivia in my arms and my pregnant wife on the floor. I gave her the baby and walked out, planning to never return. I intended to confront Kyle and then throw myself in the river."

"Oh, Jake!" Casi fell into his arms and pressed her cheek to his shoulder.

"Gail called my parents and told them what happened, but claimed she caused it. They could hear Olivia crying in the background and realized I reached my limit. As soon as I pulled in the driveway, they ran out to comfort me. I spent the night and Kyle promised he would be there within the month. I should have guessed he was detoxing; he was so damn skinny and tragic-looking, but I was consumed with my own problems."

"What part are you leaving out?" Casi directed her gaze to his face.

Jake cringed. "Years before that, I accidentally hit my mom when she soothed me during an attack. I left a bruise on the side of her face. It remains one of the worst days of my life. She never flinched, just continued to rub my back and pretend like it meant nothing. After I smacked Gail, I told them it proved I was dangerous, and I was afraid to be around my kid." He smiled as tears sprung to his eyes. "Mom said I was an angel who sometimes flew too close to the sun and remembered I was human; flawed and imperfect. She noted I had taken care of Kyle since he was born and never once hurt him out of anger. And she trusted me with her life. Gail kept the secret about what I had done. She signed us up for parenting classes at the community center and hoped it would help me cope better with stress. That was one of the reasons we stayed married so long; she believed I was a better person than I did."

"And you've proven that to be true. You're a wonderful dad." Casi tilted her head. "What was Kyle's panic about today? I surprised him by knocking him in the lake, but he was severely worked up."

"We're coming up on the twenty-year anniversary of the boating accident. I suspect he's tortured by the belief he should have saved Grady. He has nightmares sometimes."

"Was the accident his fault?"

"One of the other kids was driving the boat, and Grady's neck was broken instantly. No one could have helped him. Kyle had fractured ribs, femur, hip, and collarbone. Everyone jumped in the river to rescue kids. Kyle wasn't even conscious. He never remembered the crash, but I think he's having flashbacks."

"My poor broken husband." Casi winced.

"When Kyle was a kid, he was happy all the time. I dragged him around and made him do stupid shit. He always complied and never complained, even when it resulted in injury. The first time he stood up to me was after that thing with Amber. That's what hurt the most; he cut me out of his life. After the accident, he was lost. He didn't know which end was up, and it took him over a year to feel normal again." He pulled her closer. "The only other time I've seen him so distraught was after you hit rock bottom in LA. It sent him into a tailspin."

Casi cringed. "He's fine now. Don't forget you almost killed him when you died."

"I forgot about my near-death experience with that damn pig poke. You're right, we've taken years off my brother's life. There's something happening internally with him. I suspect it has to do with the accident, but it was strange he claimed he had a million problems."

"Yet there's only two of us," she noted.

"What's all the racket?" Kyle strained to hear Casi on the phone.

"Lia and the boys are over, and Olivia is playing with them. Katie's here, too. I suggested we have our girl's night at the house instead of a bar." She walked out to the back porch.

"Where's Jake?"

"He's out to dinner with Anna and Charlotte."

"Then why is Olivia there? It seems like every time I call, she's at the house." Kyle rubbed his temple.

"She wants to move in with Jake." Casi held her breath.

"Inform her his house is across the street," Kyle snapped.

"It's not finished. Why do you have a problem if she's here?"

"Whatever, it's fine." He sighed heavily. "I guess now that Katie's living part time in Seattle, you'll be seeing a lot more of her?"

"I've been keeping myself busy while you're away." She hesitated, and the tension was thick between them as they struggled for how to end the conversation. "I should check on the kids."

"I love you. Please don't let them destroy my house."

"I won't. I love you, too." She walked inside and corralled Austin on the sofa while relocating Tommy to Olivia's lap. "Movie and popcorn time!"

"Popcorn!" Austin yelled as he flipped over the sofa and wrestled his brother from Olivia.

"Careful!" Casi cautioned, frowning while she listened to the conversation between the women.

"You're at a disadvantage because you're a woman. I never got a fair break," Katie claimed. "A man can be as fat as hell, but still be respected in the workplace. Take it from a former porker, people will overlook your abilities if you're overweight. Don't you agree, Lia?"

Lia blushed and smoothed her top over her hips. "I don't believe it's ever held me back in my job."

"Well, you're not really fat, more like curvy," Katie assessed. "Some men like that, such as my husband."

Lia exhaled. "Well, um, I only talk to him online…"

"It's cool. We're not exclusive." Katie rolled her eyes. "But don't get your hopes up for more. We have three kids, and they come first. Also, until my paperwork is done, I must stay married."

"I understand," Lia insisted. "I'm not divorced, either."

"My dad is a player," Olivia scoffed. "Why did I get his weight issues and bad attitude, but got my mom's looks?"

As Katie launched into a diatribe on drugs to aid weight loss, Casi spoke up, "Olivia, when your dad started to eat better and exercise, the weight came off. He's in great shape now, and he has a lot more confidence. You should take advantage of being here so much and swim and hike the trail."

"Bullshit!" Katie stated. "Tell us the truth about how you stay thin. I've seen the way you eat, and Jake likes to chow down. Do you guys bang it out after a binge?"

"Katie! None of that is true. You understand better than anyone how I work out to keep in shape. I indulge in snacks, but only since Kyle is away because I'm bored. Jake and I are not lovers." Casi glared at her.

"You're smart. I'm sure your husband wouldn't be as eager to come home if you were a lard ass." She turned to Olivia. "Chunky wives are good for housework, but a guy as hot as Kyle would find a side piece in a heartbeat." She glanced over Casi's figure. "You made a mistake not locking him down with a child. In time, you'll regret not giving him the one thing every man wants; a link to immortality."

Casi felt the heat rise in her cheeks and locked eyes with Lia. "I won't even bother defending my marriage to you." She turned away while Katie continued to rant about men and superficial women.

Kyle stared at the ocean, wishing he could see all the way to Blackberry Falls. "Hey." He smiled as Lauren strolled down the walkway. "When did you get here?"

"I came to check on the progress of the kitchen with Marcos. It's almost done, and he wanted my help to create the equipment list."

"I'm happy to see you." He gave her a hug. "Are you here for the night?"

"No, we're taking the last ferry. I wanted to discuss something with you." She grasped his hand. "I need you to hear me out, and I require one thing; I don't want your answer today. Please listen and reflect on what I'm asking. You can talk to Casi, or Jake, whatever makes you comfortable."

"Ok," Kyle said.

She took a deep breath and led him to a driftwood log to sit. "I've always been a planner. I set goals for myself and make very detailed lists of how to achieve them. That's one of the major differences between me and Lia."

"Yes, you excel in that department," he complimented.

"One goal was to get my culinary education and work in every aspect of a restaurant. I want my own place one day and I'm dedicated to learning all the steps to achieve my vision."

"Are you asking to borrow money? I'm not averse to considering a loan. I should talk to Casi, especially if it's a big investment."

"I'm not quite there, yet. I appreciate your attitude, and it's comforting to know you would consider that as a possibility. My request is of a more personal nature." She hesitated. "I want you to father a baby for me."

"Lauren, no!" Kyle's eyes widened.

"I'm not asking for sex. The procedure can be done through a clinic. I sourced the information and costs, which I would cover. You're the ideal man; handsome, intelligent, with a kind nature. I regret our relationship didn't work, but if you consider the facts, there's no reason you can't give me the one thing I've always wanted. You wouldn't need to be involved. I can do this on my own, and I've calculated all the risks and expenses. This is the perfect scenario for everyone. You don't want the work or financial responsibility of a child, Casi can't get pregnant, but your amazing DNA will go on. I'm not being impetuous, I'm thirty-six and this might be my only chance."

"Jake shares my DNA and he's populated the world enough." Kyle cocked his head. "Besides, what if you meet someone and you're pregnant? You shouldn't give up."

"I'm not giving up. I'm focusing on making my dream come true. Jake's kids are adorable. Imagine if we had a girl."

"I don't want children. I like Austin and Tommy." He shrugged. "Reid is cool. Olivia is a pain in the ass, and I predict Charlotte will be headstrong."

"You wouldn't need to deal with any of that. This would be my child. If you ever want to be a part of her life, you can choose later." She straightened her back. "If Casi truly loves you, she'll support you. It honestly doesn't involve her, but she should consider what you want."

"I don't want to father a child," he said flatly.

"You research a tool for months before you buy and cautiously weigh the pros and cons of everything. I deserve the same consideration." She wiped a tear and clutched his hand. "I've been dreaming about being a wife and mother since I was in high school."

"I remember your wedding binder and the extensive research you did on a honeymoon in Italy. Some dreams must be adjusted," he said gently.

"I've accepted you moved on and will never be my husband. It's not fair how Lia bumbles through life yet has two kids with your brother. Everyone jumps to help her and now she's moved to her dream cottage. I've worked my ass off and sacrificed everything to be where I am. What if someone told you it was unrealistic to build your house on the lake?"

"That's different. I was able to obtain that myself without relying on anyone to help me."

"What about Casi? She was a disaster when you married. You did so much for her. Jake smothers her in attention and she has a mentor who built a career for her." Lauren wiped another tear. "Plus, her dad adores her. I'm alone, Kyle. I'm asking for a child to make my life complete. I've given up on the other dreams and pushed the goal for the restaurant off."

Kyle focused on the ocean. "I don't want to talk to Casi now. I must finish the job and get our life back to normal before I throw this at her."

"That's all I ask." She stood and checked her watch. "It's time to meet Marcos. Thank you for listening. You've been an amazing friend and I hope you understand how important this is to me."

Kyle waited for her to return to the resort before going to the bar. He wished he could escape the pressure clawing at him constantly, and Lauren's request put him on edge. He nodded to the managers, having made it a nightly routine to meet for a drink while they discussed the workload. "Hi, Bree." He slid on the stool beside her.

"You appear to be carrying the weight of the world on your shoulders." She ordered him a scotch with a smile.

"It feels like it."

"Wife pressuring you to come home?" someone asked.

"No, she's been wonderful. She has a career in marketing, so she's busy. She cut back on travel while I'm away to make things easier." He downed his drink and nodded to the bartender for another.

"Do you have kids?" a man asked. "My wife is always overwhelmed when I'm away. Honestly, it makes me want to stay gone longer," he confessed.

"No kids. Just a lot of other stuff. She's helping my brother at the business and with his family."

They launched into a conversation on travel and the perks of being away. Kyle was amazed at the blasé admittance of affairs while they were on location. Bree laughed and clarified, "When you travel as much as we do, you lead two separate lives. Perhaps your wife understands that?"

Kyle smiled through his discomfort of her flirting. "No, we only lead one life. I'll be happy to return to it."

"Well, you're not there now." Bree smoothed her hand over his thigh.

7

THIN ICE

Kyle parked in the driveway and sat in his truck, focusing on the glow of the sunrise penetrating the sky. He entered the house quietly and noted the futon was empty, assuming Jake spent the night with Anna. He did a double take when he walked in the bedroom, finding two figures in bed. He knew in an instant he located his brother but was confused by the proximity to his wife. He sat on the edge of the mattress, considering how to approach the betrayal. In a swift motion, he placed his hand over Jake's mouth, pinching his nose closed. Jake lashed out frantically, attempting to pry the murderous grasp from his face. Their eyes locked, and Kyle hesitated for a moment, pondering the ease of the earthly release.

"Do you possess a death wish?" Jake gasped. Kyle shrugged and glared at Casi, still peacefully asleep. "Are you kidding me?" He peeled back the covers to reveal them both fully garbed. "We were trolling Facebook and fell asleep." He punched his brother on the arm and growled, "You took advantage of my comfort zone to sneak up on me."

Kyle nodded. "Get up, I need to talk to you. Don't wake her."

Jake chuckled as he removed a crushed package of caramel cakes wedged between them. "We forgot about our snacks."

"I'll make coffee," Kyle whispered, gently moving a wisp of hair from Casi's face. "She's so beautiful."

"She is," Jake agreed. "Why are you here so early?"

"Meet me at the dock." Kyle walked to the kitchen. He brought a carafe and cups, setting them on the table between the Adirondack chairs, facing the lake. He sipped the hot brew while he gazed at the water in silence, speaking volumes with his demeanor.

Jake observed the guilt emanating from the faint lines in his face. "What did you do?"

"I'm on thin ice. Every step is uncertain, and the weight of the emotions I'm carrying is threatening to send me to a horrible death."

"That's poetic, but what does it mean?"

"Lauren requested I father her child. I said no, but she wants me to think about it. My response to dealing with it was to kiss a woman at the resort."

"You stupid jerk!" Jake shoved him. "Why?"

"She's been hitting on me for weeks. We gather for drinks at the bar and last night I drank more than I should have. I walked her to her room and kissed her. She invited me in, and I turned her down." He covered his face with his hands.

"Don't tell Casi! She's barely holding on with you away. This will send her into a tailspin," Jake advised.

"I have to tell her, it's killing me." Kyle glanced up the dock and noticed her approaching.

"Not now. Wait until you're home and you can find the right moment. You can't burden her with this and take off to the island. You know how she is," Jake whispered.

"How who is?" Casi melted in Kyle's arms.

"You." Jake nudged her. "I told him it was a bad idea to come visit if it's only for an hour."

Kyle caressed Casi's cheek and kissed her tenderly. "I'm picking up supplies from the shop, but I wanted to see you. Imagine my surprise to find a lover in your bed."

"Who? Jake? He's not my lover; no one could replace you. I must have fallen asleep while we were investigating people on the internet. I showed him some of my high-tech tricks to find information. Why is there chocolate on me?" She licked her arm.

"You're a goofball!" Kyle hugged her tightly. He nodded to his brother, realizing he couldn't devastate her just yet.

❧

"I brought Chinese!" Casi breezed through the door. "It's from that amazing place in Seattle. Wait, why are you dressed like a sports guy?"

"I'm headed to the baseball game with Kyle." Jake opened cartons and grabbed a pot sticker.

"The boating peoples. Why am I not invited?"

"Because you still think it's an aquatic sport. It's the Mariners game, and he got prime tickets from some guy at the resort." He gave her a hug. "We'll eat the food tomorrow."

"No! I'll eat it all myself!"

"Ok, Porky Pig. I'll be home late." He gave her a kiss.

"I hate you." She surveyed the empty house and sighed, stomping to the bathroom and running a bubble bath. She turned up the music and slid in the tub, armed with the food and a bottle of wine. As the water began to cool, her phone rang, and she smiled at the picture beside the number. "Hello, stranger."

"I'm in Seattle. Come to a club opening with me. Drop everything and seize this opportunity," Alix stated.

Casi eyed the half-full wine and containers. "I can be there in an hour. Text me the address so I can put it in my GPS. Can I bring a friend?"

"If she's hot. Leave your husband at home."

"My husband left me." She waited for his shocked response before she continued. "He's on a job on some island for another week."

"Crazy girl! We're on the second level. Dress hella hot."

"I always do." She rinsed the bubbles from her toned body. She shoved the leftovers in the fridge and called Katie to extend the invitation, not surprised she jumped on the opportunity. She found her old friend difficult to be around since their reunion but hoped the atmosphere of a club would perk her up, realizing it was a meager attempt to compensate for broken promises in the past. She pushed her work attire aside, perusing the contents of her forgotten club clothes. She smiled at the fond memories of dazzling onlookers in the fog-infused lounges. A slip of black material caught her eye, and she smoothed her hand over the scandalous creation. As she slid on the dress, a surge of confidence bolted through her. She styled and fluffed her blonde waves and applied heavy makeup, recreating her favorite smoky eyes. Ruby red stilettos completed the racy look, and she smiled at her reflection, finding the lost club girl she thought was gone forever.

Jake walked toward the tailgate party. He spotted his brother and shook his hand, nostalgic at their greeting. Kyle introduced him to the group from the resort, hesitating when he came to Bree. As they passed out food and beer, Jake whispered harshly in his ear, "What the hell is she doing here?"

"She's a manager at the resort." Kyle tried to downplay Bree's flirting as she suggestively ate a hotdog.

"Have you been missing your brother?" Bree observed Jake hovering at Kyle's side.

"Not as much as his wife has." Jake took a sip of his beer and waited for her to react.

"She knows I'm married," Kyle whispered. "She doesn't care. These people live in a different world than we do."

"You live in Blackberry Falls with your gorgeous, sweet wife. It would be wise to remember that," he hissed.

Kyle rolled his eyes. "Was she upset you were coming here tonight? Did she find a friend to hang out with?"

"I wish you told her yourself. She got home from work late and brought Chinese food. She was mad and claimed she would eat it all. She's probably taking a bath, masturbating, and drinking wine," Jake surmised.

Kyle smiled at the image. "I'll call her later."

Casi helped Katie finish getting ready, attempting to add more polish to the sleazy outfit. "So, you guys are going to a club?" Shane asked, wrangling the children.

"Yup, don't wait up." Katie held up a middle finger as they left.

They parked in a nearby garage and walked up the steep incline to the entrance. "Man, this is a workout!" Casi laughed, tugging Katie up the grade. They passed the long line of hopefuls and greeted the bouncer. Casi smiled as he nodded and moved the rope. She surveyed the club and ascended the stairs, negating Katie's request to stop for a drink. "They'll have booze in the private lounge." She paused on the landing and adjusted Katie's dress, caressing her long brown hair over her shoulder. "If you get uncomfortable, tell me. We don't need to stay that long."

"You don't think I can handle myself in a club?" Katie sneered. "I'm from the same place you are, Cassidy."

"It's not that." Casi exhaled and led her over to Alix's posse.

"Babe, you're severly delicious!" He directed her toward him for a lingering kiss while the crew of models sighed with envy. She sensed eyes on her, analyzing her attire of the shimmering charcoal dress skimming her backside.

"This is my friend, Katie." She swung an arm around her waist. "We grew up together." Alix nodded, not entranced by the average-looking woman before him. The evening wore on and Casi lost herself on the dance floor, lured by the rhythm and vibration. She returned to discover Katie leaning forward, snorting a line of cocaine from the coffee table. "Alix, why?" she asked with alarm.

"It's cool, Babe. She asked for it," he claimed.

"I hope you're not doing it." She narrowed her eyes.

"I'm clean." He made a cross over his heart.

"Katie, we should head home. Your kids have school in the morning, and I'm scheduled for an early meeting." Casi shifted her weight.

"Don't get all high and mighty," Katie slurred. "Remember the first time we did coke? At your kitchen table, with your mom. Jesus Christ, I just want to live a little. When did you become such a downer?"

Casi locked eyes with Alix and he held out his hand and whispered, "Release it to the universe, Babe. You're not that girl anymore."

"Monkey, I'm home. I bought you a shirt. It has the Mariner logo, so you can pretend you're somewhat knowledgeable about sports," Jake called out. He walked through the rooms, confused by the silence. "Where did she go?" he asked Dingo. The dog tilted his head, equally uninformed. Jake turned on the TV and relaxed on the sofa to wait for her return. At one in the morning, he took out his phone and texted his daughter. "Did Casi tell you where she was going tonight?"

Olivia responded, "Did you lose your child?"

"Yes, and she has an early meeting and can't be a party girl tonight."

"Try the find my phone app. That would give you her location."

"Guide me through it." He sat at the computer. She sent the steps, simplifying the process to his level of understanding. "She's in Seattle!" He typed the address in his GPS and thanked her for her help.

"Dad, why don't you ever wonder where I am?"

"Because I trust you."

"You shouldn't," she challenged.

"I trust your mom to kick your ass if you step out of line. I think we should plan a conversation soon about where you want to go to college."

"I want to come live with you. You owe me."

He rubbed his eyes, not wanting to discuss more when he was

anxious to get to Seattle. "That's fine. The house will be finished by September."

"I'll start packing." She sent a happy face emoji.

Jake parked illegally across the street from the club and shook his head. "God damn it, Casi." He strolled to the front of the line and tried to enter through the ropes.

The bouncer put a hand on his arm and shook his head. "Forget it, hillbilly, hot chicks only."

"I'm tired and not in the mood for your bullshit." Jake clenched his jaw. "Move your fucking hand before I break it. I'm picking up my drunk girlfriend and hauling her ass home. Give me two minutes."

The bouncer surveyed him, assessing he might be a challenge. "Two minutes. I'll come in there and drag you out myself if you're not back."

Jake nodded, happy not to deliver on his claim. He bolted inside, quickly scanning the club. He sighed, pushing through the throngs of scantily clad women and salivating men. After a quick search, he wondered if the app had been incorrect, but then spotted the upper level. "Of course, hobnobbing with the elite," he scoffed. He climbed the stairs, noting the more glamorous and wealthier crowd. Within minutes he discovered Casi, playfully dancing for Alix, while Katie sat with a group of models snorting lines. "You're a liar," he seethed, not pleased with her scandalous attire or the drug scene. He stepped behind her, sliding a hand up her dress to caress her silk underwear. "Surprise."

She glared over her shoulder, shocked by the advance and warm breath on her neck. "Jake!"

"Who else would have his hand up your skirt?" His blue eyes sent daggers of ice. "Hey, Alix."

"Sup, Jake," Alix replied. "Are you here to party?"

"Not tonight. Casi has an early meeting." He glanced at a young model wiping her nostrils. "She has a real job with responsibilities. Katie, I'll drop you off."

"No, thanks." She reclined on the sofa.

"I'll make sure she gets home," Alix assured.

Casi kissed him goodbye and whispered, "Please don't sleep with her, Alix. She'll try, but you must turn her down. She's married with kids and she's acting out."

"I recognize the type. You have my word, Babe." He kissed her tenderly.

Jake put an arm around Casi's shoulders, guiding her through the club. "This affection for you is fake. I'm royally pissed," he growled in her ear.

"I understand."

They walked out of the club and the bouncer raised an eyebrow. "Way to go, Bro." Jake gave him a wink, running a hand over Casi's ass in a display of his prowess.

Jake snatched the parking ticket from his window and opened the door for Casi. "You're paying this." He tossed it on her lap. She clutched the paper and stared out the window. "You can be angry I dragged you out of your little model party, but you're clueless to the ramifications of your actions."

"It was a night at a club! I didn't do anything wrong."

"You're dressed like a whore, doing coke, and partying all night. You have a meeting at nine, how were you planning on pulling that off?"

She narrowed her eyes. "Kyle has no problem with how I dress. You're the one who monitors me."

"He loves for you to dress sexy when you're with him! Not at a club with your ex and random men with their hands up your dress," he challenged.

"That was your hand! Next time I'll punch you in the face." She turned her face away. "I didn't do drugs. Katie did it with the other girls."

"And Alix?"

She shook her head. "No, he's back on track." She slid her phone from her bra. "My meeting is at nine?"

"Yup, do the math." He put his hand on hers. "You've been drinking so your car stays parked. I'll drive you back, which means you'll be lucky to get about two hours sleep. Do you have everything prepared?"

"Can we stop for donuts in the morning?"

"Yes, Monkey. And a gallon of coffee," he chuckled.

"How did you find me?"

He grinned. "I have my ways."

"You tracked my cell. Who helped you?"

"My sources are protected."

"Olivia. None of your friends are smart enough to figure it out."

"Or sneaky enough. Trouble tends to stick together."

"Don't tell Kyle about tonight. I don't want him reading more into it than what it was. He's overwhelmed and he shouldn't worry about me."

A week later, Kyle arrived home with a pizza and set it on the dining table. "I thought you guys might be tired of cooking." Casi hugged him, surprised by his lack of response as he put his hand on her hip and moved her back. "How did your meeting go last week?"

"Which one? I had four." She set out plates.

"The one Friday morning. I imagine you must have been tired after staying up all night partying."

She glared at Jake and he shook his head. "Not me."

"Does that loyalty go both ways? Or did you tell her about the woman I kissed at the resort?" Kyle hissed as Casi whirled around to glare at him. "Oh, I guess that's the first time you're hearing it."

"What woman?" she demanded.

"Her name is Bree, but it's not important. Do you want to share about your night at the club?" Kyle sat and folded his hands in his lap.

She snapped open her computer, typing at lightning speed. "I met Alix at a club opening in Seattle while you were with your brother at the baseball game. I took Katie with me and that's the extent of it."

"And you dressed like that for Alix? What about the drugs?"

"I wore a dress I've worn many times to clubs. Should I hide my body now that I'm married? There were drugs at the club, as always. I didn't do them. Why don't you tell me more about your new girlfriend? She's very attractive and educated. I bet that was a fantastic vacation for you."

"Where are you getting that information from?" He jumped up and raced to the computer. He read the bio on the company website and gasped. "You have eerily good sleuthing skills."

She opened a new search engine and did a quick evaluation until she found what she suspected. "Facebook, of course." She noted the pictures Alix posted. "I didn't think you ever went on there?" She rolled her eyes. "Lauren told you to check it out. Ignorant bitch. Did she send you a message or did she show up on the island again?"

"Why are you upset?" Kyle fidgeted, unnerved by her question.

"Answer! You're in a twist because I met with my ex at a club full of people. At least he's not trying to come between us."

"Just tell her," Jake said.

"She came to visit, didn't she?" Casi fired back.

"Yes, but not to tell me about the club. It was something else." He rubbed his temple. "How come I'm now the bad guy?"

"Because your genius is flawed by your desire for honesty. You threw yourself under the bus," Jake chuckled and grabbed a beer.

"You kissed a woman you work with. You're sharing secrets with a past lover. You're pussyfooting around the truth and you think I'm the stupid one. Go fuck yourself!" Casi stormed away and slammed the bedroom door.

"I assume it's a bad time to tell her what Lauren said?" he whispered to Jake. He rapped on the door. "Casi, please let me in."

"Go to hell. I don't want to talk to you."

He cringed. "I need my suit for the party this weekend."

She ripped open the door and stood to the side. "Sure, get your suit. I'm sure Bree and Lauren will be fawning over how handsome you look."

Kyle retrieved the clothing and stood in front of her. "Please come to the party. They have a multitude of activities planned. It would make me happy to have you there."

She nodded, and he turned to walk away. "Kyle." She put her hand on his arm. "You can kiss me goodbye."

He smiled and gave her a lingering kiss. He smoothed her hair and grazed his thumb over her bottom lip. "Eat the pizza. I bought it for you. It's your favorite with extra bacon. I promise it was just a kiss and I realize how dumb I was." He brushed away the tears from her cheek. "I'm sorry."

"You're not staying for dinner?" Jake frowned.

"I have to get back to the ferry." Kyle regarded the closed door. "I needed my suit. And to see her. Please make her come to the event."

"Am I invited?"

"Of course! Bring Anna, I've reserved a room for you."

"I'll ask her. She's kinda pissed at me because I hooked up with that hot chick, Lynne, from the cooking school."

"Why did you do that? And why did you tell Anna?"

"Stupid Katie told her. She spotted me in Seattle and texted Anna. I wasn't doing anything wrong, so I didn't lie when she asked."

"Honesty does not seem like the best policy." Kyle transferred slices of pizza to a napkin. "Make her eat. She's getting skinny again."

"She exists on junk food and alcohol. She misses you and needs you to come home. Work is boring without you." He clutched Kyle's arm. "I picked her up from the club. She didn't do anything wrong."

Kyle nodded. "It was my own guilt that convinced me she did. One more week and we can get our lives back on track."

8

FORGIVEN

"Are you packed?" Jake surveyed Casi dressing for work.

"I'm not going to that stupid thing," she sighed.

"He did something dumb, but you're always kissing guys and flirting. You're making a bigger deal about it."

"Is that what you said when he told you?"

"I said I would punch him in the face if he ever did it again. I told him to wait to confess because it wasn't fair when he was away, and I had to deal with your snotty slobbering reaction."

She half-smiled. "What did Lauren ask him?"

"I can't tell you."

"Will I be crushed?"

"She wants him to do something. He'll tell you this weekend."

"I don't like secrets." She shoved past him to put on her shoes.

"You love them, just not when you're on the outside. Get your shit together and I'll drive you to Seattle in your car. We'll save time if we leave from there."

"I'm meeting Anna at Starbucks."

"Perfect. I asked her to come, and she refused to answer me. She won't be able to resist my charm in person." He grinned, and she rolled her eyes as she pulled a bag out from under the blanket. He chuckled. "You had me worried. Where's your dress?" He sifted through the contents. "It's a formal reception. We're wearing suits."

"I'm bored with my clothes."

"What about the one you wore to the club?"

"Too demure. I prefer a dress that's better than a slap in the face for Lauren and Bree to annihilate my competition."

"They can't compete. That woman targeted my brother when he was weak. He's only a man."

"He's my superhero. He should be infallible."

Jake slid behind Anna and kissed her neck, making her jump as she typed on her laptop, oblivious to her surroundings. She narrowed her eyes and pushed him back. "Go away."

"I'll be back this afternoon to take you to the island with me. Dump our kid with a sitter, it's adults only," he directed.

"In your dreams." She turned her face away.

"You're always in my dreams," he whispered.

"Go buy me coffee, I want to talk to Casi." She waited for him to walk away. "Are you ok? What do you think Lauren wants? Did Jake tell you?"

"No, his loyalty to his brother is too deep. I don't want to go to the party." Casi slumped beside her.

"You have to stake your claim. Don't let those women try to defeat you."

"Are you coming?"

"Yes, but I want Jake to squirm. I'll be there for you." She squeezed her hand as Jake returned with coffee and pastries.

He sat beside Anna and ran a hand over her thigh with a smile. "I'll pick you girls up after work."

She shoved his hand away. "You can text me in the afternoon and I'll let you know my decision. I don't like leaving my child."

"She's our child," he corrected. "You'll come because it means spending an entire weekend with me."

He leaned in to kiss her and she put her hand over his mouth. "Don't get ahead of yourself. A coffee doesn't give you permission to kiss me."

"I bought you a pastry, too." He nuzzled her neck.

"I don't like public displays of affection."

"This weekend we can get freaky in private."

"Go to work!" She tried to hide her smile.

"I'll pick you up this afternoon. Kyle emailed you the itinerary for the activities. Apparently, this one requires a new dress, so I'll be back around four. Bye, Monkey Brains." He gave Casi a kiss. He wiped chocolate from her chin and whispered, "He loves you. You are his world."

Jake parked at the Macrae office and smiled at Anna waiting outside, busy on her cellphone. He figured Casi would be late, tending to a thousand last minute projects. As predicted, she rushed out several minutes later, laden with a laptop case and bundles of paperwork. Jake gathered her belongings and put them in the trunk. "So, we're headed to the mall?"

"Hardly," Anna answered in a clipped tone. She handed him her phone with the GPS directions and turned to Casi in the backseat.

Jake frowned and placed the phone in the cup holder. "What did you end up doing with our kid? I'll pay for the sitter."

"My sister is watching her. She and her partner are considering having a child, and they determined it would be beneficial to have a trial run."

"Your people are very calculated," Jake snickered.

"Which people? The O'Shea's or the redheads?" She turned her attention to him and drummed her fingers on the armrest.

"I believe they are the same." Jake drove to the destination and dropped them off in front while he parked. He ignored Anna's suggestion to wait in the car, but once he walked in the couture store, he reconsidered his decision. "I'm with them." He quickly joined the women.

Anna smiled and accepted a glass of champagne before directing the attendant. "I'm between an eight and ten, depending on the cut. I want something elegant that highlights the cleavage and downplays the hips. I'll consider navy, emerald, or black. No red, obviously."

Casi sat beside her, at ease in the upscale shop. "I'm not sure what I want. Something sexy in a six."

The attendants fluttered about the store, placing gowns on a rolling rack. Anna stood and handed her glass to Jake, then nonchalantly slipped out of her clothing as they wheeled the assortment over. Jake jumped up to shield her from the front window. She giggled and put her hand to the side of his face. "You're such a gentleman," she complimented, as the assistant drew the blinds.

She tried on several dresses, considering her appearance in the mirror. Jake read the doubt on her face, realizing she was adjusting to her slightly fuller figure. "You're beautiful, Anna. Which one do you like the best?"

"That's the one!" Casi exclaimed as the attendant zipped a midnight blue gown, longer in the back and slit up the side to reveal her legs. It highlighted her cleavage and accented her creamy skin and copper hair. While Anna changed, Casi stood and disrobed. Jake shook his head as she flung her bra to the side, adamant about finding a bodice with support. She tried on numerous dresses, checking with Anna for her opinion. Finally, Anna sighed and signaled the lead assistant. "Her husband kissed another woman. Check out her outrageously gorgeous body and work with it. She has the confidence to wear something sinful."

The woman nodded and rushed to the back of the store, clucking at a junior aid to follow. They returned with three dresses and Jake held his breath, growing concerned at the selection. When the final dress was arranged on her body, he jumped to his feet. "Absolutely not! You're half naked, for God's sake."

Casi winked at Anna. "I'll take it."

"Damn it, what are you trying to prove?" Jake slumped.

"I would like a silk tie to complement a charcoal suit. Consider his sapphire eyes when you choose." Anna grasped Jake's chin.

"I thought my suit was black," Jake said.

"Of course, you did." Anna patted his hand. She scanned the ties, holding them up to Jake as she tilted her head to assess. "We'll take this one."

Jake frowned at the price. "That's ridiculous for a tie. Why can't I wear the one I brought?"

"It's generic." She shrugged.

"How do you know? You haven't seen it."

"Did you pick it out, or Casi?"

"I did, with Kyle."

"Point made." She strolled to the register and Jake pulled out his wallet. "What are you doing?" Anna cocked her head.

"Paying," he said.

"We're career women and we'll take care of our own purchases. The tie is a gift." Her mouth twisted into a smile. "Don't worry, Sweetie, you can work it off this weekend."

Jake shivered. "You make me feel cheap."

"If you were a woman, you would accept it." Anna winked.

"If I were a woman, you would be a lesbian." He smiled.

They returned to Anna's condo to get ready. Jake changed to his suit, escaping Anna's clutches as she fussed with his tie. "I've been doing this since I was a teenager." He finally gave up and let her fix it to her liking. Casi swiped gel through his hair, artfully sculpting it to perfection. He grinned. "If you girls wanted a threesome, this is not quite how I imagined it."

Anna helped Casi with the last details of her hair, arranging waves around her bare shoulders. She twirled in front of them, smoothing the dress over her curves. "What do you think?"

"You look amazing!" Anna proclaimed.

Jake nodded, surveying the sheer bodice with strategically placed beaded flowers. The skirt hugged her body, accenting every curve and the perfection of her figure as it shimmied down to a pool of emerald chiffon. A side slit parted with each step, revealing her long, toned legs. She reached in her bag to extract her rhinestone stilettos and laughed. "Did you repack?"

"I added a few things. I assumed you hadn't bothered to read the itinerary and weren't prepared for the activities," Jake asserted.

"What activity is this for?" She withdrew a black lace teddy.

"Seducing my brother back to his normal self."

❧

Jake checked his phone as it buzzed with texts, uncomfortable with Anna's determination to arrive late at the resort and their refusal to allow him to answer Kyle. "Alright, let's go." He handed his keys to the valet.

"Not so fast. We'll have a drink at the bar first," Anna proposed.

"Anna! Stop torturing my brother." He scowled. "The bar is in the reception hall and Kyle has the keys to our rooms. It's show time." Anna whispered to Casi, stopping her at the door. She slid her arm through Jake's and smiled. "What about her?" He regarded Casi waiting in the hallway.

"She'll be in shortly." Anna nudged him forward.

They noted Kyle anxiously checking his watch while he stood at the bar with a group from the hotel. Relief washed over his tense face when he noticed them. "Where's Casi?" He frowned.

"She's here," Jake said before Anna could claim otherwise. "She stopped to use the bathroom."

"You didn't wait for her? She doesn't know where the reception hall is." Kyle rushed toward the entrance.

Jake put his hand on Kyle's arm. "She's coming."

A collective gasp penetrated the general chatter, and he turned to witness Casi enter. With the poise of a supermodel, she covered the distance with grace and elegance. Kyle stood speechless, unable to take his eyes off her.

"Who is that?" one of the managers whispered.

"My wife," Kyle uttered, closing the gap between them. He held her at arm's length, as if she were a delicate orchid that would shatter if he touched her. "You look incredible."

"Thank you." She planted a kiss on his firm lips.

Kyle breathlessly began introducing her. Casi extended her hand to the attractive brunette. "You must be Bree."

"I am." Confusion registered in her eyes.

Casi turned to her left. "Hello, Lauren. I hear there's something important we should talk about."

Lauren blanched as Kyle intercepted. "Um, not here. We'll do it later. Let me get everyone a drink." He handed Lauren a vodka tonic and Bree a chardonnay, then turned to Casi. "What would you like?"

"You know what your ex-girlfriend and new lover drink, but you have to ask me?" Casi jutted out her bottom lip.

"Usually you drink anything I put in front of you." His face flushed with embarrassment as the words registered in his brain. "I meant you have a wide variety of tastes, but they always drink the same thing. Not that I...." he stuttered, lost how to fix his blunder.

Jake suggested they order champagne, and the bartender added Chambord with a wink. "For the beautiful ladies."

Bree smiled at Casi. "I'm not your husband's lover. It was a tiny kiss after too many drinks. Believe me, in this business that's like a handshake. He was clear about having a wife at home and turned down the invitation to my bed, on numerous occasions."

Lauren's eyes lit up with anger and she scowled at Kyle, infuriated by the revelation of his misstep.

Casi evaluated the statement. "I realize my husband is extremely handsome, and the temptation to entice him, against his wishes, is natural. I think he's more concerned about it than I am. I have a somewhat liberal view on kissing."

The resort executive, Larry, smiled. "May I offer my services if you should feel so inclined?"

Casi threw her head back and laughed, enjoying the shocked expression on Kyle's face. "Thank you, but I'll be busy catching up with my husband. Perhaps Bree can fulfill your request?"

Larry's shoulders slumped. "I've already been there."

"It isn't worth revisiting," Bree added to a round of laughter. "There's something so charming about a small-town man."

"Interesting you should make that remark. Kyle is better educated than you, with a master's degree. He's owned his business for years and is well established in his community. You're a virtual unknown from Berkeley, who holds a liberal arts degree. In fact, you got the job with this resort through a friend, and I do use that term lightly." Casi winked.

"Master's degree?" Jake whispered, then narrowed his eyes as Kyle swallowed loudly. "Another lie."

"You certainly have done your homework," Bree said. "I'm impressed with your research skills. Can we call a truce? You're definitely someone I would like to have in my network."

Casi smiled, pleased with the result. "I've said what I had to. There is no reason to belabor the point."

Lauren indicated for Kyle to follow her to the other end of the bar under the pretense of getting another drink. He placed his order and turned to her. "I understand what you're about to say. If I was going around kissing women, why didn't I come to you?"

"Something like that. Jesus, Kyle, you preach what a devoted husband you are and then you're making out with random floozies."

He rolled his eyes. "We didn't make out! It was a stupid kiss after a few drinks, nothing more."

"Tell Casi tonight about what I asked, or I will. Don't keep stringing me along with your high morality." Her nostrils flared.

They watched the interaction at the bar and Bree smiled. "To be honest, I assumed Lauren was his wife. If I had known for one minute, he was married to a goddess, I wouldn't have attempted to flirt."

Casi smiled, curious about Lauren's angry demeanor. "I'm not surprised. How often was she here?"

"A few times. She came to see another friend but was always trying to track down Kyle. He seemed to avoid her, so I figured he was unhappily married. They had a long conversation in the garden a week or so back, and he was overwhelmed. That's when I kissed him because he appeared to need a pick-me-up."

"Did you hear what the conversation was about?" Casi pressed.

"No, but she was crying, and he seemed to be consoling her."

Kyle returned with drinks and smiled at Casi. "Dance with me."

He spun her out to the dance floor and glided through an upbeat number. As it transitioned to a slow song, she asked, "When will you tell me what's going on with Lauren?"

"We'll enjoy this evening together with dancing and delicious food, including a chocolate fountain. After we make love, we'll talk about what she asked me."

"Tell me now," she said tearfully.

"It's nothing important, that's why I don't want to discuss it now. I missed you and I want to revel in every minute of holding you in my arms and admiring your body in this scandalous dress before I take it off you."

Casi felt the burn of Lauren's scowl throughout the evening. She pushed the dreaded conversation from her mind and enjoyed the reception and making new friends. As the night wore down and yawns were witnessed, Kyle whispered, "Are you ready to go upstairs?"

"Take me to your lover's lair." She noted the pain reflected in his eyes and clarified her comment. "I meant for us. It wasn't a reference to previous activities in there."

He nodded sadly. "I kissed her in the hallway outside her room. No one has been in my suite. Not Lauren, either."

She put her hand to the side of his face. "Forgiven and forgotten. There's no more to be said about it."

"I'll get your bag from the car." He handed her the keycard and turned back to whisper, "Wait to get undressed. I want to watch you."

Anna swept up beside her as they approached the elevator. "Are you ready to rekindle the flame with your husband?"

"Yes. I'm glad I came."

"Me too. Poor Kyle was really in a twist," Anna laughed. "Honestly, I can see the desire to kiss Bree, she's kind of phenomenal."

Casi giggled. "She reminds me a lot of you."

"Exactly," Anna agreed.

Casi stood at the window admiring the view. Kyle slipped in silently, embracing her and kissed her neck. "Spectacular, huh?"

"It's a beautiful resort. I pictured you in bunk beds, like summer camp."

"The room is better with you here." He ran a hand over her hip. "This dress is incredible. How do I get it off?"

She smiled and indicated the zipper hidden in the side seam. He strolled to the closet and returned with a hanger. "I assume it was expensive, so it shouldn't end up on the floor."

"It was ridiculous!" She slipped the spaghetti straps from her shoulders and let it slide off. "Was it worth it?"

"Every penny." He hung it in the closet. He turned and smiled, admiring her figure with the backdrop of the ocean outside the window making the scene more exquisite. "Sexy panties and high heels turn me on."

She smiled and put a hand to his chest, pushing him back on the bed. "Giddy up, Cowboy, let's get this party started."

"Wow, do I need a safe word?" he chuckled, caressing her thighs as she straddled him.

"You're always safe with me." She undid his tie and smiled as she wound it around his wrists, securing him to the headboard. He moaned as she unbuttoned his shirt and pushed his undershirt up to run her tongue over his chest, gently nibbling at his skin. He bucked his hips toward her, unable to resist the sensation. His wrists strained against the fabric bonds and she smiled at him. "Did you miss me?"

"More than you can imagine," he groaned.

9

———

OWNERSHIP

Kyle brought the tray of coffee and pastries to the table by the window. "Are you ready to play baseball?"

"Is that a euphemism for sex?" Casi sipped her coffee.

"No, the actual game. I assume you never read the itinerary."

She smiled. "Jake did. He put clothes in my bag. He's become my personal servant since you've been gone."

"How handy."

"Can I be the cheerleader?"

"Do you know anything about the game?"

She shrugged. "One guy throws a ball at another guy. If he hits it, he runs around in a circle. If he misses, he whines like a baby and storms off. There's a lot of scratching and spitting."

"That's the basics," he chuckled.

She smiled at his handsome face, highlighted by the sun streaming through the window. "What does Lauren want?"

He sighed and rubbed his temple. "I told her no. She believes you should be involved and that I might change my mind..."

"About what?"

"She wants a baby and has asked me to be the father."

"Absolutely not!" She slammed her fist on the table.

"That's what I told her." He grasped her hand. "I didn't feel it was necessary to even tell you, but she said she would, and I didn't want you to think I was hiding anything."

"Why you? They have clinics for those things."

"She believes I'm a perfect candidate for the qualities she desires. I'm not doing it," he repeated.

"Conniving bitch."

Kyle snickered and eased her on his lap. "That was the entire conversation. There's nothing more to tell you."

She snuggled in his arms. "I'm sure there was more, and you've reduced it to the main bullet point. You're my husband and she must accept that."

Casi smiled when she pulled the Mariners t-shirt from her bag. "This will make me look like a pro." She slipped it on with her jean shorts.

"Yes, you'll completely confuse them," Kyle laughed.

"It's not that difficult to play, is it?"

"Well you excel at hitting and running, so you should shine." He patted her backside as they walked out.

They arrived at the field and Jake signaled them over and explained how they divided the players. "How come I'm not on your team?" Casi asked.

"Because I'm sure you suck," Jake answered honestly.

"You have Anna," she noted.

"Sure, but she's my lover. I must take a hit on that one." He grinned and Anna held up her two middle fingers in his direction.

"You get Kyle because it's unfair if we get all the good players." He winked. "Before you ask, we took Lauren."

"To keep her away from me?" Casi put a hand on her hip.

"No, she's a fantastic player, and we needed another chick." Jake smirked. "You guys got Bree. We wanted to balance Kyle's lovers, to make it even."

Kyle positioned Casi in the far-right field. He explained the basic rules, figuring most of them wouldn't apply to her. "The other team is up first. If a ball comes your way, try to catch it and throw it to me."

She inspected the glove and shrugged, finding interest in the nail polish on her other hand. Kyle smiled and strolled to his position on second base. The game ensued, and Jake's team proved to be stronger than predicted. Anna came up to bat and Larry winked, tossing her an easy pitch. Without warning, she swung expertly, sending the ball to the far-left field.

Casi clapped and cheered, "Go, Anna!"

Anna approached second base, giving Kyle a kiss. "Surprised?"

"Completely!" His eyes widened.

"I played softball in high school. I'd forgotten how much fun it is." She eyed third base.

Larry turned to Kyle as Lauren came to the plate. Kyle nodded, relaying she was a top-notch player. Larry threw a difficult curve ball, making her swing at air. On the third pitch, she tightened her grip and bent her knees, determined not to strike out. She bunted the ball, forcing Larry to run forward, allowing her to get to first base. Jake came up to bat, flipping off his brother as he assumed the stance. Kyle rushed to Larry and whispered, preparing him for his brother's performance.

"Hey! No time outs," Jake chastised.

"He's on my team." Kyle jogged back to his position.

"Hit it to me, Jake." Casi waved and twirled.

Jake sent the ball her way, realizing she was completely unprepared. She tripped over herself to grab it before haphazardly loping it to Kyle. Too late to tag out Lauren. "Good job." Kyle smiled at her awkward toss.

"You suck," Jake called from first base.

"That's terrible sportsmanship." Casi wagged her finger at him.

Lauren smiled at Kyle. "Did you talk to Casi?"

"Yup. She didn't take it well and I'm standing by my original answer." He surveyed Casi swat a fly away with her glove, smacking herself in the head.

Lauren glared at her, predicting her input. "I asked you to talk to her and then think it over. You're just regurgitating what she says. Her feelings in this aren't valid. It doesn't involve her."

"It does…" He pushed her forward as he saw Jake running toward them.

"Lauren, fucking move. This isn't social hour," Jake yelled. He collided with his brother, knocking him to the ground. "That's what you get for yapping while you should be playing ball."

"She was asking me about the damn sperm donor thing." Kyle dusted himself off. "I told Casi, and she wasn't happy."

"No doubt. Although, if you had a kid with Lauren, it might stand a chance at getting some athletic ability." Jake grinned.

Kyle smiled at Casi, who was distracted by a dog peeing on a tree nearby. "I'm fine with my little Princess."

"Damn it!" Jake swore, as Lauren was tagged out ending the inning. "Get your head in the game," he hissed as he ran past.

"Casi, it's our turn at bat," Kyle called.

She appeared confused, unsure what to do with the glove. Lauren jogged over and held out her hand. "I'll take it. Oh, and by the way, I don't appreciate your lack of understanding about Kyle being a sperm donor. It would mean nothing to you, but you can't accept he wants something greater than what you have."

Casi narrowed her eyes. "He's my husband, and every hair on his head and sperm in his body belongs to me. He's sweet and considerate and you thought you could manipulate him. It will never happen!"

"What was that about?" Kyle cringed when she joined him.

"She was complimenting me on my game," Casi lied.

After a heated discussion, Lauren took the pitcher's mound while Jake stomped to first base. Kyle arranged for Casi to be last in the batting rotation, hoping she wouldn't get a turn. The game proceeded, and Anna proved to be as skilled in the field as she was at hitting, and Kyle had to remind Casi not to cheer every time Anna caught a ball. With two outs, Casi came up. Kyle showed her how to hold a bat, tucking her backside in as she straddled the plate. "Just swing at the ones in the middle."

Lauren threw impossibly difficult pitches, making Casi swing wildly. After two strikes, she gripped the bat tighter. Lauren wound her arm, sending the next pitch directly into Casi's back, knocking her down. "What the hell, Lauren?" Kyle exclaimed, racing to help her up.

"It was an accident." Lauren shrugged.

"She walks," Larry said.

"Go to Jake at first base," Kyle directed.

"I don't want to play anymore," Casi sulked.

"After the game, we'll go back to the resort to swim and sit in the hot tub," Kyle encouraged.

"With cocktails?"

"Many." He gave her a kiss and showed which direction first base was.

She trudged over to Jake. "Are you ok, Monkey?" He rubbed her back.

"Lauren is a stupid bitch."

"Yes, she is." He kept an eye on Kyle. "Pay attention. Kyle can hit hard. When I say go, you run to each base until you reach the home plate." He watched her kick at the dirt. "Pretend there's a shoe sale. There's only one pair left in your size."

She raised an eyebrow. "What's the sale?"

"Buy one pair, get one free. Your favorite."

"How do I get two pairs if only one is in my size?"

He rolled his eyes. "Now you can do math? The other ones are those short boot things; that's the free pair. You must touch all the bases with your foot. It's like a video game, where you get points for hitting targets."

She regarded the field. "Two more and then that thing at the end?"

"Home plate. That's where the prize is." He watched Kyle swing and gave her a shove. "Go, Monkey, run!" She took off at a roaring pace, almost missing second base, but remembering to come back and tap it with her foot. She tuned out everything else and focused on her goal. She jumped on home plate and eyed Jake, who nodded his approval.

"Is it over now?" Casi asked.

Larry laughed. "We have eight more innings. Excellent run."

When the game ended, Kyle swept Casi in his arms. "Amazing run! You helped our team win."

"I doubt I was much help, but Jake's advice made the game more interesting. I wish there really were shoes at the end."

They returned to their rooms to change before heading to the pool where a barbecue was being prepared. Casi put on a floral bikini and pink shorts with a t-shirt on top. Jake and Anna met them in the hallway. "Wow, what a gorgeous place." Anna scanned the large atrium with the indoor-outdoor pool and expansive patio.

Casi cocked her head at the music, rifled with laughter and whistles. "What are they listening to?" she asked, surprised to hear Demi Lovato's song, 'Confident', being played with this older crowd.

"There she is in the flesh!" Larry cheered, as the other men added sexy remarks and catcalls.

Casi directed her gaze to where the group focused and witnessed her performance on the catwalk at the lingerie show being projected on the wall. She stood frozen, watching herself gyrate to the song. She pushed past Kyle and rushed out, bolting for the stairs.

"Turn it off!" Kyle demanded.

"We were just admiring your hot wife," Larry chuckled.

"She was a model, that's not a secret. She didn't do it to be leered at and fulfill your voyeuristic fantasies," he snapped.

"Sorry." One of the managers stopped the video. "We were discussing how gorgeous she was, and Lauren suggested we check out YouTube."

Kyle glared at Lauren. "How dare you ask me for an intimate request and then turn around and do something so callous?"

"The performance is online for the world to view! They were

surfing the web for pictures. I thought you were proud of your beautiful supermodel wife." She leaned forward and hissed, "She claims she owns you."

"The lingerie show was the week her mother died. It was a horrible and chaotic time in her life. That song represents how she was feeling. She didn't do it to be mocked or lusted after." Kyle turned on his heel and stormed out, leaving everyone ashamed.

Kyle sighed when he entered their room and witnessed Jake consoling Casi, crumpled on the floor, weeping. "I want to go home."

"The next ferry isn't until tomorrow," Jake informed her.

"We have the car, why can't we drive?"

"Because it doesn't float." He rubbed her back. "Remember we drove it on the ferry to get here?"

She nodded, angry at her ignorance. "Of course."

Kyle grasped Jake's shoulder. "I need to talk to her, alone."

Jake kissed her on the forehead and rose, meeting Anna in the hallway. "Kyle ripped Lauren a new one," she whispered.

"Good, he's been too naïve about her."

Kyle knelt beside Casi and she began to hyperventilate. "I can't breathe in here, there's no air."

"It's very stuffy. Come with me." He held out his hand and led her to the beach and straddled a log. "Sit here." He directed her across from him and looped her legs over his, pulling her forward and kissing her gently. "I'm sorry that video hurt you. There are times when I wished you never modeled. People see the shell of a gorgeous woman and make assumptions about who you are and what you represent, and they're always wrong." She started to speak, and he put his finger to her lips. "I've been avoiding this conversation because I realize I'm not myself. I'm acting out of character and have a sense of doom hovering over me." He noted the concern in her eyes. "The one thing I'm clear on is how much I love you. I hated telling you about Lauren's request because I understood the pain it would cause for something I would never consider doing. You're the most confident woman I've ever met, but for some unknown reason you lower yourself to engage in this imaginary battle for my attention. It's impossible for Lauren to comprehend what you and I have, and her jealousy inspires you to doubt my intentions. Please believe our love is greater than that and we are kindred spirits, bound together by destiny. We belong to each other."

"I was kind of a bitch to Lauren today. That's why she hit me and played the video. I realize she's jealous and I take advantage. To be honest, I'm also envious. She shares history with you and seems to excel at all the things I don't. I sense her weaknesses and tear her heart out with them. She might be my most challenging adversary."

"I would be happy to live alone with you on this island," he stated. "Jake could come visit."

"And Anna. I would miss the boys, and Lia, too. We would have to invite your parents, and mine. We'll bring Dingo and Jezebel."

"This island is getting crowded," he laughed. "Let's stay where we are and mentally tune out the bullshit."

"What's making you overwhelmed?"

He regarded the ocean. "Twenty years ago, my life changed drastically. Losing Grady was a devastating end to my childhood. I've never stopped wondering if I could have saved him if I tried harder."

"Jake said Grady's neck was broken instantly. You were unconscious..." She winced. "I searched for the records from the accident. It was tragic, but you couldn't have prevented it."

He grasped her hands. "I'm circling the drain, Casi. That's how they died. Did the report say that?"

"It said four teenagers drowned."

"At the crook of the river, there's a set of caves. You can explore them when the tide is low, but it becomes a death trap when it rises. At the far end, there's a whirlpool leading to an underground system. On that day, we crashed just outside the caves. The tide was rising, and we were sucked inside. I blacked out, but they told me I got wedged on a jagged piece of rock leading to the last cavern. They were able to reach me before I was swallowed into the abyss. It took them days to recover the remaining bodies."

"That's horrible!"

"I have a sense of being caught on that rock again, and it might release me into the dark depths of the vortex and tear me to shreds."

"I'll save you."

"I love you, Casi. Please don't give up on me."

"Never." She kissed him. "I want you to consider being a sperm donor. I was selfish with my reaction."

"No. I've made my decision."

"You were thinking about me, not what you wanted long term. I promise to stand by you if you go ahead with it. Do whatever is in your heart because that's what will make me happy."

Kyle nodded. "We could take a float plane back to Seattle if you want to go home now."

"We'll leave in the morning as planned. I overreacted to the video because it was more intimate than what I care for people to see of me. I only want you looking at me like that. I won't run away; I own the choices I made in the past."

"You are incredibly sexy and strong."

They entered the atrium and conversations halted, unsure how to greet them. Casi smiled and shed her clothing, then strode to the hot tub and slipped in. "Who's in charge of cocktails?"

Bree smiled and gave her a wink. "A round of drinks, Larry."

Anna slid over and took her hand. "You're a kick-ass woman, Casi. Don't ever allow anyone to knock you down."

10

BROKEN

Kyle walked to his truck and gazed up at the bright blue sky and decided it was the perfect day to go fishing. On the drive, he mentally prepared his evening, packing a meal, taking Dingo, and making a tour of the lake while he fished and smoked a cigar. By the time he arrived home, he was excited about his plans. He parked and steeled himself for the mess he assumed would greet him inside, hearing techno music blaring.

"Hi, Olivia," he called out. "Can you turn down the music a bit?" He stood frozen as he witnessed her smoking a joint on the sofa, bare feet resting on the coffee table, beside a spilled bottle of nail polish. Chip bags were strewn about, intertwined with snack cake packages. Olivia raised her middle finger to him in response to his question, while she texted. His anger boiled over, pushing him past the ability to reason. He stormed over and snapped off the stereo, then the TV, shaking with rage when he noticed his Google speaker was unplugged to allow access for her phone charger. "Get the hell out of my house!"

Olivia rolled her eyes as she tossed her phone to the side and grabbed the bag of chips. "I'm waiting for my dad. He's taking me to the mall."

"To get a job I hope."

"Get off my back," she said.

"I'm unclear why no one will stand up to you. You've been spoiled rotten and you're completely unaccountable for your choices. You contribute nothing to this world but expect everyone to serve you. Get a job and start being a proper member of society. In the meantime, get your fat ass off my couch and stop being a burden on your father!" He grabbed her purse to expedite her departure, accidentally snagging the strap on a chair and spilling the contents across the floor. He picked up two prescription bottles, reading the labels aloud. "Adderall? Is that for your fake ADD? Oh, anti-anxiety. For what? The stress of doing nothing all day?" He sorted through the condoms, weed, and paraphernalia, finally stopping with the bag of cocaine. "That goes well with prescription meds."

"Dad!" Olivia screeched as he entered, relaying her status as a victim while she shivered in his arms.

"Back off, Kyle." Jake fumed.

"Look at this place!" Kyle waved his hand around. "My house is not a landing pad for troubled youth."

"Knock it off, drama queen. Grow some balls and stop being a whiney little bitch," Jake snapped.

"What's going on?" Casi rushed in the house.

"Kyle's being an asshole as usual," Olivia cried.

Casi surveyed the mess and Kyle's flushed cheeks. "It's his house. If you don't like it, find somewhere else to be."

"At least someone is on my side." Kyle crossed his arms over his chest.

"I'm always team Kyle." Casi embraced him.

"She unplugged my Google," he whispered, visibly upset.

"I understand what a violation that is," Casi conceded.

"Screw you guys." Jake turned with Olivia glued to his side.

"Wait." Kyle stepped forward. "I was harsh. I planned on a quiet evening fishing and this escalated. Why don't we go to Seattle for fun?"

Jake narrowed his eyes. "Why the sudden attitude change?"

Kyle sighed. "I had a session with a therapist. I needed to talk to someone about my emotions. I believe it would be smart to follow her advice and let go of the past."

Jake balked. "Why didn't you talk to me?"

"It was essential to speak to someone who had no connection to everything that happened."

Casi furrowed her brow. "I didn't know you back then."

"True, but you've done a lot of research and I needed someone impartial." Kyle shrugged.

Her eyes watered. "You punished me for snooping."

"No, although I wish you hadn't shared the information about my master's degree. That was something I did for myself because I like the challenge of learning." He regarded Olivia. "Let me show you things from a different perspective. I judged you unfairly."

Olivia gathered her belongings while Jake perused the contents. "What prescriptions are you taking?"

"It's nothing, Dad." She tossed the bottles in her bag.

The ride was silent while Kyle hummed to himself, easing in a parking spot in the underground garage. He smiled at Casi as he opened her door and took her hand, leading them to the staircase of Pike Place Market. "Let's get fish tacos."

"I'm a vegetarian," Olivia stated.

"Cheese tamale?"

"Ok," she agreed.

Kyle placed their orders and brought back bags of food. He marched down the pier with them in tow, curious about his deter-mined manner. He finally halted at an occupied bench and opened his bag, casually eating a taco. "There are other places." Jake turned away from the homeless person at the far end.

"Sure, but I thought you would like to introduce your precious daughter to her grandmother." Kyle handed food to the woman. "Tara, meet Jake's daughter, Olivia. You remember Jakey, right?"

"Jakey?" the woman muttered, turning with glazed eyes.

"That's him right there." Kyle pointed. "Don't you recognize your own son? Of course, I've been coming here for years and you're clue-less we're related."

Casi wiped a tear, observing the woman in a daze, hair matted and missing teeth. "Kyle, let's go," she begged.

"Jake, sit and chat with her. Ask how she likes the transitional housing. I'm sure she appreciates the money we send every month to ensure she has food and medicine. Take a good look, Olivia, this is where you're headed."

"I don't understand." Olivia backed away.

Kyle shrugged. "Your dad and I were adopted. This is our birth mother. Our father overdosed when she was pregnant with me." Jake turned his back, wiping his eyes as his shoulders shook. Kyle stood and put an arm around him. "Are those tears of joy because you're so happy she's alive? I've been a horrible brother pretending she was dead."

"Why did you do it?" Jake whispered.

"To protect you! Tell your daughter about the heroin."

"Stop. Please." Jake's eyes searched his.

Kyle nodded and slid the bag of food beside Tara. "See you later. Unless you overdose, which is very likely."

Jake bolted for the car and yanked the door open when Kyle unlocked it. "I want to go home." He slumped in the seat.

"We are." Kyle set his jaw.

"No!" Jake gasped as they got on the on-ramp, realizing they were heading to Elmvale instead of Blackberry Falls.

"I need to show you things I've been hiding for years," Kyle said.

By the time they arrived at the farmhouse, Jake shook with spasms. "Dad, what's wrong?" Olivia wrinkled her nose as he trem-bled and refused to get out of the car.

"He's been having panic attacks since before you were born. Are you seriously just noticing this now?" Kyle yanked his brother by the arm.

"Don't do this," Casi whispered.

"Do what? I'm sure you've snooped and found out everything.

This will be nothing to you." Kyle shoved Jake in front of him on to the porch.

"You came to visit," Georgia said cheerfully. Her face dropped when she noted Jake's demeanor. "Sweetheart, what's going on?"

"We visited Tara in Seattle," Kyle said. "Jake didn't take it well. I came to get the file."

"No!" Georgia blocked the door.

"Yes, Mom. I can't handle this anymore." He slid past her and rifled through the den. He returned with a thick file folder. "Have a seat. This will take a minute." He regarded his brother and pursed his lips. "You already know this and have blocked it out."

"Probably for a good reason." Jake slouched on the sofa and rubbed his arm vigorously. Casi scooted beside him and leaned against him.

"Darling, would you like a snack?" Georgia brushed Olivia's hair back from her face. "I have sodas in the fridge."

"Mom, this isn't a social gathering." Kyle shook his head.

"What has your panties in a twist?" Peter joked. He frowned at the icy reception and caught Casi's expression advising caution.

Peter rubbed his temple as he settled in the chair, uncomfortable with the impending conversation. "Perhaps Casi and Olivia should go upstairs?"

"Casi's part of this family and Jake doesn't hide anything from her. Olivia is old enough to understand what's going on," Kyle said.

"You're not my real grandparents?" Olivia asked tearfully.

Georgia wiped her eyes and Peter took her hand. "We adopted the boys, but that doesn't make us less real."

Kyle handed Jake a scrapbook. "Care to relive some memories?"

Jake thumbed through the pages, seeing a picture journal of Tara and Tommy's relationship. Tara beamed as she stood sideways, embracing her pregnant stomach with a caption, "One more month until our dreams come true." He turned the page to reveal his hospital bracelet, pictures, and footprints.

Olivia gasped at the photos. "I look just like her!"

"You do," Kyle confirmed. "She was nineteen, you should keep this as a memento of how a life can topple due to poor choices."

"I don't understand why you kept this a secret." Jake shrugged. "The adoption wasn't unknown, and I'm aware of my birth parents."

"We didn't hide it." Georgia glanced at Peter. "You never asked about anything from before."

Kyle chuckled. "Keep going through it, you'll see why."

Jake returned to the book, seeing his evolution. He sighed at the childish handwriting under the pictures, 'Mommy and Jakey', with hearts. Tara began to appear withdrawn and sported the telltale bruises on her arms indicating her drug use.

"You look like Austin, huh?" Kyle pointed to the photo.

Jake nodded, running his finger over the smiling face, bright with wonder. "I don't remember any of this." The rest of the book was blank, and he turned to Kyle. "What happened?"

Kyle handed him a clipping from the newspaper with a brief mention of Tommy's death due to an overdose. "And now the fun part." He placed a birth certificate on his lap.

"Who's baby boy Petrov?" Jake asked.

Kyle pointed to the mother and the blank space for the father. "My birth wasn't as joyous." He indicated the weight of under five pounds. "Two pounds less than you, but still full-term. I assume due to drugs. I'm thankful I'm not completely demented."

"Not completely." Jake rested his head on Kyle's shoulder.

"I questioned if you were my real brother."

"I am!" Jake's eyes filled with tears. "One hundred percent."

"A DNA test confirmed it. I didn't rate a father. I guess it was advantageous to have a brother or I might have been forgotten."

"You had her." Jake jutted his chin to Georgia. "She loved you right from the beginning."

"From the age of two. Before that, I never even had a name."

"Then who named you?" Casi asked.

"We couldn't keep calling him lil' guy like Jake did. We decided Kyle was a strong name." Tears rimmed Peter's eyes. "Our tiny runt of a toddler. Plus, two letters were part of Jake's name, which we felt might be helpful."

"Because I was too stupid to spell," Jake scoffed.

"Not stupid, but troubled. And we didn't want to throw more at you than you could handle. No one read to you before we adopted you." Peter grinned. "Cartoons were your only form of education. You were drawn to the animation and bright colors. For your own peace of mind, they tested you in second grade and your IQ is above average."

"Good to know." Jake picked at his knuckles.

Georgia glanced at Peter. "Tell them how you came up with Kyle's name."

Peter sighed. "Jake constantly hushed you by saying 'no kai lil' guy' in case you would be taken away for crying. He had trouble with r's and t's. You responded to the sound and we shortened it to Kyle, which you immediately took to."

Jake regarded his brother sadly. "I named you."

Kyle grasped his hand. "How's it possible I remember him saying that?"

"He did it for years, even after you were living here. If you were scared or couldn't sleep, he would rub your back and whisper it until you felt safe," Georgia recalled.

Kyle handed him another stack of papers. "Documentation of Tara's parenting skills." Jake winced when he extracted the photo of a baby, so thin his ribs stuck out. Tubes ran from his nose and arms, and his skin glowed a bright yellow. "Feeding me was too much of a chore." The file contained more photos and reports of malnutrition, questionable accidents, and a suspected poisoning. By the age of fourteen months, Kyle had suffered two broken arms, a fractured hip, cigarette burns, and puncture marks on his abdomen. The hospital had contacted social services and the process of intervention began. "It took another four months for them to act on it. By then I had a fractured skull and heroin in my system."

"Oh, my God!" Casi covered her face with her hands.

"The social worker reported my brother pricked my belly with needles to give me medicine because that's what Tara told him they were for."

"I'm sorry." Jake squeezed his hand.

"You were trying to take care of me. There was no food in the house, and I don't want to know what you might have fed me."

"Dog food?" Jake surveyed a photo of the house, strewn with garbage and a spilled bag of dog food in one corner.

Kyle shivered. "Tara was jealous of your attachment to me. She admitted she had thrown me down the stairs to the basement. She locked the door to prevent you from retrieving me. Here's the celebration she had after." Jake sat with a filthy face, blotchy and red from crying. His lip pouted as he pushed away a cake inscribed, 'Mommy and Jakey,'. "That was the day the social worker came. You were apparently hysterical because you couldn't unlock the door by yourself."

Jake shook his head. "Locked doors. We went to foster care then?"

"You did. I was in the hospital for six weeks." He turned the page to a series of reports. "Jake Petrov indicates below average intelligence and an unnatural attachment to his sibling. He won't eat and soils himself while he sits in a corner and bangs his head against a wall. It is recommended he undergoes psychiatric evaluation and be placed in an institution."

Jake glared at him. "How long have you known about this?"

"Since I was eighteen. I was searching for my birth certificate to get my passport and I found the file." Kyle smoothed his hand over the folder.

"Why did you guys keep this?" Jake demanded.

"We were given the paperwork when we adopted you. We put it in the cabinet and never thought about it again," Peter explained.

"Throw this shit out!" Jake ordered.

"Wait, you must see the best part." Kyle gave him a letter. It was a long hand-printed plea from Tara to regain custody of Jake, who she referred to as Jakey. Her only reference to Kyle was near the bottom, which simply stated, "You can keep the other one, but I need my precious boy back."

"She never wanted me, and the feeling is mutual. It takes all my energy not to hate her." Kyle's eyes turned to ice.

"I wanted you," Georgia blurted. "You boys are everything to me. You experienced a rough beginning, but once you came here, there hasn't been a moment we regretted adopting you. We became a family."

"Even me?" Jake asked quietly.

"I picked you first." Peter grinned. "My scrappy little boy who fiercely loved his brother. You belong here with us."

Kyle exhaled and stood. "There you go, Olivia, proof you oversee your destiny. You may want to think about the choices you're making." He tossed the file on the coffee table and walked out.

Casi ran after him. "Where are you going?"

"For a walk." He kept his eyes straight ahead as she followed him through the field and over a rocky ledge toward the river. He checked his watch and turned to her with a vacant smile. "Do you want to see something cool?" He scrambled down the rocks to the river's edge. He undressed and waded in the rushing water, as she attempted to keep up. "Come on." He held out his hand. He directed her through the rapids, then swam to a calm pool of blue. "It's pretty here, isn't it?"

"You've never taken me here before."

"It's a magical place," he said, devastation registering in his sea-blue eyes. "Follow me." He dove under the water.

She obeyed, escorting him to the sandy bottom of the river. He turned back and gave her a thumb-up, then suddenly disappeared between rocks. She hesitated for a moment, unsure if she could hold her breath any longer. She pushed forward, trusting there was a passage. As she squeezed through the opening, her lungs ached from the lack of oxygen. Suddenly a glimmer appeared, and she surfaced in a cavern bursting with a kaleidoscope of light. "Wow, this is insane!" she gasped. Kyle floated on his back, softly paddling in circles. He glanced at his watch with a blank stare, then swam to the far recess. Casi joined him and gazed down the rockslide toward a whirlpool of water spinning below. "Is this where it happened?" Her eyes widened. He nodded and pressed his back against the rock and closed his eyes. The water tugged at her legs as the tide rose and fear gripped her. "Kyle let's go. Isn't this when it gets dangerous?"

He grabbed her arm and locked eyes with her. "Swim back to the rocks on the shore. Wait for me there and don't come back."

"No! I won't leave you."

"Now!" He braced himself as the water surged higher.

"Please, Kyle!"

"Trust me. I'm right behind you."

She searched the cave wildly as the air gap receded. She forced through the water and swam toward the inlet and pushed against the current, spinning violently with an undertow. The tranquil pool bubbled, possessed with the storm within. She hesitated at the opening, torn with leaving him behind but assessing she required her strength to cross the now raging river. Emerging from the crashing waves, she fought to stand on shaking legs. Strong hands grasped her from the shallow edge, and she flailed in Jake's arms.

"Where's Kyle?" He carried her to shore where Peter frantically paced.

"There's a cave," she shivered.

"No!" Jake charged back in the river.

Peter peeled off his denim shirt and wrapped it around her. "Did he go inside?" His voice shook.

She nodded, unable to speak as the tears overcame her. Peter paced the shore, wringing his hands and muttering to himself, oblivious to the raging river soaking his jeans to the knees. He lunged forward at the sight of the brothers emerging. "Why did you go there?"

Kyle collapsed to the ground, shaking as he clung to his knees and rocked. "I had to see if I could do it."

"No, your boat flipped, and he broke his neck." Jake shook his head.

Kyle touched Jake's cheek. "You're a stronger swimmer. If you had been at the party, you could have reached him."

Jake's face contorted. "You've blamed me all these years?" He shook his head as he absorbed the blow. "I told you I would meet you after because I wasn't in the mood to celebrate your trip to Europe."

Kyle rested his head on his knees, letting the tears fall. "I wanted you to support my decision and put me first."

Jake swung an arm over his shoulder. "You're right, I was selfish. But guess what? The accident still would have happened. I would have been drinking with you guys and cheering you on. When the boat crashed, I would have saved you, faster than anyone else could have. You would have sustained a similar degree of injuries, but I'll accept responsibility for the extent of them." He turned Kyle's face toward him. "I couldn't have saved anyone else because you're the only one who matters to me. I'm not a hero, I can only handle being your brother."

"I saw him float by me." Kyle's eyes turned to a liquid blue. "I was tumbling in the water and his face appeared. His eyes were open, and he had an expression of terror. I reached out for him, but he slipped away. I should have tried harder. I failed him."

Peter exhaled and spat in the water. "Right after the accident, Amber ran to the house and told us what happened. I bolted here and saw the wreckage. Kids were screaming, and the river ran red with blood. You hit right there on those rocks." He pointed to the outcrop. "It was late in the day and the tide had risen. You kids were naïve, but we knew about the whirlpool of death waiting below. We told you to stay away from this side of the river! You had to push the limits and race each other past the fork." He shook his head. "This is where my brother died when he was only eight. I warned you not to come here."

"We were going too fast and Grady missed the turn at the fork, I told him to cut back after the rocks. The river was calm. It shouldn't have happened." Kyle's face crumpled.

"Grady was driving the boat?" Casi asked.

Kyle nodded. "I never told anyone. I didn't want people to blame him."

"None of you were familiar with this stretch. There are submerged rocks, and that's what the boat got caught on, spinning you into the outcrop." Peter surveyed the water churning. "We almost lost you."

Kyle noted the anguish on his father's face. "Did you bypass

Grady to get to me? I can't live with that burden!"

Peter turned to him. "You can't let this go, can you? No one could help Grady. We did our best."

"Maybe he would have been paralyzed, but you let him drown."

"God damn it, Kyle! He was decapitated! I recognized his dragon tattoo, and I pulled him out..." Peter gasped. "He wasn't whole anymore. I tried to hide him from Nicole, but she appeared at my side. You were unable to grab him, because there was nothing to hold on to."

"Oh, God." Casi covered her mouth and willed herself not to throw up. Kyle sobbed in his hands as Jake rubbed his back. The color drained from their faces.

"I made Nicole promise not to tell you. I urged you to give her Grady's Europe money to pay for college because I wanted her to be far away from you. It was a huge burden for an eighteen-year-old girl, and I paid for the remainder of her tuition. Years later she attempted to pay me back, but I refused to take it. Grady always protected her, and she had to live the rest of her life alone. It wasn't fair." He ran his hand roughly through his hair. "That day tore our hearts out. No one came out unscathed. We didn't think anyone survived the vortex." He turned to Jake. "I broke down because I knew when I told you your brother was gone; I would lose you too. Earl insisted on making one last sweep of the cavern. There's a notch at the top of the slide, and you had gotten caught, dangling above like a puppet." Peter pointed to Kyle's scar under his right rib. "Earl said Mother Nature snatched you back before the devil took you."

A sob escaped Jake's lips as he hugged his brother tighter. "She understood I couldn't live without you."

"They tied a rope around your leg and dislodged you moments before the air gap disappeared. They loaded you in the ambulance and we didn't know if you would survive, but I held on to you and pleaded for you to fight. It took days for the remains of the kids to appear once the vortex ripped them apart. It's not an easy journey. The team in charge of the rescue had to live with what they witnessed. By then everyone was accounted for, and no one's life remained untouched by the tragedy. We all bear the scars; some are just invisible." He crouched in front of Kyle. "You've kept it bottled up and lived your life flawlessly. Don't throw it away because of past tragedies. Let this go now.

Kyle glanced at Casi. "I've been talking to Nicole a lot lately. She's the one who recommended the therapist."

"She would be a good person to do it." Casi regarded her hands.

"The therapist said I should stop trying to fix everyone's life, especially my brother's," Kyle smirked. "She wanted to write me a prescription for anti-depressants."

"Will you fill it?" Casi asked nervously.

"I don't require drugs. I'm not depressed, more like overwhelmed." He looked out at the river. "It helped to talk to someone with a perspective about what we had gone through, but she made me more unsettled. I must move forward."

"I agree." Peter squeezed his shoulder. "You've been patient with everyone as they figure out what they're doing in life. We'll support you as you sort through this."

"I've been a mess lately." Kyle turned to Casi. "I'm sorry."

She snuggled against him. "I'm by your side forever."

Jake shoved her. "Team Kyle? I'm the original cheerleader. Obviously, I'm unable to state that in front of my daughter after Kyle bullied her."

"I didn't..." Kyle sighed. "I've been derailed for too long with this. I need to throw away all my stupid mementos from a trip we never took." He poked his fingers in the dirt beside him. "It's best to bury the past."

"Can I see your maps before you throw them away?" Casi asked.

Kyle shook his head. "The ones stashed in my backpack at the back of the closet that I've never shown you?"

Casi grinned. "I would like to hear about the red stars."

"My itinerary for Europe. Those were the places we planned to visit. I did a lot of research to figure out what the highlights were based on our common interest, and budget."

Casi laughed. "You were always a data nerd?"

"I'm organized." Kyle chuckled. "You can paw through it again, before I throw all that crap out."

"I could make you a scrapbook."

"There's no point keeping things from somewhere you've never been." Kyle stood and brushed the dirt off. "I'm sorry I freaked out." His eyes paled. "Casi, I put you in danger. You shouldn't trust me."

"Too late. You have my undying loyalty." She shrugged.

Olivia glared at Kyle as he entered the living room. "Grandma says I must stay here because I have a negative impact on your life."

Kyle cringed. "I'm fine now, Mom."

Georgia pursed her lips. "We were distracted as a family with all the new additions." She eyed Jake. "Olivia has been waffling for a while, and I'm insisting she stays with us until we decide on the best path." She straightened her back to let them know it wasn't up for discussion.

Peter nodded. "Perfect, I could use some help around the farm."

"I'm not doing manual labor." Olivia jutted her chin out. "Dad, tell them I'm figuring out what I want to do on my own."

Jake surveyed the room. "I'm sorry Olivia, but I can't help you at this moment." He shrugged when her eyes widened. "The contents of your handbag suggest you're in trouble and I've been too lenient because of my own guilt. Stay with your grandparents and maybe it will expedite some tough choices you need to make."

"Jensens are contributors, not takers." Peter asserted.

"I'm not a Jensen! I come from white trash so it's my destiny to be a loser." She sulked.

"I gave you the name that was given to me. It's time you live up to it." Jake kissed her cheek and turned to Georgia. "Thank you. Let me know if you need money for expenses. I can bring by clothes later in the week. She can suffice with what she has here already."

"Nothing fits me!" Olivia burst into tears.

Georgia rubbed her back. "We'll tackle that issue too."

11

PITY PARTY

"Do you want to go to a party at Nicole's tonight?" Kyle leaned against Casi's desk and straightened her papers as he spoke.

Casi set down her laptop and glanced around her office, distracted by her marketing campaign. "What kind of party? It's the middle of the week."

"It's not really a party. It's the twentieth anniversary of the accident." He lined pens alongside the paperwork. "We're getting together for drinks with people who were there that day."

"Oh, a pity party." She frowned at his precise rearrangement of her workspace. She glanced at the sadness written on his face. "I'm sorry, that came out wrong. I think it would be beneficial for you to be with your friends. Honestly, I would feel out of place. Would you mind if I pass?"

"It's fine. You have a lot of work to do."

"Do you want me to go?"

He ran his hand over the doorjamb, inspecting the wood. "No. You're right, I don't think anyone else is bringing spouses and Gary is out of town at a game convention."

"I'm leaving on a business trip to Toronto tomorrow, but we'll talk about it when you get home, ok?" She grasped his hand and gave it a squeeze.

Casi sat at the counter finishing a report on her laptop as she sipped a glass of wine when Jake stormed in the house and surveyed the living room. "Is Kyle home?"

"No, he's at Nicole's. They're doing a memorial thing for the twentieth anniversary of the accident." She shrugged and entered data.

"Why aren't you with him?"

"Because I have a business trip in the morning and it seemed like something he should do with his friends." She elbowed him as he attempted to access her keyboard. "Knock it off! I'm in the middle of a report. Get the iPad if you want to play Candy Crush."

"Make it go to Facebook."

She giggled at his lack of technical skills before saving her document and opened her account. "Who are we trolling?"

"Your husband. Go to Nicole's page."

She frowned at his frantic manner, until the pictures loaded, and her heart dropped. The memorial spun into a drunken college party with bottles and drugs on full display. Kyle lounged shirtless with Nicole suggestively snorting a line from his ripped abs. The pictorial continued as the partygoers posed seductively, using each other for props. Casi slammed the computer closed when the last picture revealed Nicole undoing Kyle's zipper with her teeth while he ran his hand through her hair with a grin. "What the hell is he doing?" Casi whirled around to look at Jake.

"Spinning out of control." Jake rubbed her back. "I'm driving over there and shutting this party down."

"Don't!" She wiped her eyes with the back of her hand. "He can fucking stay there. I have an early flight and I can't deal with his bullshit." She stormed toward the bedroom. "How did you find out about the pictures?"

"Olivia called me when she noticed Kyle was tagged. Can you block them?" Jake grabbed her hand.

"Not my problem," she hissed.

❧

Casi stared at the clock with bleary eyes while she gathered her belongings, trying to assess if she had everything after a long sleepless night. She heard the front door and froze, unsure how to proceed. She hoped to be gone by the time Kyle came home, but also felt guilty leaving for a trip before she knew if he was alright. He stood sheepishly by the door, realizing she was well informed of his activities. "My phone died. It wasn't safe to drive home, so I stayed at Nicole's." He kicked at the floor with the toe of his shoe.

"Wore down the battery taking pictures?"

"It wasn't how it appeared." He stepped toward her.

"No, Kyle! I'm late and I don't have time to deal with your problems. Who would have believed I've become the adult in this relationship? Party all you want. Bring Nicole over here to hook up, I don't care anymore. When I get back from my trip, I'll find a new place to stay." She flung the strap of her bag over her shoulder and pushed past him.

"Casi, please listen!"

"Talk to your shrink, Kyle. I'm not interested in your bullshit." She held up a middle finger as she slammed the door.

Jake waited at her car, anticipating a blow up when he noticed Kyle's truck drive in. "Come here, Monkey." He opened his arms. She fell against his chest, sobbing. He hugged her tenderly. "You can't leave like this. Go back and give him hope, you owe him that."

"I can't be around him. I hate him!"

"You have every right to be angry, but he never gave up on you when you were acting like a moron." He dabbed her tears with a handkerchief.

"This is why I didn't wear makeup." She exhaled and turned back to the house.

Kyle glanced up from where he stood at the coffeemaker, surprised to see her. "Did you forget something?"

"Yes." She rushed toward him. "I'm beyond angry and I don't have time to talk about it. I'll be back on Friday, and I'll give you a chance to explain."

He enveloped her in his warm embrace, breathing against her neck as he spoke. "I'm so sorry! I swear I didn't have sex with Nicole. What you saw in the pictures was all that happened."

She put her hand to the side of his face and nodded. "I'll call you tonight from the hotel. I love you." She kissed him softly.

"I love you, too. I'm done with this angst. I promise it's behind me now," He let go of her begrudgingly.

"I'm glad." She brushed her fingertips through his.

She walked back outside as Jake finished cleaning her windshield. "Your bag is in the trunk and I checked your oil." He held the door open for her. "Make sure to text when you land. Have a safe trip." He gave her a kiss and waved as she backed out, then went inside and sat at the counter, watching his brother pour coffee. "How much more are you going to put us through?"

Kyle handed him a cup. "That was the end. We got out of hand with the pictures, but we're ready to move on."

"Did the cocaine help with that? Or was it hooking up with Nicole that did the trick?" Jake narrowed his eyes.

Kyle blushed. "I drank too much, but no drugs or sex. She tried, but as drunk as I was, I never forgot I was married. It helps to be totally in love."

"Nicole doesn't love Gary?"

"She married him for the stability. I figure growing up the way they did in the trailer park made her choose a man who is financially responsible. Grady's death and having to hide the tragic outcome was brutal on her." He rubbed his temple. "How do I fix things with Casi?"

"You're lucky she's as smart as she is beautiful." Jake snickered, "Unless we're talking about directions or time. She can't grasp those concepts."

Kyle smiled as his eyes watered. "She's priceless."

"You hurt her, but she'll come around. Stop being a useless zombie and return to the man she fell in love with." Jake stood and put his arm around his brother's shoulders. "We don't function well without you as our guide and I'm not cut out to be the responsible one."

Jake smiled as he watched Kyle video chatting with Casi at the wood shop. In the four days she had been gone they spoke every morning, and he was pleased to see his brother's confidence and stability return. Concern flickered in Kyle's eyes, and he began to pace nervously. "What's going on?" Jake whispered, as the screen filled with Casi's tearful face.

"It's just turbulence," Kyle relayed calmly, going into a lengthy explanation of air pockets and thermal layers. A vein protruded from his temple, indicating his placid expression was a lie.

"Hey, Monkey Moonshine," Jake cooed, smiling at the phone. "Are you on your way home? We miss you."

"We might not make it," Casi sobbed as the video shook violently. "This is costing a fortune to call, but I'm terrified we'll crash."

"The cost is unimportant." Kyle smiled, and he gripped the workbench as the picture pixilated. "Keep talking to us and we'll go through it with you."

Jake rubbed Kyle's back, sensing he was panicking. "Hey, did I ever tell you about the time when we were kids and I had this awesome idea to build a treehouse? The problem was, the only tree strong enough was about twenty feet up. Can you believe Kyle actually listened to me and carried the lumber up there?"

"Is that the treehouse that's still there?" She glanced back nervously as baggage toppled from overhead compartments.

"Yup. You'll have to check it out," Jake said.

"Kyle said only you two are allowed in and there are spiders inside."

"We'll make an exception for you and we'll ensure it is spider-free." Jake quickly launched into another story from their childhood.

After thirty minutes, Casi rubbed her neck and smiled as the captain announced they would be making an emergency landing in Chicago. "I think it's over." The passengers cheered in relief. "I'll call you from the airport."

The screen went blank and Kyle exhaled and turned to Jake, resting his head on his shoulder. "I wondered if that was my penance; to have the perfect life snatched away because I didn't appreciate it."

"Maybe it was a wake-up call?" Jake hugged him. "You have an amazing life, a darling wife, and an incredible brother. What else could you want?"

Kyle grinned. "I want nothing more and it's time to acknowledge that permanently."

12

CEREMONY

Casi rushed in the house, apologizing for being late. "We were stuck in Chicago for over six hours! I'll shower and be ready for the wedding in a flash. Where's Jake? Is he getting Anna?" she asked breathlessly.

Kyle smiled and embraced her. "Jake is picking up Gail and the kids. He's not taking Anna because he wants to be supportive of Gail and spend time with Olivia. We're not in a hurry. It isn't our wedding and we'll get there at our own pace. Take a shower and relax. Do you want me to make you something to eat?"

"I ate four bags of chips and a donut. That should hold me until I start boozing." She giggled. "Realistically, how much time do I have?"

Kyle checked his watch. "Forty-five minutes."

"Done." She sprinted to the bathroom. She spun around and jumped in his arms. "I missed you!"

"I missed you, too." He gave her a kiss. "Forty-four minutes."

Casi cringed when Kyle sat on the vanity while she toweled dry. "Am I out of time?"

"No, you're fine." He set a glass of wine on the counter. "I wanted to talk to you about something before we left."

"Can we not do this now?"

"It's not about Nicole. That will take a lot more time to apologize for. While you were gone, I wanted to put my life back in order and prove I'm the same man you married."

"Ok." She set down the blow dryer.

"I realized I hadn't addressed the sperm donor thing with Lauren, and I had been purposely avoiding her because I didn't want to deal with it. You said I should do what was in my heart and you would support me."

"I meant it." She gripped the edge of the counter.

"I went to the clinic..."

"Oh!" Casi gasped. "Um, so what happens now? Has she already done the in-vitro?"

"No, Casi!" Kyle embraced her. "I never wanted to be a father, not even from afar. I couldn't sire a child and not be involved. I don't care what you claim, it does involve you and our marriage. I have everything I want right here, with you. I had a vasectomy."

"Why?"

"My body belongs to you and that includes my sperm. I never want you to question if I'll change my mind. My choice is permanent. I only told Lauren I made my decision and not to ask me more about it. I was clear my role in her life is as a friend, and that's where I draw the line."

"Was she alright with that answer?"

"I hope. She texted me she's bringing a date to the wedding. I wanted to tell you before you saw her so there wasn't animosity between you."

She took a sip of wine and smiled. "Did you get a shave?"

"I'll let you check it out after the wedding. We need to ensure the equipment still works." He wiggled his eyebrows. "You have plenty of time. I'll put on a TV show, so you aren't pressured."

"Polar bears and ice caps?"

"The migratory habits of blue whales."

Kyle did a double take when she entered the living room. "Wow! What happened to the navy dress you bought?"

"I could tell by your face when I showed it to you that you

thought it was dowdy. I texted Mary Ann a picture of this one and she said she had no problem with me wearing it." She smoothed the plum chiffon skirt.

"It's super sexy. I love it." He twirled her around to get the full effect. "The other one was too uptight for you."

"This is more fun. I bought it in Toronto."

"A Canadian dress for my Canadian girl." He brought his hand to the side of her face and gazed in her eyes. "You were never the problem. It's important you understand that."

"I'm your partner and I can't shut you out when you're going through a tough time."

&.

Kyle circled the parking lot in search of a spot, to no avail. "This is a big wedding." He noted a limousine pull up. "The bridal party just arrived."

"Should we wait in the car until the ceremony is over? We could make out." She slid a hand up his thigh.

"Very tempting." Kyle grinned. "But I don't want you to miss out." He pulled beside the limousine. Mary Ann stepped out, and he smiled. "You look lovely. Casi's plane was late. Can you walk slowly so she can duck inside while I find parking?"

"Take your time," Mary Ann giggled. "This will be a lengthy ceremony and I'm guzzling champagne to get through it."

Gail held out a glass for Casi as she got out of the car. "Have a drink with us. That dress is amazing on you!"

"It's exciting to wear something less conventional than my regular work attire." Casi kissed Mary Ann's cheek. "You are a beautiful bride."

Mary Ann clinked her glass. "Cheers to husbands, including Gail's ex, who's being a rock star today."

Gail smiled. "He took Olivia to the mall to buy a dress early this morning to ensure she wasn't rushed. He picked us up at the house, so we could arrive as a family."

"Is Olivia doing better?" Casi asked.

"It's been excellent for her to be with her grandparents. She seems calm and happy," Gail reported.

Kyle jogged over and Casi downed her second glass of champagne. "See you inside, Mrs. Petrov."

Kyle took her hand and whispered, "Is that Tucker's last name? That's the same as our birth father."

She considered the information and shrugged. "It's like Smith; there are millions of them. I doubt you're related. Although Petrov means Peter's, so it's like you always belonged to your dad."

His eyes lit up, and he grinned. "I love that idea."

They hurried up the steps, hand in hand, and swung open the broad doors to the church, accidentally creating a scene. All eyes turned in expectation of the bridal party. Jake stood and waved them over. "Nice entrance," he chuckled. "You're stunning in that scandalous dress, Monkey. I'm relieved to see you on solid ground."

"It was unbelievably scary," she whispered, as the procession began.

Kyle nodded at Lauren, quickly analyzing her date. "He's a douche," Jake said in a hushed tone.

"Perhaps, but remember it benefits us all if Lauren has a boyfriend."

Jake nodded. "Your wife looks super hot, by the way."

"She does." Kyle ran his hand over her bare back. "Did Lia bring Shane?" He peered down the pew.

"Yes, it's their first date. She texted me and asked if it would be weird and I told her to go for it," Casi said.

The ceremony began, and they took their seats, smiling at the happy couple. Tucker's daughters, Sacha and Siena, beamed as they became a family. Kyle smiled as Casi's eyelids flickered as the priest droned on. He secured his arm around her to ensure she didn't slip from her seat when he noted her waver. "Just a little longer." He kissed her temple.

"The champagne and wine are catching up to me." She gave him a sleepy smile and leaned against him.

"We can greet everyone and sneak out if you're tired. You've had a hell of a rough day."

"A quick cat nap and I'll be ready to go." She winked. "I still have to check out Lauren's date. Plus, there's food to be eaten."

Kyle smoothed his hand over Casi's arm as the bridal party began to exit. "It's time for cake." He chuckled when her eyes flew open and she bolted upright. "Well, almost. The ceremony is over though." He laced his fingers through hers and shuffled with the crowd to the reception hall. Outside the church, he halted and directed Casi to the side. "Um, do you remember me mentioning someone named Lindsey? A woman I dated a while ago."

"Is she here?" She surveyed the throngs of guests. He nodded toward a woman attempting to camouflage a bulging belly with her wrap, as she straightened her too-tight dress. Casi cocked her head, not picturing Kyle with the frumpy woman. "She's the pharmacist at the drugstore."

"Yes, and she's married to Bruce."

"The guy who comes for sports night," she confirmed. "Why are you telling me this now? I'm aware of your legacy of lovers."

"She may still have a slight crush on me. She can become quite vocal about it when she drinks." He smiled as she approached and leaned into an awkward hug. "Wow, Lindz, are you..." he stopped mid-sentence as Bruce shook his head, drawing a hand across his throat behind her. "You look pretty." He froze. "You've met my wife, Casi?"

"We haven't been formally introduced, but I've seen you around town. I love your dress, it's amazing on you." Lindsey wrapped her arms around her. "We're sitting at the same table." She clapped and moved place cards to ensure Kyle sat beside her.

They turned to greet other couples, and Casi whispered, "Were you about to ask if she was pregnant?"

Kyle blushed. "She's had a bunch of kids. I assumed she was expecting."

"Another hopeful would-be Mrs. Jensen who ditched you to find a man who wanted children?" She nudged him in the ribs.

"Something like that. She was the first girl I dated in Blackberry Falls." He glanced back at the swell of guests and directed her to an alcove. "I met her at a beach party, and we had fun hanging out at the lake, swimming, and playing sports. Lauren and I immediately connected because we had a lot of common interests."

"Boring." She rolled her eyes. "Unless you want to give me the dirty details I would rather hit the bar."

"Lindsey was super hot back then, cute in her bikini. She was outgoing and fun." His eyes danced with amusement. "I hooked up with her, but texted Lauren the next day by mistake, which didn't go over well. We kept it casual for years as we continued to build the business. Lauren and I became close friends and supported each other in our goals. One night at the bar, I announced we bought the building. Lindsey declared I must finally be ready for a relationship, and I joked it might be time to start settling down. She made sure everyone knew she was first in line. I didn't realize she had also been dating Bruce and dropped him instantly, which crushed him." He noted the crowd thinning. "Eventually, she pushed for more. Sex was great, and I liked going out to do things, but I remained clear about not wanting kids and marriage wasn't a priority. We continued to be off and on for years. Finally, Bruce pressured her for a formal commitment, and she told me she no longer wanted casual hook-ups, so we called it quits."

"Until?" Casi raised an eyebrow.

"I was dating Lauren, and she wanted to take things slowly. Painstakingly slow." He winced. "It had been four months or so. I took her to Elmvale to meet my parents, upon her insistence. She loved my mom and tolerated my dad. I could see the wheels spinning in her head, planning our future. I freaked out."

"And had sex with Lindsey?" Her eyes lit up.

"Yup. At the bar. In the bathroom stall," he chuckled. "Lia told Lauren, and I figured that ended our relationship."

"She doesn't give up, does she?"

"Bruce had been on the verge of proposing to Lindsey and was heartbroken. I apologized and promised it had been a onetime thing.

I asked Lauren for another chance and we worked things out. Bruce and Lindsey got married and everybody was happy." He clenched his jaw. "A few years later, we were hunting and out of the blue, Bruce turned his gun on me and demanded to know if I was sleeping with his wife."

"Oh, my God! Was Jake there?" Casi's hand flew to her mouth.

"Yes, and about six other guys. Jake pointed his shotgun at Bruce and calmly told him to drop his weapon or he would blow his brains out. I can still remember that damn barrel at the base of my skull," he shuddered. "Bruce started crying, saying he was a mess because he knew Lindsey was cheating. I swore it wasn't with me and that Lauren and I were planning to get married." He read the doubt in her expression. "It was the truth! She was screwing the UPS guy, not me. He dropped the gun and Jake hit him so hard, he broke his jaw. We voted he couldn't hunt with us for a year and one of the guys took away his gun to protect Lindsey." He shook his head. "Unfortunately, it made me realize I didn't have feelings for Lauren. This poor desperate man was ready to kill his friend over an assumed affair with his wife. If I found out Lauren cheated, it wouldn't have bothered me. In fact, I didn't think I was capable of loving a woman like that." He cupped her face. "Casi, I love you with all my heart. The party at Nicole's turned into a drunken sob fest. I promise I only hugged her when I arrived and nothing else happened."

She brushed her lips to his. "I believe you. I understand the turmoil inside you about losing your friends and regrets from the past. I'm sorry I lashed out in anger." She smiled. "The turbulence on the plane was a reality check to how quickly we can lose everything in an instant."

Jake strolled over and smacked Kyle on the back. "Lindsey's here. All your girlfriends will be at one table, except the one who just got married."

"Perfect, they can socialize with your ex-wives." Kyle winked. "Oh, and here's your new pal." He turned and smiled as Shane approached with Lia.

"Hey, Cassidy." Shane hugged her enthusiastically. "I hope this isn't weird. Lia and I have been talking online, and it seemed like an opportunity to get together socially..." His cheeks flushed with embarrassment.

"I'm happy you're here," Casi said.

Lia's eyes lit up as she introduced him to the table of guests. Jake grinned and shook his hand. "Nice to see you again."

"The pleasure is all mine." Shane gave him a wink.

Lauren approached and linked arms with a slight man, with thinning brown hair cemented with gel, who had an air of boredom. "This is my friend, Dalton." Her brow furrowed as she noted him lustfully scrutinizing Casi's attire.

Kyle extended a hand, drawing his attention away from her cleavage. "Hello, I'm Kyle, and this is my wife, Casi." He leaned in and gave Lauren a warm hug.

Without warning, Dalton pulled Casi toward him and embraced her. "I see this is a friendly crowd." He slid a hand across her backside.

Kyle clutched Casi's elbow to reclaim her. "We'll get drinks."

"Ew," Casi breathed as they strode to the bar.

"Sorry, I wasn't prepared for that." Kyle shivered.

"She's a looker." Dalton watched her walk away.

"Yes, my brother's wife is beautiful." Jake stepped forward and hissed in his ear. "Hands off!"

Dalton smirked. "In my experience, women dress like that to get attention. I just gave her what she asked for."

Jake's eyes ignited with rage and Shane slid in with a harsh body check, shoving Dalton into the coat rack. "Oops, sorry, tripped over my own foot. Us hockey players can be a bit rowdy in public." Shane nodded to Jake and Lia smiled as she smoothed Shane's jacket.

"Linz, are you still vodka cranberry?" Kyle returned with a tray of drinks.

"You know it!" She eagerly reached for the cocktail.

"Aren't you pregnant?" Dalton eyed her.

"Do you work with Lauren in Seattle?" Casi interrupted, giving Lindsey time to compose herself while Bruce rubbed her back.

"I'm consulting at the restaurant. My family owns a winery in the Columbia Valley, and I'm a sommelier." He wrinkled his nose at his glass of cabernet. "I'll bet you've never met one of those before."

"I can't say I've ever wanted to." Casi turned to Lindsey and struck up a conversation about Blackberry falls, giving her full attention.

The evening progressed, and the drinks flowed. The Russian food was a big hit with diverse flavors throughout the extensive menu. Casi grinned when Kyle set a large platter filled with an array of desserts in front of her. "Is this all for me?" She grabbed a fork.

Kyle chuckled. "I brought it for the table, but you can have first pick."

Jake reached over and took a cookie from the plate noting Dalton perusing every bite that went into Casi's mouth. As he curled his lip and began to comment, Jake cut him off. "Why don't you help yourself? You seem fascinated by the selection."

Dalton redirected his eyes to Jake. "Dessert makes you fat."

"It does?" Shane stopped mid-bite before letting out a hearty laugh. "Screw it, these are too incredible." He moved the plate toward them. "Try it."

"Oh, I'm fine." Lauren shook her head.

"You have to taste this." Casi held a pastry out to her. "I can't place that unusual spice." Kyle began to answer but noted the glimmer in Casi's eye and smiled at her including Lauren in the conversation.

Lauren took a small bite and brushed crumbs from her lips. "Anise."

"Delicious, huh?" Casi beamed.

"Yes, it is." Lauren nodded. "Is there princess cake? It has raspberry and almond. Technically it's Swedish, but it's a delicacy that would definitely be included in an elaborate Russian wedding."

Casi perused the assortment and Kyle jumped up. "Sorry, I guess I forgot that one. Can I get anyone else something?"

"I'll take another drink." Lindsey held up her glass.

Mary Ann made the rounds, visiting each table and joining in the festivities. She saved their table for last, encouraging Gail to join her. Jake pulled Gail on his lap, teasing her as he whispered in her ear.

Kyle tugged Casi to the dance floor for a Latin number, twirling and dipping her low as he gazed in her eyes. Lindsey grabbed Lauren's hand across the table. "When did he learn to dance like that?"

Lauren tucked a strand of hair behind her ear. "He took lessons. Casi really likes dancing, so he surprised her."

Lindsey moaned. "He's so sexy! I remember when he did those line dancing classes with you." Lauren's nostrils flared at the offhanded remark.

Bruce clenched his jaw and Jake nudged him. "Kyle is completely in love with his wife. His entire focus is what makes her happy."

Bruce watched as Kyle and Casi got swept up with the mass of Russian dancers when the song changed. He glared at his wife, analyzing his friend's physique. "I understand, but it's emasculating when she acts like that."

Jake nuzzled Gail's neck. "I'm a pretty slick dancer too. Do you want to see my moves?"

Kyle returned, flushed and laughing as relatives held on to Casi, weaving her into their circle. Mary Ann smiled when Tucker whirled around in a fit of aerobatics. Casi clapped and grasped his hand, twirling with him to the center. Kyle turned his attention to the table and pulled Mary Ann toward him. "This is a fantastic wedding!"

Mary Ann smiled and gave him a kiss. "You've been a great friend, thanks for introducing me to Tucker. My life blossomed into something wonderful." She glanced at her stepdaughters dancing with family and grabbing Casi to stay with them. Tucker danced to Mary Ann and enticed her to join the group, making her giggle with his enthusiasm and antics, encouraged by his relatives cheering.

Kyle brought more drinks and offered Olivia a cocktail. She raised an eyebrow. "I'm only nineteen."

"This is an international crowd. Let's pretend you're Canadian." He placed his hand on top of hers. "I owe you an apology. I've had a lot going on lately, and I shouldn't have taken it out on you. I'm sorry I was harsh and said things I truly regret."

"It's ok." She shrugged.

"It's not." He squeezed her hand. "I had no right to dictate what you should do."

"Grandma says it's because you care about me." She glanced away. "She said you appear strict, but you protect your family and help them make good choices for their futures."

He swung an arm around her shoulders. "She's your real Grandma. The other one may have given birth to us, but she's not part of who we are. I was wrong to spring that on you. I lashed out at your dad and you got caught in the crossfire."

"Grandpa said I'm a Jensen, and that's all that matters."

"What can I do to make it up to you?"

She brushed a hair from her face and turned away. "You care more about the boys than you do about me. You've never liked me, and you judge me. I'm a bitch around you because I'm left out."

"I was nineteen when you were born, and I felt you were a responsibility my brother didn't need at twenty-two. But you changed him. He stepped up to be a good father. I was jealous you took a piece of him away from me." He gave her a heartfelt smile.

"I've always been envious he loves you more than anyone else in this world." Her lip trembled. "I don't fit in anywhere."

"He loves me differently. Our early situation made us closer than a lot of brothers, but that doesn't mean we can't also love other people. The new kids haven't made him love you less either. It's easier for me to show my feelings for them because I'm older and my home life is stable."

"And because they're boys."

Kyle considered her comment. "I'm not sure what to do with a niece. Reid likes fishing and outdoor things. What do you enjoy?" He cocked his head.

"I'm floundering. You assume I don't care about my weight, but I'm overwhelmed. I can't focus on anything else." She pushed her cake away. "I've tried to diet." She regarded her reflection in the window. "I wanted to do that course, but it's expensive and you didn't consider it valid since it's not college."

"The class on Vancouver Island? Perhaps I should have asked you more. Would you like to share what it's about?"

"It's a twelve-week seminar on healthy eating and nutrition. I wanted to take it before I chose a college." She inhaled sharply. "High school was hard enough; I don't want to be a fat college student. I realize it's pricey, but you earn credits."

"Huh, that sounds like an interesting course. I apologize for not paying attention when you mentioned it. Can you forward me the information and we can check it out?"

"You would actually consider letting me do it?"

"I am happy to let you choose the programs which suit you the best. College isn't for everyone." He kissed her forehead. "I care about you and although my delivery was horrible, it's important that you succeed in life."

"I figured you would be intrigued because it involves cooking." She fumbled with her napkin. "We could make meals together sometime?"

He nudged her and grinned. "We could teach your dad and Casi how to eat better. They seem to think donuts are a food group."

"Casi's friend, Katie, said I should try diet drugs, but they made me loopy and wired."

"Stay away from that crap, and any advice from Katie. You're making a smart choice with the class and I'm happy to finance whatever you need to be successful."

She smiled. "I'm the one who saw the pictures of you on Facebook and called Dad. He told Casi."

"Not my finest moment. That woman was someone I dated in high school, and for the record, nothing happened past what you saw in those stupid photos." Kyle winced.

"You didn't cheat on Casi?"

"Never!"

"What about the drugs?"

He grimaced. "I'm sure you were pleased to see I am a hypocrite. I didn't do any that night, but I've had my share of wild parties. I'm not a saint in any respect."

"I wanted Casi to take the pictures down. You deserved privacy."

She shook her head. "Dad slept with my friends."

"What? When?" His eyes became sapphire spheres.

"It was over a year ago, before Austin was born. My friend Zoe, and another friend Crystal."

"The tattoo girl in Seattle? She's your friend?"

"Yup. It took a while before I realized the older hot guy she hooked up with, was Dad." She shivered. "They said they took pictures, but somehow they all got erased. Casi?"

"Yes. He called us to help him. We didn't want any record. It was a bad choice on his part. He didn't realize that girl was so young."

"It's gross he slept with a random girl!"

"Absolutely! He was freaking out about the baby and kinda went off the rails." He chuckled. "But then he straightened out and had two more surprise babies and got married. And divorced."

She rolled her eyes. "That's why you can't have photos like that on Facebook. You must be the sensible one, not the half-naked partier. I don't want my friends talking about how sexy you are."

"I'll try to do better."

"When you dated Lauren, you never invited us to do anything. I rarely went to your house until you married Casi. I'm sorry I took advantage, I wanted to be included in your life."

"You're welcome back anytime."

"I'm glad my dad has a house across the street. He should be close to you. He's kind of dumb sometimes." She smiled at Jake as he eyed them from across the table and tried to hear what their conversation was about. "He's so much sweeter since Casi became his friend. He always seemed mad before. He's happier since he lost weight too."

"He is." Kyle nodded. "I'm happier that he's healthier and feels better about himself. My brother is very important to me."

The single women were called to the floor for the bouquet toss and Jake cheered on Gail and Lia, making them blush. Lauren tried to bow out, but Lia pulled her up with the group. As the women stood uncomfortably on display, Mary Ann turned with a smile and made an announcement. "I'm changing things up. I refuse to throw this in the air and make you fight for it in desperation to be the next bride. I was very content as a single woman, and Tucker will now be a perfect partner." She untied the ribbon on the bouquet and handed each woman a rose. "Instead, I'm giving you each a flower with the hope you'll find your true love, but not abandon yourself in the process." She knelt before her stepdaughters. "Sacha and Siena, I love you. I'm thrilled to be part of your family and I'm thankful to be able to watch you grow and one day find a partner to share your journey with."

"That was beautiful!" Casi wiped a tear.

Lindsey raised her glass, making a slurred speech about tainted love. "Kyle, how did Casi finally seduce our elusive bachelor? I mean, she's super gorgeous, but you were so adamant about never getting married." She thumped the table for emphasis.

Bruce rubbed his forehead in annoyance, trying to remove the drink from her hand. "Lindsey, stop."

"No really, we all want to know." She staggered to her feet. "Right Lauren? You tried for years and almost had him in the net, then swoosh, he swam away!" Her cocktail sloshed and Lauren's cheeks were ablaze as Dalton looked between her and Kyle.

"Absolute blind love, Lindsey." Kyle held his hands up. "I met Casi and my heart stopped. From the first kiss, she owned my soul."

"That is so fucking sweet!" Lindsey continued, hiccuping and uttering nonsense as she swayed. Kyle jumped up, swiftly directing her to the nearest exit, anticipating what was about to happen. He managed to get her to a planter and held her hair as she vomited, rubbing her back and consoling her. Jake stifled a laugh and redirected traffic from the area. Lauren rolled her eyes, muttering criticism under her breath. Casi glanced out the window and engaged the table in conversation, drawing attention away from the unfortunate woman. Kyle quietly strolled to the bar and asked for a wet towel and glass of water, then returned to the patio to tend to Lindsey. Jake gripped Bruce's shoulder and whispered, "Why don't you get the car and meet us out front. Let's not make her come through here."

"Thanks." Bruce stood and gathered Lindsey's purse and shawl, apologizing to the table for his wife's behavior, specifically to Casi.

"Hey, we've all been there." Casi put a hand over her heart.

"Some of us can control our drinking," Lauren challenged.

"Perhaps, but I'm sure you've had moments where you regretted your actions." Casi gave her the death glare and Lauren scrambled out of her seat with a hurried excuse to use the bathroom.

"Why don't you share all your shameful escapades." Dalton leaned forward and drummed his fingers on the table.

"I don't relive my past." Casi stood as Kyle came back. "My present and future are with my husband." She whispered, "You're a good guy. Thanks for always being the knight in shining armor there to save the day." She kissed his cheek and exited to the hall while he refilled her champagne. She pushed open the door of the bathroom and noted Lauren dabbing her eyes.

"I don't need another lecture." Lauren glared at her in the mirror.

"Actually, I came to make sure you were alright." Casi leaned against the counter. "You might find it easier to be my friend."

"It's too late for that." Lauren disposed of her paper towel.

Casi shrugged. "For the record, I supported Kyle in whatever decision he made concerning your request. I'm thrilled he chose not to, but I would have stood by him if it had gone the other way."

Lauren nodded. "He told me. He said he wasn't comfortable doing it."

"Perhaps Dalton will be a good match?"

"It's obvious you don't like him." She set her jaw.

"I don't care for his comments, but I don't know him. Often men are jerks in public because they're insecure."

Lauren gave her a half smile. "He's really smart and knows a lot about wine." Her eyes lit up. "His family is considering putting a restaurant at the winery, and maybe that would be a good project for me."

Casi noted the insecurity etched in her face. "It sounds like an intriguing opportunity." She put her hand on Lauren's arm. "I've heard you're a talented chef and I understand it's your passion. I hope this turns out to be everything you hoped for." She stepped forward and smiled. "If we stop wasting our energy hating each other we can discover more positive interactions in the future."

13

LIL' BEE

Casi stood in the parking lot of Coffee Junction, casually texting, while Kyle knelt before her and re-laced her boots. Jake observed them, then snatched the phone from her hand. "What's wrong with you? My brother is on his knees tending to you."

Casi held her hand out. "Give it back!"

Kyle straightened the hem of her pants and smoothed it over the boots. "There you go. They should stay laced now. I must have gotten weather proofing wax on the laces, so that's why they were slipping."

"Thank you." She gave him a kiss.

"You're a spoiled brat." Jake frowned at the contact on her phone. "Why are you texting Shane?"

"Jeez, don't get in the middle of him and Katie, or Lia." Kyle shook his head. "He can figure out his own mess."

"He asked my advice." She rolled her eyes.

"I hope your answer was to divorce the first wife before taking on a girlfriend?" Kyle grinned. "Of course, his new best friend might have a different answer?" He poked Jake in the ribs.

"Our conversations are private." Jake chuckled when he noted the devastation in Kyle's eyes. "We're not women; we don't talk about feelings. I invited him to sports night."

"Is that code for a hook-up?" Casi giggled.

"No, it's that thing we do weekly at my brother's house. The night you get plastered at Happy Hour," Jake replied. "Oh wait, that's vague, the Monday nights."

Casi laughed. "Whatever. His relationship with Katie is complicated because of the green card. Lia understands, but I don't want her taken advantage of." She hesitated at the door. "Kyle, I also received a text from Olivia saying how excited she is to start her course. Did you think this through and ensure you're not setting her up for failure?"

"Are you questioning my ability to guide my niece in a productive direction?" Kyle scoffed.

"What classes?" Jake cocked his head.

"She expressed interest in a course on Vancouver Island. I discovered it can be applied toward an AA degree, which I'm encouraging her to continue to a BS in Health Sciences," Kyle said.

"Seems lofty," Jake asserted.

"We've been spending more time together, and I assessed if she can apply her energy to her studies rather than running in circles, the outcome will be beneficial."

"How did you phrase it to her?" Jake grinned.

"If she finishes the first six weeks and enrolls in the full two-year program, I'll pay for her to complete her degree at the college of her choice. If she decides furthering her education is not beneficial, she'll be required to get a job." Kyle nodded with satisfaction.

"How are you the hero when I'm paying for it?" Jake narrowed his eyes.

"I'm taking care of her expenses." Kyle smiled. "You've got four more to save for." Kyle pushed open the door and stopped, causing Jake to bump into him. "Hey, Lauren. I didn't realize you were in town this weekend."

Lauren smiled and hugged him. "I spent the night at my mom's. Lia and I went out to dinner with Dalton and Shane."

"Cozy." Jake shoved past his brother and grinned as a man brought in a huge bouquet, understanding Casi's text, 'Make her feel special'.

Lia's face lit up as she signed for the delivery, happily setting them on the counter on full display. "Casi, look!" she exclaimed.

"Wow, gorgeous! From Shane?" Casi asked.

"Yes, isn't that sweet." Lia's cheeks blushed with excitement.

Jake smiled. "Your new boyfriend is doing it up right."

"Do you see how envious Lauren is?" she whispered. "She told me he would be gone the minute I slept with him."

"I wasn't gone," he noted. "Sex isn't a commodity that has a onetime use. Speaking of that, I would like to keep the by-products of our lovemaking a few more days? We're headed to Elmvale for my dad's birthday and they enjoy seeing the boys."

Lia threw her head back and laughed. "You crack me up! If you're away, I'll invite my new friend over for the weekend."

🐝

Casi sat on the floor at the farmhouse surrounded by beautifully written letters radiating a faint scent of perfume. She willed herself not to pry but was overwhelmed by the revelation. She grabbed her phone and texted, not trusting herself to do the right thing.

Kyle stood in the doorway, responding to her text. "Is this the bad thing you did? Snooped through my stuff, again?"

"I was searching for something else and this box fell out. I'm aware I shouldn't go through it, but it's obvious they're love letters and I can't tear myself away from this treasure even though my heart is shattered." She wiped a tear.

Kyle sprawled on the floor beside her. "Would you like to reveal the original purpose of your covert mission?"

"I would prefer not to at this time."

He surveyed the disarray of the closet. "My backpack? I told you what was in there, why snoop when I'm not around?"

"May I take a rain check on the truth?"

"Fine, but I won't forget it's on the back burner." He picked up a page and smoothed his hand over the perfect script signed with a hand-drawn bee. "I've told you about my Aunt Libby, Dad's sister. I called her lil' bee when I was a child, and it's been our thing ever since. She sends me letters from her travels and signs it with a bee."

"Can I read some?"

"Didn't you already?"

"No, I read, 'My Darling Love,' and stopped."

"Excellent control." He chuckled. "They aren't private. My aunt is a writer, so they're very descriptive and imaginative. I hated throwing them out, and sometimes I reread them. Her travels to Scandinavia are what inspired me to want to go there. After the accident she kept my spirits up with tales from abroad."

Casi smiled at the account of a safari. "When can I meet her? She sounds amazing!"

"Hopefully this Christmas. I believe she'll be back in town."

"Does she write to Jake?"

"Not a lot. Letters were more my style. She sends him cool things like shark's teeth or warrior stuff. She understands her audience."

"Do you write her back?" She sorted through the note cards.

"I used to write often. Now it's mostly emails and phone calls." Kyle shifted his gaze to the ceiling. "She's the one I talk to about things that are troubling me."

"So, you've spoken to her recently?" Casi asked softly.

Kyle turned to face her. "Yes, I called her the morning after Nicole's party. She suggested I talk to you and not be afraid to show my weakness." Casi gathered the envelopes and carefully put them back in the box. "Bored already?"

"No, they're fascinating, but they weren't written for me. She loves you very much and the tales are meant for you."

Kyle smiled and put the box away, discretely moving his backpack to the corner of the closet. "Ready to go to the treehouse?"

"Am I still allowed even though I broke your trust?"

"I don't hide things from you. I prefer certain events to remain private only because it hurts to talk about them and nothing positive will come from it." He held his hand out to her.

"Alright Monkey, spider patrol is done," Jake called from the deck surrounding the treehouse.

Casi scrutinized the safety of the ladder and worn exterior. "I changed my mind. I don't want to go up."

"Too late, you're committed." Kyle indicated how to climb the ladder.

"I'm scared." She leaned against him halfway up.

"I'm right behind you," he breathed in her ear.

"Come on, Monkey Face, show us your climbing skills," Jake called down. "The view is amazing from up here."

Casi clasped the board above her head, shaking as she rose higher. "Focus on where you're going." Kyle steadied her foot as she slipped on a broken rung.

Jake reached down and tugged her up the last few feet, before giving his brother a hand. "We did a decent job thirty years ago."

"You should have anticipated you would be taller." Casi ducked under a crossbeam.

Kyle chuckled. "It seemed huge back then."

"Shane thought it was cool," Jake remarked.

Kyle whirled around to face him. "You brought him to our tree-house? What about the code?"

Jake shrugged. "We invited her, I thought it was open season."

"Now I don't feel special." Casi pouted. "Did you and Shane make out?"

Jake shoved her and observed his brother's defeated demeanor as he sat cross-legged at the window surveying the river below. "I haven't been here since college. Why would I bring Shane?"

"You like hanging out with him." Kyle picked at a weathered board.

"He's cool, but he's not my brother, or my best friend," Jake assured him.

"What's your attraction to him?" Casi sat beside Kyle.

Jake sat back and stared at the river churning below. "He's an outsider and I understand that. The difference between us is he embraces what makes him different, and I never did."

"Different how?" Kyle wiggled his eyebrows.

"Not gay." Jake rolled his eyes. "Neither of you gets it because you're beautiful and easy going. Everyone loves you the instant they meet you. Kyle, every girl wants to sleep with you and guys clamor to be your friend. Casi is the same but reverse the sexes. You wouldn't understand how it feels to be awkward."

"You're super handsome." Casi touched his cheek.

Kyle put his hand on Jake's. "If I'm still your favorite, you can be friends with Shane."

"Don't I get a vote?" Casi sulked.

Jake sighed. "Is there a dark history I should be aware of? Remember, it's not only about me, but Lia and the boys."

"Shane is super sweet. He's one of Joey's close friends and the guy you call when you need a ride, or pot," she giggled. "My surprise at his relationship with Katie isn't because he's not cool…"

Kyle cocked his head. "Because Katie can be cruel, and you wondered why she chose a mellow guy?"

Casi pursed her lips. "Katie is high maintenance and Shane was the fun guy you always want at the party or on your team if you're a sports person." She surveyed Jake and nodded. "You are a smart match for him, someone he can bounce things off and give him sound advice. Since he's in Seattle so much he should have American friends." She wagged a finger. "You may only bring him here with your brother's permission."

A shadow darkened Kyle's face. "After you left for college, I used to come up here by myself and think about what life would be like when I left this town. The last time I came here was the day of the accident." His face crumpled. "I brought Grady. I wanted to show him this vantage point. In the whole year we fought, I had never broken our vow." He pointed toward the bend in the river. "I told him we needed to be careful of the undertow after the rocks because it was unpredictable. He said we could navigate it together, just like we would in Europe. We hadn't told anyone, but our tickets were for the next day. We wanted to announce it at the party that night. I didn't even tell Mom and Dad."

"You weren't going to say goodbye to me? Your plan was to fly thousands of miles away and forget you had a brother?" Jake fumed.

Kyle regarded the turbulence below. "I found the adoption paper-work the beginning of the summer when I was applying for my pass-port. I was pissed at Mom and Dad for not telling me." He turned to Jake. "I hated you for being wanted, when I wasn't. I became detached from everyone and everything that summer. I wanted to get away and start my own life." Casi slid on his lap and he leaned his chin on her shoulder. "Grady was right. Once we passed that bend in the river, our lives changed forever."

❧

Nicole answered the door and smiled. "I anticipated a visit."

Casi handed her a basket of cookies. "I liberated these from Geor-gia's kitchen."

Nicole directed her toward the living room. "Is this a warning to stay away from your husband or are you requesting an apology for my outrageous behavior?"

"Neither." Casi glanced around the room. "Your home is extremely well decorated. I never noticed before during the parties."

"Thank you. Tea or alcohol?"

"Is it too early for a cocktail?"

"Is it ever?" Nicole laughed and walked to the bar. She came back with a colorful concoction. "I didn't have sex with Kyle."

"He told me." Casi took a sip.

"Did he tell you I tried?" Nicole looked away as her eyes watered. "More like begged. I even offered to add another girl to the mix and really go crazy." She smiled sadly and regarded her chest. "I used to be flat as a board until Gary bought me these. I attempted to get Kyle to check out my new curves, but he didn't want any part of it and insisted on leaving. One of the guys stopped him and took away his keys. We were all too hammered to drive. He slept out by the pool, by himself. A few of us went back to my room and played out the orgy fantasy."

Casi raised an eyebrow. "Did that help console you?"

Nicole shook her head as she broke down in tears. "I convinced myself life with Gary was boring and I needed to shake it up. I felt ill when I woke up and saw the nude people in my bed. Kyle had already left, and I sent him a lengthy text to apologize for being out of control." She squared her shoulders. "Gary wants a divorce. He saw the pictures on Facebook and confronted me. Luckily, he had taken them down remotely, so the audience remained limited. It's beneficial to be married to a computer geek."

"The pictures were a bad idea," Casi agreed.

"I don't know who took them. I have kids!" Her face contorted.

"Gary must recognize it as a onetime slip. Have you told him everything about Grady?"

"Only that my brother died in a boating accident." She surveyed the room. "This property used to be a trailer park. We lived here with my mom and stepdad. He was a bastard who hit us when he was drunk. Grady tried to protect us. But my mom wouldn't leave. After he died, Peter paid for my college in Spokane..." Her face blanched.

Casi grasped her hand. "Kyle knows the truth."

"Oh, God! Did I tell him when I was drunk? I'm mortified!" She clutched her chest in horror.

"Peter told him. Kyle was suffering from terrible nightmares. He was convinced he could have saved Grady."

"It wasn't possible." Nicole sobbed.

"Peter feels guilty for making you keep the secret."

She wiped her tears. "I lost my brother, but he was Kyle's best friend. He had his own injuries and terror to face as well." Her shoulders slumped. "When we came back from Japan, I found out they turned this property into custom homes. I insisted we buy this one, even though someone had an offer on it. Gary thought I was crazy, but he outbid them to make me happy."

"He'll come around. He's hurt, but he loves you."

"He's staying at his brother's, but he said we'll talk this weekend." She pointed to a box on the mantel. "Grady hated this place and was desperate to get away. What did I do? I stuck him on display to spend eternity in the hell he tried to escape."

"Actually, that's the purpose of my visit." Casi smiled.

14

SECRETS AND LIES

"*D*arling, it's official! I'm moving to Seattle and opening a salon," Dylan exclaimed. "We're having a celebration and you will be my special guest."

"When is it?" Casi checked her schedule on her laptop as she balanced her phone while he rattled on.

"Thursday at six but come at four so I can do your hair. I don't want you to look like a hag and scare off potential clients."

Casi giggled and made a note to reschedule her afternoon meeting. She realized Dylan hadn't made the decision to relocate on a whim, and her support was crucial for a successful transition. After she hung up, she perused her calendar, figuring out how to adjust the timeline to accommodate the party and meet with Jake to finalize their plan. She opened a new tab, determined to finish the monthly report to allow flexibility of her schedule.

Kyle grasped her shoulder. "What are you working on?"

"Jesus Christ!" She jolted in her seat. "You scared the crap out of me."

"Sorry, you seemed completely engrossed in your work. I guess you didn't hear me come in."

She closed tabs. "I'm working on my financial report."

"That turns me on when you talk numbers." He slid a hand under her blouse and caressed her breast.

"I'm sure it does." She swatted his hand.

"Are you denying me your love?" He kissed her neck.

She smiled up at him. "I can give you quick and dirty. Ten minutes, tops."

"Wow, the romance keeps growing in this relationship." He chuckled.

She stood and slithered out of her clothing. "The clock is ticking."

He wrapped his arms around her and leaned her back against the table. "I admit it's a bit intimidating to perform on this tight schedule."

Jake strolled in the house. "Kids in the room. Reel it in."

Kyle glared at the intruders as he fumbled with his jeans. "I thought you were out with Anna tonight?"

"Schedule conflict. Anna's sister needed her, and Lia went with Shane to some wine bar thing with Lauren. Obviously, I have the boys."

"Which sister?" Casi re-buttoned her blouse.

"Who knows? She has a million of them and they're all bossy." Jake chuckled and opened the fridge. "What are you making for dinner?"

"I was planning on an intimate meal." Kyle frowned at Austin climbing over the sofa as he hit Tommy with a pillow.

"Not happening." Jake smacked him on the back. "Try again Thursday."

"I can't." Casi poured a glass of wine. "Dylan is moving to Seattle and opening a salon. Isn't that wonderful? He's having a party on Thursday; do you want to come?"

"I have a truffle lecture with Lauren." Kyle rubbed his temple.

"Chocolate? Bring me samples." Casi held a thumb up.

"Sorry, mushrooms." Kyle smiled.

"Ick, don't bother." She shivered. "They smell like teen boy feet."

"It'll be a fascinating lecture. The speaker is from Italy and that's what he does for a living. Can you imagine how exciting it would be to go there?"

"I imagine Italy would be a wonderful place to visit." She winked at Jake and slid her hand over his in the pretense of getting a napkin.

❧

Casi entered the sleek salon and clapped when Dylan appeared from behind a curtain holding a glass of champagne. "Tell me I've made the right decision moving here. I'm freaking out!" he gasped.

She embraced him. "Best decision of your life. Brian is amazing, and stable. Crazy people like us require an anchor. Your own salon? Please, that's fabulous."

"I can't believe how Brian and I clicked. Who would have guessed two Hollywood babes like us would find love in a hick town?"

"Seattle is a cosmopolitan city," she corrected.

"I was referring to Blackberry Falls. That's where Brian is from."

"I forgot. This will be heaven having you here all the time."

"Your hair will thank me." He frowned at her roots. "We're going shorter; you've fallen into the dreaded bun-head thing again. Brighter highlights and for kicks I'm popping in a pink streak."

"I'm a professional businesswoman, I can't have LA hair."

"It's stylish-trendy. You sell skincare and you should exemplify modern and sophisticated. Please tell me you brought something sexy to wear." His lip curled in response to her blouse and skirt.

Casi smiled and cranked the stereo. She slid out of her clothes, giving him a shimmy in her skimpy lingerie. "Wait until you see the scandalous dress I brought." She downed her champagne and held it out for a refill.

Dylan filled her glass and twirled around her as she danced. "At least you've maintained your outrageously hot figure. I feared I would find you in Spanx and pantyhose with a minimizer bra."

"I'm a layered woman. Professional exterior over a sexy core."

"It suits you," he agreed. "Sit and let's catch up." He draped her with a cover as he excitedly shared his plans for the salon.

Two hours later, with a final spritz of hairspray, he declared her glamorous enough for the party. Casi smiled at the tousled style, highlighted by a vibrant streak of pink. She decided she could twist it into a professional chignon, hiding her wild side, but pleased with the statement. She changed into a glimmering sheath of silver, plunging to her belly button, and barely covering her lace panties. She spun around, slightly dizzy from the champagne. He gave her a kiss of approval as Brian entered leading a group of friends eager for the event. Introductions were made, and refreshments set out. Casi mingled with the guests, a walking display of Dylan's talent. The champagne flowed, and the conversations ensued, breaking into dancing and laughter. Casi socialized with Brian, leaning against him and teasing him about his perfectly coiffed style when an attractive man with dark wavy hair sauntered over. "Switched sides, again?"

Brian blushed, keeping his arm around Casi's waist. "This is Casi, Dylan's best friend from LA. That's how I met him." He locked eyes with the man. "She's Kyle Jensen's wife."

"No fucking way!" He grinned. "Good for him."

Casi cocked her head. "Are you a friend of Kyle's?"

"I used to be. I'm Lance Harrison." He waited to see if the name registered. "Lia's and Lauren's brother."

"You're out of jail?" She blinked in surprise.

"I was never there. I was banished from Blackberry Falls due to my sexual orientation." He bent his wrist to demonstrate.

Dylan slid on a counter. "Oh goody, are we finally telling her?"

"Perhaps we shouldn't..." Brian started.

"What?" Casi spun to look at them. "Since when do we keep secrets?"

"You're familiar with my tawdry past, Darling." Dylan pulled her to lean against him. "This story is Brian's, and it's juicy! Go on, spill. She's marvelous at keeping her mouth shut."

Casi drew her thumb and a finger across her lips like a zipper.

Lance grinned. "Gorgeous and funny. Our boy Kyle sure hit the jackpot."

"And these are real." Dylan cupped her breasts.

"Wait, does this involve Kyle being gay?" She shivered. "I don't want to hear about his escapades."

Lance broke into laughter. "Your husband is straight, don't worry. I'll let Brian begin the story."

Brian sighed. "I grew up in Blackberry Falls and I dated Lauren from the time we were fifteen."

"Oh, I like where this is going." Casi snuggled in Dylan's arms.

"After we graduated, I moved to Seattle to attend college. Lauren and I planned to get married at twenty-five, the ten-year anniversary of our relationship. She had it all organized; the fancy wedding, honeymoon in Italy, buy a home in Blackberry Falls, and start a family. She wanted to own a restaurant and I would be an accountant and keep the books. She delayed culinary school and worked while I went to college, so she could start saving."

"Didn't you realize you were gay?" Casi shrugged.

"I tried to hide it. She was determined to make it work, and it seemed like a comfortable life."

"But she figured it out?" Casi concluded.

Lance jumped in to finish. "Yup, the day she found us in bed together!"

"Oh!" Casi covered her mouth.

"I confessed I had been dating men in Seattle and it wasn't a onetime slip. She was hysterical and told her mother. I agreed to let everyone believe I cheated on her and that's why we broke up. She got sympathy, and I got my freedom." Brian held his hands up.

"And Lance was banished?" she added.

"I was ordered to literally straighten up and fly right; follow our Christian values," Lance mimicked. "Lauren wanted nothing to do with me, but Lia begged me to pretend to be straight. She was afraid I would move away, and we've always been close." He raised an eyebrow. "You're aware my sister dated Kyle, right?"

"Painfully aware." Casi rolled her eyes.

"She fell head over heels in love with Kyle and the fairy-tale life she planned with Brian was transferred to him. He wasn't interested in most of what she wanted, but I believe he liked how steadfast and determined she was. At some point, he must have communicated their sex life was lackluster. So she tried to spice things up and they took sexy pictures with her new phone. I discovered them on her computer and copied them. They made super masturbating material."

"Gross! Your sister and my straight husband?" Casi gagged.

"Obviously, I photo-shopped her out. Kyle's a god." He exhaled. "Lauren caught me and flipped out. She threatened to tell Kyle, and I told her to go ahead because I had read the texts where he had asked her to delete them once he sobered up."

"What happened to the pictures?" Casi narrowed her eyes.

"Lauren destroyed my computer. I'll bet she has the originals. She's still in love with Kyle."

"I realize that," Casi confirmed. "They are together tonight at a lecture thing with her new boyfriend."

"Dalton." Lance wrinkled his nose. "He's a prick."

"Do you talk to her?" she asked.

"She won't have anything to do with me. After the picture fiasco, my mom said I was Satan's spawn and threatened to turn me into the police for selling drugs." He smiled. "I had a little side business. I was sick of them and their Christian principals, so I took off for Seattle. I stayed with Brian for a bit and then made my life here. I talk to Lia all the time and see her on occasion. I was shocked when she married Jake! Her kids are super adorable though."

"You've met them?"

"She brings them to my apartment. I'm her friend Joe, in case they repeat anything to my mother."

"Joe who bakes cookies?" Casi smiled.

"Lia wants her own coffee shop and I'm helping her come up with recipes for the pastry case. She mentioned you've been ultra supportive about the idea and even Jake's behind it. She's smarter than people think, she's just timid." He waved his hand around the salon. "I'm an interior designer so obviously I would decorate it." He fiddled with his nails and frowned. "Lauren tells Lia she'll never be able to follow through with her dream because she can't commit to anything. I realize she's jealous of Lia's kids, but it crushes her to be demeaned constantly. What do you think of this new guy she's dating?"

"Shane's wonderful. His life is chaotic, but Lia's isn't perfect either. She's enjoying being with him and hopefully that's enough for now." Casi reached for his hand. "Why are you allowing your family to treat you like a convict?"

"I've served enough time." Lance smiled and picked up her phone. Brian leaned into Dylan, while Lance stood to his other side, sandwiching Casi in the middle. They posed for a series of pictures, getting more flamboyant with each one. They voted on their favorite, and Casi sent it to Kyle.

Kyle was discussing the lecture with Lauren and Dalton, determining their preferred application for truffles when his phone beeped. He smiled at the picture, confused by the caption, 'Guess who's not in jail?'

He texted back, "Your party got a little wild, huh? Do you need a ride home? I must say, that dress could land you in prison."

She giggled at his naïveté. "Look closer."

"Your hair is amazing. Is that a pink stripe? I'm turned on imagining how it appears from the top of your head."

Casi showed the men his reply. "Blow job," they said in unison, imitating the action.

"Do you recognize the man beside me?"

"Kyle, did you want to get a drink?" Lauren repeated, frustrated with his attention to his phone, figuring it was Casi.

"Sorry. Sure." He enlarged the photo. "I'm trying to determine what Casi's asking me."

Dalton peered over his shoulder and whistled. "You let her go out dressed like that?"

"She wears what she wants." Kyle shrugged. "And I'm sure everyone is gay at this party. Wait, is that Lance?"

Lauren paled and grabbed his phone, wanting to slap the coy smile off Casi's face as she posed with her brother. "It's hard to tell. He's been gone for years."

Kyle interpreted the first text and caught Lauren's glare. "Oh. Let's get that drink. It looks like Casi's having fun. I'll pick her up after."

"Your wife is a party girl, huh?" Dalton scoffed.

Kyle opened the door for Lauren. "Casi enjoys a lot of things in life. She's confident and outgoing." He whispered to Lauren as she walked past, "Did you want to go with me?"

She shook her head, blinking back tears. "I don't want anything to do with Lance. He's out of my life forever. You can tell Casi to go to hell."

Lia smiled as Austin showed her what the Google Home could do, amazing Jake with his grasp of technology. Kyle pushed through the door, wrapped around Casi as they moved in unison toward the bedroom. He had his hand up her dress while she unzipped his pants.

Jake called out, "The living room is not an appropriate location for sex."

Kyle glanced up from Casi's cleavage to notice them sitting on the floor with the boys. "What's wrong with your house?"

"I don't have internet and Austin wanted to show Lia his toy."

"Casi, I love your hair!" Lia admired.

"Thanks, Dylan did it. He's moving to Seattle and opening a salon!"

Lia glanced at Kyle. "I thought you went to the lecture."

"I did. I picked Casi up, so she didn't have to take an Uber. Also, I was curious to meet someone." He grinned as Casi turned her phone to them.

"Joe!" Austin cheered.

Jake peered closer. "Is that Lance?"

"Where did you see him?" Lia's eyes watered.

"He's one of Dylan's friends." Casi clasped her hand. "Why did you go along with the story?"

Lia shook her head. "My mom told everyone he was in jail

because she hated his lifestyle." She turned her head away. "I couldn't tell them I was still in contact with him."

"He's a nice guy and misses you as friends." Casi smiled. "He wasn't sure if he would be welcome here."

"I don't care." Jake shrugged. "Why did Austin call him Joe?"

Lia wiped a tear. "I take the boys to see him in Seattle and I worried my mom would find out."

Jake grasped her hand. "He's their uncle. Invite him over and make him a part of their lives. I'm assuming it's your mom who has a problem, but that's her issue."

"Lauren won't talk to him because he had a thing with Brian."

"Who cares?" Kyle said.

Lia narrowed her eyes. "Lauren was engaged to Brian! They had been dating since they were fifteen. I knew he cheated on her but didn't figure out it had been with Lance until we were in Vegas."

Kyle glanced at Casi and she stifled a laugh. He frowned, understanding Lauren's reaction to the photo revealing her secret. "That's not amusing."

"If you're taking Lauren's side against her brother because he got it on with her gay fiancé, you're not getting any tonight." Casi crossed her arms over her chest.

Kyle rolled on his back and chuckled, "I'm always on your side, Casi. Let's move to the bedroom and finish tonight on a high note."

"Wise choice." She patted his hand.

15

———

HAUNTED

"Merry Christmas," Casi moaned, waking to Kyle's warm tongue. The chill of the early morning air nipped at her skin, intensifying the sensation. He shoved the pillows to the side and slid up against the headboard, pulling her on his lap. He cupped her breast as she arched her back.

He gripped her waist as he climaxed. "Good morning, Sunshine."

"That was a superb way to wake up." She snuggled against him.

"You remember Lauren and Dalton are coming for breakfast?" He smiled as he heard his mother greeting people at the front door.

"Annoyingly early, as always."

He chuckled. "It's after ten; you slept like a log."

"I was exhausted," she yawned.

"Work has been busy for you lately."

She bit the inside of her cheek to avoid smiling. "I've been working on something else, too."

"Or someone."

"Excuse me?" She grabbed his chin and forced him to look at her.

"It wasn't a complaint. I'm referring to the amount of time you spend with Dylan in Seattle. Or maybe it's Katie? Either way, you haven't had any spare time."

159

"How is that not a complaint?"

"It is. But it wasn't to incite an argument. It's Christmas and I want to spend every minute with you." He kissed her and threw back the covers. "Get dressed, it's time for coffee and cinnamon rolls."

She bounded across the bed, tackling him to the floor and straddling him as she clasped his wrists together over his head. "I'll be stuck to you like glue. You'll be so sick of me by the new year, you'll be begging for space."

They strolled in the living room after helping themselves to coffee and Casi made the rounds of greeting everyone. She snatched a cinnamon roll before snuggling beside Kyle. Jack surveyed Dalton's gaze following her, specifically interested in her breasts under the loose-fitting sweatshirt.

"Boys, can one of you help me with this turkey?" Georgia called as Lauren joined her in the kitchen. Jake jumped up and raced Kyle, laughing as he shoved him against the doorjamb. Georgia smiled, recalling their childhood antics. "Kyle, can you start another pot of coffee while Lauren helps me with the seasoning?"

Casi got up to refill her mug and Jack cleared his throat. "Honey, can you come here for a second?"

"Do you want more coffee?" She picked up his cup.

He secured his arm around her waist and whispered in her ear, giving her a pat on the hip, and she nodded in agreement. Dalton studied her departure and grinned. "We can see who she likes to call Daddy."

Ava's eyes went wide, and Jack snapped, "That's my daughter you're making lewd comments about!"

Kyle returned, confused by the commotion and the anger written on Jack's face. "Did I miss something?"

Ava grasped Jack's hand. "We were getting to know Dalton, and he hasn't made the best impression."

Kyle observed Casi coming back in fully dressed and turned to Dalton sulking on the sofa. "I hope we won't have a problem going forward. I won't tolerate you making my family uncomfortable."

Dalton held his hands up. "A bad joke, that's all."

"You might need to work on that sense of humor." Jake squeezed his shoulder, making him wince with pain.

Kyle nodded and smiled as Georgia and Lauren returned. He picked up a brightly wrapped gift and placed it on Casi's lap. "I made you something."

Casi opened the package and extracted a handcrafted jewelry box, complete with inlay in an intricate design. "It's absolutely beautiful!"

"It's a Japanese technique called Urushi." He explained how the wafer-thin layers were glued together to create the pattern within the wood. He smiled. "I had a lot of free time since Casi has been working so much. I found a class at the community center and I was impressed with the instructor who allowed me to come to his studio to perfect my technique."

Jake shook his head. "You're an incredible artist."

"I think it suits Casi." Kyle kissed her.

"Weird layers glued together, somehow creating a beautiful result," Jake interpreted. "Perfect."

"Rude!" Casi giggled. She inspected the tiny drawers inside the box. "What's this?" She held up sparkling earrings with a spray of diamonds.

"Replacements for your missing constellation necklace and diamond earrings." He whispered, "Because you're my universe and your mother will never take away what we have together."

"I love them." She brushed away a tear. She cleared her throat and retrieved a package. "Dad and Ava, I wanted to do something special this year. I hope you like it."

Ava opened the box. "You had the tapes converted to DVD's?"

"Blu-ray." Casi nodded.

"When are they from?" Jack asked.

"Years ago." Ava smiled. "Can we take a peek? I don't remember what we recorded."

"A wild sex tape," Jake suggested.

"Unlikely," Ava blushed. She noted Jack's hurt expression. "We're from the era before they recorded every personal moment."

"Unlike Casi and Kyle on the cruise." Jake chuckled.

"That was unintentional." Kyle laughed.

Casi raised her middle finger to Jake and put the disk in the player. The screen lit up with a backyard scene and Casi stood motionless, watching her young self, laughing and twirling on the grass. A handsome blond man grabbed her and threw her in the air, and Jack gasped. "Jamie."

Ava stifled a sob and Casi asked, "Should I turn it off?"

"No, leave it." Ava gazed at the television. "It's been so long."

Jake's face registered pain. "He looked a lot like you, Jack."

Jack sighed. "He did." His eyes locked on the image of Jamie playing with Casi, chasing her and smothering her in kisses. "Oh," he moaned when a young Ava entered, rubbing a pregnant belly. He reached over and took her hand, unable to turn away from the joyous scene.

"I didn't realize you had children," Lauren said.

"I don't," Ava said flatly. Jamie planted Casi in her mother's lap and Sonya shoved her to the ground before lighting a cigarette and inspecting her nails while she jotted notes in a journal. Undaunted, the little girl ran to Ava and flung herself against her legs. Ava swooped her in her arms, kissing and hugging the two-year-old with genuine affection. When Jamie wrapped his arms around them and kissed her tenderly, sweetly greeting the child, Ava jumped up and hit the mute button. "I'm not prepared for this." She sucked in air. "Please turn it off."

"I'm sorry I never considered what might be on it." Casi winced.

Ava took the disk with a shaking hand and gave her a meek smile. "I love the gift. It's more than I can handle now." Her eyes swept to Lauren and Dalton, and she brushed a strand of hair behind Casi's ear. "I would love to watch it with people who understand the tragedy."

Casi nodded. "You truly loved me, didn't you?"

"You've always been my little girl."

They finished opening gifts and Casi slipped in the kitchen while

Jake cooked bacon. "Are they staying here all day? I want to give him his present."

"Just do it." He glanced in the living room and noticed everyone engaged in conversation. She nodded in agreement and bolted up the stairs.

Casi walked casually in the living room. "I was thinking we might skate later. The river gets frozen, right?"

"It should be by now," Kyle agreed.

"Your mom said to check for skates in your closet, so I searched for them," she said, as Georgia raised an eyebrow.

"I wouldn't have girl's, but maybe there are some in the basement."

"I found this." She held up his backpack.

Kyle recoiled. "I intend to throw that away."

"It seems incomplete," she pushed. "Can I see the itinerary?"

He shook his head and reached in the bag, yanking out the crumpled paper. "What's the point of this?"

"Ava and I were going through scrapbooks, and I discovered she backpacked through Europe. Can we compare your routes?" Casi bit her lip.

Jake watched as his brother fidgeted, visibly becoming agitated. "Ok, Monkey Brains, spill it. Stop torturing him."

Casi placed papers in Kyle's hand. "I'm screwing up on my personalized gifts this year and causing more pain. You require closure and the best way to get that is to complete what you started twenty years ago."

Kyle surveyed the documents. "Tickets to Scandinavia? But how..."

She put her finger to his lips. "I got a check from the termination of the Sand and Surf line. I don't want the money. This is the perfect opportunity for us to get away and do this trip."

"When did you get a check? I didn't notice an irregular deposit."

"Three months ago. Ava cashed it to keep the secret." She smiled. "That's what I've been sneaking around doing."

He sorted through the papers. "Jake's coming?"

"Hopefully that's a good thing," Jake said. "It was Casi's idea. She felt we should experience this together."

Kyle nodded. "It's ideal. How much of this have you planned?"

Casi took his hand. "I booked the tickets, but you're in charge of planning everything else. I'm not sure which countries you were interested in, except I noted your original destination began in Copenhagen. You're the leader and we're your faithful followers. Wherever you want to go, we're beside you. You can recreate the itinerary you had with Grady or expand it to suit your grownup self."

"Grady was fascinated with the Vikings, trolls, and legends. His tattoo was a dragon, which he designed himself." Kyle grinned. "Can we still backpack and take the train?"

Casi's smile tightened. "Sure, it sounds exciting."

Jake chuckled. "I can't wait to witness you roughing it."

"It's Europe." Casi shrugged. "I'm sure they have modern conveniences." Doubt flickered in her eyes. "It's your trip, plan away. I'll transfer the remainder of the money into our joint account."

"Maybe we could include Italy?" He turned to Ava. "Didn't you live there for a while?"

Ava smiled. "I would love to help you plan. I have friends who will arrange a culinary tour for you."

"Yay." Casi giggled, unaware of the sadness emblazoned on Lauren's face.

"Casi, this is incredible. I'm speechless." Kyle exhaled.

"There's one other part." She glanced at Lauren and Dalton. "I visited Nicole..."

"Because of the party," he mumbled.

"To talk to her about something important." Casi produced a box. "She wants us to take Grady's ashes with us and spread them in the locations you planned with him. She's convinced that's what he would want."

Kyle gasped and put his hand to his face. Casi leaned in and hugged him, as Jake stood up to block them from view. Georgia sobbed in her hands and Peter rubbed her back, wiping his own tears.

"Are you happy? I intended to do it in private, but I couldn't wait any longer to tell you," Casi whispered.

"It will be an amazing tribute." He nestled against her. "Thank you for not giving up on me."

"We both harbor ghosts in our past. We're stronger together and we can't ever give up." She embraced him.

Dalton smirked and looked at Lauren. "He's crying about going to Europe. I've been five times. What did you ever see in this guy?"

Peter stood in response to a knock at the door and leaned close to Dalton. "Until you suffer a severe loss, you can refrain from judging others."

Georgia opened her arms as Austin ran toward her. "What a lovely surprise!"

"They were excited about Christmas at your house." Lia fidgeted by the sofa. "Um, this is my friend, Shane."

Jake smiled and extended a hand. "I'm glad you guys are here."

"Is this ok?" Lia hugged him and whispered, "You said you wanted the boys. I didn't realize Lauren would be here."

"It's perfect. Casi told Kyle about Europe, and he's a little undone. It's a lot for him to process."

"Hello, Mr. Roberts." Shane blushed. "Um, and Mrs. Roberts."

Ava smiled. "You can call us by our first names now."

Shane turned to greet Lauren and Dalton, making small talk awkwardly.

"Not with your wife today?" Dalton asked.

"We do a Christmas eve thing with her folks. Katie took the girls up to Whistler for a few days to go skiing," Shane stated.

"How old are your children?" Georgia smiled.

"Annabelle is seven, Isabelle is five, and Lulubelle is almost three."

"Casi gagged. "Were you high when you named them? I'm going to have a field day with nicknames."

"Katie chose them." Shane cocked his head. "You've been friends with Katie again for months, how do you not know their names?"

"I have zero interest in children." She pulled Austin on her lap and bit his neck while he shrieked with laughter. "Except these two."

Kyle looked up from his map. "How long have you been planning this?"

"Remember the day I discovered your love letters? I was searching through your backpack for your itinerary." She smoothed her hand over his. "I realized that day at the river that you needed to complete your journey."

"What letters?" Jake asked.

Kyle smiled. "From Libby."

"My sister, the writer." Peter shivered. "That woman can weave a novel out of a thread of truth. She's unbelievable."

"She's a wonderful storyteller," Georgia praised.

"Too wordy for me," Jake shuddered. "I like when she visits better."

"Well then, you are in luck today." Warm arms slid around Jake's neck as a beautifully dressed woman leaned over the sofa.

Kyle's face lit up. "You're here!"

"Of course, my beautiful love." Her smile expanded, and she cupped Casi's face. "Your description did not do justice to this divine creature." Casi sank into her warm embrace, entranced by her delicious scent and beauty.

Kyle smiled. "I sent you pictures from our wedding."

Libby's eyes danced over Casi's features. "You could show me a photo of the Taj Mahal and it would never compare to witnessing the exquisite beauty in person." She brought her face close to Casi's. "I was compelled to meet the woman who stole my baby boy's heart and evaluate if she was worthy of such a fine man."

"Am I?" Casi asked.

"You are a precious gift sent from heaven." Libby nodded.

"Geez, are you a writer for real?" Dalton scoffed.

Libby regarded him. "I am. What is your career?"

"I'm a sommelier." He winked.

"That's a big word for a little man," Libby stated. Dalton started to reply, and she held up her hand. "Please don't bore me with useless words. At my age, I don't have patience for drivel. I had a sommelier once, and he was all pomp and no pump." Casi giggled as Peter tried to shush his sister, redirecting her to greet the other guests. "Who is this fine specimen of a man?" Libby planted a lingering kiss on Jack.

"He's my father," Casi said. "And my step-mother, Ava."

"Beautiful." Libby clasped her hand and leaned in to kiss her cheek. "You have a unique aura. You've had immense pain, but your soul is majestic." She smiled. "Your eyes are divine, like moonlight on a summer's eve."

"Thank you." Ava smiled broadly.

Libby turned. "Where are my love bugs?"

Jake chuckled and rounded up the boys while Libby fussed over them and gave them loud kisses. There was a knock at the door and Peter opened it to discover Earl wringing his hands with an expression of devastation. "I can't find my way home."

Libby rushed and embraced him. "Your home is here, Sweetheart."

"I'm confused," Earl confessed. "I thought you were gone."

"I came back to see you," she assured him.

"To make sure I'm alright?"

"Yes." She directed him to the living room. "Peter was about to make us Bloody Mary's."

"Libby, it's not even noon." Peter frowned.

"Which is why I'm not having a martini, Darling." She waved him away.

Peter eyed Casi. "I'm assuming you want one too?"

"Absolutely. I love your sister." Casi grinned.

"You're cut from the same cloth." Peter began making drinks.

There was a commotion on the porch and Jake swung the door open. "What do you want? Can't you knock like a normal person?"

The slight man squared his shoulders, visibly intimidated. "Is my father here? We were at church and he disappeared."

Jake called over his shoulder. "Earl, Frankie's here." He moved to allow access to the family of five.

Frankie shook his head and glared at Earl. "This is the last straw. We've talked about the nursing home and obviously it's time."

"Earl, how did you get here if you were at church with the family?" Peter peered out the window to the driveway. "Please tell me you didn't walk."

Frankie rolled his eyes. "We took two cars since we don't fit in my BMW. He insisted on going early to practice the piano. He's been playing it for over fifty years, you would think he could at least remember how to do that."

Peter nodded. "He likes to warm up. The cordial thing would have been to go with him and keep him company. You rarely come around and can't seem to grasp routine is important for him with the dementia. You throw him for a loop when you alter his schedule."

"This is a family matter." Frankie turned to leave.

"Yes, it is." Libby adjusted her wrap. "So, we'll be taking care of him."

"He's my father," Frankie said.

"He's my husband." Libby straightened her back, and the room fell silent.

Peter froze and read his sister's nod to mean he shouldn't challenge the statement. Frankie stammered and paced, trying to process the information. "When did that happen?"

Earl beamed. "I always intended to marry Libby; she just took her time accepting my proposal."

Libby patted his hand. "We were married last February. The house belongs to you and your brother as you already transferred the title. Do what you wish with it since he'll be living here from now on."

"What about the money from his business and life insurance?"

"Your father is still alive," Libby spat. "He will spend his money as he sees fit. If you would like to visit him, you may contact Peter to find a convenient time. Please pass the message to your brother."

"And his grandchildren?" Frankie snarled.

"May also visit." Libby glanced at the sullen teenagers. "If they're expecting more than that, too bad."

Jake escorted them to the door and waited for them to peel out of the driveway before asking, "Am I the last to know?"

Peter glared at Libby, then Kyle. "What have you done?"

Libby stood and put a hand to the side of Peter's face. "I keep in touch with Earl and he seemed to be more forgetful. I had Kyle check up on him and he noticed the same thing."

"Why would you exclude me?" Peter snapped.

"To protect you, Darling," Libby said. "How would it appear if his business partner took over his affairs? Those ungrateful sons would tear you to shreds." She smiled at Earl. "But as his wife, I automatically gain control. We married last year in Seattle to ensure he was considered of sound mind. Kyle was our witness, and we explained everything to Earl, including how we would live at the cottage when the time was right."

"Thanks for inviting me." Jake glared at Kyle.

Kyle shrugged. "It was the day Tommy was born."

Libby hugged Jake. "I only came for the day to make it official. I needed to tie up my affairs before I could extend my visit."

"How long are you here?" Peter held out her drink.

Libby smiled. "If it's alright with you, I would like to come home."

Peter's eyes watered and he pulled her in his arms. "It's about time you stopped roaming the world and came back to us."

16

THE QUEST

"*A*va gave me a check for the balance of the Sand and Surf money, and I deposited it in our joint account." Casi walked through the front door and stopped in her tracks when she observed Kyle carefully considering the contents of his backpack spread out on the table. The box with Grady's ashes was in the center and he jotted notes on a pad of paper, lost in concentration.

He placed items on a food scale and wrote the numbers down, reorganizing piles. "I've made a list of what everyone should bring. We'll research backpacks this weekend." He directed his gaze to her.

"We have four months!" She laughed and headed to the shower.

He followed her and leaned against the counter. "Have you ever backpacked before?"

"I carried one in high school. It had books and stuff in it."

He grinned and quickly undressed to join her. "Put everything on the bed that you want to take. I'll help you decide what's essential." He kissed her neck as he stood behind her, sliding his hands over her breasts. "The best way to experience Europe is to stay in local dwellings, perhaps a few hostels?"

"This is your trip, plan whatever you want to do, and I'll comply."

They returned to the living room to find Jake poking through the piles on the table. "You're not taking all this shit, are you?"

Kyle snatched the travel book from his hand and placed it on the stack, lining it up precisely next to another. "I'm in the process of deciding what's important."

Jake put his hand on his shoulder. "What's the most significant thing about this trip? Say the first thing that comes to your mind."

"Honoring Grady," Kyle blurted.

"Fine." Jake moved the ashes to one side. "Who made the itinerary and how did you choose where you wanted to visit?"

"I did, and we decided together what would be cool and feasible in the time we had. There were twelve sites we deemed crucial."

Jake regarded the paper. "That's what these stars are?" Kyle nodded, and Jake handed him the map. "I doubt Europe has changed much in twenty years. Get rid of the books and travel guides. Use the internet for research. Lighten your load, brother."

Kyle sighed and stacked the books and guides, handing them to Jake. "Take them to the recycle bin before I change my mind."

Casi picked up Grady's ashes and shook them. "Can you put him in a Ziplock or something? This is kinda heavy."

"Casi!" Kyle yanked the box from her clutches as Jake laughed hysterically. "Respect the dead!"

"We put my mom in a damn t-shirt and threw her in the ocean." She crossed her arms over her chest.

"That was different. Plus, it was my favorite collared shirt," he mumbled. "He'll be in my pack. It doesn't matter how much it weighs."

"Should I take my laptop or just my iPad?"

"Neither. We're not bringing electronics. We'll bring my phone for emergencies and use the camera while it's in airplane mode. I'm sourcing European chargers." Kyle condensed the contents on the table.

She laughed and then surveyed the brothers. "This is a joke, right? I need at minimum my iPad and phone. I'll buy a charger."

"Where will you charge them? We'll be sleeping on trains and in hostels. Wi-Fi will be spotty at best. We also can't risk the liability of expensive electronics in our packs. I'm buying money belts for our cash and passports." Kyle put a hand on her shoulder.

Jake chuckled as she started to cry, shaking from the revelation of what they were embarking on. "It'll be ok, Monkey. There's a whole world outside of your phone."

"What is this nightmare I signed up for?" She shivered. "I'm calling Anna."

"Why do you think she's only coming for the last few days? That city-girl wouldn't make it on a cross-country trek." Jake headed outside.

Casi rushed after him. "You agreed this would be helpful for him. You never told me how much I would need to sacrifice."

"Suck it up, Buttercup. Your husband requires you to be a trooper. Staying in fancy hotels and Americanizing the experience won't accomplish anything. He must let go of the past and it was your idea for him to complete the trip." Jake tossed the books in the recycling bin.

"I can't handle two weeks without technology."

"It's not about you." Jake winked.

Kyle smiled at Casi when they returned. "I'm prepared to start doing my research. Tell me what you want to see, and I'll add it to the itinerary. We can stay in some nice hotels if that makes it more palatable."

"I'm happy to tag along with you and discover amazing places. My experiences in Europe have been limited to hotels, nightclubs, and airports." She grinned and turned to the sink to fill a pot of water for pasta. "Of course, I'd be down for checking out one of those sex clubs if we go to Amsterdam."

Kyle raised an eyebrow. "I can fit that in."

"Hey, the little guy is walking!" Kyle watched Tommy take a few shaky steps across the floor.

Jake turned from the Tv and nodded. "Cool."

"Casi?" Kyle nudged her. "Tommy is walking."

"Huh? Oh good, it's about time." She kept her eyes focused on her computer screen.

Kyle frowned and checked the calendar. "His birthday is tomorrow. He's one day faster than his brother." He waited for a response. "What are the plans for his big day?"

Casi sighed, saving her documents. "What day?"

"Tommy's first birthday is tomorrow," Kyle reiterated. "I'm sure you didn't forget, especially after making a big deal about Austin's last year. We don't want the little brother to be snubbed."

"He doesn't understand the difference," Jake chuckled.

Casi noted the anger rising in the flush of Kyle's cheeks. "Of course, we know it's his birthday! The party is on the weekend to make sure everyone can come. Tomorrow will be a low-key family dinner with just us."

"And a cake?" Kyle asked. "Homemade, not from Costco."

Casi forced a smile. "Lia and I are making it. He's lucky since he gets to celebrate twice." She patted the baby on his head.

"He's not a dog." Kyle frowned. "He wants his party to be special and meaningful, with a scrapbook chronicling his first year."

"Jeez, you expect a lot," Casi giggled.

"He shouldn't be less important than his brother. When Austin took his first steps, everyone cheered for him. You rarely acknowledge Tommy."

Casi sighed, "It was exciting when Austin did stuff because it was new, now it's repetitive and lacking the wow-factor."

"Spoken as an only child," Kyle chastised. "I'm taking Tommy with me to the store to choose ice cream for his party."

"Be my guest." Jake watched him leave and turned to Casi. "Oh my God, I totally forgot. Please tell me you really are planning a party this weekend?"

"I am now." She cringed. "This is a crazy week and the last thing I can handle is a needy kid with expectations of a grand party."

"Are you referring to Kyle?"

Casi giggled. "How the hell do real parents do it? I can't juggle work responsibilities and party planning."

"We are real parents and there is no do-over. Especially with the fair-patrol on red alert. Pull this together and make it spectacular or your husband will be crushed."

❧

"How do you manage to do this with a full-time job?" Georgia exclaimed as she entered the festively decorated living room.

"It was more challenging having it inside." Casi suppressed a yawn. "But I wanted everything perfect for our little nugget."

Lia swung an arm around Casi's waist and surveyed the colorful tablecloth and party supplies surrounding a brightly decorated cake. "I can't believe I forgot my son's birthday," she whispered.

"Tell me about it. Kyle had a conniption fit! We did it though, and I think everyone bought the email glitch on the invitations."

Kyle held Tommy's hand as they walked to the presents. "I'm glad the dad is on top of things," Jake snickered as he joined Casi and Lia.

Kyle sat cross-legged and put Tommy on his lap while they thumbed through the scrapbook, pointing to pictures and reliving the memory. A cut-out stuck to his thumb, and he raised an eyebrow at Casi. "It seems as though the glue is still tacky."

She strolled over and reattached the piece. "The damn scrapbook is done, and that's all that matters."

"CeCe." Tommy reached for her.

Casi smiled and cuddled him in her arms. "You're not forgotten little guy, maybe overshadowed at times." She regarded Austin twirling around the decorations and commanding attention.

Kyle grasped her hand and brought her to his lap. "This was more for me than him. I still have some issues to work out."

Casi turned to kiss him. "You were right to demand he was noticed. Life gets busy, but these kids are our priority. Twenty years from now I won't remember what report I did, but these are the memories I'll cherish."

Kyle adjusted the straps on a backpack and tugged, almost knocking Casi over. He chuckled and repositioned her. "Is that alright on your shoulders?"

"It's comfy," she shrugged, engrossed in a text.

Jake shook his head and grabbed several free weights from the shelf, zipping them in her pack. She tipped back, and Kyle took her phone. "Jake and I will take most of the weight, but you must practice having items."

"Like my iPad?" She grinned.

"Clothes, food, and water." He gave her a kiss. He sighed and picked up a pack, inspecting the dimensions. "This is a lot better than my other one. It was all I could afford back then, and now they're much lighter."

"Buy a new one," Casi encouraged. "Can I get mine in red? Black seems basic and industrial."

Kyle chuckled. "They're not designed to coordinate with your outfit." He turned to the salesclerk. "Does it come in red?"

"Red, navy, and black," the associate answered.

Kyle sighed. "We'll take one of each. One more thing to let go."

"I get the black one. I'm not into fruity colors," Jake insisted.

Kyle shrugged. "I'm happy to take blue."

"It suits you." Jake winked.

Kyle filled the basket with additional items and waited in line. He took out his credit card and Casi reached in his wallet. "Use the joint account. We're spending my money before we dip into our reserves."

"Why don't you save some of it?" Kyle asked.

She shook her head. "That business escalated into a nightmare and forced me to make poor choices. I work hard for my money now and I deserve every penny of it."

He rubbed her back and handed the associate the card. "This is closure for both of us, huh?"

Kyle checked his watch as they drove and took a sharp left into a parking lot. "What are we doing? We don't need groceries." Jake frowned.

"Wait here." Kyle jogged to the store. He returned and handed Jake several bags. "Fill our packs and let's go for a hike." He jutted his chin to Casi, still intent on her phone.

Jake grinned and divided the canned goods and water bottles, purposely making Casi's bag the heaviest. Kyle drove to the overlook and parked, taking her phone and locking it in the glove box. "What are we doing?" She surveyed the surroundings with confusion.

"Trying out our new gear." Kyle placed her hiking shoes in front of her. He helped her adjust the backpack and checked his watch. "We don't want blisters, so five miles?"

"What's our average for the trip?" Jake secured his pack.

"Around ten, with breaks. Some days could be a little longer." Kyle charged ahead of them.

"Do breaks mean coffee shops and restaurants?" Casi asked with growing concern.

"More like to go to the bathroom." Kyle grinned.

"In a proper restroom." She narrowed her eyes when he pretended not to hear. "This blows." She gritted her teeth. "I'm a trooper, so it's all good."

"You might have to add in some entertaining stuff for her if you want to return with a wife," Jake cautioned.

"I've adjusted my itinerary to reflect a middle-aged man and a princess rather than two teen-aged boys." Kyle jogged up the hill.

"I'm not middle-aged, asshole," Jake called after him.

"Have we gone five miles yet?" Casi wiped her brow. "It's starting to rain, and I have to pee."

"Time to practice." Kyle gave her a thumbs up. "We're only about halfway. The weather in Europe will be similar, so you have to get used to rain." Casi stomped to a cluster of plants, yanking down her jeans. She squatted, and the pack knocked her off balance, sending her over the edge in a flurry of screams and obscenities. Kyle rushed after her, trying not to laugh as she untangled herself from the bushes. "You may want to take your pack off first." He offered her a hand.

"What's the likelihood of finding toilet paper and hand wipes?" She threw her pack to the ground.

"I'll add that to the list." Kyle smiled. "Can you drip dry?"

"Give me your handkerchief." She held her hand out. "I peed on my leg."

Kyle chuckled, and she readjusted her pants and wrestled the pack while he extracted leaves from her hair. "Should we call it a day?"

"I would appreciate that." Her lip trembled.

"Glass of wine and a hot bath?"

When they reached the truck, she tossed the pack and rubbed her shoulders. "I'm not concerned about distance, but I can't carry this weight."

"It's sixty pounds and the real one will be about thirty, so you should be fine." Jake poked her in the ribs.

"Bite me, Jake," she replied.

"Maybe when we get to the sex club." He smacked her behind.

"Why are you wearing yellow pants?" Jake surveyed his brother.

"They are supposed to be fawn." Kyle sighed. "Do you think it's the lighting in here?" He walked to the living room.

"Now they are more like dirty mustard." Jake curled his lip.

"Damn it, these were the last of the things I ordered, and it took weeks to arrive. They're lightweight and have tons of pockets," Kyle lamented. "Do you think they'll fade if I wash them?"

"Doubtful. It's unfortunate because they seem practical. I planned on bringing jeans, but I like the weight of these pants; quick wash and dry." He felt the material on Kyle's pocket. "What color did you get me?"

Kyle frowned. "My other pair is camel which is also weird."

Jake picked up the package and grinned. "They're pink. That's what you get for not considering me."

"Wow, those are bright. Are you embracing the European culture?" Casi giggled as she entered the house.

Kyle explained his dilemma and placed a bag on the counter. "Yours are bisque, which I assumed was cream colored."

"Figures you bought her some," Jake sulked.

"These are white," Casi noted. "Which will be dirty grey after one day of travel. I appreciate the gesture, but we should stick to black or navy since I'm sure washing will be limited."

"I figured fawn would be brown, like a deer." Kyle frowned.

"A deer with jaundice?" Jake suggested.

"This is a bad omen. I assumed I was prepared and now it's unraveling." Kyle tugged off the pants and tossed them in the box.

Casi checked the tags. "The store is in Seattle. I'll go tomorrow and return these and buy normal colors. And I'll get two pairs for Jake."

17
____

TORTURED SOULS

Casi listened to Kyle chatting on the phone as she angrily folded laundry. She was pleased he immersed himself in research for their trip, but wasn't thrilled he regularly consulted Lauren about highlights and tours. When she snapped at him one evening, pointing out Lauren had never even been to Europe, he sweetly said, "It's always been her dream. She has researched a trip to Italy from the time she was sixteen, and as we both realize, she's been let down for a honeymoon, twice. Let her enjoy the details, it will only make our trip better."

He hung up and observed the pile of clothes on the bed. "Did you make sure to use the non-fragrant detergent I bought for our hiking clothes? We don't want to get a reaction."

"Yes, for the millionth time." She wrestled with a pair of leggings.

"I take it you're not as excited as I am about this trip. We can still make changes; we have three weeks." He gave her hand a squeeze.

She sighed and tossed a shirt on the bed. "I'm sorry. The itinerary is perfect. I'm attempting to finish a dozen projects before we leave, and it's stressing me out."

"We've been slammed, too. We have Riley working overtime to handle the orders, but we're pushing deadlines."

"You made sure Amy can stay at the house while we're gone? I love Lia, but I can't handle having her living here."

"Amy is lined up, and I told her Riley could come stay with her. Jake's worried about leaving the boys for so long, but Gail said she would help out," Kyle detailed.

Casi wrapped her arms around his neck and kissed him. "You understand I get crazy before a trip. I'll dial it down a notch." Her phone rang, and she grabbed it from the nightstand, frowning at the number. She pushed the ignore button, growing concerned at the multitude of calls from the mysterious Los Angeles area code. On the occasions she answered, a heavy breather made references to her mother. She assumed it was one of her drug dealers and hoped he would give up calling.

"Problem?" Kyle frowned.

"Wrong number."

❧

The brothers parked in the driveway and noted Lauren had already arrived. "No Dalton?" Kyle grabbed several bags from her car.

Lauren glanced away. "He had a family thing."

"Gosh darn, I was hoping to spend the evening with him." Jake grinned. Kyle shook his head and piled groceries in his arms.

Lauren smiled. "I realize you guys don't like him. He comes off as pompous, but he's interesting once you get to know him."

"I appreciate you coming over to cook this meal with us. I want Casi to learn about unique ingredients before we get to Italy to enhance her experience." Kyle closed her car door.

"I wish I was going with you." Lauren squeezed her eyes closed and bit her lip. "It's a place I've always wanted to see. Your whole trip looks amazing."

"You'll get there someday." Kyle stroked her back and turned toward the house. "Who's here?" He winced at the screaming from inside.

"Katie? She's giving Lia a bad time," Jake suggested.

Lauren shook her head. "Lia shouldn't be dating him until he's divorced. She's setting herself up for heartbreak, again."

Jake mimicked her behind her back as Kyle shoved him. They walked in the kitchen to witness Casi ranting on her cellphone hysterically, while she grasped a manila envelope with tattered edges. "I don't want any part of it! Stop fucking calling me! No. No. No!"

Kyle rushed to her side, and she pushed him away. "Hang up," he ordered.

"I will hunt you down! She deserved better than this and I'll make you pay." She hurled her phone, smashing it to pieces, as it hit the patio doors and a crack splintered across the pane.

"Goddamn it, Casi!" Kyle stormed toward her. "We're leaving in four days and now I have to arrange to get that fixed."

"I can't go." She paced frantically.

"Whatever deadline or situation you have can wait." Kyle grasped her arm. "We're not doing another hysterical meltdown before this trip."

"I need to fix this." She grabbed at pictures as they tumbled from the envelope.

Kyle snatched a photo and glared at her. "Are these in distribution? I didn't almost die, so these could be seen by the world." He narrowed his eyes. "Where did the money for the trip really come from? Are you lying to me?"

She slapped him so hard across the face she left a handprint. "Don't you dare! You have no idea." Her hand shook as images littered the floor. "My mom..."

He knelt beside her and hissed, "Don't ever hit me again. I don't give a fuck about your mom. The day we threw her in the ocean was the best day of my life, and I never want to hear you mention her again."

Her eyes went wide, and she lunged at him, wildly swinging her fists and scratching. "I can't trust you! They're right, it was your fault."

Jake grabbed her arms. "Monkey, stop!"

Kyle stood and slipped his wedding ring from his finger, slamming it on the table. "I'm done with you and this ridiculous behavior." He wiped blood from his face as he turned his back to her.

Casi yanked her rings off and threw them at him. "This marriage is over!" She twisted from Jake's grasp. She snatched her purse and bolted out the door, and the grinding of metal penetrated the house.

"Probably my truck." Kyle gripped the counter.

"Go after her," Jake warned.

"No. I'm tired of chasing her. She'll calm down and come back." He picked up her rings from the floor and set them beside his. "I can't keep playing this insane game."

"You didn't even try to find out why she was upset," Jake said.

"Her mom was a useless tweaker. I can't even escape her drama from the grave." Kyle opened a beer and shrugged.

"I'm going home. Don't come knocking on my door when you realize what a stupid idiot you are," Jake snarled.

Kyle leaned against the fridge and exhaled. "Apparently dinner night is cancelled. I'm sorry to disappoint you." He rubbed his temple. "My life with her never gets easier."

"We can still cook. You shouldn't be alone." Lauren hid a smile and smoothed her hand over his arm.

"I've lost my appetite. I'm sorry it ended this way." He dropped the wedding rings in a cup and set it on a shelf.

"I'll call you tomorrow and see how you're doing."

Casi pounded on the door until the snap of a lock vibrated. "Casi? It's late. What's going on?" Mary's face registered alarm.

"Mom sent you a package and I want it," Casi demanded.

Mary crossed her arms over her chest. "Some things are best left alone. Your mother loved drama; let that be buried with her."

"She's not buried! Why didn't anyone tell me cremation was a violation of her religion? You're all hiding things from me. I can't trust anyone."

"She didn't practice her religion, and cremation was the best solution. What were you going to do? Carry around her body for six months and then drive it back to Canada?" Mary rolled her eyes.

"I need what she sent. Too many people are at risk."

Mary retrieved a heavy package. "I received this the week she died with a note asking me to keep it safe. Your mother's behavior was erratic, don't follow in her footsteps."

Casi grabbed it and smoothed her hand over the surface. "She alerted someone. And they want it. They sent me horrible photos, including that stupid editorial I did." She broke down. "My life is unraveling."

"Casi, let's talk about this with Kyle..."

"No! He's a liar. I have to handle it on my own."

"Honey, where are you going?" Mary rushed after her down the hall. "Don't run off without a plan." She stormed back to her apartment and grabbed her phone, dialing angrily. "Ava, the shit has hit the fan. Someone has figured out what we have done."

Casi drove haphazardly to a well-lit lot near the freeway and parked. Her hands shook as she opened the package, curious why it was the subject of blackmail. Tears fell on the first few pages of the journal as she read the beginning of the poorly written chronicle of abuse Sonya suffered from an early age. Pieces of the puzzle came together through the revelation of deep-seated corruption and control by what appeared to be a cult. No one was spared Sonya's wrath, implicating Ava of having intimate knowledge. "You're all a bunch of liars!" Casi pounded her steering wheel. It was disheartening to learn how much her mother truly loathed her, literally since conception. She closed the book, unable to read more. She regretted throwing her phone, shivering as she realized her life was about to take a serious turn.

§

Kyle opened a bottle of whiskey and poured a tall glass, omitting the ice. He wanted to take the edge off his anger and required the infusion of alcohol to calm the rage boiling inside. He ran a finger over the crack in the glass door and shoved the broken remains of Casi's phone with his boot.

"Fucking nutcase." He finished his whiskey in one gulp.

He poured another and surveyed the pile of pictures strewn across the floor. He realized she had worked extremely hard to overcome her past and prove herself as a professional woman. He refilled his glass, bracing himself to examine the photos as he bent to gather them. He frowned at the unprofessional photography, making an experienced model appear awkward in a skimpy swimsuit. He tried to see the photo from the standpoint of someone who didn't know her. Her bountiful breasts were on full display, competing for attention with the rest of her incredible figure. A casual onlooker would stop there, not glimpsing upwards to the withdrawn expression and glazed eyes. The memory of how they discovered her hours later made him shudder while he sorted through the pile. He descended deeper into drunken despair as he witnessed the drugs capturing his beautiful wife. He gasped when he extracted the next stack of photos, unsure when they had been taken. The setting was familiar, and he was nauseated by the pictorial of drugs and sex forced on an unwilling participant. He buried his head in his hands, unable to handle more of Casi involved in the drugged-out orgy when he identified the location as her loft.

"Goddamn it, Casi!" He threw the scant remainder of the whiskey bottle toward the patio door. The crash of glass brought relief as it shattered to the ground. He staggered forward, intent on discarding the pictures in the fireplace. He found himself suddenly on the ground, unclear how he ended up there. He stared at the ceiling, pushing Dingo back, when the dog whined and tried to tend to his master. "Stop, there's glass," he slurred, attempting to stand. He noticed blood trailing down his arm and considered continuing to the lake and ending his pain for eternity.

"Go away!" Jake yelled.

"I need help."

"Too late." Jake yanked the door open to continue his diatribe. He stepped back, assaulted by the sight of his brother covered in blood in a heap on his doorstep. "What the hell did you do?" He tried to source the stream and noted a long gash on his right forearm, which seemed to be the most severe of the cuts. "Stupid idiot." He wrapped his t-shirt around his brother's arm.

"The pictures..." Kyle attempted.

"Have you heard from Casi?" Jake assisted him to the truck. "How much did you drink?" Kyle shook his head, unable to answer either question.

Thirty-two stitches and a violent episode of vomiting, and they were back home a few hours later. Jake surveyed the scene as he walked in the door, piecing together what occurred. He helped Kyle to bed, giving up on undressing him and only removing his boots. "Sleep it off, Buddy." Jake smoothed Kyle's hair from his forehead. "She'll be back."

Jake strode to the living room, assessing how to remedy the disaster. He swept the floor and glared at a long shard of glass smeared with blood, realizing it had been the weapon to tear through the flesh of his brother's arm. After taking measurements of the door, he put away the remainder of the groceries left over from the failed dinner. He checked on Kyle, setting a glass of water and aspirin at the bedside. "What the hell is it about those pictures?" He eyed the blood-spattered images with distaste. With resolve, he picked up the stack, not wanting to see his sister-in-law displayed that way. The images brought back the memory of that day; Casi drugged out of her mind, and Kyle being shot.

"Monkey, you're so much better than this." He flipped through the erotic poses which he didn't find particularly sexy. He smiled at the thought of her bouncing around in cotton underwear and undershirt, oblivious to how gorgeous she was in a natural state. The overly made up woman with glazed eyes and breasts overflowing a bikini top wasn't nearly as hot, in his opinion. He frowned at another set of photos, taken at a different location. He paled as he recognized the brick wall of the loft and wondered when the party had occurred. Casi seemed to be the only woman surrounded by several men. One was holding a needle, while another assisted with the administration of what he assumed was heroin. He understood why she was hysterical; someone had the originals and threatened to expose them. She would be recognized, and her new career would be destroyed, possibly putting Mary's company at risk. He went to the bedroom and sat on the edge of the bed, rubbing Kyle's back as he shuddered in his sleep. "We'll fix it." He regarded his brother, heartbroken for another tragedy thrust upon him.

Jake glanced up as Lauren entered, holding two coffee cups. He turned back to Riley and continued replacing the glass door. "He's still sleeping. Leave it on the counter and he'll call you later."

"Wow, she destroyed that door." Lauren gasped.

Kyle stumbled out in response to the voices, visibly defeated when he noted Casi wasn't one of them. "She's not back?"

Lauren approached him swiftly, handing him a cup. "What happened to your arm?" Her eyes widened at the expansive bandage with blood seeping through.

"I cut it." He sipped the latte, hoping it would calm his raging headache. "How did you get the glass so fast?"

"It's three in the afternoon." Jake chuckled.

Kyle tried to focus on his watch. "Has she called?"

"She doesn't have a phone," Jake reminded him. "Do that tracking thing and see where she's used her credit cards."

Kyle traipsed to the computer. "No credit card purchases, but, wait, she used her gas card. Damn it! LA."

Jake sighed. "She must have driven straight through."

"She charged it about an hour ago. Where's my phone? I'm calling Alix."

"Are you guys still going to Europe?" Lauren asked casually.

"Sure, but Casi's out. You can take her place," Jake snapped.

Kyle shivered as he considered the ruined trip. "We have a few days still. She'll come home."

18

HOSTEL TAKEOVER

yle paced the living room, frantically checking his watch. "Should we call the airline and see if we can get a refund? We'll tell them it's a family emergency?"

"Alix said she left LA yesterday. Were there additional gas charges today? She must be on her way back." Jake gripped his brother's arm to make him focus. "He didn't give you more information?"

"No, only that she had been there. He wouldn't elaborate." Kyle bent over the computer and cringed. "She got gas in Elmvale. She's probably informing Mom and Dad our marriage is over."

"Call Mom and see if she was there."

"No! I don't want to explain everything when I don't understand what the hell is going on." Kyle clenched his fists. He redirected his gaze to the front door when it opened. "Casi, thank God you're ok. I was desperately worried about you."

"I'm fine." She ran to the bedroom. "I need my passport."

"We have everything in our backpacks." He stood in the closet watching her throw clothes in a suitcase. "We can make the plane if we leave now."

She studied him with bewilderment. "I'm not traveling to Europe!"

"Talk to me. I'm sorry I reacted badly. I didn't understand. I should have listened. Please don't leave." He blocked the doorway.

"Go to hell." She shoved past him. She collided with Mary, who stood arguing with Jake in the living room. "Why are you here?"

Mary wrenched the suitcase from her hand. "You're going to Europe."

"No, I'm not!" Casi burst into tears.

"You're not safe here." Mary pulled her in her arms. "Give me time to cover your tracks. Please do what I ask."

"What's going on?" Kyle scanned the tense faces.

Jake shrugged. "We're not privy to the intel. Our orders are to take your wife far away and not make contact with anyone."

Mary put her hand to Kyle's cheek. "Sonya left a mess and Casi tried to clean it up." She turned and frowned. "She created a bigger problem."

Jake stepped toward her. "I'm not leaving my kids if they're in danger."

"Casi is the only one at risk." Mary propelled her forward. "Go on your trip and forget about what happened."

Casi drew the back of her hand over her eyes. "I hate everyone."

"I understand." Mary kissed her cheek. "I'll drop you at the airport."

Casi staggered in a circle. "I'm not packed." She eyed her suitcase.

"I finalized everything for you." Kyle stared at the floor.

Jake grabbed her hand. "Do you have tampons?"

Kyle winced and checked the calendar. "I didn't think of that."

Casi grabbed her backpack and suitcase and rushed to the bathroom. "I'll need my makeup as well." She stopped at the door and bit her lip. "Can I at least change?"

Kyle surveyed her outfit, obviously borrowed from Alix, of skinny black jeans and a graphic t-shirt. "We'll wait." Mary checked the time, and he whispered, "What the hell is going on?"

"Follow your itinerary. This will all be forgotten soon." Mary set her jaw.

Kyle frowned. "That's not putting me at ease."

They drove in silence, unsure how to start a conversation that wouldn't escalate to an argument. Mary dropped them off at the curb, hugging each of them. She whispered in Casi's ear. "Give me a few days and then find an internet café and make contact."

"I deactivated my accounts."

"Wise." Mary nodded. "Work email?"

"Still intact."

"Check it on Sunday." Mary smoothed Casi's hair. "Was it worth it?"

"I threw my life away."

Mary patted her hand. "Let me see how deep this runs. Were you at least careful to not make waves in LA?"

"I only used my gas card. I went to Alix's, but I didn't stop for coffee or go anywhere I would be noticed."

They walked to the ticket counter and checked in while Kyle handed out passports and helped Casi secure it in her money belt. "I can do it." She pushed his hand away.

He turned and walked ahead of them to the security line, angered by her response. "Ease up, Monkey. He's had a hard couple of days." Jake kissed her cheek and directed her to the opposite line with a nod.

She drifted through the inspection, holding her breath while they checked her bag. She casually took her backpack and swung it over one shoulder, strolling toward the gate. When she neared the restroom, she stopped and glanced back, watching to see if Kyle made it through.

The TSA agent asked Kyle to step to the side as the contents of his bag were inspected. When he explained what was in the wooden box, the agent shook his head. "It's unacceptable to carry human remains across international borders without a seal from the crematorium. Do you have paperwork?"

"We're spreading his ashes in Europe. He's been dead over twenty years."

"Sir, that's illegal. It cannot go on the airplane." He motioned to another agent to remove the box and handed Kyle forms. "Twenty-one days to retrieve it from the airport or it will be disposed of."

Kyle's nostrils flared as he filled out the form and shoved it back across the counter. Jake slid an arm around his shoulders when he stormed away from the security. "We have time for a drink before we board. Unless you're still drying out from your bender."

Kyle gave him a half-smile. "This trip is sucking. The most important thing to me was to spread Grady's ashes, and I completely failed him, again. Why are we even going?"

"We have two weeks to discover the places you've always wanted to go. Casi will snap out of her mood. Everyone will be happy."

"What do you think happened in LA?" Kyle surveyed Casi slumped in a seat with her knees to her chest.

"Something to do with Sonya. That bitch won't stay dead." Jake stopped to buy coffee. "She was getting mysterious calls which were upsetting her."

"Why didn't you tell me?" Kyle took the tray.

"I figured Sonya owed someone money, and they were trying to get it from Casi. You had enough on your plate with your fragile mental state." Jake handed Casi a cup, and she sipped it without saying a word.

They boarded and secured their backpacks in the overhead compartments. "Did you bring a book or something?" Kyle stepped aside to let Casi settle in the middle seat.

"I just want to sleep." She buckled her seatbelt and closed her eyes.

Kyle touched her arm when they landed in New York. "Sweetheart, there's a layover before our next flight. Are you hungry?"

She lunged forward, gasping awake. "What's going on?" She scanned the interior in terror.

Jake grabbed their backpacks and directed her up the aisle. "You slept like a log for five hours. We're in New York."

She gazed out the window, unable to formulate anything in the dark rainy night. She surveyed Kyle's arm as he assisted her. "What happened?"

"I fell and cut my arm on the glass door." He shrugged.

"I thought it only cracked."

"It did, until I threw a whiskey bottle and destroyed it." He pulled her aside when they approached the gate. "Can we talk about this? Why don't you trust me?"

"I don't know what's real anymore."

He pulled her to his chest. "Our marriage is real." He grimaced at his bare finger. "I wish we put our rings back on before we left."

"It's not going to matter."

❧

They landed in Copenhagen and wearily grabbed their backpacks, exhausted by the travel and difference in time zones. Kyle reset his watch and suggested Jake do the same, then considered Casi. "You won't know the time without your phone."

"Just tell me what we're doing. I'm happy to not make decisions." Casi noted him analyzing the clock on the wall. "My only suggestion as the more seasoned traveler is not to compare here to home. Follow this time zone and you won't get jet-lagged."

"Is that how you handle the difference between LA and Washington?" Jake swung an arm around her shoulders. "Come back to us, Monkey. We love you and it's killing us to witness you suffering in silence."

Kyle watched her sulking in Jake's arms and guided them through the security checkpoint. "We can take the train to the main district and walk around to explore sites. It's possible to see quite a few since it's early."

Casi put her hand on his arm, "Kyle, you're the planner; start walking and we'll follow. You don't need to give us a detailed report on all our options."

Kyle rolled his eyes and led them to the train. They arrived at StrØget about twenty minutes later, disembarking and regarding the surrounding scene. "This is amazing." Jake smiled at the commotion and bustle, stepping out of the path of bicycles. "What an incredible city."

"Not to sound like the dad, but it's important we don't get separated." Kyle eyed Casi. "We don't have our phones to contact one another."

Casi stopped to smooth her hand over a pair of wool socks in a storefront, letting the sensation soothe her, "I won't wander off."

"Are you feeling ok?" Kyle came behind unintentionally startling her.

"Fine." She adjusted the hood of her sweatshirt. "I'm cold." Kyle nodded and brought the socks to the counter to pay for them. "I don't need more things in my backpack."

"I'll carry them." He secured them in his pack and turned to her. "Can I hold your hand? I don't like this disconnection from you. It's crowded here and we have a few miles to cover. I would feel better if I wasn't worried."

Her lip trembled, and she slipped her hand in his. She listened to his detailed history of the sites around them and relaxed to the cadence of his voice. She watched the tourists on the boats in the canal and noted the colorful buildings in Nye Haven. "This is beautiful."

"It's outstanding." Kyle's eyes lit up at the remarkable statues and ornate buildings along the way.

"I'm already loving this." Jake beamed at the view.

Kyle stopped and swallowed loudly. "The Little Mermaid sculpture."

"Hmm, small, but pretty cool." Jake shrugged, jumping over rocks to get a better view. He looked back at his brother and cringed. "Was this one of the stops on your itinerary?"

Kyle kicked at a stone. "Grady always rooted for the underdog. I wanted to put some of his ashes here. It would have been a point that determination is all it takes to make history."

"Did you consider your locations with their significance to what Grady meant to you?" Jake observed his agitated manner.

"To me and Nicole. Grady would never have been a famous artist, but his friendship mattered." His eyes flashed midnight blue. "I failed him."

"No, you didn't." Jake unzipped the front pocket of Casi's back-pack. He put his hand in Kyle's with a grin.

Kyle opened his palm and frowned, regarding the tampon. "Great, that's awesome, being teased about acting like a hormonal woman."

Casi raised an eyebrow. "You may want to reconsider that state-ment and think about the strong women in your life and how insulting that is."

His eyes welled. "I can't do anything right in your opinion. I get it. This trip is a waste of time and it's only prolonging the inevitable demise of our marriage. You don't care about me and you sure as hell aren't concerned a redneck kid never got a chance to see the world."

She reached over and tore open the wrapper, pushed the appli-cator and extracted a roll of paper. "I do care." A tear slid down her cheek. "Grady is perfectly portioned in convenient segments to spread where you will. We kept half for Nicole to do a memorial, but he still filled more than twelve tampons, so he gets bonus locations."

Kyle stepped back with wide eyes. "What was in the box?"

"Debris from the fireplace." Jake grinned. "It was her idea; I was tasked with opening it and switching the ashes. I was very respectful. Apparently, your wife is quite the smuggler. This isn't her first-time carrying contraband across the border."

"My first human remains, unless you count my mother." She frowned. "Perhaps this is becoming a habit."

"We should still claim the ashes at security, so we don't appear heartless," Jake suggested.

Kyle smiled. "This is ingenious. Did Nicole know about your method?"

"Only Jake." Casi took his phone. "Nicole asked for pictures at each location. I think she'll be amused by the vessel."

Kyle stepped across stones to approach the statue. "Well, Grady, here's to new experiences." He untwisted the paper and held it up in the gentle breeze. The ashes danced in the air as if they were joyful to be freed from captivity. He returned and gave Casi a kiss delicately on her unresponsive lips. "Thank you."

"It's legal to drink on the street in Copenhagen." Casi smiled.

"I think we could all use a beer." Kyle looked over his shoulder. "We can check out the Round Tower on our way."

Casi tugged at his sleeve. "I haven't eaten in three days."

Kyle's face fell with the realization he had overlooked that fact. He scanned the area and pointed. "711's are amazing here. Food and beer."

They traipsed down the cobblestone street and entered the well-stocked store. Casi watched the clerk taking a hotdog wrapped in bacon and insert it into the center of a bun precisely designed to hold it. She smiled and winked at Jake as they observed the concentration on the young man's face. When the remoulade bulged from the top of the bun and he handed it to the customer, Casi broke into hysterical laughter.

Kyle bit the side of his cheek. "We'll take three." He selected several tall cans of Danish beers and set them on the counter.

Jake dispensed the hot dogs and held up the camera as Casi took a bite. "Stop!" She laughed and put a hand over her mouth. Her face blanched. "You're not posting this on Facebook, are you?"

Kyle rubbed her back as she began to shake and cry. "We're not using internet. The phone is in airplane mode until we get to the hotel. I promise we won't post any pictures that make you uncomfortable." She nodded, and he stroked her cheek. "You can trust me. I don't know why you doubt that."

Jake opened a beer and handed it to her. "Cheers, Monkey Moonshine. There are brighter things on the horizon."

They wound their way up the spiral ramp in the Round Tower, stopping to gaze at the city below. At the top, Casi leaned out the window, teetering over the ledge. Jake bolted toward her and Kyle caught his arm. "Let me talk to her." He slipped behind and wrapped her in his arms, gently rocking her. "I love you, Casi. Why can't that be enough?"

She gazed back at him with tear-filled eyes. "I've done something horrible and ruined our marriage.”

“I don't accept that.” He kissed the top of her head. “Always and forever.”

She pointed to a stall in the street below. “Viking wine.”

“Let's give it a try.” He smiled and held out his hand.

“Wait.” She tugged him back. “Maybe this could be a bonus location for Grady? You can see the whole city from here.”

Kyle's face radiated with a bright smile. “It does put things in perspective from this vantage point.” He unzipped the zipper on the front pocket of her pack and fiddled with the wrapper. “How do you do this?” She laughed and showed him how to access the interior. “Huh, pretty nifty.” He glanced back to ensure they were alone before casting the ashes to the breeze.

“Good call.” Jake smiled. “That kid would have loved this city.”

They slid past a group ascending the tight stairwell and tumbled to the street to race each other to the vendor. After a dozen samples, more generously poured for Casi, Kyle noticed her beginning to sway. She unabashedly flirted with the man dressed as a Viking while he charmed her with his accented description of the product. Kyle clenched his jaw and withdrew his wallet. “We'll take one.” He gripped the paper-wrapped bottle and checked his watch. “We should probably find our hotel. I would like to get an early start in the morning.”

“I think we should find a bar.” Casi turned down an alley.

Jake noted the irritation in his brother's face. “I'm exhausted. Let's call it a night and troll the bars tomorrow.”

Casi shoved her hands in her pockets and trailed behind them without saying a word, lost in her dark thoughts.

Kyle scratched his head as he checked his map and back to the sign indicating they reached their destination. “It's supposed to be a historic hotel.” He frowned at the shabby exterior.

“It's a landmark alright.” Jake grimaced. “Is that how you spell it in Danish?” He grinned at the sign that clearly read, ‘Hostel,’.

Casi charged ahead. “Let's hope it's not like the movie where they attempt to steal our organs in the night.”

Kyle approached the front desk to check in and held out his hand for a key. The clerk scoffed and indicated the signs above adjoining hallways. "Well, goodnight boys." Casi headed to the dorm for women.

Kyle rushed after her. "Wait! We can go somewhere else."

She shook her head. "I'm tired. I've had an unbelievable few days."

"Can I at least get a kiss?" His expression was pained. She brushed her lips to his and looked down when he pressed something soft in her hand. "Take your socks. You might get cold."

She smiled sadly and turned down the corridor without another glance.

"I hate this!" Kyle seethed as Jake placed an arm around his shoulders.

"It's one night. She'll sleep it off and be her normal perky self in the morning." Jake patted his back.

"She's been gone three days and I have no idea where the hell she was or what she's done. There's something sinister I'm not aware of, yet I'm being blamed for causing it. I don't know what to do."

Jake nodded. "We will get through it." He squinted in the men's dorm and shook his head as he surveyed the rows of bunks. "It's exactly like juvenile hall." He tossed his backpack on the bottom bunk and indicated for Kyle to take the top.

"Hey, that's mine," a scrawny man claimed, pointing to his belongings on the mattress.

"Find a new one." Jake pulled off his shirt and flexed his cobra tattoo as he shoved the bag to the man.

"No problem." He quickly retreated.

Jake flopped on the mattress with his back to the wall, ensuring he had a clear view of the door. "I expect better accommodations going forward."

"I'll double-check my reservations." Kyle undressed and vaulted on the top bunk, staring at the water-stained ceiling. He kneaded his bare ring finger and sighed, considering Casi was only a few yards away, but the emotional distance was unfathomable.

19

TROLLS

"Icould've robbed you." Jake peered at Kyle, inches from his face.

Kyle chuckled and put his hand over Jake's face. "I trusted my big brother to take care of me." He yawned. "I was awake most of the night worrying about Casi. I guess I passed out sometime this morning."

"We're kicked to the curb at eight. We should shower and sneak in the women's dorm to kidnap our girl." Jake wiggled his eyebrows.

"Let's hope she's still there." Kyle sat up and smacked his head on an overhead pipe. "I think I'm done with staying in hostels. This may have been cool when I was eighteen, but it's a hassle now. Where's the shower?"

"Grab your stuff, you'll love this."

Kyle followed him and gasped when they entered the community shower room. "Are you kidding?"

"Just like high school, huh?" Jake stripped off his clothes.

"Or jail." They showered quickly, keeping an eye on their belongings as the room filled with weary travelers.

Kyle checked his watch repeatedly while they waited in the lobby for Casi. "Do you think she understands we have to be out of here by eight?"

"Yes, she can read." Casi appeared beside them.

"Oh, good, you survived prison." Jake gave her a hug.

"What did you think of those showers?" She shuddered.

"Kyle dropped the soap, which wasn't a wise start," Jake joked. "Did you enjoy girl on girl prison sex? Or pillow fights in the dorm?"

Casi rolled her eyes. "It was exactly like that, and then we braided each other's hair. Actually, it was similar to a model apartment with less attractive girls."

"Did you watch your bag at all times?" Kyle unzipped her pack to investigate.

She pulled away from his touch and crossed her arms over her chest. "I have my passport, but do you know what's missing?"

"What did they take?" Kyle cringed.

"Not they, you." She tapped her foot in annoyance.

"I didn't do anything!" Kyle looked at Jake frantically.

"Exactly!" She narrowed her eyes. "No money or credit cards, not even my phone. I'm completely dependent on you. I assume that thrills you to no end to have absolute control over me."

"I..." Kyle flushed. "We were rushing." He opened his money belt and sifted through the contents. "Each country has a different currency."

"Forget it." She pushed past them through the door.

Kyle grabbed her arm more aggressively than he intended. "Sorry." He stepped back. "Did you want me to carry your socks?"

Tears rolled down her cheeks. "I don't want to hate you."

"Then don't! I swear I have not done anything intentionally." He moved toward her and she put a hand to his chest. He glanced down to see the soft pink socks, and he nodded before transferring them to his backpack.

"They were really warm. Thank you for buying them." She wiped her face. "Can we get coffee?"

"Of course." Kyle surveyed the street and smiled. "Crepes with Nutella?"

Casi followed his gaze. "They smell delicious."

They watched the batter being spread on the circular griddle and waited for it to turn a golden brown before getting flipped over and filled with the creamy Nutella. The server folded it in quarters and wrapped it in paper, handing it to Casi with a nod. She took a bite and grinned. "Scrumptious."

Kyle paid and led them to a table where he spread out his detailed map. "We were able to see a lot of sites yesterday." He regarded the grey sky. "It might rain today, but we should be able to check out the Forgotten Giants." He grinned and waited for them to be excited. "They didn't exist when Grady and I planned our trip, but he would have loved them." He showed them photos and explained the layout.

Jake surveyed the enthusiasm in his brother's face. "They're fantastic. Maybe one could be a bonus location for Grady?"

Kyle nodded. "That would be fitting. The artist, Thomas Dambo, intended for the trolls to encourage people to get out in nature and explore. They also provide shelter and one contains twenty-eight bird houses." He pointed to his itinerary. "If we have time when we get back I'd like to tour Christiansborg Palace. There are ruins beneath it from around eleven hundred AD."

"Was that there when you planned your original trip?" Casi blinked.

Kyle's mouth dropped and he scanned her face for signs of a joke. "Yes, I'm sure it was."

Jake chuckled and poked her. "What year do you think he graduated?"

Casi considered her comment and blushed. "Oh."

Kyle smiled. "I doubt any of us slept well last night."

"That twenty-mile hike will wake us up, though." Jake read Kyle's map.

"We don't need to see them all." Kyle shrugged. "There are two fairly close together. We'll take the train to the beginning of the trail."

They stopped at a 711 kiosk before the train station and filled their backpacks with water and snacks. Jake unzipped Casi's bag and she whirled away from him. "Why is it so full?" He asked.

Kyle stepped toward her. "There should be plenty of room. I only put the clothes we agreed on and a few toiletries. Do you need me to carry more?"

"No!" Casi retreated. "I like it the way it is."

"Alright." Kyle exhaled. "I'll take your water." He glanced across the street as they approached the station and jogged to an ornately decorated building. "I'll be right back."

Jake caught Casi's arm when she tried to follow after him. "Give him a minute." He eyed her. "What's in your backpack that you're trying to hide?"

She stared at her feet. "It's my stuff."

"More contraband? You didn't bring your iPad, did you?"

"No." She moved toward Kyle as he crossed the street.

"I booked us rooms for tonight. It's a cool old hotel." Kyle smiled and directed them to the train.

When they stepped to the platform several stops later, a loud boom vibrated in the air. A gush of rain released from the clouds and they ran for cover. "I guess this trip is cancelled." Jake huddled beside them.

"Not necessarily." Kyle winked. He searched through his bag and produced three small packets, handing one to everyone.

Jake shook out the plastic poncho and pulled it over his head. "You thought of everything."

"I tried." Kyle surveyed Casi. He cautiously helped her figure out how to get the poncho over her head and smoothed his hand over her. "Good? The rain should stop soon. There are a lot of flash storms."

"If we don't get struck by lightening, we should be fine," Jake agreed.

After five miles of hiking, the sun was out in full force and Casi stopped to yank the poncho from her sweat-soaked body. Kyle winced as the plastic tore and willed himself not to complain. He consulted his map and pointed. "Number four should be over there." He proceeded through the forest and came to an abrupt halt. "Maybe there's another way."

Jake stepped beside him and shook his head. "We didn't walk five miles to turn back." He charged down the steep hill, grabbing saplings as he slid in the mud. At the bottom he peered through the trees and yelled, "I see it!"

Kyle turned to Casi. "Do you want me to go first in case you slip?"

"I can do it." She dipped her toe over the edge and bit her lip. "Actually, can you hold my hand?"

He smiled and steadied himself on the grade, showing her the best route to take. When they reached the bottom, he held her hand a moment longer, unwilling to break the connection between them.

A group of young tourists from Germany clamored into the ice bar, phones in hand, taking selfies. Kyle sighed as he watched Casi's annoyance, realizing it was directed at him. "I'm sorry you don't have your phone. Is it not possible to enjoy everything we've seen without documenting it on Social Media?"

She turned and glared at him. "I had a great time today discovering the trolls and seeing the palace. You've taken plenty of pictures and I can look at them later. Although, I'm sure Lauren is enjoying the photos you texted her."

Kyle blushed. "We left abruptly. I thought it would be nice to show her we're having a good time."

"I asked you to not post pictures of me. You said I could trust you." Her lip quivered.

"I only sent pictures of the sites. I didn't even mention you were with us." He moved closer to her on the fur-lined seat. "We're in a bar entirely made of ice, filled with amazing sculptures, drinking cocktails. How can you possibly be unhappy?" He stood and walked to the bar for a refill. A young attractive woman immediately slid to his side, enchanted by his handsome face framed by the fur parka.

Casi gritted her teeth. "He doesn't understand."

"How can he? You are confusing as hell." Jake shook his head. "Laughing one minute and a surly bitch the next. Spell it out, psycho, before you completely destroy my poor brother."

Casi jumped to her feet and strode to the other end of the bar to strike up a conversation with a group of men. She flirted and accepted the drinks they bought her until she could barely stand. Kyle eyed her and slid closer to the enamored woman at his side. He caught Casi's attention and shrugged, daring her to make the next move. She stumbled toward him and grabbed his arm, not realizing the pain she caused to his wound. "I want the truth. Did you give anyone the keys to the loft?"

Kyle scowled. "You know the real estate firm had them. Who cares?"

"Not the set you left with them. Did you have more?"

"No..." His face clouded. "Yes. A buyer was interested, and the real estate office was closed. I realized I still had the key you gave me when you lived there, so I sent it to them. What does it matter?"

"My mother was living there at the time!"

"I told them that." He ordered a refill. "Honestly, I'm embarrassed at how the place may have looked when they went to inspect it."

"Why didn't you tell me?" Casi's eyes watered.

Kyle inhaled sharply. "The truth? I knew you weren't rushing to sell because it was a free place for her to stay. I wanted to be done with the loft, and with her. She made zero effort to improve her situation. You saw the state of the place when we cleaned it. It was disgusting."

"What did you intend to do with her if the loft sold?"

He regarded the frost on the edge of his drink. "I hadn't planned that far ahead." He wiped the condensation from his glass. "Are you trying to get me to say our lives are easier with her gone? You would think so, except she keeps coming back to haunt us."

Casi slapped him and turned to the woman, who stood in embarrassed silence. "He's all yours. I want nothing to do with him."

She ran from the bar and threw her parka at the front desk. Jake jumped up and tugged at Kyle's arm. "Let's go."

Kyle shrugged him off. "She's already gone. I'm fine right here." He smiled at the woman as she cuddled closer to him.

Jake grabbed Casi from the sidewalk. "Go back in."

"I can't." She wept in his arms. "Which way is the hotel?"

He frowned at the bar and wrapped an arm around her shoulders as she shivered against him. "I'll take you back but tomorrow we need to have a serious discussion. This argument is bullshit."

"He killed my mom."

"He wasn't even there when she died." Jake's mind flooded with pieces of conversations and he wondered if he missed clues, unsure how far Kyle may have gone to eliminate the perceived threat of Sonya in Casi's life. "We've had a long day and exhaustion is making you crazy. Sleep and we'll talk to him in the morning while we have coffee." He escorted her to the room, waiting for her to brush her teeth and settle in bed. He checked his watch and clenched his jaw at the disaster that was unraveling.

Golden streaks peeked through a clouded sky. Kyle rubbed his face and pulled his jacket tighter, aching from the cold. He jogged up the path, entering the hotel silently. He slipped in the room, casting a glance at his wife, relieved to see she was alone, but unclear what events may have unfolded during the night. He brushed his teeth, considering what to do next. Stripping away his clothing, he eased under the covers, watching Casi in a fitful sleep. He rolled on top of her, placing his mouth over hers as she woke. He kissed her with desperation, expressing himself where words failed him. She responded, clinging to him as a sob escaped. "Sweetheart, I want you," he breathed. She parted her legs, welcoming him. As he thrust, she gasped, and he searched her eyes for answers. "Am I hurting you?" he asked, praying nothing happened to her in LA.

"No." She wrapped her arms around him. "Don't stop."

He communicated his love and desire, coaxing her to respond. As he neared climax, he sensed her hesitation. "What's wrong?" She gripped her legs tighter, bringing her hips to greet him. Without a word, she made it impossible for him to resist. He shuddered against her, breathing heavily into her neck. "Why did you hold back?"

"I can't give in." Tears streamed from her eyes to the pillow.

"I didn't sleep with that woman. I went to her hotel, but I couldn't bring myself to cheat. I'm sure I gave American men a bad reputation when I ran out without an explanation. I slept on a park bench because I wasn't ready to come back." He stroked her cheek. "I can't handle what's going on between us."

She touched the bandage on his arm. "What really happened?"

"After you left, I started drinking. I looked at those pictures and freaked out. I threw the whiskey bottle through the glass door and it shattered. The events after that are hazy, but I think I tripped and fell on a shard of glass. Jake took me to the hospital to get stitches, and I was seriously hung over the next day." He locked his eyes on hers. "The truth is I cut myself intentionally. I wanted to mitigate the pain in my heart."

She pulled him closer and cried against his shoulder. "I'm sorry."

There was a knock at the door. "Monkey, are you awake yet? Do you want to get coffee and one of those delicious crepes?" Jake asked.

Kyle opened the door. "Sorry, her husband came back, you're out of luck."

Jake pretended to be appalled by his brother's nudity as he pushed past. "Lucky for you, I'm not interested in your girl; too many issues. I'm surprised she let your cheating ass back in her bed."

"I didn't cheat," Kyle reiterated. "That woman was pretty, but I'm not into casual sex anymore."

"Get dressed. I'm ready for breakfast." Jake reclined on the bed. "Are these mattresses made from straw?"

"Ugh, is that why they're lumpy?" Casi tumbled from the bed and walked to the bathroom.

"That's what they used back then." Kyle followed her. He surveyed the tiny stall with the chest level shower head. "Do you want to go first?"

"We can both fit," she said. "This seems like the kind of place with limited hot water, so we should conserve."

He put his hands to the sides of her face. "I don't care what happened in LA, or who you were with..." he hesitated, "I love you. I need you to tell me what's really going on and how it relates to your mother. My only crime is naïveté, you must believe that."

After a cup of coffee, Jake smoothed his hands across the table. "I realize today is our final day in Copenhagen and we have lots of places to see." He crossed his arms over his chest. "I refuse to leave until Casi shares what's going on. Kyle waited twenty years for this trip, and Casi was excited as one of those yappy dogs to arrange it. Suddenly, in the last week, everything became unhinged. If it's because I'm here and spoiling your fun, I'm happy to trek on by myself."

"It's not you." Casi gripped his hand. Pain emanated from her eyes as she took a deep breath. "A man has been calling and texting me over the last few months. He threatened to distribute the photos if I didn't comply."

"Does he want money?" Kyle asked. "How did he get the pictures? I thought we got all the original data things."

Casi smiled at his lack of software knowledge. "My mom made a copy of the flash drive the day of the shoot. She kept it as collateral to use against me if I didn't obey her."

"What about the other pictures? They were taken in the loft, after we were married." Kyle's face crumbled. Casi burst into tears and he grasped her hand. "It's ok, you don't have to tell me what happened. The pictorial was enough. I only wish you trusted me and shared about the drugs. Is this an ongoing issue?"

Casi yanked her sleeve up to expose her inner elbow. "I've never done heroin and for the record I've never participated in a gang bang either!" She glared at him. "Why did you give that man a key?"

"Did he hurt you?" Kyle's eyes flashed with rage.

"That wasn't me in those pictures! It was my mom," she gasped.

"Your mom has brown hair." Kyle cocked his head.

"You noted the hair color in that cluster-fuck?" Jake gasped. "I saw nudity, sex, and drugs. I recognized the loft and assumed it was Casi..." He grinned. "The boobs looked like you."

"Ugh." Casi shivered.

Kyle fidgeted with the tablecloth. "I tried to find a reference point for when it happened. The kitchen had been remodeled, so I knew it was after we got back together."

Tears ran down Casi's face. "My mom dyed her hair when she returned to LA. She thought it made her look younger. Remember, you saw her?"

"Casi, she was in a hospital bed, in a coma." Kyle winced. "Why are you upset about the key? I understand it was callous of me not to be concerned for her welfare after it sold, but you must admit she hated me as well."

"She did." Casi nodded. "And me." Tears bubbled up again.

Kyle grasped her hand. "I'm truly sorry her death is hard on you. For your sake, I wish she was alive and sober enough to try to be a good mother."

Casi dabbed her eyes with a napkin. "The man who contacted you was not a buyer. He wanted the location of the loft to confront my mother."

"Your mom wouldn't be hard to find." Kyle shrugged. "Why would he need a key?"

"She had a journal that contained information which he felt could incriminate the people he worked for." She gasped for breath. "They intended to search the loft without her knowledge, but she must have surprised them when she showed up." Her lip trembled. "Kyle, the loft wasn't just a mess because she was a slob. We cleaned up a crime scene!"

20

BLACKMAIL

Casi wrapped her arms around herself while they stood in line for the ferry. Kyle put an arm over her shoulders and kissed her temple. "Why can't you give us more information? You drop a bomb and then get up and walk away like everything is normal."

"I'm not trying to be cagey." Casi glanced around at the crowds. "I don't know who I can trust and I'm fearful I've put you and Jake in danger. There were people surrounding us all day, and I thought we would have freedom at the amusement park, but it was even more congested."

"Tivoli gardens was awesome," Jake said.

"See? There are eavesdroppers everywhere." Casi giggled.

Kyle smiled, enjoying the precious moment of her good mood. "We have an eight-hour ferry ride with a private cabin. Can we talk tonight?"

"What do you mean by private?" Jake frowned. "You left me all alone last night already."

"You sat outside Casi's door until I returned." Kyle grinned.

Jake shrugged. "You knew I wouldn't leave her unprotected."

"I appreciate it." Kyle bumped his shoulder. "Private means a room for all three of us. Bunks and a bathroom. It won't be fancy, but it's unlikely we will be overheard."

Kyle guided them down the hallway to the interior cabin. "Basic amenities." He surveyed the all white room with four bunk beds and a tiny bathroom with a stall shower.

"I like it." Jake reclined on a bed.

Casi cocked her head. "I guess I'm on top?"

"Yup, right here, baby." Jake patted his stomach.

"In your dreams." Casi laughed and hoisted her backpack.

Kyle grabbed the bag as it tipped from the bunk and secured it. "There's more than clothing in here."

"Give me time." She glanced away.

"I won't push." Kyle squeezed her shoulder. "Are you hungry? There's a dining car."

Casi swung around and fell in his arms. "I do love you. My brain is overwhelmed by what I found out."

He hugged her tightly. "Don't carry the burden alone. Let's eat and come back to relax and hang out."

Casi curled up beside Kyle on the bottom bunk and sipped her cocktail. "The calls began out of the blue. At first, I figured it was a wrong number, but he had too many facts about LA and my mother. He spoke in circles and seemed unclear about his intent. I kept hanging up, but he threatened me."

"Why didn't you tell me?" Kyle asked.

"Because it involved her, and you made it clear you were sick of all the problems she caused. I wanted it to go away."

He laced his fingers through hers. "My issue was her problems hurt you. I didn't intend to make you deal with things on your own."

Casi nodded. "Work has been busy, and I came to terms with things regarding my mother and wanted to focus on the positive stuff. Ava and I have been spending time together and memories surfaced of her from my childhood. It was a pleasant surprise." She sighed. "Katie has been kind of a drag and I slightly regret re-friending her."

Kyle chuckled. "Honestly, I agree you didn't have a choice."

"I prefer Dawn, and you have wonderful friends in Blackberry Falls, why do you want that deadbeat in your circle?" Jake yawned.

"Let's park my annoying friend for now." Casi held out her glass for a refill. "I'm setting the scene for where my mind was when I got the calls."

"Duly noted." Kyle emptied the whiskey in her glass.

"I felt invincible." She pursed her lips. "I took the high road with Lauren and we called a truce on our war."

"Imaginary battle." Kyle laughed. He regarded her expression. "I'm proud of you for rising above and being the better person."

"I assumed he wanted money and somehow had knowledge of the payout from Sand and Surf, so I offered it in exchange for whatever photos he claimed he had."

"How much?" Kyle asked.

"A little over twenty-thousand."

"He wanted more?" He cringed. "You can't make a deal with a blackmailer. We should have contacted a lawyer."

"He was adamant about a journal and how people would pay a lot of money to get their hands on it. I explained I didn't know anything about it and threatened to turn him over to the police if he didn't stop harassing me. The calls ended, and I used the money for the trip instead."

Kyle rubbed his temple. "You've been dealing with this since summer? You should have included me."

"You were preoccupied with Grady and I couldn't add my crap to your emotional pile. I was proud of myself for standing up to him."

"What changed?" Jake asked.

"Ava's reaction to the video at Christmas made me concerned there were still secrets in the wings," Casi said.

"She was upset to see herself pregnant and Jamie alive," Kyle said.

"There was more. Mom was writing in a book, and Jamie said

something Ava reacted to. Did you notice she muted it before we turned it off?"

"I think you're fishing." Jake selected a small bottle from the tray.

"I asked her if I could come over and watch the rest of the videos with her and she's suddenly always busy," Casi said.

"Maybe it's too sad for her," Kyle suggested.

"I asked if Mom kept a journal and she was evasive. They were best friends and shared everything. I told her about the caller and what he wanted, and she freaked out and made me promise not to involve the police or share information with anyone."

"That's odd," Kyle frowned.

"I suggested we contact my mom's sister, Simone, and see if she had information and she begged me to leave it alone. I gave up and figured I would leave it in the past." Casi shivered. "Then the calls began again. He implicated you and inferred you were hiding things. He told me about the key and how you insisted we throw everything away after she died."

"That was your decision!" Kyle balked.

"I realize that. I told him it was a bunch of junk and if he wanted anything, he could check the dump. He insisted something must have been mailed before she died." She covered her face. "You never told me her ashes arrived. I assumed you would hide something she sent you as well."

"I arranged for her ashes to come to the wood shop, and you agreed. I didn't tell you they arrived because it was unnecessary until you decided what to do with her. Nothing else came," Kyle said.

"He sent the pictures to my former name. He wanted me to understand he was in control."

"The editorial was tacky but wouldn't have ruined your career. He didn't have much leverage." Kyle opened a bag of cookies and handed her one.

"They're embarrassing, but I agree. The photos of my mom were upsetting." Her eyes filled with tears.

Kyle pulled her closer. "They were difficult to look at, especially when I thought they were you. I assume they drugged and raped her. That was a horrible thing for you to witness."

Casi sobbed uncontrollably and Jake reached over and squeezed her hand. "I'm sorry, Monkey. You understand we are sickened that happened."

"No, they..." she struggled to get the words out. "They killed her! She didn't overdose. They administered it."

"What?" Kyle blanched. "Did he tell you that?"

Casi jumped to her feet and tugged the zipper open on her backpack, yanking a set of photos out. "Look!"

Kyle recoiled. "I destroyed these."

"You tried." Jake rolled his eyes. "I found them scattered by the fireplace and hid them in your desk. How did you find them?"

"This is another set." Casi cried. "I took them from his apartment in LA."

"Oh, God." Kyle pulled her to his lap. "You met with him?"

"Just look." She pointed to the photos.

Jake slid beside Kyle and wrinkled his nose in disgust. "What are we looking for?"

She shuffled the pictures and guided them through the assault. "They tortured her to find the location of the journal." Tears streaked her cheeks. "She must have told them she mailed it for safe keeping, and they decided she was no longer of use to them. They killed her to shut her up."

Jake's eyes welled at the now obvious order of events. "How did they know she had it in the first place? What does it contain?"

"Are you sure it exists?" Kyle asked. "Why would people take her seriously? Anyone can write fiction."

"You should read Libby's books," Jake chuckled. "Talk about an imagination!"

Casi exhaled. "Remember the commune where we took my mom's ashes? Ava was sketchy as hell and insisted we didn't tell Simone who I was."

"That was strange." Kyle agreed.

Casi inhaled sharply and shoved her backpack on Kyle's lap. "It's real. It's full of hate and crazy rants, but it makes compelling accusations. The cult members penetrated Hollywood, the government, and giant corporations. Mom may have been a drugged-out floozy, but she knew a lot of secrets about powerful men. No one cared until she threatened to expose them."

Kyle extracted a heavy book from her backpack. "This is immense! You've been carrying it the whole time?"

"I didn't have time to read it. The stories are so convoluted and I'm unclear how much is true." She rubbed her shoulders. "It weighs a ton."

Kyle flipped through the pages. "This is full of conspiracy theories?"

"Family secrets too." Casi set her jaw. "Ava claimed I died in that accident when I was three."

"Why?" Kyle scanned the pages.

Casi bit her lip. "She won't talk to me." She slumped beside Kyle. "The pictures were sent to my work address and I couldn't figure out how someone from LA had made the connection to me. My business cards have my phone number and email, but no address. I remembered my mom asking for it before I went to LA that last time. She said she was sending something special for me." She blinked away tears. "I was excited about the bungalow and forgot about it."

"Mary intercepted the package," Kyle breathed. "She's friends with Ava and somehow it's intertwined."

Casi nodded. "That's what I figured. I went to Mary's and forced her to give it to me. I called Ava when I got to LA and she was hysterical. She demanded I return home, and I asked her why my mom had written that I died in the accident. She hung up on me and refused to answer after that."

Kyle furrowed his brow as he read a passage. "The compound is a community of divine beings. The purpose is to methodically and silently infiltrate the major infrastructure and gain control of the universe."

Casi swatted Jake when he laughed. "You would be shocked to

hear who they claim is involved. My grandfather was a significant politician who was murdered for knowledge he possessed."

"Kennedy?" Jake feigned surprise.

"Perhaps. She used code names and weird symbols."

"I'm quite intrigued." Kyle turned a page.

Casi put her hand over the text. "My death wasn't interesting?"

"Disturbing," he admitted. "Government conspiracy and secret societies are fascinating."

"It's full of that shit. I skimmed over it to more personal things about my mother. The philosophy is hung up on numbers."

"Numerology." Kyle's eyes lit up.

"Three is the age when children officially enter the religion."

"The trinity. Three is a significant number." Kyle nodded.

"Fact wizard," Jake snickered.

Kyle frowned. "I'm suggesting it makes sense. A lot of religions don't baptize children until an older age."

"How about thirteen?" Casi posed.

"Age of adulthood in the Hebrew religion," Kyle said.

"And this one. Girls marry at thirteen. My mother was a child bride, given to a man many years older."

"Three times older? If they are following a pattern." Kyle smiled as he watched her attempting to do the math. "Thirty-nine."

"Gross. The book contains symbolism and ceremony, like how they prepared for my mother's ashes."

"You demeaned their faith." Kyle cringed. "Not only did you have her cremated, but you stole the remains."

"Thanks for pointing out the obvious." She pouted.

"Old men marry little girls and that's not a scandal?" Jake asked.

"No one cares about that part. If it's labeled as religious there's a free pass. The girls are expected to produce children within a year. It's their divine purpose." Casi waited for the term to resonate.

Kyle shook his head. "And your mother still believed that? She was in her twenties when she had you."

"I wasn't her first," Casi said. "She had Sebastian when she was almost fourteen. She loved him dearly."

"Does he still live at the compound?" Kyle asked.

"He's dead. She killed him," she said.

Kyle's eyes flew to the journal. "All that's in here? What was her motive?"

"It's not a crime thriller, Kyle." Jake shook his head. "It's doubtful any of it's real. Sonya was a crackpot searching for attention."

"There's a very detailed description of the difficult delivery due to her small hips." She looked sideways at Kyle. "I take after my father's side."

"I love your figure." He gave her a kiss.

Jake gagged and Casi continued, "That's when she began the journal. He was deprived of oxygen. It was assumed he would die, so she was permitted to keep him to help her mourn until he passed. He survived but was brain damaged. At the age of three, when he was supposed to be baptized, she was forced to hold him under the water until he died. The ceremony was to release him to the after world where he would be reincarnated. They told her he would come back to her and be perfect if she was a true believer."

"That's disgusting," Jake scoffed.

"It broke her heart," Casi said. "She ran away from the complex and hitched her way to Vancouver. She was seventeen and all alone."

Kyle sighed, "I'm sorry she had that life. That must have been hell."

"She met my dad and fell in love. She got pregnant to make him marry her but aborted the baby when they told her it was a girl. She wanted Sebastian back. Simone convinced her it wasn't possible because she broke her ties to the compound."

"Why didn't she return?" Jake asked.

"She met Ava and Jamie. She discovered a life outside the complex and shared her past with her new best friend, who promised to guide her. She became pregnant with me and wanted to terminate again, but Ava convinced her I would be a blessing."

"Good," Kyle snapped.

"I wasn't. She hated me," Casi lamented. "I didn't have Sebastian's sweet nature, and I resembled my father. She disgraced her family by having a child out of wedlock since her marriage wasn't valid. Her punishment was the curse of a daughter who would never be divine."

Kyle wiped her tears. "You're perfect in every way." He frowned at the book on his lap. "Why do you have this? Wasn't it why the man was harassing you?"

"I drove all the way there and each time I stopped for coffee I read more passages and became angrier. There were notes tucked within the pages and one was a threatening letter ensuring my mother would meet a horrible death if she didn't shut up. It was from Simone. She seemed to be my mother's only contact, and they used a P.O. Box in Prince George."

"No one leaves the compound?" Jake asked.

"At thirteen, the boys are sent to private schools around the world to become future politicians and influential men. Think about famous people who have children but pretty much keep them hidden until their teenage years. I think they're members of the cult."

Kyle shrugged. "I don't follow the lives of those people. Their offspring mean nothing to me."

Casi rolled her eyes. "They return at thirty-nine to take a wife and basically knock her up before carrying on with their lives outside the walls. Some are athletes, actors, and directors, with covert affiliation to the religion. They're not involved in raising the children and only participate in ceremonies and reproduction."

"A baby making factory," Jake reasoned. "Keep the perfect ones and kill the imperfect. Survival of the fittest."

"All the women stay there?" Kyle asked.

"They only have one purpose," Casi concluded.

"Your mom was excommunicated when she left?" he said.

"Pretty much. Simone was her only contact and granted her favors for accomplishing tasks on the outside." Casi cringed. "They seem to have a variety of levels; the pure who produce children, the subordinates who can't conceive..."

"Three to thirteen," Kyle offered enthusiastically.

Casi frowned. "You are too excited about this."

Kyle grinned. "What are the other tiers?"

"A few, like my mom, who are shunned but can perform duties to win favor for the afterlife. That's why we had to bring her back. Although she didn't spawn children for the cult, she acted as a liaison. I believe she was too desperate to realize she was used as a pawn in their scam."

"What kinds of things did she do?" Jake asked.

"She knew which producers were into child porn and movie stars with weird sexual appetites. That's what she documented in the journal. Names, dates, and even pictures."

"I understand how that could be a problem." Kyle tapped his forefinger to her nose. "I'll bet that's why you died!"

Jake surveyed Casi. "She looks alive."

"Ava probably tricked them." Kyle nodded. "She took off to Vancouver and pretended you were dead." He searched through the book. "Is there a passage that discusses half-breed children and their use?"

Jake fell back on his bunk in a fit of laughter while Casi jumped to her feet and pulled pajamas from her backpack. "I think we have had quite enough of this journal for the night."

Jake rubbed Kyle's shoulder until he woke up. "Ouch," he groaned, trying to twist the kink in his neck. He surveyed Casi wound around his chest as he was wedged against the side of the bunk. "Damn, I guess I fell asleep while I was reading the journal."

"I tried to move her, but she cried out, so I left her where she was." Jake shook his head. "You'll both be sore today. Take a shower quickly, we are getting ready to dock."

Kyle yawned. "Was there an announcement?"

Jake held up a tray of coffee and pastries. "I saw the shore and talked to the crew. What's our plan?"

Kyle rubbed his face. "Oslo is a pretty big city. I considered going farther up north, but if we want to fit in Italy, we probably shouldn't waste time."

"This is your trip." Jake yawned. "Do what interests you."

"I need to find an internet café." Casi climbed over Kyle and staggered to the bathroom. "Today is Sunday?"

"Yes. You need to contact Mary? You can call her if you want. We can use the phone for a small fee," Kyle said.

Casi leaned against the door and tossed her clothes on the bed. "I must be cautious. I've deactivated or rather scrambled, my social media accounts. I'll use my work email as I would if I were traveling." She noted Kyle's lustful expression. "Did you retain any of that?"

He blushed. "No, I was too busy admiring you."

She laughed and continued to the bathroom to shower. "Are we taking a train to town?"

"Not only can we walk, there is a castle ruin that we can check out on our way in!" Kyle's face beamed. "Oh, but maybe you need to get your email sent so we should do it on the way back." He scanned his map.

"The café can wait. I'm excited to explore the castle." Casi smiled and noted Jake giving her a thumbs up behind Kyle's back.

They climbed the hill to the stone wall of the castle and took pictures, posing as they laughed and investigated the ruins.

"This is so cool." Casi peered out at the port from the rise of a hill and turned slowly to take in her surroundings.

"Casi, are any of these real?" Kyle sorted through the tampons.

"As in really meant for my vagina? Pink is intact. Blue is Grady. I'm not due until we get back, but it would totally suck to be without them in case it screws up. Honestly you would have done me a favor when you signed for the tubal ligation if you had requested a hysterectomy. What's the point of having a period?"

"You would have gone into early menopause which brings a whole new set of issues. I won't pretend to understand what you have to deal with each month, but I was only attempting to save your life not permanently alter your body." Kyle's cheeks burned.

"Sorry." She gave him a hug. "Lia's concerned she's entering menopause, and she says it's horrible. Apparently, her family gets it early which is why Lauren is panicking about having a baby."

"God, I hope that doesn't make her as psycho as when she was pregnant." Jake shuddered. "Kyle, why are you laughing?"

"Not about that." He chuckled. "I was thinking how awful it would be if Grady ended up in an unintended destination."

"Poor innocent Grady will never touch the inside of a woman," Jake joked. "You should put him up there just for the experience."

"He was a virgin?" Casi's eyes widened.

Kyle shrugged. "That may have changed by the last summer."

"You gave in to him?" Jake poked him in the ribs.

"He wasn't gay." Kyle rolled his eyes. "He was shy and didn't have an older brother imparting his sexual experiences."

"Those were the days," Jake whistled.

"Grady sounds sweet," Casi said. "Was he older than Nicole?"

"They were fraternal twins," Kyle confirmed.

"Oh, that's even sadder." Tears sprung to her eyes.

"He had a rough living situation and buried himself in books. We got along because he was smart and loved to discover new things."

"Unlike your dumb brother," Jake mimicked.

"Jake was jealous of him and called him Fraidy-Grady. He got the dragon tattoo to show he was tough. And he insisted on driving the boat that last day to prove he could keep up," Kyle sighed.

"You think he finally got laid?" Jake asked.

"He didn't want to be inexperienced when we came to Europe. He aimed to be prepared for hot Scandinavian girls." Kyle chuckled.

"Did he tell you who he banged?" Jake pushed.

"He didn't say, but I suspect it was Amber." Kyle punched his shoulder.

"That little hussy!" Jake shook his head.

"He acted weird when she came around. I figured she seduced him to get back at me, except I didn't care."

"I'm happy he got to experience the wonderland of a woman's body." Jake smoothed his hand over Casi's backside.

She pushed him away and pointed to a tower. "Put him up there! He can be the king for all eternity."

Kyle's face lit up and Jake dropped to his knee to give him a boost.

They watched him climb carefully, avoiding crumbling rocks. "Hurry up," Jake whispered as people began hiking toward them.

"All done." Kyle called, sliding down the opposite side of the wall.

Casi and Jake ran to greet him and noted him hunched over. "Are you hurt?" She bolted toward him.

Kyle shook his head. "This damn bandage is falling apart. When we find the café, let's look for a pharmacy to get supplies." He smiled at them. "I appreciate you guys helping me do this. I feel like he's here with us on the journey. I know he would be thrilled to be free."

Tears filled Casi's eyes. "I don't care about that stupid religion. I put my mom where she belonged, and I'm glad they don't have her."

"You did the right thing, Casi. Your mom was a disaster on earth, but you released her. They have a marker for her in the compound, probably beside the baby they made her kill." Kyle reached for her hand.

Jake pushed between them. "I almost forgot." He opened his wallet and held up their rings. "Put these back where they belong."

21

PLANES, TRAINS, AND FERRIES

Kyle bundled their souvenirs in his backpack and gave them a satisfied nod. "Oslo is amazing, but should we push on and get to Sweden? I haven't booked reservations..." He bit his lip. "Ok, this might be crazy, but I came up with a new plan!" His face beamed with excitement. "We can take the train to Stockholm, which is about five hours. If we sleep, then we can do a quick tour and catch a flight to Helsinki, which is about an hour. Guess what that gives us time for?"

"God, just tell us before you wet your pants with excitement." Jake grinned. "We're happy to try every mode of transportation."

"Perfect, because after a fourteen-hour ferry ride we'll be in St. Petersburg, Russia! Imagine how cool that would be."

"Don't we need visas?" Jake asked.

"Not if we enter by sea. We have seventy-two hours." Kyle surveyed their responses and frowned at Casi, kicking at the dirt. "Too much? We could revisit the map. Ugh, were you serious about the sex clubs in Amsterdam? That would be backtracking, but I guess we could squeeze it in."

Casi gave them a meek smile. "The club was a joke. I only desire to have sex with you and we can get freaky in our own home. I had a great time today, but we never made it to an internet café." A tear slid down her cheek and she swiped it away. "I'm afraid I've permanently messed up our lives, and this vacation is prolonging the inevitable shit storm at home."

"You were the one being blackmailed," Kyle said.

"I realize but..." she looked around frantically. "I killed a guy!"

Jake's eyes widened. "Let's find that café pronto, and then I want to hear the dirt on this little escapade."

Kyle pulled her in his arms. "If we must move to keep you safe, we will." He furrowed his brow as the rain began. "Do you still have your raincoat?" He eyed Casi. "I assume you need a new one. It's a good thing I packed extra in case of emergencies."

Jake chuckled and tugged on his poncho. "You think of everything. Who knew we would need protection from the law as well as the rain?"

"Perhaps not fashionable." He read Casi's expression. "It's lightweight and it'll keep you dry. It pays to be prepared. Aren't you thankful that even with our last-minute glitch we were able to pull this trip off?"

"Would the glitch be when my life imploded?" Casi cocked her head.

"That's the one." Kyle grinned.

❧

Casi logged on a computer while Kyle ordered coffee. She rubbed her neck, stressed about what the message might say. She scrolled through the numerous emails, relieved there weren't any from the LA stores. She noticed one from Mary with the subject, 'All clear', and read through it while Kyle moved to the side to give her privacy. "Ok," she exhaled.

"Is that a good ok? Or are we moving to Europe permanently?" Kyle cringed. "By the way, how much danger are you in and should I be concerned about the welfare of Dingo and Jezebel?"

"Or my kids, secondary to your dog." Jake punched him.

"Ouch." Kyle laughed and rubbed his arm.

"Everyone is fine. Buy me a pastry and I'll fill you in."

"Your desire to eat is a healthy sign." Kyle leaned in to give her a kiss. "So, Dingo is alright?"

"Yes." She smiled. He returned with a plate full of cookies, marzipan, croissants, and chocolate confections. She bit into a pastry, critiquing the flavor. "I think the butter is better here."

Jake put his hand over Kyle's mouth before he launched into a detailed account of how they churned butter in the region. "Spill the beans, Monkey Breath."

Casi plucked at the paper under the pastries. "What time is the train? I would rather talk about it in our cabin."

Kyle checked his watch. "We can make it if we leave now." He surveyed Jake hovering to his side. "It's only a five-hour trip and there weren't cabins available. Are you guys alright with traveling coach class?"

Jake directed his gaze to his feet. "Will we sit together?"

"Yes, the seating is for four." He glanced back at Casi. "We can sleep in our seats and discuss what happened in LA when we get to Sweden."

"Stockholm syndrome." She giggled and cocked her head. "Jake, are you alright? You seem jittery."

Jake exhaled and shrugged. "I'm unnerved by your revelation." He held his hand up when Casi began to speak. "I don't care if you're a stone-cold killer. You took off from the house in a panic and since then our lives spun out of control. My brother has a questionable injury, most likely self-inflicted. You confronted a maniac by yourself and confessed to a crime." His eyes turned to ice. "I failed both of you and I can't catch my breath for fear there's something sinister around the corner. Casi, you're acting like one of those demented Jack-in-the-box toys; sweet and fun with lively music until a crazed clown jumps out to scare you. I'm afraid to let you out of my sight and although it appears pathetic, not to mention playing havoc with your romantic reunion, I can't back off."

Kyle squeezed his hand. "We want you with us. None of that was in your control, and the circumstances would've been more severe if you hadn't been there. We need you to keep us safe."

"Besides, we got it on the other morning in Copenhagen." Casi grinned.

Jake rolled his eyes and Kyle chuckled. "True, and we have a lifetime to catch up on being intimate." He glanced at his watch and bundled the pastries into his backpack. "How fast can you guys run?"

❧

Kyle's eyes fluttered open, and he bolted forward in alarm. "Why are you crying?" He pulled Casi in his arms.

"I'm trying to make sense of this." She sighed and glanced at the photo in her trembling hand.

"Did you take that from my backpack? We agreed I would carry everything and when we were in a safe place, we can go over it." Kyle eyed his unzipped pack at her feet.

"I couldn't sleep." She rubbed her neck. "Something was bothering me about the disaster at the loft."

"Everything about how she treated that place irritates me." Kyle frowned. "Sorry. What specifically stands out to you."

"Excellent job, Kyle." Jake chuckled, still reclined with his eyes closed. "I see you've been reading those relationship books on communication."

Kyle blushed. "I don't need them. I read the journal, and it's incredibly convoluted. This catastrophe made me understand we have issues that might tear us apart." Casi's eyes bubbled with tears. "I don't listen to you properly. I either shut you down or I charge ahead to fix things without looking at the bigger picture." He took her chin in his hand. "You leap into things without giving me a chance to process what's happening. We possess drastically different approaches to trauma." He kissed her gently. "We need to be more patient and trusting of each other."

"It's fixable." Casi sniffed.

"Completely," Kyle agreed. He leaned back in his seat and tapped the photo. "Tell me what you see. Pretend I'm blind and you have to help me understand what's happening in the picture."

Casi took a deep breath. "The clutter is methodical, like someone had been searching for something." She scowled at the photo. "There are clothes on the floor that are off season. Mom wouldn't have been wearing them."

"You're thinking like a detective." Kyle nodded.

"Or the fashion police," Jake chuckled.

Casi pointed to a pile near the bathroom. "Navy shoes and a black dress. Mom wasn't bright, but she knew how to dress properly. It was common for her to throw an outfit on the floor when she staggered home from a club, but these items wouldn't be lumped together. She studied fashion magazines and was obsessed with looking high class. Even blitzed out of her mind, she wouldn't make a faux pas like that."

"Intriguing." Kyle studied the photo. "Wait, she also didn't cook. She always got ready to eat or take out. I bought that set of pans at Target, but she would have no reason to have them out on the counter."

Jake leaned forward. "I'll contribute in my area of expertise. Alix and I found a lot of random drugs, including heroin." He pointed to the last photo. "But no paraphernalia to administer it."

Kyle nodded. "Someone took away the evidence, and we tossed the remainder."

A tear slid down Casi's cheek. "They tortured her to get information. If she'd had the journal, there would be no reason not to give it to them. She knew they were coming but hid it in a place they couldn't find it."

Kyle inhaled. "She alerted them. I bet she offered to sell it. That's why she stashed it. She never intended to expose them. It was a money-making scam."

Casi clasped a hand to her mouth. "Mom was celebrating that night at the club because she figured she had outsmarted them." She narrowed her eyes. "And us. She laughed when I told her about the bungalow. She never had any intention of living there. She was convinced she was coming into money." She yanked the journal from

Kyle's backpack. "She hated me and wanted to prove she didn't need me. I was a meal ticket for her when I was modeling, but once I asserted myself, she was done."

"She was a damaged person." Kyle kissed her temple.

"I'm shattered!" Casi pouted.

Jake patted her knee. "You're not broken, just a bit cracked."

She laughed and nodded. "I wonder who she would have been given different experiences?" She scanned the first pages and came to a passage. "Sebastian was the love of my life, sweet and complacent. When I held him under the water, I experienced his soul leaving his body and part of me died with him." She shook her head. "She loved him so much. I didn't think she was capable of that." Tears fell on the page as she continued. "The girl was six months old, and I regretted every day allowing her to use me as a vessel to bring her to earth. I listened to the wrong people who promised to be there. Instead, they only wanted her, and I was left alone. I tried to return her; I held her under the water, wanting her to slip away like he had. I knew it would be best for everyone. He found me too soon. She was his priority. She was the only one he loved." Casi looked up. "The entry date is after I was born. He is my father. He caught her trying to kill me. He thought she had postpartum depression, so Ava took care of me."

Kyle closed the journal. "Does Mary's subject line, 'All Clear', mean the guy is dead? Should we contact people and make sure they're alright?"

"No one is home. Amy and Riley took Dingo and Jezebel to visit her family in Spokane. Dad, Ava, your parents, Libby, and Earl, are all on Vancouver Island."

"And my kids? One look at Facebook and someone can figure out they're important to you," Jake snapped.

"Lia took our boys to Shane's in Canada and Anna's in Portland. Gail has the other kids in Marin visiting her family."

"That was in the email? It's a map for a kill list!" Kyle's eyes widened.

"It was a code. She understands how I am with puzzles. We would do it when she didn't want my mom to understand our messages. She uses the first letter of the name as a product, the location is a song lyric, and so forth. The email reads like a marketing proposal informing me that when I get back from the convention in Tokyo, the orders will be shipped." Casi smiled. "The storm that was expected from the West has subsided, so there should be no problem with the delivery."

Kyle kneaded his hands. "What were you doing in Elmvale?"

"You were thorough with your investigation," Casi noted.

"I was trying to find you," he said softly.

"I went to see Gary. I required his help to eliminate my online presence. I deactivated my accounts, but that's an obvious trigger when someone is trying to disappear. He created a false identity to redirect to a generic account and not link me to any family, friends, or locations. My recent posts have indicated I'm in Tokyo at a convention." Her eyes welled. "My relationship status is blank, and it appears I'm based in LA."

Kyle fell back in his seat. "I hate that."

"I'm sorry. I had to make sure you guys were safe if anyone came looking for me." Casi grasped his hand. "I couldn't make you a target."

"I thought Gary was a game designer?" Jake said.

"Gary has hidden talents I recognized immediately. His games are embedded with twists and turns. He's brilliant." She smiled. "Kyle should be thankful he was able to remove the party pictures from Facebook while he was in Japan. He blocked the source and sent them a warning email to destroy all the photos."

"Who posted those damn things?" Kyle asked.

"Nicole's oldest kid came home from a sleepover. She wanted to punish her mom and let her dad see what was going on. Gary located the IP address and pretended he was threatening legal action."

"Are things ok with Gary and Nicole?" Kyle sighed.

"It wasn't you that caused the problem. He was pissed about the orgy, which you weren't a part of." She poked him. "Nicole told him about Grady and why she acted out. Gary loves her and is willing to overlook what happened. When I suggested we spread Grady's ashes, she was ecstatic, and she wants to have a memorial in the summer as the final piece of letting go."

§a.

"I'm not eating that." Casi pushed Jake's hand away.

"You're in Finland. You can't be uptight," he insisted.

Kyle took a piece of the jerky. "Reindeer, huh? Tasty."

Jake shoved a fork in Casi's mouth. "Yummy, moose."

She wrinkled her face and swallowed. "It tastes like venison." Her eyes lit up as she regarded the glass cases brimming with delicacies at the market. "Is that princess cake?"

Kyle pulled out his wallet. "We're definitely buying that."

Casi rolled her eyes as Jake continued to offer her treats. "Fine, I'll eat Rudolph, but I get a whole cake to myself."

"Buy two, Kyle." Jake grinned and put the meat on her tongue.

"Surprisingly delicious." She smiled.

Kyle handed out trays laden with cakes and directed them to a park area. He pointed up the street. "There's a church built in a rock with a glass ceiling. What do you think of it as a place for Grady?"

Casi tucked hair behind her ear. "Sounds good. We'll be in Russia tomorrow? How long will we be there?"

Kyle hesitated, determined to unlock the hidden question. "We can spend up to three days. Is there somewhere else you would rather see?"

Casi sighed. "Mary requested we come to Austria. I told her we don't have time, but I sense that she will not be satisfied with that answer."

Kyle extracted his map and drew his finger over the route. "St. Petersburg is my main interest. We can do it in a day." He took her hand as they walked and surveyed the bustling city. "I really want to visit Tallinn." He smiled at her blank expression. "Estonia. Still nothing, huh?" He chuckled. "The old city is surrounded by a stone wall with secret passages."

"I want to go there!" Her face lit up.

"Perfect. We can also do that in a day which will leave us extra time to go to Austria." He brought her hand to his lips to kiss. "I love spending this much time with you."

"Ah, thanks." Jake bumped his shoulder with a grin.

"Yes, both of you." Kyle noted Casi scrambling up the rock wall with surprising agility. "Hey, it says no climbing!"

"I can't hear you. Come up here and tell me." She smiled. He quickly joined her and she handed him the roll of paper. "I unwrapped it for you. There are a lot of tourists, so be quick."

Kyle gave her a kiss and ascended the last few feet to the top. Jake noted security pointing toward them and shoved Casi. "Do something."

She glanced at Kyle, lost in his task, and swiftly removed her shirt. "It's so hot up here." She fanned herself and sauntered to the side, drawing the full attention of onlookers. She smiled at the security team as they scrambled to help her down from the boulders. "Thank you, gentlemen."

"No climbing," one said in a thick accent.

She batted her eyelashes. "I'm sorry. I was distracted by the beautiful landscape and I didn't notice the warning."

He nodded and watched as she slowly slid her t-shirt back on. "It's much cooler down here." She gave them a sweet smile and walked away as Jake and Kyle rounded the corner to meet her.

"Nice diversion," Jake snickered.

She slid the neck of her shirt aside to reveal her chaffed shoulder. "This would be a good time to point out that although I appreciate you doing my packing for me, a sports bra would have been a better choice."

Kyle frowned at her reddened skin. "I thought I was supposed to make sure they match your underwear."

She laughed. "You did a good job." She crossed the street. "I'm sure they have shops where I can buy athletic wear."

Jake grinned. "It may not be comfortable, but that black lace did a stellar job of distracting the authorities."

22

RIVER OF TEARS

Casi tossed and turned on the upper bunk, wetting her pillow with tears. She scooted to the side and peered over, greeting Kyle's sympathetic eyes. He reached out to her, and she laced her fingers through his. "Did I wake you," she asked.

"No, I couldn't sleep. I keep replaying everything from our fight to what may have happened in LA. That journal is cursed, and it has my mind reeling with conspiracy theories." Kyle exhaled.

She vaulted from the bunk and climbed in with him. He smiled and turned on his side, securing her between him and the wall. "We can make this work." He wrapped her in a warm embrace. "Are you ok? I appreciate you putting on a brave front and making this trip fun. We won't push you."

Kyle chuckled as Jake squeezed in at the foot of the bed and arranged Casi's legs over his as he shimmied against the wall. "He says we because I can hear every word. I hope you weren't thinking this was a good place to get intimate." Jake grinned.

"Certainly not with you two feet away." Casi laughed. She gazed at Kyle. "Right now, I need to feel safe and work through everything jumbled in my head. I had such an epic meltdown at the house. I can never see Lauren again. You'll need to cut her out of your life."

Kyle chuckled. "I'm not proud of my behavior either. I switched to autopilot because I was pissed you were hitting me. I shut down."

She stroked the scratches still etching his cheek. "I'm sorry. It was immature and ghetto." She winced. "I inherited my mother's nature."

"No, you didn't." Kyle hugged her tighter. "You implode when you're overwhelmed. She hit an innocent child."

"You were innocent." Casi locked eyes with him. "I should have come to you in the beginning. That man convinced me you were hiding things from me and couldn't be trusted."

"I didn't know it was related to the key. I'm guilty of jeopardizing your mother's safety," Kyle admitted.

"He called from an LA number." She paused, and they waited for her to work through the details in her mind. "He knew too much about me, yet only from a business standpoint. He addressed the pictures to Cassidy Roberts. Yet they were sent to my work."

"That's odd." Kyle tapped a finger on his bottom lip. "You haven't used that name since you left Canada. What's the affiliation?"

"Simone!" Jake said. "She wouldn't have known you changed your name."

Casi's eyes widened. "True, and she said she knew me when we went to the commune. Do you think she blames me for my mother's death?"

"Maybe. Did you meet the man who called?" Kyle asked.

Casi took a deep breath. "After I received the pictures and made the connection to the journal, I picked it up from Mary. I drove to LA..."

"You called Ava," Kyle interrupted.

"Yes, from Alix's phone." She closed her eyes to focus on the facts. "I also called the man and told him I had what he wanted."

"Then why do you still have it?" Kyle shivered unintentionally.

She put her hand to his mouth. "This part is difficult. Please let me say it all in one go. I won't be brave enough to tell you later." He nodded, and she shifted her gaze to Jake, who gave her a thumbs up. "I arranged to meet the man at his apartment. His voice sounded familiar, and it was unnerving." She noted Kyle's eyes turn to deep blue with concern. "I took Alix with me. I also had him buy heroin, and he demonstrated how to use it." She pressed her hand firmer when Kyle's lips twitched to speak. "Not on himself. He used a banana. He waited on the sidewalk while I went up to the third floor. It was a crappy place, and the elevator was broken. When he answered the door, I realized he was one of my clients."

Jake raised his hand. "Then why did he call you Cassidy?"

"I'm unclear why. He said he was acting as a broker for a wealthy client who wanted to purchase the journal. He was willing to give me the original copies of the photos if I complied."

Kyle pulled free from her grasp. "You trusted him?"

"No." Her eyes glazed. "I intended to kill him." Tears flooded her cheeks. "She was a terrible mother, but she didn't deserve that punishment!"

"No, she didn't." Kyle rubbed her back. "Was he involved?"

She nodded. "He had already given me details over the phone, which proved it. He knew about the scars on her wrists and the mole on her back. A guy she slept with wouldn't have noticed. He took pleasure in tormenting me with how she begged for them to stop."

Kyle locked angry sapphire eyes with Jake. "He deserved to die!"

She cried on his shoulder for a moment and took his hand, squeezing it to give herself courage to continue. "I faked being dumb enough to fall for his offer. I produced the journal and asked for the originals. He teased me and said he wasn't sure if he still had copies on his laptop..." She gasped for air. "He said he knew I loved to dance at nightclubs and put on a show, and if I slept with him, he would give them to me."

She erupted in sobs and Kyle clenched his jaw as he comforted her. "It's ok. I understand what you had to do."

Jake smoothed his hand over her hip. "We love you, Monkey."

She clung to Kyle. "I told him to undress and sit on the bed to watch me dance." Her eyes paled to a watery green. "I took off my top and moved toward him, and then when I knew he was turned on, I dropped to my knees." She grabbed Kyle's chin as his face crumpled. "I injected him with the heroin in his balls!"

"Hell, yes! That's my girl." Jake cheered. "That must've hurt like crazy."

"Alix told me it would be a fast overdose with the amount I injected. He went into shock and then started sputtering and foaming at the mouth."

"You ran to Alix and got yourself somewhere safe?" Kyle's body shook with rage as he pictured the scene.

She pursed her lips. "While he was writhing in pain, or whatever happens when you overdose, I searched his apartment. I stole his laptop and any flash drives I could find. I found Alix and got the hell out of there. He didn't want the details of what conspired, and he disposed of the evidence from the drugs."

"You put him in a tough place," Jake commented.

"I know." Casi wept.

"Honestly, I feel he owed you for initiating the editorial in the first place," Kyle wiped her eyes with the corner of the sheet.

"That's what he said." She rubbed her eyes. "We called 911. I couldn't live with being a murderer."

"What did you tell them?" Kyle gasped.

She bit her lip. "I set fire to his apartment. He was a smoker, so it would be plausible. I figured it would take care of anything I missed and erase my presence. I pulled the fire alarm to alert the residents. Alix used a fake name and told the dispatcher he was walking by and saw smoke." Her lip trembled. "The fire was minimal and could easily be contained. I figured they would discover him, and his fate would be in their hands."

"Given the response time in LA, I'm guessing he's dead." Jake laughed and noted the pain in Casi's eyes. "He deserved it."

They stood on the dock and assessed their appearance in a filthy window as fellow passengers gave them sideways looks as they passed by.

Kyle patted a rogue patch of hair down after licking his palm.

"How did we miss the announcement for disembarkation? The whole point of getting a cabin was to sleep and take showers."

"We talked all night and fell asleep in one bunk." Jake shrugged. "Not only do I have a cramp in my neck, you wouldn't let me shower."

"There was no time. They were banging on our door." Kyle turned away as he broke into hysterical laughter at Casi's attempt to smooth her hair.

Jake grinned. "You look homeless."

"You have hair like a hedgehog." She stuck her tongue out at him and frowned at Kyle. "How are you still handsome? We slept on top of you."

"It's my fate." He gave her a wink. "We can clean up at a Burger King before the river tour." He grabbed Jake's arm as they strolled through the park toward the green coffee kiosk. "Anna!"

"Where? I thought she was meeting us in France." Jake scanned the park.

"The movie. The last scene. This is the location they were in." Kyle began taking pictures with his phone. He gave Casi a sheepish grin. "Can I send a photo to Lauren? She'll be beside herself."

Casi crossed her arms over her chest. "Did you see that movie with her?"

Kyle blushed. "You were out of town. I asked if you wanted me to wait and you said you weren't interested in spy thrillers."

"Fine, but make sure I'm not in it." Casi shuddered. "I don't want my appearance documented." She strolled through the garden, easing the tension from her shoulders as she noted the surrounding beauty. She exhaled and released pent-up annoyance at the friendship between Kyle and Lauren as she watched him smiling while he held his phone at an angle. "All done? Did you send her some of these lovely flowers?" she asked, joining him by a symphony of roses.

"Huh? Oh, I sent her a photo of the gate. I wanted to copy that sign. What do you think of it? I'll make one for our garden." Kyle pointed to a brass plaque on a stone. "Life is not measured by the number of breaths we take, but the moments that take our breath away."

She slid her hand in his as tears filled her eyes. "I love it. It's perfect for us. You should put a Grady-bit here."

Kyle laughed. "Good thought. Can you hand me the paper part? It seems disrespectful to eject him from a plastic tube." He wandered along the path in search of the ideal location. After he tipped the ashes gently to the breeze, they wafted through the air to settle at the base of a tree."

Jake jogged up beside him and slipped something in his hand. "Perfect."

Kyle observed the pocketknife in his palm. "Where did you get this?"

"There are a million souvenir shops here. I thought it would be a cool keepsake." Jake shrugged. He smiled at Kyle's envious gaze. "I bought two. You've been busy keeping us on track and I didn't want you to miss out. I also noticed a vodka bar that I want to visit when we finish the river tour."

"Thank you for thinking of me. We'll visit the bar for sure." Kyle gingerly stepped on a rock out of sight behind the flowering bushes and knelt to carve Grady's name. "There you go. You made it to a whole new place, even though your world ended before you were ready. I wasn't prepared to say goodbye so soon, but it feels right to bring you with us. I hope you would agree." He smoothed his hand over the deep carving. A breeze kicked up, and he sat back on his heels, watching as the ashes danced along the garden's edge. "I'll take that as a sign."

They strolled the streets hand in hand, while Jake took ownership of the camera. "More architecture and fewer pictures of women," Kyle suggested.

"The women in Europe are beautiful." Jake smiled. "Naturally pretty, not all fake and made up."

"They are." Kyle smiled at Casi.

She shoved him away. "I know I look like crap."

He pulled her in his arms. "That was an honest compliment. Even with your hair looking like a mop and no makeup, you are lovely. I want to drown in your beauty."

Jake grabbed his arm and redirected him. "You might drown in the river if you don't pay attention. We're here."

A group of backpackers waved them over to the side of the boat. "Come join us. Is this your first time in Russia? We stayed in a horrible hostel last night so avoid it at all costs," one girl claimed.

"We're only here for the day. We have a busy itinerary we're trying to get through." Kyle smiled and slid beside them.

"Oh Americans. You're so friendly."

"My wife is Canadian." Kyle smiled at her attempt to smooth her wayward hair. "Where are you from?"

"Sidney by birth and now we're trekking in from Italy on our way to Norway," the bearded man said. "Been an epic trip so far. How about you?" They shared their itineraries, impressed with Kyle's sophisticated system of information and planning. "What are the stars for, Mate?"

Kyle glanced away. "We're spreading the ashes of my high school friend. He always wanted to travel here."

"Sorry to hear that. Did he recently pass away?"

"No, it's been twenty years. It had been our plan to come to Europe after graduation, but he was killed in an accident."

"That's a shocker. Good on you for doing right by your mate," he said as his group nodded in agreement.

"It's been an amazing journey." Kyle smiled brightly and pointed. "Wow, look at that palace!" The Australians nodded and pulled out cameras, encouraging Kyle to share his in-depth knowledge of the area.

One man gave Kyle a list of shops to buy from ensuring they didn't get pegged as tourists. "The Hermitage is crazy packed, but you must go!" He described the paintings and sculptures and Kyle's eyes lit up.

Casi noted his reaction. "I definitely would like to see that."

"Are you sure? I know museums aren't really your thing." Kyle shrugged.

Casi laughed and put a hand on his knee. "I'm not into art galleries because I've seen enough with Alix to last a lifetime. I would enjoy being a tourist and discovering original works of art." She smiled. "With you."

Kyle leaned over and kissed her. "Thank you for making this trip special. I can't believe all the amazing things we're experiencing."

Casi struck up a conversation with one of the travelers as they floated under bridges and sipped champagne. When the boat docked, the girl gave her a hug and handed her a slip of paper. "Let's connect on Facebook. I would love to see how the rest of your trip goes." She winked. "Feel free to post pictures of your husband and his brother without shirts."

Casi tucked the paper in the pocket of her backpack. "This is surreal to be on this trip and not post anything. It's like I'm in a dream."

Kyle nodded and regarded his hands. "When do I get to be your husband again? It seems like we're living separate lives in the dark web."

"Let's talk to Mary in Austria. I'll need Gary's help to resurrect my accounts to their former status." She smiled and held out her hand. "For now, you could be my secret lover."

23

WALLS WITHIN WALLS

Jake rubbed his shoulders and stretched as they stood on the sidewalk. "Where to?" He yawned.

Kyle chuckled and scanned their appearance. "I was overly ambitious with this itinerary. I don't think it's realistic to spend a day in each place and expect to sleep while we travel."

Casi rubbed her eyes. "The ferry is plausible. But the bus wasn't comfortable. I also need a shower. Are you planning to make us wash up in a fast-food restaurant again?"

"Oh, I could go for a hash brown." Jake grinned.

Kyle smoothed his map over the ledge of the stone wall. "This city is enchanted, and we should give it our full attention."

"I'm ready." Casi stood up straight and saluted him.

"I appreciate your loyalty." He gave her a kiss. "Which is why I called ahead and booked a hotel room. I realized our budget is self-imposed and we're not high school kids with limited funds." He noted excitement in Casi's eyes. "Yes, it's a real hotel with showers and beds."

"I might cry." She fanned her eyes.

Jake kicked at the edge of the wall. "It seems like a waste of money."

"Well, you can sleep in the hall if you want to. I booked us a double room." Kyle waited for him to comprehend what that meant.

Jake shrugged. "I'm sure you want to be alone with Casi."

"We can make out in the shower. I just want to sleep in a real bed." Casi grinned and slipped her backpack over her shoulders. "Can we go now?"

"Yes. It's about three miles. Walk or bus?" Kyle asked.

"Let's walk. I don't want to wait for a bus and my butt is numb from riding on that last one." Casi strode ahead.

Jake smacked her on the behind. "Can you feel that?"

She frowned. "Yes, stop being a pervert."

He laughed and pulled her into a head lock as they walked, rubbing her hair into a severe style. "Wow, humidity and you don't mix."

She shoved him away. "I will smother you in your sleep."

"Remember, she has experience." Kyle chuckled and blanched when Casi froze. "I'm sorry. It seemed funny before I said it."

"I haven't come to terms with my killer status yet." Her lips curled into a smile. "So, you may want to watch yourself."

"I'm not afraid of you." Kyle swung her in his arms and twirled her around. "Wow, that's the old city!"

Casi's eyes widened. "Should we go there now?"

Kyle checked the time and scanned her appearance. "Let's check in and get cleaned up. The shops are open late, and we'll have tomorrow too."

She put a hand on her hip. "I noticed you looked at me first."

Kyle smiled. "Jake looks like crap too but it's less noticeable on him."

❧

Casi laced her fingers through Kyle's as they strolled to the old town. They posed for pictures at the stone walled entrance, highlighting the incredible architecture in the background. Casi halted at a storefront and peered through the window at sheep made from wool. "We should get that for your mom, it's adorable!"

Kyle led the way inside and perused the shelves. He turned and smiled when he noted the unusual food items. "Would it be alright if I bought a few things for Lauren?"

"You don't need to ask permission. She's your friend and would love to try these. Just make sure you buy some for us too." Casi patted his hand.

Jake held up an auburn bear with long fur. "Do you think Austin would like this? It's genuine alpaca."

"He's too young and would destroy it." Casi observed how gently he was stroking the fur. She reached over and smoothed her hand over the bear's head. "It's so soft. Why don't you get it and it can be a special toy that he can play with under supervision?"

Jake frowned at the price tag. "It's super expensive."

Kyle squeezed his shoulder. "Get the tan one for Austin and the black for Tommy. It's better than bringing back t-shirts they'll outgrow."

They continued winding their way through the cobblestone streets, stopping to taste marzipan and chocolates. They settled in a booth at a restaurant decorated with reclaimed wood and antiques. Kyle slid out from the bench and walked toward the back, taking an impromptu tour. He struck up a conversation with the chef who welcomed him into the expansive kitchen. He came back twenty minutes later, shaking his head. "The one mistake I made with my house was putting in a generic kitchen. I wish I had the experience of travel before I committed to a style." He slumped in his seat and picked up the menu.

Casi shrugged. "Couldn't you remodel?"

"You have zero idea what that entails." Jake kicked her foot under the table. She kicked him back and pointed a thumb to Kyle's sullen appearance. He inhaled and narrowed his eyes at her. "With our experience, it wouldn't take long to change out the cabinets and countertops. What would you prefer?"

Kyle sighed. "It would be a waste. I bought everything high-end, and we spent a lot of time on those cabinets." He surveyed the unique color variations of the wood of the cabinet across from them. "I love the character of this place. This would be perfect."

"If you want to do it, I will help you. I'll take anything you don't need and put it at my place. It would be awesome to have it." Jake smiled.

Kyle looked up. "Really? That's a great solution." He closed his menu. "I'll try the rabbit burger. It sounds delicious."

"Yuck!" Casi shivered. "That's horrible."

"It's no different than a chicken," Jake said.

"They're cute and fluffy." Casi crossed her arms over her chest. "They were your childhood friends. My, how time has hardened your heart."

Jake rolled his eyes. "Fine, I'll have the venison."

Kyle yawned and pulled his t-shirt off. "I guess we should go to bed early. I would like to see the rest of the old city in the morning and find the cheese shop the chef told us about. We'll take the late afternoon flight to Berlin." He wrinkled his nose as he sniffed his shirt. "We need to find a laundromat."

Jake scanned Casi, smiling at Kyle as he continued to undress. He picked up his key and shrugged. "I'm not tired yet, and I noticed a bar down the street with a lot of hot Scandinavian chicks. I'm going to head out for a bit."

Kyle regarded his clothes in a heap. "Do you want us to go with you?"

"I'm sure you can entertain yourselves." He gave them a wink as he left.

"We're all alone..." Kyle began as Casi flew into his arms. "I like where this is headed. Shall we take it to the shower?" He walked her backward to the bathroom, peeling off her clothing on the way. His mouth claimed hers as he reached in the stall and adjusted the water temperature. He brought his hands to cup her face. "I love you so much. It kills me to imagine the danger you were in."

Her eyes welled. "Can you forgive me for what I did?" Her hands trembled as she smoothed them over his chest. "I'm so afraid of losing you. My life became whole when we found each other."

"You'll never lose me." He pressed his forehead to hers. "You don't need to be forgiven, and it has not changed my feelings for you." He stepped over the threshold and held out his hand. "Our marriage cannot be tarnished by jealousy and hate from others. Our bond is sacred." He ran his tongue over her collarbone. "And eternal."

She she wrapped her leg around his waist. She clung to him as the passion intensified and she cried out for more. Her body shook with the release of stifled emotions and the pleasure he coaxed from her. "Don't stop," she breathed, wanting the moment to last forever.

After what seemed like hours, he shuddered against her, locking his lips to hers to capture her moans. He smiled and lathered the soap. "We should bathe before this water runs cold."

She shivered. "It's already chilly."

Casi's eyes lit up when she noted the blow dryer on the counter. "This is heaven." She locked eyes with Kyle in the mirror. "I've loved every minute of this trip. The monumental hikes, discovering sites, using every mode of transportation, and trying new foods." Tears welled, and she blinked them away. "I was terrified after what happened and sickened by what I learned. You're my superhero and you always make me feel safe. I love you with all my heart and I'm disgusted by how I pushed you away." Her gaze traveled to the blood-spattered bandage on his arm. "I hate that I hurt you."

He stepped behind her and wrapped her in a warm embrace. "My arm will heal, and it was caused by my own ignorance. This trip has been amazing and I'm looking forward to the next leg of this epic adventure."

Jake opened the door and surveyed Kyle reclined on the bed. "Where's our girl? Did she get bored with you and head out on the town?"

Kyle shifted his gaze to the bathroom. "She's been in there awhile. I think she's doing her hair, although I heard a lot of water running."

Jake knocked on the door and Casi opened it with a smile. He glanced past her and grinned. "Did you start a laundry service?"

She laughed and slid past him to scamper on the bed beside Kyle. "I took advantage of having a tub and washed all our clothes."

"Oh?" Kyle cocked his head. "Will they be dry by morning?"

Jake shrugged and undressed. "I might as well wash these. Either everything will be dry, or we go naked as a team."

Kyle winced as he felt the clothes hanging from the shower curtain rod. "Still pretty damp. I don't think the humidity in these countries is helping."

"I'm sorry. I assumed it was a smart thing to do." Casi slumped on the bed and regarded the clock. "Could we blow dry them?"

Kyle turned to the clang of a cart in the hallway and bolted out the door. He returned with a broad smile. "I asked the maid if we could sneak our clothes in the hotel dryer, and she agreed. That's one way to ensure a tip." He grinned and gathered their clothing.

Jake chuckled. "Make sure you give her more than just the tip, we want to ensure our clothes are good and dry."

Kyle rolled his eyes and dashed to the hall, clad only in pajama bottoms. Casi turned to Jake and smiled. "He has no idea how handsome he is and the effect he has on women."

"He never did." Jake shrugged. "Even as a baby, he had a magnetic quality. It's more than his dashing good looks though, he has a pure soul that promises redemption just from being in his presence." He patted her knee. "Look what he did for you."

She clasped his hand. "Thank you for taking care of us. I put you in a terrible position and hurt your brother."

"The scratches and cut will heal." He put his arm around her. "Don't push him away. You two are connected, and it's counterproductive to run around fighting demons on your own."

§

"Where did you get that dress?" Jake frowned at the platinum sheath barely containing his sister-in-law as she stepped out of the Burger King.

"I bought it yesterday at one of the shops when you guys went to use the bathroom." She smiled and took the drink he was holding. "Let's go check out the nightclub."

Kyle shrugged and took her hand, leading them to the alley. "We can spend a few hours here, but then we need to head to the train station."

Jake surveyed the area. "This place is surreal. Witnessing the devastation of the holocaust and actually touching the rubble of the Berlin wall were beyond my expectations of what we would experience on this trip."

Casi kicked at a rock with her shoe. "You're being a downer."

"Sorry, I forgot your highlights were getting a beer and a pretzel in Germany." Jake poked her.

"Actually, the pretzel was dry." Casi exhaled. "I understand the atrocities that took place. It was incredible to put some of Grady's ashes at the wall and Check Point Charlie." She tilted her head toward the sound of the disco music. "It's important to let go. It doesn't make the evil nonexistent, but I believe in redemption and living in the moment." She paused at the door. "It's like Grady's death. We can't wallow in what happened. He becomes immortal because we acknowledge the tragedy and allow ourselves to love again. We can either build walls to isolate ourselves in misery or tear them down and be brave enough to carry on."

Jake kissed her temple. "Your compassion and love are endless." He grasped her hand. "I'll never let anyone destroy that."

§

Casi laughed as she stumbled to the street. "I haven't heard those songs since the '80's, on my dad's cassette player. That was awesome!"

"Hey, pretty lady. Want to come play with us?" A dark shadow emerged from the alleyway.

"Jake!" Casi whirled around to get his attention.

"Back off!" Jake barreled from behind and launched himself toward the voices. A crash of a bottle thundered through the night as it shattered against his skull.

Kyle pushed Casi back to the door. "Go inside, now!" He ran toward his brother as several men tackled him, kicking and punching at the wild man in their clutches.

Casi banged at the locked door. "Help!" She watched as Jake was overpowered and Kyle flew at the mob, fists swinging. She flung off her shoes and crept along the wall. She noted one end of the alley was barricaded and the only way out was through the mass. Her nostrils flared as Jake was forced to his knees and kicked in the face. When the man reached for his money belt, Jake bucked his head forward, shattering the man's nose. She focused on the placement of the group, imagining it was like a video game and sourced the weaknesses. With a swift swing, she struck the assailant holding Kyle's arms in the temple with the heel of her shoe. He staggered back and Kyle reached in his pocket to withdraw his knife. With a flick of his wrist, he sliced the man's forehead, forcing him to cover his face in pain. He crumpled to the ground as the flow of blood blinded him. Kyle drew the blade over the wrist of the man restraining his brother and Jake jumped to his feet, quickly extracting his own knife. Kyle grabbed Casi's hand and yanked her toward the exit. "Run!" He glanced back, assessing the men were only temporarily disabled.

After several blocks, they made it to the luggage storage by the train station. Kyle slammed the locker shut and pulled on his backpack, thrusting Casi's in her arms as he stormed away. She ran after him, crying out as the gravel tore through the flesh of her bare feet. Kyle stopped and glanced back, exhaling as he turned around and knelt beside her. She reached out and wound her arms around his neck. "I'm sorry! Are you angry because I wore this dress? I wanted to have fun at the club. I didn't mean to make us targets for those thugs."

Kyle sat back on his heels and rocked her in his arms. "I'm not upset about your outfit. The shoes made a good weapon. They would have come after us no matter what you wore. They intended to rob us, and I can only imagine what they had in mind for you once they disabled us." He gave her a sad smile. "You called Jake to rescue you. Is it because you don't think I can protect you?"

"Damn, I had a hard time fighting those guys." Jake spat. "They kept multiplying."

Casi shook her head. "I yelled for him because he was behind me. You were paying the bar tab." She smoothed her palm over his cheek. "I knew you wouldn't give it a second thought to join in."

Kyle sighed. "I feel like I fail you so often."

Jake squeezed his shoulder. "Obviously, we do best as a team. Even the monkey did her part to protect us." He knelt and unzipped Casi's backpack. "I would like to suggest you change for the trip though. That dress is outrageously hot, but it might be best if we get out of Germany without unwanted attention."

A whistle blew and Kyle put his hand over Jake's. "Let's get on the train. We have a private compartment. We need to get cleaned up and we could all benefit from a cocktail."

Casi stood and took Kyle's hand. "I'm ready for pajamas and my fluffy pink socks."

He leaned over and kissed her. "You'll still be unbelievably gorgeous."

The attendant glanced over their bloodied faces, torn clothing, and Casi's bare feet. He shook his head and waved them on board without a word.

24

UNRAVELLED

Mary paced the platform, grinning as the train approached. "Oh my, you look like you require a decent meal. And a bath." She hugged each of them, hesitant to let Casi go. She frowned at the bruises on the brothers' faces. "Were you mugged?"

"They tried." Jake shrugged. "They got a beating, including a high heel to the face from this one." He slid his arm around Casi's shoulders.

Mary shivered. "Did you enjoy Scandinavia?"

"We loved it, especially Tallinn. Did you know it existed?" Casi climbed in the back seat of the car.

Mary laughed. "Yes, I've been there. It's enchanted." She drove to the top of a winding road and parked. They viewed the mountains and pastures with sheep grazing and wildflowers in bloom.

"How did you live in LA so long?" Kyle asked. "This has similarities to Washington, so I can see the appeal there at least."

"I was born there and stayed until I completed my goals." Mary smiled and led them to an expansive stone patio overlooking the valley. "My husband, Lars, is from Austria, which is why we maintain two homes."

Casi stopped in her tracks as a tall figure came toward her. "Daddy? Why are you here? Oh my God, what happened? Where's Ava?" She clasped her hands to her face as he hugged her.

Ava grabbed her arm and yanked her from her father's embrace. "You should have left it alone! You put everyone at risk."

"Stop!" Jack pushed between them. "You said we were surprising them because we won a vacation. I sense you have an ulterior motive."

"You are dense at times." Ava exhaled..

"I'm sorry." Casi began to cry and Kyle pulled her in his arms.

"I don't think you should be the one apologizing." He glared at Ava.

"There's no point trying to protect you anymore. I'm exhausted, and I've been betrayed for the last time." Ava threw her hands in the air with defeat.

Mary sighed. "I invited Ava here to talk to you about the journal. I'm sure it has caused… confusion."

"That's the understatement of the year." Kyle reclined in a chair and tucked Casi beside him protectively.

"What journal?" Jack asked.

"This one." Kyle tossed it on the table between them. "Who knew Sonya was such a prolific writer? It would have been nice to have some warning on what it contained." He pointed a finger at Ava. "You've been lying to her."

Mary sat beside Ava and patted her hand. "She didn't know about it." She eyed the heavy volume. "I can't believe you brought it to Europe!" Her eyes shifted to Ava's, and they shared a moment of silent reconnaissance.

Casi jumped up. "Stop hiding things. Why are you two conspiring against me? I'm not a special needs child who requires caregivers. I don't like you talking about me behind my back."

"The universe does not revolve around you." Ava glanced at Mary. "Our history began way before you were born."

"You were lovers?" Jake wiggled his eyebrows.

Ava shrieked with laughter. "Jesus, Jake! No, we're…"

"Sisters," Mary concluded.

"What?" Casi staggered back and cocked her head. "Really?"

Mary smiled at the shielded glances between their vastly different skin tones. "Same father, different mothers. My mother was from Nigeria and she was a model in LA. Our father saw fit to get her pregnant and run back to his upper-class family in Idaho. She struggled to raise me but was a rising star in the modeling world. She was fatally shot one night when we stopped to get milk from a convenience store on the way home from a casting. I was six when I entered foster care. My mother kept letters from my father, and I made it my mission to confront him when I was eighteen." She shifted her weight on the bench. "It's funny how people misuse the word 'abandoned' when they have no idea what it truly feels like."

Ava slipped her hand over Mary's. "Twelve years later, she showed up at our house and read him the riot act. He lied, of course, and said she was mistaken. The letters told a different story where he stated he couldn't leave his sick wife but would eventually send for her. My mother was never ill, and he had no intention of leaving."

"I said my piece and left." Mary smiled at Ava. "This scrawny little white girl came running after me down the street begging for the whole story." She squeezed Ava's hand. "She had the most unusual eyes, and I was intrigued by her determination."

"I couldn't believe I had a sister. I was sixteen and she seemed worldly, fired up about how successful she would be and didn't require anyone to take care of her." Ava grinned. "I was enamored by this exotic creature."

"I finally gave her my address and told her she could write, but not to get her hopes up because I was a woman with a goal and had no time for a long-lost sibling. She was relentless with letters, and I would occasionally write back. I liked to impress her with my accomplishments. I put myself through college and was working as an intern for one of the fashion houses." Mary straightened her shoulders. "I remembered being with my mother and the energy in the chaos. As I got older, I saw a lot of her in some of the scared young women trying to find success in that world. It was important they had someone to depend on with the multitude of false promises."

Kyle surveyed the women. "Why would you keep your relationship hidden? You're both successful women."

"It was my choice," Mary stated. "We kept in touch, but we hadn't grown up together. I didn't want to explain to strangers why I had a white sister. They would always assume I was adopted or the product of an affair."

Ava sighed. "We had a DNA test and we're blood related. My father eventually admitted the truth to me, including how in love he had been with Mary's mother. He felt trapped by our social standing and pressures of raising a family." She regarded Jack. "I was determined to not be like him; I would love who I wanted regardless of society's expectations."

Mary nodded. "We became close when she attended UCLA."

Ava laughed. "Which my father only allowed once I agreed to be a debutante. My mother was livid when I moved away, or as she would say, threw my life away."

Jack set his jaw. "Why didn't I know she was your sister? What else are you hiding? I'm beginning to question this head injury you claim I have, or is it more accurate that you're a pathological liar!"

Mary threw her head back and laughed. "Get off your high horse, Jack. You have put Ava through hell, and with all the bullshit we had to cover up over the years, having a secret sister has come in handy."

Ava giggled. "It has been a wild ride."

Casi studied Ava's slumped shoulders, "What happened in the video that you didn't want me to see at Christmas?"

Ava exhaled. "It was Jamie."

"I imagine it was difficult to see him," Kyle said.

"Actually, it was lovely. I was caught up in the magic of that time and almost missed it." Ava cringed.

"What?" Casi asked.

"He called you Sofia." Ava broke into tears. "He was singing, Sofia sunshine, this little girl of mine, when he put you in my arms."

"Am I your daughter?" Casi gasped.

"You're not making sense!" Jack's cheeks burned with rage. "I know my own child."

"Of course." Ava bit her lip. "You just don't remember her name."

"I assume you've read the journal?" Mary turned to Kyle.

"What is in this thing?" Jack grabbed the book and flipped through it as papers littered the patio. He snatched a photo and his face paled as he turned to Casi with tears in his eyes. "Why?"

Casi gathered the rest of the pictures and dumped them in his lap. "It's not me! It's the woman I believed to be my mother, being raped and murdered."

Ava bolted forward and captured her in loving arms. "She was your mother. That part is true. This escalated faster than we could control it. You must understand we wouldn't have allowed that to happen to her."

Kyle slid the book from Jack's lap. "It's too disturbing to read. It basically documents Sonya's upbringing in a cult and their infiltration through positions of power. It's the ranting of an unstable woman." He gazed at Casi. "And her vicious attack on her daughter."

Casi wiped her face with the back of her hand. "Dad did you realize she had a child when she was thirteen?"

Jack cocked his head. "That's not true."

"Sebastian," Ava confirmed. "She loved him. Without realizing it, you did the exact thing she would have wanted for her burial. She spent hours on the rocky point writing in her journal and gazing out to sea. She said she pretended the buoy was him, waiting for her to come and play in the water. She wanted nothing more than to be with him." She took Jack's hand. "She drowned him when he was three on orders of the cult because he was brain damaged at birth." She followed his eyes to Casi and nodded. "Yes, she was trying to drown her too, because she wasn't Sebastian."

"Sonya had deep regrets about leaving the compound." Mary smiled at Jack. "She was only seventeen when you married her and had no idea how to live in the outside world."

"She was twenty-one. I saw her paperwork when I hired her as a hostess." Jack frowned when Ava shook her head.

"She needed a job." Mary shrugged. "The only skill she possessed was how to please a man in bed. Six months of being a prostitute on the streets of Vancouver was risky. She traded favors for a license with a new birthdate to increase her odds of getting a stable job."

"She was a terrible driver," Jack noted.

"She taught herself," Ava said. "Once she had the ID, few people looked beyond her great figure to validate anything on her resume."

"It was a hostess job, there weren't a lot of skills required." Jack blushed. "So, I married an underage girl?"

"Who was already married," Mary pointed out. "She aborted the first baby with you because it was a girl."

"Was that because she wanted a boy or for fear the cult would claim the child?" Kyle asked.

Mary smiled. "You were thorough in your reading."

"It was difficult to stomach and poorly written," he assessed.

"She was obsessed with bringing Sebastian back." Ava inhaled sharply. "I persuaded her to keep Casi. I was convinced she would love her once she held her and it would mend her broken heart. I didn't know gender was important." Her eyes turned to steel grey. "I wasn't aware she would be able to bargain for her return to the cult by offering a female child as collateral."

Kyle cocked his head. "It said the community is inbred with what they believe to be superior qualities. The women are kept inside with the sole purpose of breeding and the men integrate into society in key positions, returning their wealth to the cult. Any children born outside of the religion are deemed unworthy."

"Sonya struggled with living in a world where women could accomplish as much as men. She was threatened by Jack's attachment to Casi and was terrified of what her future held. She made a deal with Simone to return to the compound if she sacrificed her daughter on her third birthday." Ava locked eyes with Jack. "You told her you wanted a divorce. We were taking Casi, or Sofia, with us to open a restaurant in Bellingham."

"I don't remember." Jack rubbed his temple.

"The compound prepared a ceremony to cleanse Sonya of her

sins. At her age she would have been considered a low-level member, but she was honored at the opportunity to go back. The scouts were directed to pick up Sofia at the park. She had a red balloon tied to her wrist."

"She told you all this?" Kyle asked.

"I intercepted a letter she received from Simone. We used my post office box because Sonya didn't have her own…" She regarded her hands and sighed. "She could be childlike at times, unable to do the simplest of tasks. I thought I was helping her to keep in contact with her family." She looked up. "I had struggled with my own family relationships and we had become close. She had begun acting strange, nervous and paranoid. I read the letter and realized what her plan was." She shuddered. "She was elated at the prospect of returning. I figured we would get ahead of the scouts and grab Sofia. Sonya had already left with Simone." She bent over in pain. "We had the accident, and it was a race against time after that." She angrily swiped tears from her face. "I never had a chance to mourn! My priority was your safety."

"I'm sorry." Casi pushed between her and Mary and wrapped her arms around her. "Is that why you changed my name?"

"You did." Ava laughed through her tears. "Jamie loved the name Cassidy and chose it for our daughter. He would play with you and rattle on about Butch Cassidy and the Sundance Kid. He was always making up rhymes and songs. He was very animated. When we were taken to the hospital, you got confused because we rarely addressed you by your own name. You used to sing to the baby, and I guess it appealed to you, so you gave the nurse that name." She brushed hair from Casi's face. "I almost had a heart attack when they brought you to me and called you Cassidy. You also claimed I was your mother. I saw the opportunity and wrote Sofia Roberts on the death certificate. I took you back to the apartment and your mother had returned. She was hysterical when she realized you hadn't gone with the scouts. I gave her the choice to get back together with Jack if she agreed with the story and your new identity. She sent the death certificate to the cult, with an edit of the birthdate. I took you to Vancouver and had a new birth certificate issued."

"How?" Casi asked.

"When I was in foster care, I lived in some horrible homes." Mary rolled her eyes. "As a teen I moved in with the most incredible family. They taught me how to be a strong woman and I became very close with the daughter, Mildred. She was an international model and was completely stunning on the runway. She's a force to be reckoned with and runs an empire, with some activities that are underground." She winked. "I contacted her to issue new documents."

Casi frowned at her father. "Dad, you weren't suspicious of a sudden name change? Your wife and daughter were missing, and your brother was dead. You never questioned anything?"

"I was in a coma." Jack swallowed.

Ava regarded Mary. "We knew his mental state was delicate. I brought you to him before we left and called you Cassidy, ensuring you responded. When he asked about Sofia, I cried and insisted he stop asking about the baby. He was confused, but we made him believe his memory had gotten altered in the accident."

Kyle suppressed a laugh. "You two are devious! Did you bribe Casi with treats to listen to commands?"

Mary smiled. "We gave her chocolates as rewards."

Casi shivered. "I feel completely violated."

"You? They brainwashed me." Jack looked at them with distrust.

Ava shrugged. "It all happened according to plan until Sonya became pregnant with a son."

"She named him Sebastian," Jack cringed.

"She thought he was returning to her. When she lost the baby, something inside her broke forever." Ava glared at Jack. "I warned you she was unbalanced."

"You should have told me the truth," he accused.

"I couldn't!" Ava sobbed. "When I came back Sonya threatened to take Casi to the commune. She was still of value until fourteen. I had to wait and keep her safe from the sidelines."

Kyle sat forward. "Casi would have been given to the elders as a mistress because she wouldn't have qualified as a wife. They would have sacrificed her on her fourteenth birthday because she was too old."

"That's disgusting!" Jack roared.

"You read all that in the journal?" Casi asked. "I stopped after she droned on about how much she hated me, and I was confused by the conspiracies and rituals."

"I read every word. It's a horrible religion and your mother was a monster," Kyle seethed.

Ava patted Kyle's hand. "It's what she grew up with. She didn't know how to be a mother." She clucked her tongue. "You couldn't even call her mum, it wasn't allowed, only mother, and eventually mom in LA." She rubbed Casi's shoulder. "After you turned fourteen, I relaxed." She smiled at Jack. "Which is why I encouraged you to leave your marriage. The threat of taking Casi away was gone." Her eyes hardened. "But she couldn't let me have that. She destroyed what we had to prove she had control."

Jack winced. "I was a pawn in her game, apparently."

Mary scoffed, "Oh please, my heart breaks for you."

Jake snickered, "Jack is lied to, manipulated by women, and confused by his offspring. Sounds like my life. How does this involve the guy in LA?"

Ava gazed out at the fields. "You were never supposed to go in the compound, only deliver the ashes and leave. You had dropped off the map. You evolved from Sofia to Cassidy to Casi and changed Roberts to Jensen. The trail was cold."

"Until?" Casi winced

"You received the check for the Sand and Surf payout, made to Casi Roberts. It was sent to your work address. Simone figured out who you were and probably sent someone to track you in LA. They used Cassidy to scare you and send a sign that they knew you." Ava twisted her fingers together. "I let my guard down after your mother died." Tears rolled down her cheeks. "It's my fault they killed her."

"Why?" Casi's bottom lip trembled.

"When you moved to LA, I still watched out for you. I urged you to make it on your own without our assistance, not to be cruel, but I believed it was the final step in removing any trace of you from their radar. It was excruciating for me to not be a part of your life."

"You were there." Mary turned to Casi. "She sent money and helped with all the decisions for your future. She wanted you to get your degree, and we planned the business together and ensured you acquired the skills. She has always looked out for you." She smiled. "Do you know what Macrae skincare stands for?"

"You said it was a family name," Casi offered.

"Yes, our maiden names. Mary Achike, Casi Roberts, Ava Easton."

"It's a code!" Casi clapped. "I'm honored to be included."

"Safely tucked between us." Mary patted her hand.

Ava sighed. "After Sonya seduced Jack again, I told her she was on her own. I would no longer protect her from the multitude of ignorant choices she insisted on making. My only request was she let you live your life."

"Without guidance, she became negligent with negotiations," Kyle concluded. "She spoke to the wrong people."

"Yes. I told her to burn the damn journal, but she was convinced it was valuable. She sent it to you before she died," Ava stated.

"Did she realize they were coming for her?" Casi gulped.

"She thought she had a business deal. She assumed the journal was protected and she convinced them to pay her. It was undercover members of the cult who arrived. They didn't believe it existed and tortured her as a punishment for threatening to disclose their actions and locations."

"There's more than one?" Jake asked.

"They're all over the world. Sonya was correct that it's a conspiracy." Ava swallowed. "They lured you to LA to see if the journal was real, and to find out if you were Sonya's daughter. They intended to kill you."

"God dammit! Why didn't you protect her?" Kyle jumped to his feet.

"She moved faster than we could get a plan in place!" Mary grabbed his arm. "I didn't know what was in the package. We were unaware Sonya had been murdered. The death certificate said she overdosed."

Kyle clenched his jaw. "Was Simone behind this?"

"She informed them Casi was alive and working out of LA. A satellite team arranged for contact and used a low-level associate to do their dirty work." Mary sighed. "Your mother was not a priority to them. They threw her to the wolves to satisfy Simone's request."

"She wanted her sister dead?" Casi asked.

Mary put her hand on Casi's. "Simone was jealous Sonya lived outside the community. That festered when she met you and Kyle. She didn't realize you had a troubled relationship with your mother, and she saw how distraught you were and willing to risk your life to honor her in death."

"I wanted to do the right thing." Casi wiped a tear.

"You did. She's exactly where she wanted to be. I'm sorry I was unaware Simone would target you." Ava sighed. "She's five years younger than Sonya. After she ran away, Simone had to take her place with the husband she abandoned. She has not had an easy life."

"I'm going back there to punch her in the face!" Casi threatened.

Ava laughed. "Even if I thought you were able to remember the directions, it would be a wasted trip."

Kyle chuckled at her insinuation. "Why?"

"I've already been there and put her in the hospital. Your mother and I had a falling out, but I continued to protect her. She didn't deserve to be hurt, and when they came after you, I wouldn't tolerate it. I called child protective services and reported the abuse to have the children removed. I burned that horrific place to the ground." Ava spat.

"And caused a small forest fire in the process." Mary laughed. "Which luckily was contained."

"That was unintentional." Ava blushed.

"What do we need to fix in LA?" Jake asked.

"Already handled." Mary nodded. "Alix called me while he waited outside the building. I explained to Mildred it was an emergency, and she saw you pull the fire alarm before you left. She ensured he was found dead."

"I killed him," Casi mumbled.

"Sadly, he was smoking in bed and caught himself on fire. It was tragic they couldn't get to him in time. You rendered him unconscious, but our team finalized it. Nothing was retrieved from his apartment. All his files and computers were destroyed."

"Handy to have a friend like Millie," Jake said. "She sounds bad-ass, when can I meet her?"

"One day," Mary said.

"Is Casi completely safe?" Kyle held his breath.

"Simone revealed her location in BC and put the entire community at risk. An informant reported the journal was a hoax, and they only had the name Cassidy Roberts, who no longer exists. The leaders are too busy protecting much bigger fish to concern themselves with a lost descendant of a low-level commune." Mary smiled. "You are safe."

25
<hr>

AFFAIRS OF THE HEART

"Stop pacing, you're driving me crazy," Ava snapped, making Jack halt in his tracks on the bedroom carpet.

"I'm sorry to annoy you. I'll try to process everything I learned in a civilized manner." Jack glared at her.

Ava gave him a meek smile. "I never intended to be dishonest. I weighed the outcome each time and opted for the best choice."

"Like lying to me about my daughter?"

"Only her name. Everything was to protect her."

"Why didn't you tell me from the beginning? Obviously, I would put Casi... or Sofia's safety first."

"Above everything else, blindly and foolishly as a devoted father would."

"Why must I defend my love for her? Are you jealous of a child?"

"She's a thirty-three-year-old woman," Ava corrected. "I have never been jealous of her, but continually let down by your choices."

"That's not fair." Jack ran his hand through his hair.

"I love you, but it exhausts me to defend my actions and bolster you up, both of you."

He sat beside her on the bed. "What if we put the past to rest? No more excuses or questions. Everything is on the table?"

She twisted her hands together. "It is."

"You throw out my indiscretions with Sonya, but you omitted your retaliatory affair with Craig."

"From my band?" Ava blushed. "How did you find out?"

"You came home crying uncontrollably and wouldn't let me near you. I destroyed your trust. You wanted to leave me, but we have too much invested in the restaurant. An affair evened the score." He stroked her cheek. "You wanted me to be aware, to punish me."

"Craig has been a close friend over the years, and he understood what I required. It didn't make me feel better, only weak and hopeless."

"Thank you for not calling it quits on our marriage."

Ava bit her lip. "The worst part was everyone found out. What kind of a woman stays with a cheating husband?"

"One who recognizes he's better than his flaws?"

"I've been so crazy in love with you literally since the day we met. I should have my head examined."

"I've loved you just as long. It's been a difficult journey at times, but we were meant to be together." He smoothed his hand down her back. "Remember how Jamie encouraged us?"

"He walked in when you were comforting me when I was having contractions. He freaked out about being a father and wanted you to take his place." She smiled. "He said I already carried the last name so when we arrived in Bellingham, we could claim I was married to you."

Jack nodded. "He promised us two years at the restaurant to build a name, and then he wanted to head out to see the world. I hoped he would fall in love with the baby and change his mind."

"I wish he had gotten the chance." Ava swiped a tear away.

"I do too." He kissed the top of her head. "We lost so much." He tilted her chin up to make her look at him. "Thank you for your sacrifices to ensure Casi's safety. I wouldn't have her without you. I'm eternally grateful."

"Look at you bright and clean," Kyle smiled when Casi padded out to the terrace.

"I feel amazing. I was told there was wine out here, but was that a rouse to pry me from the tub?" She glanced around the patio.

"Lars is expected home shortly." Mary produced a bottle and glasses. "I prefer to keep some of our history private. He has a difficult job and I don't burden him with details outside of our home."

"Can you be specific?" Kyle asked. "We unloaded a boatload of issues."

"He knows Ava is my sister because we were together in Germany at a Christmas fair when I met him. I've told him she married Casi's father, and he understands I'm very attached to her step-daughter and she's an integral part of our company."

"No talk of Sonya, LA, or conspiracies," Kyle confirmed.

Mary surveyed the meadow stretching toward the mountains, bursting with wildflowers. "My life here is simple. No drama or Hollywood bullshit. In fact, that was my motivation for moving to Seattle. I'm close to the people I love and live in a beautiful environment."

"Like how we are at the lake." Casi shivered. "Until this stupid journal intruded on our lives. Should we give it to the police?"

"I doubt there is enough evidence of criminal activity." Kyle eyed the thick book. "Even with child protective services involved, this does not provide solid ammunition." His sapphire eyes pleaded with Ava's. "Can we destroy it? I want this nightmare over."

"Yes!" Jack poured the wine. "Let's put the past behind us and separate ourselves from this cluster-fuck. No good will come from revisiting the trauma. Sonya made her choices and we make ours. We won't stop the cult and I can't have my family at risk."

"I agree." Ava rose as a portly man with glasses arrived. "Lars."

Mary smiled, quietly tossing the journal in the stone fireplace, and nodded to Kyle. He knelt on the terrace and built a fire, watching the flames lick the edges of the pages before it ignited.

"Are you chilly?" Lars regarded the scene.

"No Darling, we wanted to get rid of trash weighing them down on their journey. It's of a sensitive nature, so we decided it was best to burn it." Mary made the introductions, seamlessly moving away from talk of the journal.

"This is your golden girl?" Lars embraced Casi. "I hear wonderful things about you. I hope you will visit the manufacturing plant. You have many admirers."

Mary nodded. "We're planning to come tomorrow, after spending the morning at the spa and then lunch. The men will entertain themselves in town." She smiled. "I'm sure Kyle has researched sites he would like to visit."

"Have you become injured?" Lars observed Kyle's tattered bandage and scanned his bruised face.

"This is nothing." Kyle brushed a hand over his cheek. "My stitches are giving me trouble. I've replaced the bandage several times, but I ran out of gauze and it got messed up after an alley fight in Berlin."

"Well, let's take a peek." Lars directed him to the table.

Mary laughed at Kyle's concerned expression. "Lars is a doctor."

Lars clucked his tongue when he peeled back the gauze. "Darling, fetch my kit. We should remove the stitches and prepare a new bandage. I'll give you supplies to take on your journey."

Kyle regarded the blotchy, swollen area. "I was supposed to get the stitches out, but we've extended our trip."

"We'll fix you up good as new," Lars promised.

Mary returned with a black bag and he withdrew a set of tools, working methodically after sterilizing his arm. Kyle watched intently, posing questions and investigating more of Lars' background in microphysics. "He's in heaven." Jake smiled at his brother.

"I figured they would get along." Mary beamed.

Kyle glanced over at Ava. "Since we have you here unexpectedly, can we discuss which areas of Italy would be the most beneficial? My itinerary is flawed due to inaccuracies in transportation and lodging."

"What? The hostel was awesome!" Jake chuckled.

"I would be happy to call and make provisions for you." Ava smiled.

"Why don't you join us?" Casi slid beside her. "You know the area and Kyle could maximize his time."

"Oh, we should get back to the restaurant." Ava bit her lip.

"Why? We have stable employees and I'm sure Roxy can handle the bar." Jack smiled. "I'll make the reservations."

"Maybe Ava should do it," Casi giggled.

"I'm not inept." Jack rolled his eyes. "You think only Ava and Kyle can plan a vacation? I'm pretty swift on a computer."

"You really aren't." Casi nudged Ava. "We'll give you a test run."

"Put Ava with me, there'll be plenty of room." Jake winked.

"Not happening." Jack laughed. "Mary will you two join us?"

"Thank you but Lars has a medical convention he's speaking at this week. We've been to Italy numerous times and it would be ideal for you to be together as a family," Mary insisted.

"I'm so excited." Casi joined Kyle and wrapped her arms around his neck and whispered, "I'm sorry for all the crap I brought along. I promise it's behind me now." She glanced at his arm as Lars removed the stitches. "Yuck! That's horrific. You said it was a small cut."

"It appears worse because it's swollen," Kyle assured her.

Lars surveyed the couple. "This is a minor injury. In time the scar will be the only indication of a difficult time."

Kyle nodded, thankful for the reassurance. "This trip has been amazing! I've seen more than I ever thought I would, and it's a huge honor to fulfill the dreams Grady had. Your crap hasn't ruined the trip. It forced us to focus on what we value."

"And who." She laced her fingers through Kyle's. "If it hurts, you can squeeze my hand."

"Thank you. Seeing Europe with you and Jake has been incredible. Age has brought a different perspective and instead of being excited about cute girls and drinking in pubs, I'm engrossed in the history and culture."

"Plus, you are traveling with the prettiest girl," Lars added.

"Absolutely." Kyle squeezed her hand.

A fluttering photo caught Casi's attention, and she bent to retrieve it from the edge of the patio. A young version of her mother holding a small boy, smiling radiantly at the camera. She slid beside Ava. "I've never seen pictures from her youth. She said memories were a waste of time."

Ava smiled at the image. "She was only fifteen. Many horrible things happened after that. She lost her innocence long before we knew her and lived through a lot of pain."

"Did she ever look at me like that? I don't recall her holding me." She caught Ava's eye and sighed, "It doesn't matter. This girl is gone and the woman she turned into was a tragic shell." She ignited the photo in the embers. "I'm my own person and revisiting the past won't change the outcome."

"You are perfect the way you are," Ava said.

Jake nodded toward his brother. "Experiences and environment mold us, not our lineage. Who would have thought the forgotten baby of drug addicts would grow into an amazing man?"

"And you're both so handsome." Casi kissed his cheek. "Hey, speaking of kids and the boatload you've fathered, did you contact Anna?"

"Do the words bounce around inside your head and tumble out in a random order?" Jake shoved her. "Yes, she said we could meet in Bordeaux. I pretended to listen, but I'll require Kyle to make the actual plans."

Kyle nodded, still watching the removal of his stitches as he launched into a thorough explanation of Bordeaux's wine region in the south of France, including the history, and covering the culinary traditions before saying, "It will be an excellent experience."

26

CIAO CHOW

*J*ack answered the door and raised an eyebrow at Jake standing in the hallway wearing only a towel. "Are you lost?"

"Where the hell is the bathroom?" Jake peered over Jack's shoulder. "Is there one in your room?"

He glanced around. "Honey, where's our bathroom?"

"Down the hall." Ava pointed the way.

Jack opened a door. "What's in here then?"

"Our room," Jake stated. "Which is not a suite. It's two twin beds that sag in the middle. This place blows."

"Where's the bathroom?" Casi stepped through the connecting door.

"That's the question of the hour," Jake said.

"We have a sink for brushing your teeth," Kyle chuckled.

"I bet people piss in it," Jake said on his way down the hall with everyone in tow. They stopped in the doorway, surveying a toilet without a seat, under a shower head. "That's convenient." He removed his towel.

Kyle grimaced at the dingy stall. "The history here is cool, but I'm not hip on the shared facilities. You should wear shoes." He noted the thick mold in the grout.

"Too late." Jake stepped under the stream. He regarded his companions. "This is not a spectator sport. Close the door."

"Damn, is this the line?" a weary man called from the hallway.

"Yes, give us twenty minutes." Kyle removed his shirt.

"Back off," Jake warned.

"I'm getting prepared." Kyle stuck his head out the door. "Jack get towels and Ava can hold your place."

"Ava can join me," Jake smirked.

"You're done." Kyle shoved him aside.

Jack wove his way through the increasingly long line. "Jesus, this is insane. I grabbed these from your backpack." He handed towels and sandals through the gap in the door.

Kyle slipped on shoes and tossed their clothing in Jake's arms. "Casi hurry, it's lukewarm. Where's the soap?"

"I used shampoo." Jake pointed to a cake of soap growing hair. "You can use that if you want."

"Ugh, no." Kyle put his arm around Casi's waist as she stood on top of his feet. "Don't want to take a chance of making contact?"

Jake smiled as he caught Ava's eye, admiring his lean physique through the partially open door. "All this hiking is paying off, huh?"

She blushed and turned away. "It certainly is."

"Hurry up," someone called from the back of the line.

"I suggest you shower in tandem," Kyle advised Jack. "No hot water."

"Jake, guard the door." Jack shivered. Jake nodded and positioned himself outside, like a Greek god wrapped in a towel protecting the temple.

They laughed about the shower experience over dinner. Kyle insisted on ordering a selection of entrees, eager to try each one. Jack chose the wine and Ava and Casi picked desserts to share with a variety of coffee. "Ava, what's your opinion of my itinerary?" Kyle dipped his spoon in the tiramisu.

"Hey." Casi slid the dish away from him.

Kyle smiled. "I had to get a bite before you stole it."

She took a bite and smiled. "Correct, this one is all mine."

"I don't think so, Piggly-Wiggly." Jake reached over her.

Jack laughed, putting his arm around his daughter as Ava answered Kyle's question. "You've chosen the proper variety of cities to see the highlights of Northern Italy."

"Where else would be interesting?" Kyle asked enthusiastically.

"Well, we visited Venice, which was full of history although dirtier than I expected. Florence is certainly beautiful, but the accommodations are poor." Ava eyed Jack. "Someone failed to check the ratings."

"I love the proximity to the Duomo and major attractions." Kyle nodded. "We should insist on private bathrooms, though."

"May I suggest Tuscany?" Ava asked. "There's a villa for rent and it would put us in a central location. It's where my friend lives and he can arrange the food tour and perhaps a cooking class if that interests you."

"Fantastic!" Kyle's eyes lit up.

"Yay," Casi mimicked.

Jack laughed. "How about making salami in Genoa?"

"Oh, I love that!" Casi raved.

"Italy was never on my original itinerary with Grady. I based my interests on what Lauren suggested. She's knowledgeable about the area, but I'm glad you guys are here to give us more direction." Kyle caught Casi's eye roll and smiled. "Imagine the joy you'll get rubbing it in her face about all the great places you went to in her dream honeymoon location."

"Now there's a silver lining." Casi laughed.

Jake nudged Casi, noticing her eyelids flutter as she leaned against a tree, warming her face in the Tuscan sun. "Pay attention."

"Why? This is Kyle's thing, and my dad is totally into it. I enjoyed learning how to make fresh mozzarella, but the talking part is tedious." She yawned, observing everyone nodding eagerly as the lecturer spoke. She smiled and nudged Jake. "Ava's flirting with Lorenzo."

Jake snickered when Ava asked a question, tucking a strand of hair behind her ear, as Lorenzo leaned toward her in response. He turned to Casi suddenly, catching her off guard. "Beautiful girl, what intrigues you about Italian cuisine?"

Casi plastered a smile on her face as the group waited. "Perhaps the terroir and how it influences the outcome of a pungent fungus such as a truffle. Would you agree the earthy under-notes are richer in this area?"

Kyle's mouth dropped as Jack raised an eyebrow at her complex answer. Lorenzo was charmed by her expertise. "This is exactly the kind of contribution we need to stimulate a deep culinary conversation. Come taste these pates I've made and tell me what you think." He offered her a platter.

Casi perused the array of samples and gave Kyle a wink. He shook his head, seeing through her dedicated student façade. "That little sneaker! She stole Lauren's answer from our Italian tasting menu to score samples."

Jack grinned. "I told you she has a remarkable memory. She doesn't seem to pay attention, but somehow the information seeps in. She rarely studied in high school but pulled A's and B's."

"She's extremely bright," Ava agreed. "Men underestimate that."

"Are you jealous your boyfriend is flirting with her," Jake teased, putting an arm around her shoulders.

Ava glanced away momentarily. "No, he flirts with everyone. Lorenzo and I have known each other for years."

"Ah, the mysterious history of your European life."

"Jack is aware. Another dream not realized."

"The relationship?" Jake cocked his head.

"The child." Ava exhaled.

Jake kissed her on the cheek. "You would have been an amazing mother. There was a little girl who needed you then, and she still does."

"Thank you," she whispered.

Lorenzo sliced off long strips of prosciutto and placed it on top of a sliver of mushroom brie on crostini. He held it to Casi's mouth, encouraging her to try it. She smiled and took a bite, not bothered as he brushed the crumbs from her lips. He invited Ava to join them, preparing another combination with a truffle infused salami. Kyle frowned at Jack. "He's poaching our women."

"Yes, he is," Jack replied, waiting patiently for Lorenzo to hand samples back to them, not as carefully arranged.

When the tour concluded, Casi nudged Kyle to give Lorenzo a tip. "He was so informative, huh? I can see why you like these food lecture things."

Kyle chuckled. "You had a much different experience than we usually do."

"You didn't enjoy it?" she asked with disappointment.

"It was excellent. I'm pointing out the extra attention, which is not customary in a typical tour." He shook his head. "You don't even notice."

"You mean because I stole Lauren's boring speech and made it more heartfelt?" Her eyes twinkled with amusement.

"Your delivery was polished. I totally believed you knew what you were talking about." He gave her a kiss.

"I was hungry and figured it was the best way to finagle snacks."

"You know how to work it." He turned to shake hands with Lorenzo. "The tour was awesome, thanks for the valuable insight."

"Your wife is as intelligent as she is beautiful," Lorenzo replied.

"I can't argue with that." Kyle smiled.

Jack's jaw dropped as he saw Casi striding toward them, clad in the tiny dress she bought in Berlin. "Darling… aren't you cold?" he stuttered, as Ava suppressed a giggle.

"A little, but it's the only dress I have." She shrugged. "It took a bit of effort to get the blood off my shoes, but I don't think it's noticeable."

"I can see why you were mugged, with all your assets on display." Jack winced when she glared at him.

"Being the dad of a woman never gets easier." Jake grinned.

"I suggested she wear a sweatshirt," Kyle offered.

"We're going dancing, that would be dumb." Casi rolled her eyes.

"You look beautiful." Ava looped her arm through hers. "Europeans are a lot less uptight."

"They're like mother and daughter." Kyle watched them walking with arms linked, laughing as men turned to ogle and whistle.

"They are," Jack agreed. "I'm sorry Ava wasn't more a part of her life growing up. She would have been a wonderful mother."

"Casi needs her now. Things worked out the way they were supposed to," Kyle suggested.

Jack grasped his arm, noting a rack of pashminas. "What do you think?"

"Perfect. We'll appear thoughtful." Kyle grinned and approached the woman selling the scarves and pointed to Casi. "Which one for my wife?"

She considered the beautiful woman and selected a colorful wrap with fuchsia tones and gold thread. She held it out to him and took the money from Jack. Kyle casually walked behind Casi and placed it over her shoulders. "In case you're chilly. We thought it was prettier than a sweatshirt. Do you like it?"

Casi stopped and regarded the perplexed trio of men, eager for her opinion. "It's beautiful, thank you." She artfully arranged it to create a stylish wrap, ensuring she was well covered.

Ava smiled. "Men love to admire gorgeous women, but it throws them when their daughters grow into one. Dad still sees you as his little angel."

"Yes, I do." Jack opened the door to the restaurant. "Do you remember your seventh birthday?"

She grimaced. "Didn't Mom take me to dinner in Vancouver?"

"I had just moved back from Europe and was working in Burnaby. Your mother didn't like how much time we spent together and insisted on taking you out when your dad had to work," Ava said. "We used to spend hours on the phone commiserating about the accident." She turned to Casi. "You were in a mopey phase, tears one minute and hyper the next. Dad was in a twist about what to do. It probably stemmed from Mom's increasing drug use and we understand now there were things you didn't share with us."

Casi slumped in her seat. "I remember being lost. I didn't click with kids at school because I was embarrassed by Mom's antics and outrageous behavior and chose to keep to myself. What is the point of bringing this up?"

"I didn't intend to remind you of a bad time," Jack said. "Things weren't great for me either. The night of your birthday I had a double shift, and Mom insisted on taking you to an upscale restaurant in the city. I hoped it meant she was showing interest in you, finally. I got a call from the maître di, explaining a little girl had been sitting alone for several hours and the mother couldn't be located."

"Yup, she left me," Casi scoffed. "She did drugs with the busboy and took him home instead."

"Apparently." Jack winced. "I left work even after my manager threatened to fire me. You had fallen asleep at the table, so sweet and innocent. I picked you up and realized your dress barely covered your bum and I was furious your mother had taken you out like that. I paid the bill, which was all the money I had. Most of the tab was alcohol because you only ate a piece of cake. I drove straight to Burnaby to see Ava."

Ava giggled. "He was distraught about the dress! You were all legs, growing into your figure. The dress was much too small, and you weren't old enough to pull it off, like you are now."

Casi laughed. "That's what this outfit reminded you of? A tragic moment in my life when I was inappropriately dressed?"

"You were seven," Jack asserted. "I quit my job and moved us to Burnaby. Ava got me a position as a general manager at her restaurant and I told Mom she could come with us or go live her own life."

"Too bad she followed," Jake reasoned.

"She didn't know what else to do," Jack explained. "We discovered Casi was much brighter than we realized, and her previous school was too crowded for her to excel. In the new class, she instantly made friends and was at the top of her grade."

"That's when I met Dawn, Katie, and Joey," Casi said.

"Like moths to a flame," Jack chuckled. "They competed for your attention. You blossomed that year."

Ava patted her hand. "Shane's grandmother babysat you."

"Mrs. Dunham?" Casi shook her head. "Pieces of this puzzle are coming together. I stuffed all those memories down because I only remembered the bad things."

"It's time to let the positive ones shine through." Ava squeezed her hand.

Casi surveyed Kyle reclining against a boulder on the bluff, overlooking the port in Genoa. He was lost in thought, scribbling in a notebook. She noticed a range of emotions filter across his face, reflected in his deep blue eyes. "What are you writing?" She set a glass of wine beside him. "A letter to Libby?"

"I sent her a postcard from Austria. I'm making notes on the itinerary." He snapped the notebook closed.

"Like what? I figured it was written." She sat cross-legged on the grass.

Jake arrived with a plate of cheese and meats and placed it on the rock. "The food here has been my favorite so far," he reflected.

"Is that what you're writing about?" she pushed.

"It's just thoughts, Casi," Kyle stated. "It's not important."

She shrugged and gazed out at the sea. "My life is an open book, and even my mother's past is on display for everyone to judge and react to. You don't share your feelings, yet this journey was about helping you deal with what happened." She plucked blades of grass and twisted them together.

Kyle handed her the book. "It's basically a journal. It's not private, but it seems dumb to reflect on how I viewed things when I was eighteen. None of that is important now."

"I don't want to read it. I was curious why you were pensive."

Kyle flipped it open and ran his hand over a page. "When we were first planning this trip, I made a list of the sites and what our expectations were. I considered it interesting to compare the perception to the reality. It doesn't work anymore, because it's twenty years later, and Grady isn't here."

"Sure, it does," Jake asserted. "The algorithm is more complex. You have a different perspective, and it's intriguing to compare it to where you were at eighteen. Terrible shit happened, but this is still your first experience in Europe. Write it down."

Kyle grinned. "This is my list." He showed them the neatly detailed columns. "Red is mine and blue was Grady's." They read through them carefully, comparing Kyle's initial responses and how he felt after. "I tried to imagine how Grady would have reacted."

"I think you nailed it," Jake said, realizing the importance of the sites in each place. "Other than sleeping with chicks in each country, we've done it all. Maybe Casi can try out accents."

"No, I suck at that," she laughed. "But I'm willing to have sex in every country. We missed a few places, should we go back?"

Kyle blushed. "The list is literally where I wanted to sleep. It wasn't about sex. Remember, I hadn't had the college experience and had only been with a few girls. It intrigued me to sleep in different locales, such as in a castle."

"My innocent brother," Jake snickered. "Now you can start a new list; places I banged my hot wife."

"It's supposed to be a reflection, not a tally," Kyle asserted.

Casi slid closer. "Ok, we've slept in a hostel and castle. When did you spend the night in a field?"

Kyle sighed. "In Copenhagen, when we got in the fight. I slept on a bench, but it was in a park. I'm considering that to be a field."

"Dammit!" Casi covered her face. "You even turn my stupid shit into something positive. You are the best man on earth."

"You should remember that." Kyle kissed her. "The advantage of age is I'm more appreciative of things."

"Plus, you have money to stay in better places," Jake said.

"True, but I'm not ruling out the original ones." Kyle grinned. "Anyone up for finding a barn?"

❧

"Are you sure you don't want to come to France?" Casi looked between Jack and Ava.

Ava regarded Jack and smiled. "We loved spending time with you guys in these beautiful towns and experiencing Italy, but I've booked a bungalow in Capri. We want a few days together before heading back to the whirlwind of the restaurant."

Jack radiated love as he took Ava's hand. "It's our extremely overdue honeymoon."

"We're happy to take your souvenirs with us. I've already paid for check-in bags and we have plenty of room." Ava eyed their bulging backpacks.

"There's space for your scandalous dress," Jack offered.

Casi giggled. "We're off to the French Riviera, I might need it if we hit the town for some nightlife."

"Have fun." Jack hugged her. He turned to Kyle and extended his hand. "Thank you for keeping her safe. I'm grateful for such a fine son-in-law."

"My pleasure." Kyle shook his hand.

Ava took Casi aside to transfer items to her suitcase. "Are we good?"

"Better than good," Casi confirmed. "I love you and I appreciate everything you did to protect me, including sacrificing being with the man you truly loved for so long."

27

TOPLESS IN ST. TROPEZ

$\mathcal{K}$yle plastered a smile on his face, not wanting to let his disappointment show as they stood on a beach in Nice, France. "We could buy towels and find a spot over there?"

"By the bathrooms?" Jake sneered.

"It's crowded, huh?" Casi said, sensing Kyle was out of his element. "Let's take a quick swim and move to a better place. I stole towels from the hotel in Florence. I took them to wrap my treasures we bought, but now that I've transferred them to Ava's suitcase, we can use them."

"Casi! They'll charge us." Kyle winced.

"Nope, I stole them from the housekeeping cart. It was a crappy hotel that cost way too much money." She grinned.

Kyle shrugged. "True. The theft is justified."

"You better have three," Jake sulked. "You always forget me."

"I liberated four. You take half of my food and drink from my water bottle. It's hard to forget you're here." Casi poked him in the stomach.

"You're delaying my reunion with Anna for your own personal needs. The French Riviera was not on Kyle's original itinerary. He added it for you." Jake shook a towel. "That's selfish."

"You'll see her in two days. Come on let's go swimming." She stripped down to bikini bottoms.

Kyle shook his head. "When did you change?"

"She's always been a wild woman; no change," Jake joked.

"On the train. I wanted to be ready to hit the beach. Hurry up." Casi strolled to the water's edge.

"Join your half-naked wife. I'll take first watch on bags." Jake's jaw dropped as Kyle put on trunks in full view. "Have you no shame?"

"Nothing to be ashamed of." Kyle winked.

Kyle treaded water beside Casi and surveyed Jake, flexing his tattooed arms when a group of teenage boys came too close to their area. "That's why the enforcer picks the spot. He protects our territory."

"Has anyone ever challenged him?" Casi asked.

"Very few dared. He realized early on violence was an effective way to deal with his panic attacks. After juvenile hall, it became his defense mechanism to make people back down. His anxiety isn't weakness; that son-of-a-bitch is fearless."

"You're not scared of anything either. You don't act as tough as him, but I've never seen you afraid." Casi paddled out past the crowds.

"I don't worry about much." Kyle swam beside her. "Except losing you. That scares the shit out of me."

She wrapped her arms around his neck. "That will never happen. Sometimes I require distance, but I won't run too far away."

"As long as you come back." He kissed her as they bobbed in the waves.

They stretched out on towels to warm themselves, and Kyle smoothed a hand over Casi's stomach. "I should buy sunscreen, you're fairly pale still from the winter. Keep an eye on her while I go up to that shop. I don't want any of these guys taking pictures of her." Kyle nodded toward a group of tourists.

Jake moved closer to Casi, ensuring the men were aware they were being watched. They casually moved down the beach, finding other women to photograph. Kyle returned with sunscreen and a brochure. "Want to go to St. Tropez? There's a ferry that takes about two-and-a-half hours."

"Yes! When does it leave?" Casi bolted upright.

"We could head to the pier and get in line." Kyle surveyed her attire. "Would you mind covering up for the trip?"

"You don't want to see her boobs bouncing all over the place if the water gets rough?" Jake teased.

"That comes under the heading, 'for my eyes only'," Kyle said.

"Yes, it does." Casi put on her top with a shirt over. She stood and brushed sand off her legs, then secured the towel around her waist. "Better?"

"Still gorgeous, but well covered," Kyle praised.

"This is what I expected from the French Riviera." Casi twirled to view the expanse of turquoise water and a white sandy beach.

"You've never been here before?" Kyle asked.

"I was invited to come on a yacht, but Mary wouldn't let me. She felt it was important to distance myself from the pussy posse, as she put it."

"I'm sure those celebrities totally respect the bikini crew as intelligent young women," Jake asserted. "Until they bang them."

"Exactly," Casi said. "I heard enough stories from models about being wooed into the sack, then tossed out when the guy was done. Alix was just as bad. Like most celebrities, he had a woman at home and his pick of hussies on the road."

"You're my only woman." Kyle extended a hand to help her jump from the pier.

"You're my main one, but I have hussies on the side," Jake laughed. "Don't tell Anna I said that."

"I don't repeat anything that would get you kicked in the balls." Casi quickly disrobed to dive in the water.

"She's too comfortable in that state of undress." Jake shook his head.

"She's a beach girl," Kyle agreed.

Jake arranged the towels, pleased with their improved location. "Maybe we should camp out here instead of going back tonight. I'll bet hotels are super expensive."

"It's gorgeous," Kyle said. "I'm unsure if it's safe to camp on a beach."

"Don't worry, you have your big brother to protect you." Jake grinned.

"True." Kyle slapped him on the back as he stood. "Who's that guy talking to Casi? He seems familiar with her."

Jake narrowed his eyes as a paunchy man leaned in to hug her. A group of stick-thin young women hovered nearby, glaring at the curvaceous blonde, flaunting her assets in bikini bottoms. Casi pointed to the brothers, then waved them toward her. "This is Reggie, he's one of the photographers I used to work with in LA."

"I always wondered what happened to my favorite model, Casi Roberts." He whistled. "You still look amazing!"

She noted Kyle's frown. "I became Casi Jensen and I live in Washington. Do you remember Mary?"

"Of course, the ball-buster who kept the girls in line," he snickered. "I haven't seen her around lately, did she retire?"

"She moved to Seattle. She started a skincare line and I work with her as a representative."

"I can see why. You're still the hottest girl around," he complimented.

"She is, but she's also a professional businesswoman. You would be stunned at her skills on the computer," Kyle interjected.

Reggie nodded. "You were off the chain with social media, so I'm not surprised. I'm glad to hear you're doing well. Where are you staying? I would love to catch up on the gossip in LA."

Casi shrugged. "Heading back to Nice, I think. We're backpacking, so we haven't decided."

"Oh, that's pricey! Stay on the yacht with us. It belongs to Deshawn Matthews, and that's his crew," Reggie noted. "He's in Monaco at a poker tournament, so we're hanging out."

"He doesn't take his women with him?" Jake asked.

"He took the top tier. These are the bottom feeders." Reggie surveyed Casi. "You were never part of those crews. Obviously, you were much better than them."

"Better at making choices," she clarified. "You said DeShawn Matthews owns the yacht?"

"The rap star," he said.

"His girlfriend ran me down in Malibu and broke my pelvis. I would say he can accommodate me for the night." She jutted her chin out.

"Damn, I remember that!" Reggie exclaimed. "Did you hear about her? Got so drunk, she drove right off a cliff. Poof, gone to the next world."

"Wow, that's a terminal ending. I can't say I'm surprised." Casi turned to Kyle. "Do you want to stay on the yacht?"

"Is that even a question?" Kyle laughed.

❧

Casi shook her head as they toured the deck, speckled with topless women lounging around the luxurious vessel. "Slick, huh?" Reggie asked.

"And the bastard couldn't pay my medical bills," Casi scoffed.

"Were heading to a nightclub later," Reggie said.

"I have the perfect dress," Casi smirked.

"You're getting a lot of mileage from three-inches of material." Kyle tickled her ribs.

"You said to pack light."

They strolled in the casino and Casi's face lit up. "Now this is nightlife!" She sauntered through the throngs of partygoers to the bar. "I'll have a whiskey sour."

"You certainly fit in," Kyle observed.

"It's like a James Bond movie," Jake whispered.

"There are tons of celebrities here," Reggie stated.

"Is that DeShawn?" Casi pointed to a well-built man surrounded by groupies as he played cards at a private table.

"Yes, but you can't go in there," Reggie said. "It's a high stakes game, and it's invitation only."

"Bullshit." Casi walked toward the roped off area and stood with a hand on her hip and a haughty expression. The bouncer nodded and moved the rope aside, granting her access.

"She has no boundaries," Kyle said. He attempted to follow, but the bouncer put his hand on his chest and shook his head.

Jake rushed to his side and Kyle whispered, "We'll watch from here. If it gets rough, we'll bust in."

"Your call," Jake seethed, surveying the scene.

DeShawn grinned as Casi approached, mesmerized by her knockout figure in the scandalous dress. "Hey girl, what's up?"

"Do you recognize me?" Casi asked.

"I'll get to know you, real quick." He unabashedly checked her out. "You're slammin'."

"My name's Casi. Does that ring a bell?"

"Did we fuck?" His shoulders sagged. "You ain't no baby mama coming to collect, are you?"

"Not per se, but you did fuck me up. Or rather, your girlfriend, Brittany, did when she ran me down in your car. You can hardly tell I had a broken pelvis, huh?" She spun slowly around.

"Hell no. You lookin' fine!"

"That's your answer? Not, sorry my lame-ass girlfriend maimed you and left you for dead?" She grabbed a stack of chips from the table and tossed them at him. "My medical bills were over twenty-thousand dollars. That means nothing to you, does it?"

"Ma'am, please don't touch the chips." The dealer halted the game.

"Whatever." She turned to leave.

"Wait, Casey." DeShawn grabbed her arm.

"It's Casi."

"Girl, don't leave like that. You get how that life works; lawyers and publicists and shit. I know who you are, you're the hot model who goes with Alix Grey. They said you was alright."

"I'm not with him anymore. I'm married." She held out her left hand. "To a wonderful man who handles his responsibilities."

"Brittany was a crazy bitch. You heard she kicked it? Drove off a cliff. Her ass was so drunk."

"Don't you accept responsibility? You understood she had a problem, and you allowed her to drive your car and live a life that perpetuated her addiction."

"I should own that." He took out his wallet. "I'll pay your bills and extra for the pain and suffering."

She smiled. "The pain and suffering helped me achieve the life I have now, and that's a fantastic place. If you want to be a real rock star, you'll take that money and do something decent with it. Help someone who's having a hard time. I'm not talking about a rehab donation to get your name in the papers, but a legitimate contribution to something important."

"I was a foster kid, maybe I could help some ghetto kid who doesn't have a chance to get ahead?" His eyes lit up.

"You've done well for yourself, DeShawn. You're throwing away money on gambling, booze, and hookers. Imagine what a tiny percentage of that would do to turn around the lives of people who are suffering. You have an opportunity to be a role model. Seize it and do something amazing." She squared her shoulders.

"You are one hell of a woman. Are you sure you don't want to spend the night with me? I will rock your world."

"My husband already does." She gave him a wink. "I will enjoy your yacht," she said under her breath.

"What happened?" Kyle asked as she embraced him.

"He apologized for the accident and agreed to pick a charity to donate money to as retribution. He offered it to me, but I realized I have all the riches I require. Suddenly, I'm a grownup."

"You do adulthood very well." He gave her a kiss.

"That was an amazing experience." Kyle regarded his winnings from the casino. "We can add this to our travel money."

"That was surreal." Jake gave Casi a hand to step on the deck of the yacht.

Casi narrowed her eyes as she surveyed their belongings. "Damn it." She dropped to her knees to check for missing items.

"What did they steal?" Kyle panicked. "We brought our money and passports with us."

Casi marched through the models strewn about the yacht, roughly grabbing at them to request the missing items. "Should we let her handle this?" Jake hovered behind her.

"Yes, she can be the female enforcer," Kyle agreed.

After a thorough search, Casi sauntered over to a wisp of a girl perched on the bow. "Hand it over, bitch."

The girl pouted in false remorse. "The worldly traveler can't spare a little? I recognize you from LA. The golden girl who won't remain defeated. You think you're better than us, snatching the attention and booking the best jobs."

"I haven't modeled in years. I'm not your competition," Casi said. "Don't blame me for your lack of success."

The girl sniffed and placed a joint to her lips, holding a lighter to the tip. "You're not the only one who can smuggle pot."

"No, Grady!" Kyle gasped.

"Don't do it," Casi warned. "It's not what you think."

The girl took a deep draw, running her tongue over pursed lips. "Tastes like shit. I expected a better buzz from a diva like you."

"It's the ashes of my husband's dead friend," Casi said. "It's not even fresh, more like twenty-years old."

"Bullshit." The girl gagged. "Gross, are you serious?"

"Grady doesn't appreciate your callous disregard for his feelings." Casi snatched the half-smoked paper. "You can keep my swimsuit since you probably tried it on, but I want the tampons, pocketknife, and phone."

Kyle whispered to Jake, "Did you notice how quickly Casi assessed what was missing from our bags?"

"She's a practiced snooper." Jake nodded.

"She has an astute knack for decoding puzzles. It's remarkable."

"Brilliant mind in a hot body," Jake agreed.

The girl slid from the railing and reached in a bag to produce the items. "Do you think I'll get sick from smoking that?" she sobbed.

"No, but one day someone will punch you in the face for stealing their stuff." Casi regarded the downtrodden girl and softened her tone. "These parties aren't what they're billed as and don't help your career. Distance yourself from this crew and focus on your goals. You'll make it if you try."

The girl's face crumpled to a pitiful expression. "You were always my idol. I wanted to be like you."

"Then don't stop at party girl. Push past that and gain some skills outside of the catwalk. You should envy who I am now because I'm so much better than I was." Casi flashed her a brilliant smile.

28

CONFESSIONS AND CANELÉ

Casi staggered up the hill, barely able to move her legs. When she came to a crashing halt, teetering on the edge, Kyle lunged toward her. He grabbed her backpack, but her arms slipped through, and she rolled effortlessly to the bottom of the gulley. "Are you ok?" he asked.

"I'm so damn exhausted; I can't climb this mountain." She flopped on her back and spread out her arms and legs. "Leave me here and continue to the station. I've reached my limit."

Kyle jogged down and knelt at her side. "It's just a few miles, and it's more of a hill than a mountain. You can sleep on the train and when we get to Bordeaux, I'll book us a fantastic hotel."

"No, you won't. It'll be like the last few hovels we've stayed in. My sweet nature is gone. I can't take another minute of carrying that stupid backpack or sleeping on trains. Let the earth swallow me."

"Can I have one last kiss before you die?" He hovered over her with a smile penetrating his deep blue eyes. "You've been a good sport. I'll carry your pack the rest of the way." He kissed her and offered a hand. He frowned when he noticed her limping. "Did you hurt yourself?"

"My lower back is tweaked from sleeping on the hay in the barn. The knot will work itself out if I keep going." She winced.

"Get on." He crouched to give her a piggyback. "Jake, take our bags."

"You don't have to carry me," she said.

"It's a free ride. You weigh about the same as my pack," he teased. "Plus, you get to hug me the whole way."

"That's a definite bonus," she said.

"Hey, you have a monkey on your back. Does it feel like when you were in college?" Jake jogged up the hill and smacked Casi on the backside.

Casi kissed Kyle's neck as she sang show tunes. "You make it enjoyable to carry you." He turned to kiss her.

"Don't worry about me carrying three backpacks," Jake pointed out. "It's not like I'm tired."

"A few hours and you will be in your lover's arms," Casi noted.

"Among other places." Jake chuckled.

"Alright, Princess, this is where your ride ends," Kyle announced as they reached the platform.

"You're my knight in shining armor." She slid to the ground.

"Or at least his horse," Jake snickered.

❧

The train creaked into the station and Jake leaped from his seat, spotting Anna standing on the platform. "Do you think he's excited?" Kyle watched his brother weave through the crowd.

"Every bone in my body aches." Casi yanked on her backpack with a sigh. "Please don't force me to stay in a hovel tonight."

"I had Anna make the arrangements," Kyle said.

"Thank God!" Casi rushed to give her friend a hug.

"You look like transients!" Anna patted down a clump of Jake's hair. "Shall we go to the hotel and you can shower before I have to be seen in public with you?"

Casi surveyed Anna's perfectly coiffed outfit and glimmering styled hair. "Yes, please lead us to civilization."

Anna looped her arm through Casi's, sensing her despair. She rattled on about plans for Bordeaux and Paris, stating she'd made reservations for dinner and packed proper clothes, figuring they would be a disaster. Jake nudged Kyle and whispered, "The drill sergeant is taking over. You better set her straight."

"I'm too exhausted to battle her," Kyle moaned.

Casi began to cry as they entered the exquisite lobby, adorned with oil paintings and antiques. Anna put an arm over her shoulder and soothed her. "I assumed you deserved a fancy hotel after your messages." She grasped Kyle's arm as he walked toward the front desk. "Everything is taken care of. This is my treat."

He started to challenge her but read the defiance in her face. "Thank you," he said instead.

"Kyle, we're kept men. These women are paying for everything on this trip," Jake noted.

"There's still Paris." Anna gave him a wink.

"And dinner tonight," Kyle asserted. "Were you able to get reservations at the restaurant I suggested."

"Is that a necessary question?" Anna rolled her eyes. They rounded a corner, and she handed Kyle a key card. "We have adjoining rooms, but don't make a habit of visiting."

"It's a shame you live all the way in Seattle. It would be awesome if you were located across the street from me." He quickly opened his door.

"That could change one day," she called out.

"Are you accepting my offer?" Jake asked.

She put a hand to his chest. "Do you want to take a bath?"

"Alone?"

"No." She disrobed.

He watched her run the water, aching with desire. "How's Charlotte? Was it hard for you to leave?"

"A little," she admitted. "My sister is thrilled to babysit. She's moved forward with her plans and is expecting in June. She enjoys the practice."

"How did she get pregnant?"

"Men are only required for a small part of the process." She adjusted the temperature.

"It's not only lesbians who believe that," Jake challenged. "I'm insignificant in your life, Anna."

She got in the tub and slid on top of him. "Before I respond, you must answer a question."

"Shoot." He braced himself.

"Did you have sex with Casi?"

"Are you out of your fucking mind?"

She grinned. "I sensed there was something weird going on with you guys and I wondered if things escalated."

"A friendly kiss to having sex is one hell of an escalation. She's gorgeous, but she's my brother's wife. I love her like a sister, not to mention he would be devastated if I crossed that line with her. She is his world." He exhaled. "What did she say that made you think that was remotely possible?"

Anna smoothed her hand over his cheek to calm him. "She said some terrible things happened, and the guilt was killing her."

"We came on this trip to help Kyle put things in his past to rest. Casi got unexpected shit dumped on her about her mother, who won't stay dead. You think I'm weak and dependent on my brother, but I wasn't a third wheel on this vacation; they needed me."

"You're the strongest man I know, and not just physically. That's why I push you away. I'm afraid to depend on you." Anna kissed him.

"Do you love me?" He twirled a strand of her hair between his fingers.

"Completely."

"My history with women is complicated, but loving them has never been part of it. You can't push my feelings for you away; they're real. What you see is what you get with me, there is no hidden agenda."

She nodded. "You get anxious sometimes..."

"Did Casi tell you anything about that?"

"No. She's like an overprotective mother when it comes to you. I see it, Jake. I notice when Kyle swoops in to rescue you from an emotional situation. Lia was intimidated by your armor. But I'm not. Trust me to be there for you," she said.

"I don't like talking about things in my past."

"Perfect, because I'm not interested. I'm not an emotionally deep person who wants to gab about feelings. This is not a façade, I'm a strong woman," she said. "Can you live with that?"

"Are you proposing to me?"

"I'm proposing we move forward with our relationship and from here on out, we're exclusive." She smiled.

"I guess I better tell all my girlfriends I'm taken."

❧

Casi sunk into the tub with too many bubbles and giggled. "I'm never coming out!"

Kyle pulled her toward him, laughing as she slipped from his grasp. "You always overdo it."

"There are twelve layers of dirt to remove."

He took a washcloth and stroked it over her skin, lovingly scrubbing her. "I'll help you reach every inch." Time passed while they soaked until the water turned to lukewarm. He cocked his head and glanced at his watch when there was a knock at the door. "It's too early for dinner, and I was hoping to take a nap." He rinsed off and wrapped a towel around his hips.

"I hope it's room service. I'm starving!" she called out.

"You can't eat. I want you to be hungry for tonight's dinner." He spoke to someone at the door and came back with a grin. "Anna arranged a couple's massage."

"Sounds fantastic! I don't need to participate, do I?"

"I'm fairly certain we are side by side." He glanced back at the tables being set up. "I've never had a massage, professionally."

"Are you concerned you'll get a hard on?" She noted the concentration on his face.

He frowned. "No, but I should check on Jake. This might not be a smart surprise for him." He nodded to the masseurs. "I'll be right back."

Anna rolled her eyes when she opened the door. "He's in the bathroom trying to figure out an excuse to get out of it."

Kyle knocked loudly. "Jake, it's me."

Jake glared at Anna. "I'm not into this kinky shit."

Kyle chuckled. "It's couple with an apostrophe, not as in plural. Casi and I have our own team."

"Oh." Jake blushed when Anna giggled. "You could have said that."

"They're professionals and it's not sexual. It should relieve your sore muscles," Kyle indicated.

Jake whispered, "What if I get a woody?"

Kyle grinned. "Remember when Mom used to rub your back? Pretend it's her touching you."

"That's weird," Jake scoffed. "That could work."

"Enjoy it and chalk it up to a new experience in Europe." Kyle returned to his room. He smiled at Casi, stretched out on the table. "Is it easing your pain?" He threw his towel on the bed.

The masseuse gasped and Casi laughed. "Kyle! You're not supposed to walk around naked. Let them drape you with the sheet."

"I'm unfamiliar with the process." He followed the hand gestures of how to get on the table. The masseuse began the deep tissue treatment, and he relaxed under her touch. He heard a slow moan escape from Casi, and he turned his head and grinned. "Is this a happy ending massage?"

"I forgot I wasn't alone. It's incredible on my aching feet." She bit the pillow to suppress a grunt.

"There is an image I adore." He grasped her hand.

After a long and luxurious session, they quietly announced it was over and motioned to the bed. "What are they telling us?" Kyle whispered. "This isn't about to get kinky, is it?"

"I guess they're leaving and are suggesting we take a nap?" Casi interpreted. "Do you have cash for a tip?"

"Oh, of course." Kyle quickly handed them bills with a nod.

"Merci," the woman said, giving them a pleasant smile.

Kyle joined Casi in bed, noting she was already fast asleep. He cradled her in his arms, breathing in the scent of lavender infused in her silky skin. He awoke an hour later, refreshed and revitalized, having the benefit of the bath and massage. He slid his hand between her legs and watched a smile touch her lips. She pulled back with a start, confused by what was happening. She exhaled deeply. "Oh, it's you."

"Who else would it be?"

"I questioned whether I fell asleep during the massage."

"We're alone in our very comfortable bed. I'm offering to provide the happy ending." He ran his tongue over her earlobe.

"Please do. I have enough energy now for a proper orgasm."

"Did you love it?" Anna strolled arm in arm with Casi.

"The bath was divine, the massage was magnificent, and the bed is incredible! The great sex topped it off." She slapped Kyle on the backside.

Anna giggled and gave her a squeeze. "I missed you! I must admit I was worried when you were acting squirrelly before you left. Did you work through whatever it was?"

Casi shrugged. "My mom left a journal chronicling her life. It was upsetting and disgusting. I never had a connection with her, but it shocked me to learn I didn't know her at all. It took some time to come to terms with everything, but I discovered Ava was more significant in my upbringing than I understood."

"That's why you're so much like her," Anna said.

"You think I am?" Casi asked with surprise.

"Sure. People notice how breathtaking you are right away, but it takes a while to see there are significant layers to you. Ava is a woman of deep insight and strength. I admire her."

"I overlooked our bond because I resented her for taking my dad away. She makes me feel calm and loved, which draws me to her.

They surprised us in Austria, and we went to Italy together." She stopped suddenly. "My mom wouldn't have done that. She never considered my needs. I still can't comprehend why she hated me."

Kyle reached over and took her hand. "Because you represent everything she could never be. Maybe it was her upbringing, or she was defective. Honestly, the best thing you can do is move past it and live your life. You'll never understand her motives."

"I had a brother. He would be roughly Jake's age." Casi giggled and cried at the same time.

"Well, now you have Jake." Kyle tried to hide a smile.

"Yup." Jake narrowed his eyes. "Screw you guys! You're laughing because that kid was slow in the head."

"What happened to him?" Anna asked with alarm.

"We're not laughing at Sebastian, or his condition," Casi said. "It just struck me as funny." She turned to Anna. "My mom was thirteen when she had him. He died when he was three."

Kyle nodded, understanding she wanted some details to remain private. "That had a lot to do with why she was an oddball."

"I'm sure it was excruciating for her. It's hard to understand..." Anna started to say.

"Please, don't." Casi rushed ahead. "Every woman on this planet tells me I'll never know what it's like to be a mother. I get it, ok?"

"Casi, stop," Anna demanded. "That's not what I was about to say. Remember, I was there when Katie lectured you on the subject and I defended you?"

Casi nodded and wiped a tear. "Only Ava understands."

"She has certainly been through a lot. My comment is about having a child at a young age." Everyone turned, and she nodded. "I was fifteen. Jake and Casi are aware, but for the record, Kyle, I was raped. That was traumatic enough, but it wasn't until months later I realized I was pregnant."

"You never told me that part," Casi said.

"I never disclosed it to anyone outside my family. I was catholic, and it was a sin even though I had no part in it. My father proclaimed it was my punishment for being promiscuous and sent me to a convent here in France, which is why I speak French. They wanted me far away from the gossip chain and informed everyone I was doing a semester as an exchange student. I gave birth to a daughter, and I wasn't permitted to hold her. She would be twenty-two now. I've gone between hating her for being created, to devastated I never got to be part of her life. Jake, you think I'm too attached to Charlotte, but no one will ever take my child away from me again." She burst into tears.

"Anna, I'm sorry." Jake embraced her.

Kyle squeezed Anna's hand, reeling from the revelation. "I'm glad Charlotte was conceived in love. You deserve that."

"She was." Anna wiped her eyes. "I arrived in Paris as planned and visited the convent. They wouldn't give me any details on her but allowed me to leave my contact information. I spent a few days wandering around aimlessly, wondering if I would recognize her if I spotted her on the street." She shrugged. "Your mom was a wacko, Casi, but perhaps a bit of it came from losing a child."

"I'm sure it did." Casi smiled. "Oh, and she was born into a cult. That may have been part of it."

Anna laughed. "That's insane!"

Kyle stopped at the restaurant and held the door. "Is everyone hungry? This is my treat and we're ordering everything on the menu."

"Yes, and I pre-ordered the soufflés when I made the reservations," Anna confirmed.

Casi gasped with delight as the courses were brought out. "This is crazy delicious. Do I want to hear what's in it?"

"Fois gras? Probably not," Kyle said. "Just enjoy it."

Casi shrugged. "Why not? You only live once."

"Unless you keep getting reincarnated like your mother," Jake joked, poking her with his fork.

"She can stay dead this time," Casi said.

"Are you alright? You don't have to eat it if you don't like it, there's plenty more on the way." Kyle watched her push food around her plate.

"It's tasty. I was thinking about Ava and how terrible I was to her when I was a teenager," Casi confessed. "I wish I hadn't been so self-involved and realized how much she loved my dad."

"It's normal you were jealous," Kyle soothed.

"The day before my fourteenth birthday, I was hanging out at the mall with my friends." Casi settled back in her chair.

"Shocking," Jake teased.

"Ava walked by and we were cruel with calling her names and tormenting her about having an affair with my dad." She cringed. "Katie led the charge, and it seemed funny until I noticed the torment in Ava's face."

"What did she do?" Kyle asked.

"She confronted me and said I was ungrateful for everything she had done for me in the past. I was embarrassed, and Katie continued to mouth off, but Joey made her stop because we looked stupid when Ava took the higher ground. The next day she came to my school with homemade cupcakes and a beautiful gold heart necklace. It was my first real diamond. That's why she had been at the mall, she was shopping for my birthday." Casi frowned. "I was such an idiot back then."

"More like uninformed." Kyle squeezed her hand. "We all have moments we wish we could redo. Thankfully, Ava loves you enough to see past the hurtful times and cherish who you've become."

"I hope." Casi shivered. "It's interesting how the three of us normal folks are the ones with regrets and Jake is squeaky clean."

"I don't believe you're normal." Jake smiled and slid up the edge of his shirt to reveal his tattoo, 'However long the night, the dawn will break.'

"Yes, we realize the drug reference." Casi rolled her eyes.

"When I was sixteen, I couldn't control my panic attacks, and they were getting worse. Some losers were teasing Kyle, and I wanted to get back at them, so I had sex with their sister and told the whole school how wild she was in bed."

"Marsha," Kyle sighed.

"Kids called her marshmallow." Jake cringed. "Actually, I gave her the nickname, and it stuck."

"Was she pudgy?" Anna asked.

"Kind of," Jake admitted.

"That's horrible," she chastised.

"I realize that now. And I served my penance by becoming fat later in life. I understand how hurtful it was. I used her to piss off her brothers, and it backfired."

"What did they do to Kyle?" Casi gasped.

"The fight started because they stole his skateboard and beat him while they restrained me. They wanted to make him cry," Jake growled. "They called him baby Jensen."

"I was thirteen," Kyle stated.

"He wouldn't give in," Jake said. "I yelled for him to stay down, but he kept getting back up. I was livid when they finally let him go."

"I never got my skateboard back." Kyle frowned.

"What did you do to Marsha?" Anna snapped.

"I didn't force her," Jake assured them. "She had a crush on me, and I invited her down to the river. Everything was consensual."

"Until you blabbed," Casi shot back.

"Yes, we covered the part where I was unkind," Jake said. "Her brothers beat the shit out of her, and she came back to school pretty banged up. I realized my retaliation hurt her by mistake. I apologized, and she said she was fine."

"Glad it all worked out." Casi reached for the bread.

"Don't fill up," Kyle said. "There's still more."

"I know, escargot." She smiled as the waiter approached with a steaming platter. "I want this for the garlic butter."

"The story didn't end there." Jake snatched her bread. "My mom heard what I had done and was furious. She insisted I take Marsha to the homecoming dance for retribution."

"I hope she turned you down," Anna scoffed.

"She was thrilled to go with me. Everyone figured I had a trick up my sleeve and would embarrass her at the dance. She tried hard to look pretty in a thrift-store dress, and I brought her a corsage. I treated her very well."

"And then you banged her," Casi concluded.

"She wanted to go to the river," Jake said. "After we had sex, she said it had been the best night of her life."

"You are absolved of your behavior," Anna said.

"We're getting to that part." Jake grinned.

"Dang, drag a story out, why don't you? Can I have my butter soaker back?" Casi eyed the roll.

Jake tossed it on her plate. "Then she held a gun to her head and declared she was ready to end it, just like her sister had done several years before. Apparently, the brothers were assaulting her, and she reached the end of her rope."

"That's horrible!" Casi paused mid-bite. "Please tell me you stopped her."

"I thought you were bored with my story," Jake said.

"We must hear the end now," Anna coaxed.

Jake nodded. "I lunged at her and grabbed the gun. I promised to help, and I drove her to our farm to tell my parents what was going on. Dad and I went to her house and confronted the family and lied that we had taken her to the train station to get away from them. She was gone by the time we got back and I'm not sure what happened to her after that."

"That's bullshit," Casi said. "You can't end the story that way!"

Jake shrugged. "The police questioned me up and down, but I didn't have information on her whereabouts."

"Which was the plan," Kyle smirked.

"You know?" Jake gasped.

"I called Libby when you left. She told me to lead Marsha to the railroad crossing and wait with her until she arrived. She came about an hour later," he said.

"Where did she go?" Jake asked.

"Libby took her to Portland, and she lived there until she finished school. Marsha changed her name and she's doing very well. I keep in touch with her on Facebook." Kyle smiled.

"Why didn't you tell me any of this?" Jake frowned.

"Immunity," Kyle grinned.

"Plus, you assumed I could handle it," Jake surmised.

"Finish your homeless story," Kyle challenged.

"After everything happened with Marsha, I took a bus to Seattle and searched for her. I ended up running into Tara. I guess I resemble Tommy..."

"Your son?" Anna asked.

"My birth father, which is why my son has his name. Austin's middle name is Peter, who is my real dad." He grimaced. "Does that sound callous after your confession?"

"Not at all. I hope she was adopted by parents who love her as much as yours do. They deserve the title," Anna assured him.

"If this story degrades into you having drugged out sex with your mother, I don't want to hear it." Casi shivered.

"You are sick in the head," Jake gagged. "I let her inject me with heroin. It was amazing, and I couldn't get enough. I lived on the streets with her for a few weeks, stealing and panhandling to get money for my next fix."

Kyle glared at him. "The first few days, Dad was pissed and said you must figure out how to live on your own. He assumed you would run out of money and come home. Mom was beside herself with worry and begged him to find you. After a month, Dad got scared and wondered if you were dead."

"We had gone in a van to Olympia," Jake said. "It got cold, and the rain started. The high was harder to obtain and didn't last as long. I got pneumonia and ended up in the hospital. Tara told them my name was Tommy Petrov, and I didn't have ID on me. I could have died, and no one would have known. Thankfully, my aunt Libby found me."

"Libby had friends and networks everywhere, so it didn't take her long to locate him." Kyle regarded Jake sadly. "I was thirteen. You were my world; you're a selfish bastard."

Jake squeezed his shoulder. "Libby came to the hospital and ripped me a new one. She said my family loved me and if she ever heard I touched hard drugs again, she would ship me off to Timbuktu. I didn't know where it was, but she made it seem scary. She's an amazing storyteller and she sat by my side telling me tales of her travels and the people she met. When I was well enough, she brought me home."

"Why did you choose that tattoo?" Anna asked.

"I hadn't been perfect about my promise. I tried heroin one more time, but messed up and blew out my vein." He exposed his inner elbow. "That scared me off the hard stuff but life didn't seem important. Several years later, after Kyle got in the accident and I had deep regrets, Libby reminded me there's a light at the end of the tunnel. We picked this one together because she believed it was significant. She got the same one on her ribs."

"I love her," Casi expressed before finding interest in the duck confit with figs on crostini.

After dinner, they strolled along the cobblestone streets and Casi walked ahead of them and flirted with the locals, who were appreciative of her charm. Jake turned to Kyle and whispered, "She got weird at dinner. Why?"

Kyle smiled. "You broke her trust."

"When? I never did anything behind her back," Jake promised.

"You told your homeless story to the table. She likes being your confidante. It makes her feel close to you," Kyle informed him.

"Damn it. I felt obligated since Anna shared something so personal."

"That was a shocker. It explains a lot about her personality."

Jake shrugged. "She said she was always a cold-hearted bitch. The assault only made her more controlling."

Kyle nudged him. "Go talk to your buddy."

Jake jogged up to Casi, slipping his hand in hers. "Are you pissed I shared my drug story without telling you first?"

"Nope, it's fine," she said in a clipped tone.

"Do you want the background on my cascade tattoo?"

"Not really. It's a bunch of symbols of the Pacific Northwest. You're a true-blooded Washington boy. Obvious."

He squeezed her hand. "Do you understand why Kyle got the salmon?"

"He's a Pisces and fisherman," she yawned.

"True but I chose it because it's a fighter. It swims upstream against remarkable odds and always returns home." He moved his shirt to expose his arm. "I have the same one to represent Kyle. You see how it has the bear, eagle, and wolf around it? They're protecting him. It's my secret symbol. Not even Kyle is aware."

"Don't all those animals eat fish?" she asked.

"Not in this scenario."

"Your dad has an eagle tattoo on his arm," she noted.

"Yup, and Mom?"

"She can be the wolf because you're more like the bear."

"You're not going to reveal what her real one is?"

"Nope, but can you add me?"

"Monkeys aren't indigenous to the Pacific Northwest." He pointed to a sun symbol close to his shoulder. "I guess you've always been there."

"I love that!" She flung herself in his arms.

"Monkey Brains, you're my number one receiver of information. Anna's not interested in my background, and I wouldn't share it with her, anyway. That homeless stint was a dark time in my life, and I wasn't anxious to admit to it. Anna's confession made me weak. I'll tell you another secret." He whispered in her ear.

"On the last night?"

"Don't let the cat out of the bag."

"I won't." She made a cross over her heart.

"Well?" Anna surveyed the group.

"This is the most divine thing I've ever eaten," Casi declared.

"It's crispy on the exterior and remarkably moist inside." Kyle took another confection from the plate. "I need to learn how to make them."

Anna nodded to the proprietor of the small shop who held out her hand to Kyle, leading him to the kitchen. "What an incredible cabinet!" Kyle examined the 16th century intricately detailed piece, complete with porcelain inlay. He turned to Casi. "This is what I would have in the kitchen. It would set the stage for the whole remodel."

As the proprietor spoke, Anna translated, ensuring Kyle understood each step of the canelé making process. "She's explaining the importance of letting the dough rest and how to coat the molds with beeswax. She keeps the ingredients in that thing and uses it for proofing bread too."

Kyle smoothed a hand over the detailed French pastural scenes. "Sure, the enamel enclosure is perfect for a controlled environment and even has a cast iron grate where you would put hot water underneath. I always wanted a Hoosier cabinet, which is a similar design."

"It would be odd in your kitchen, which is modern and commercial. I figured you liked that sterile appearance." Anna cocked her head.

"The rest of the house incorporated materials from the area, and I knew exactly what I wanted. When it came to the kitchen, I went with function and..." he trailed off.

"What Lauren wanted," Casi finished.

"It wasn't important to me, and she had a better grasp of what worked. If I were to design the space today, it would be much different." He smiled at Casi. "And I would consider your input."

"Honestly? I hate it." Casi blushed. "It's not homey like the farmhouse and has zero personality. You get snappy when I cut on the granite, but isn't that the point of having a giant counter?"

"Not for cutting." Kyle frowned. "It's bad for the knives and can scratch the surface. Would you enjoy cooking more if we designed the space together?"

"Yes." She wrapped her arms around his waist. "I've enjoyed the classes we've taken, especially in these places rich with history."

"We can create our own unique place." He gave her a kiss. "I'll also make you a special cutting board to encourage proper technique."

"Oh boy." Casi laughed.

29

CITY LIGHTS

"Kyle, how do I check if I have money left?" Casi asked as they strolled the Champs-Élysées.

"Spend what you like," he said evasively.

"I want a zero balance when we get back. You've paid for things with your own money and Anna covered the hotel in Bordeaux." She turned to look at him. "I'm sure you keep a tally."

He smiled and extracted a notebook. "Fine. You still have about two thousand dollars and we have my winnings from Monaco. You could go on a shopping spree in Paris?"

A smile radiated across her face. "Fabulous!"

"I'm in." Anna linked her arm through Casi's.

"Can that happen on the last day?" Kyle asked. "I would like to see the Louvre and Arc de Triomphe."

"I would like a croissant and a latte," Casi countered.

After coffee they walked to the Louvre and Jake feigned disinterest while Kyle took pictures and made notes. Anna nudged Casi and whispered, "Your husband is darling."

"He is," Casi agreed.

"This is the Mona Lisa?" Kyle asked with confusion.

"Yes, the painting is a lot smaller in real life," Anna said.

"Unimpressive." Kyle grinned. "Like they say about Jake."

"Are you referring to that guy?" Jake pointed to a statue. "If I had that tiny dick, I would keep it covered."

"Take your shirt off and pose." Casi grabbed the camera.

"Stop being a tourist." Kyle tried not to laugh as his brother replicated the poses with serious concentration on his face.

A security guard rushed over, chastising them in French. Anna explained they were Americans and rolled her eyes. She pretended to move them along, waiting until the guard returned to his post. "Hurry and get in there, Kyle." She pushed him toward a row of statues.

Kyle sighed and peeled off his shirt, flexing as he imitated the statues. Tourists began taking pictures, and he turned to Jake. "I guess this is what it's like to be a model."

After their tour, they admired the chalk paintings and architecture while they shared a paper bag filled with pastries. Kyle stood in the middle of the sidewalk, overlooking the Seine. "Casi, do you think our life is boring?"

"Why are you asking?" She brushed crumbs from her lips. "No, I don't."

He shrugged. "Reflecting on our daily routine seems dull compared to these places with so much history and culture. I love living on the lake, but perhaps there's more out there for us?"

"There isn't," she said. "Our world is perfect in our beautiful home. We have the children and pets to love and entertain us. Our careers are fulfilling and provide the means to travel wherever we want. I could not imagine being happier or feeling our life is more complete." Her eyes lit up as they walked by a shop. "Hey, this is like the scene on that cabinet you loved at the canelé shop. It represents what I'm saying, a lovely setting, and I believe the families are gathered inside those adorable cottages, thankful for what they have." She peered closely at the design.

"Wow, gorgeous. Let's buy them!" Kyle smoothed his hand over the design. "Microwave and dishwasher safe? That's awesome."

"I'll take your white plates," Jake yawned.

"If I move in, I want something more exciting," Anna declared.

"You're moving in?" Jake asked.

"Maybe." Anna engaged in conversation with the shopkeeper to arrange payment and shipping.

Casi glanced at the total. "Nice, that will suck up a good portion of my remaining money and it's for something truly special."

"What about my Monaco winnings?" Kyle put his hand over hers.

"How incredible would it be to buy lingerie in Paris? I bet it's super sexy." Casi gave him a wink.

"I think it would be a wise investment." Kyle grinned.

Casi looped her arm through Anna's directing her to a shop while Kyle took pictures of a cathedral. "Can you contact the proprietor in Bordeaux?"

"I've already arranged a shipment of the canelé," Anna giggled.

"Excellent." Casi glanced back. "I want that cabinet he fell in love with."

Anna raised an eyebrow. "It was beautiful and an incredible piece of history, but what the heck would you do with it?"

Casi put a hand on her hip. "Every time I hit a bump in the road, I realize what I value most in my life. Kyle and I are living with a kitchen we don't love because it's practical. We have plenty of money to make changes and it would be something unique we did together. Everyone cooks at our house and it's the heart of our home."

"Ugh, if I move in with Jake will I be required to cook?"

"Yes," Casi laughed. "He came up with the idea for our garden last year, and it has been hugely beneficial. I'm bringing back tons of treasures and ideas to incorporate and make it even more special. I want that feeling of unity inside the house as well. Neither of us has a family history we're tied to and we can embrace whatever appeals to us. Plus, I'm finally taking a stand and ridding the last bit of Lauren from our relationship."

"You are incomparable." Anna gave her a squeeze.

"We've reached our final destination," Kyle announced as they stood on the viewing platform at the top of the Eiffel tower.

"That's cryptic." Jake chuckled before noticing the shimmer of sadness in his brother's midnight blue eyes. "This is Grady's last spot." He put an arm around his shoulders. "You've been an amazing friend to him and honored Nicole's wishes. This has been the journey of a lifetime for all of us."

Casi slid between Kyle and the railing. "We've gone through hell and back, again."

Kyle directed his gaze to her. "It's been monumentally therapeutic to bring Grady here." Tears welled in his eyes. "He has a marker in the cemetery in Elmvale, but there's nothing in there. He's a footnote in an unknown novel. We refer to what happened as the tragedy without considering the lives lost and their significance to the world."

"Family and friends went on different journeys than they might have. Your innocence was crushed and twenty years later, your best friend matters. You brought him here to recognize his value. The memorial at the river should do the same. They aren't heroes because they died, but destiny was altered when the boat crashed. We don't know who Grady would have been as an adult, but I'm certain your friendship would have carried on." Casi exhaled. "You've brought closure to Grady's journey. Let that bring you comfort."

Kyle kissed her softly, finding solace in her warmth. "Thank you for helping me be the best man I can and reminding me I am human." He unwrapped the paper and lightly shook it until the last ash danced in the breeze. "Goodbye my friend."

Jake slid beside him and sang, "We've known each other since we were nine or ten." Kyle's eyes welled and he joined in to sing the lyrics from Seasons in the Sun as they watched the ashes glittering in the moonlight.

"I would like to point out that Terry Jacks is a Canadian songwriter." Casi grinned. "We should definitely play his song at the memorial."

"Your random knowledge freaks me out." Jake eyed her suspiciously.

Casi slipped Kyle's phone from his pocket and angled it to take pictures of them with the incredible backdrop. "Our last night in Paris." She smiled and winked at Jake.

Kyle smiled. "This was a perfect ending. Shall we walk around the city and enjoy the evening?"

"Excellent idea. I just need to do something first." Jake reached in his pocket and got down on one knee. "Anna O'Shea, will you marry me?"

"What are you doing?" Anna gasped and scanned the platform packed with tourists taking an interest in the sudden proposal.

Jake smiled. "You wanted me to be a man and stop depending on my brother. Luckily, he was too caught up in his own drama and Casi had her head in the clouds. This is my decision and I'm asking you without any strings attached to be my wife. I only have two requirements; we live in my house and you have to understand I have two other kids."

"Four," Kyle coughed in his hand.

Jake grimaced. "Ugh. Four kids. The older set aren't too much work. The new batch are coddled by Casi and shared with their mother, so you won't have to do much there. It's important to have them all grow up together."

Anna grinned. "What the hell, this time I'm betting on love. Yes, Jake Jensen, I will marry you." She extended her left hand to let him slide the ring on. She leaned forward and kissed him. "Now get up, you know how I feel about making a scene in public."

"Oh, thank God she accepted." Kyle whispered to Casi. "Did he tell you he was going to do that?"

"Yes." Casi grinned. "Did you know?"

"I had no idea. The crazy bastard did this all on his own." Kyle hugged his brother. "I guess we'll be neighbors, Anna."

She held up her hand. "Let me process one thing at a time."

Casi admired the ring and raised an eyebrow. "Jake, did you pick this out by yourself? When were you alone?"

"I bought it in Italy because I figured Anna would want something unique. Ava helped me when you guys were at the beach." Jake smiled.

"It's beautiful," Anna said. "When did you decide?"

"I've had the idea since we started planning this trip," Jake admitted. "I assumed the Eiffel tower was the ultimate romantic spot, and if you declined, it meant you were heartless."

"True." Anna laughed. "Now Casi will be my real sister, and my ex-lover will be my brother-in-law."

"Let's leave that part out of the toast." Kyle winced.

"My first marriage was a disaster." Anna grasped Jake's hand. "This time, we've got the children to consider."

"Which is why I want you to live in my house," Jake reiterated. "I'm hoping that can happen fairly soon."

Anna smiled. "Why don't we have the wedding at the lake this summer? A simple affair with our friends and family. Casi will be my maid of honor and Kyle, I assume, is the best man?"

"Third time is the charm." Kyle grinned.

Jake chuckled. "You aren't toying with me, are you? You seem to find it humorous to string me along."

"I'm serious," Anna said. "Now I have things back on track and I'm ready to commit to raising our daughter together."

"This has been an eventful evening for our last night in Paris," Casi declared. "I can't believe we leave tomorrow."

"I propose we don't waste time sleeping." Kyle held out his hand. "Let's check out clubs and do this town up right."

"We can stay out until the sun comes up and then take my new lingerie for a test drive." Casi wrapped herself in his arms for a lingering kiss.

"I like the way you think, my Sunshine Girl." Kyle twirled her around.

"Do you think we can be as happy as them?" Anna asked.

"We should try. It's an exceptional way to live," Jake concluded.

Always and Forever

HOMEMADE MOZZARELLA CHEESE

Makes 1 pound

1¼ cup distilled water

1½ teaspoon citric acid

¼ teaspoon rennet

1-gallon whole milk, not organic

1½ teaspoons kosher salt

1. Place one cup of water in a small bowl and stir in citric acid.
2. Place ¼ cup water in another bowl and add rennet.
3. Pour the milk in a large pot and stir in the citric acid solution. Heat the milk just below simmering (90 degrees), stirring gently.
4. Turn off the heat and stir in the rennet solution. Count to 30 and stop stirring. Cover the pot and let sit for 10 minutes.
5. After 10 minutes, the milk should have set, similar to silken tofu, and the whey should appear mostly clear. Cut into 2-inch cubes.
6. Heat the curds to 110°F while gently stirring to separate the curds from the whey. Remove from heat and use a slotted spoon to remove the curds and place in a glass bowl. Discard the whey.
7. Sprinkle the curds with salt and press into a ball to extract as much remaining whey as possible. Place the bowl in a microwave for 30 seconds. The cheese must reach 135 degrees to be stretchable. Carefully fold the cheese into itself (using a latex glove will help with the heat) until it becomes smooth and shiny. It may be necessary to place it back in the microwave several times to achieve the proper result. Shape into a ball or cylinder while stretching.
8. When the cheese is bright white and smooth, cover it with a mixture of 1 teaspoon salt mixed with 1 cup water. Cover and refrigerate.

THE CATWALK SERIES CONTINUES WITH LOVE

Love Triumphs Despite Tragedy and Jealousy

Dreams are shattered. Bonds are broken. Deception creates chaos and doubt. Will relationships withstand the crush of betrayal when the truth is discovered?

A summer wedding promises love and opportunity, while an autumn union brings misery and distrust. When lives intertwine, and an affair is uncovered, prompted by a malicious motive, Kyle and Casi attempt to rise above the drama, desperate to preserve their unique bond.

Casi falls victim to a trauma that crushes her confidence as she is forced to keep secrets and defend the people she loves. As lies unravel, she is pressured to reveal the truth. Overwhelmed by the circumstances and convinced they are each responsible for the treacherous outcome, one brother goes off the rails while the other is caught between loyalty and love.

Will the belief in always and forever be enough to protect Casi's and Kyle's marriage, or will harsh circumstances finally overcome their faith?

The final book in the Catwalk Series finishes with shocking revelations and a triumphant conclusion.

Love - Love Triumphs Despite Tragedy and Jealousy

Canadian-born author, Suzy Quenneville-Orpin, has always had a vivid imagination and a keen desire to write. Suzy views the world through her own narrative, weaving in the fascinating challenges, triumphs, and lifestyles of the people she meets. An unapologetic daydreamer, Suzy's early experiences in Toronto and Woodland Beach, Ontario provided the perfect upbringing to fuel her creativity and discover the wonder of the roads less traveled. A move to the West Coast brought new opportunities and a deep appreciation for the Pacific Northwest.

Follow Suzy to discover more about the Catwalk Series.
www.sqorpin.com
www.facebook.com/sqorpin
www.twitter.com/authorsqorpin
www.instagram.com/sqorpin
sqorpin@yahoo.com
Amazon.com/author/sqorpin

www.ingramcontent.com/pod-product-compliance
Lightning Source LLC
Chambersburg PA
CBHW061634190726
48289CB00006B/1598